PAUL D COOMBS is a writer of stories mired in either one or all of the strange, the gothic, the dark, and the beautifully tragic. He lives on a rock, floating in space where he inhabits a small clutch of islands known as the United Kingdom. Born in Cardiff, Wales, he now lives in the splendid and sepulchral North West of England.

The Great Orme is Paul's debut novel. Paul has numerous short stories published in anthologies, magazines and podcasts. His collection of dark speculative short stories, *For Strangers Only*, published in 2023.

Find Paul at pauldcoombs.com or on social media:

Twitter (X): @Coombsy101010
Threads / Instagram: @pauldcoombs
Bluesky: @pauldcoombs.bsky.social

THE GREAT ORME

PAUL D COOMBS

Northodox Press Ltd
Maiden Greve, Malton,
North Yorkshire, YO17 7BE

This edition 2024

1

First published in Great Britain by
Northodox Press Ltd 2024

Copyright © Paul D Coombs 2024

Paul D Coombs asserts the moral right to
be identified as the author of this work.

ISBN: 978-1-915179-41-8

This book is set in Caslon Pro Std

This Novel is entirely a work of fiction. The names,
characters and incidents portrayed in it are the work of the
author's imagination. Any resemblance to actual persons,
living or dead, events or localities is entirely coincidental.

All rights reserved. No part of this publication may be
reproduced, stored in a retrieval system, or transmitted, in any
form or by any means, electronic, mechanical, photocopying,
recording, or otherwise, without the prior
permission of the publishers.

This book is sold subject to the condition that it shall not, by
way of trade or otherwise, be lent, re-sold, hired out or
otherwise circulated without the publisher's prior consent in
any form of binding or cover other than that in which it is
published and without a similar condition including this
condition being imposed on the subsequent purchaser.

For Claire, Millie and Eliza
Always with love

Last exit on yesterday

Chapter One

I guess most people wait for justice. We didn't. And that was our mistake. We meted out justice like small gods. We were the kittens that killed the lions. We became the lions, but instead of free and brave; caged and mean. Now, I have to stop our descent into cruelty. I have to liberate us. For the sakes of our victims, we must confess.

The old house is too big for me and yet I could never let it go. Too many memories keep me snared, penetrating like meat hooks deep into my flesh. I should've sold up after my mother killed herself. I can't help but think how disappointed she'd be in me.

Leaving the house, I shut the front door; knowing when I open it next, I'll have instigated our fate; condemned myself and my six closest friends to spend the rest of our lives in prison. We deserve it, though.

'God forgive us,' I whisper, glancing above the door to the black and grey stained-glass porch screen depicting a bird of prey, a mouse grasped in its talons. I glance back over my shoulder, feeling certain the house is staring back at me, its two jutting black and white gabled windows and barge boards at the top like huge lidded-eyes glaring down on me. Sections of red bricks bleed through dirty white-blistered paint like old wounds through skin.

I surface into the town's canopied shopping streets, the January afternoon so cold it cuts deep to the bone. Passing pastel-coloured hotels, I head for Llandudno's North Shore, to the wide-open sea, where I can find space to think. I need a final moment of clarity, one that will validate I'm finally about to do the *right* thing. Upending the lives of the old gang, the thought of their reactions on reading the message I was about to send, enough to conjure a wash of hot blood right through me. Once sent, there would be no

The Great Orme

recall or *undo*. The damage would be done.

It was my call and always had been, ever since we were kids; our gang, the best of friends, with me, their leader. Now, at twenty-nine, I think back to when we were teenagers, when we killed for the first time.

They should never have murdered the old man. He'd done nothing wrong other than kill his dog. They didn't have to do it. People have their own minds and sometimes need to use them. The dog was called Biscuits; a great name. We treated him as if he was ours. We loved him. On our way to school, sensing our approach, he would bark furiously, demanding our attention. Every day, we'd enter the old man's garden uninvited, and fuss over the gentle golden Labrador, giving him the treats we'd pilfered from our homes. And every time, the old man never coming out to see us, watching from behind the window, curtains parted ever so slightly.

I remember that morning vividly, steep streets bathed in the amber light of a low-slung orange sun. It seemed the stillness and silence of the summer shadows belonged to us. It seemed everything belonged to us. But it's the way I burned within I remember most – with outrage, injustice, and hatred for an unfair world.

The seven of us were on our way to school, as usual, already friends for life. We stopped at the garden gate and waited for Biscuits to bark and pant with excitement at our arrival, but that morning he didn't show and, unusually, the gate was locked.

We climbed over the fence to be confronted by a murderer and the murdered.

The old man stood there smiling at us, pale lips stretched thin on his craggy face. Oversized black sunglasses covered his eyes, and a faded-blue peaked cap embroidered with "I love the Great Orme" sat on his head. Hunched over a shovel, and leaning on it, he'd been waiting for us. Before him lay Biscuits, but not the Biscuits we knew. The dog's severed head, a butchered and bloody mess, brown eyes glazed, lolling tongue limp on the concrete court.

I don't think we ever ran so fast. We scaled the fence and ran to our safe place – the old house, my mother's house.

It took us a while to calm, for me to calm them, their distress and anger a fierce and potent potion. All the while, it became clear to me what must be done. It was, I explained, a good thing they must do, in fact, a far better thing than they had ever done before. I must admit my surprise to their ready acceptance. It was then I suppose I first felt the power I wielded, not over them, but for them. Which was when it all started to go wrong.

That night, we scaled the old man's fence again. I remained in the garden to keep watch while the others crept along the side of the house to the crumbling shed adjoining it. The shed door was all rotted wood and gave way easily as I knew it would; I had completed a reconnaissance mission an hour earlier. Stepping over Biscuits' stinking "bed", a filthy old blanket stuck fast with dried shit and hopping flies, they navigated a floor filled with empty beer cans. All wearing gloves, they did as I instructed, loosening and removing the cracked glass in the window to the bathroom, climbing through, until all the others were inside the old man's home. Easy.

I admit to some nerves while I waited outside in the dark, the only sound the electric hum of streetlights and the odd clank and scrape of faraway noises that could be late-night treacheries of other sorts. It was then I got to thinking about the power each of us has, the power we never seem to exercise, everyone's quiet acceptance of a life half-lived, their acceptance at injustice, abuses, and corruption. I concluded the world would be a better place if only we all acted out of fairness, righted wrongs ourselves instead of waiting for society to rectify itself, or worse, ignore them altogether. I wondered why we complicated everything. Certainly, my mind was decided. Even at that age, I knew I was charismatic, my personality magnetic. People seemed to sense a maturity in me beyond my years and I lapped it up. And so, being susceptible, stressed, and emotionally vulnerable, my six friends turned to me, became my devotees. In many ways, I felt like a protective parent to them.

The memory is old but remains fresh, and my skin still

prickles at the sense of injustice at the old man's brutal killing of Biscuits. Yet, my conscience stabs harder still at my own involvement – our retribution, and at night it kills me over and over again. I can't go on like this.

This cardinal piece of the Welsh coast is incomprehensible: a peremptory edge of the world, all jutting bones, salt-caked scents, and the sea an eternal barrage of feral waves like a thousand searching tongues. Clothed in pale grey, the tides pulling me; I veer towards the beach, a skirt of sand, shingle, and rock. People walk briskly by, propelled by sniping winter winds, and with their hoods pulled tight, scarves wrapped around their necks and chins to protect against the bitter intrusion. No one notices me and I feel like a minor character in my own story. Each and every one of them will soon know who I am, what I've done, what *we've* done, the depths we descended. I'm appalled at myself, at us. I can only pray that late is better than never.

Standing on the sandy shore, I gaze up at the skeletal pier hanging off the mainland like a deformed limb. But, as always, here, at the Northern edge of Wales, my eyes and heart are drawn by the towering expanse of huge limestone headland that dominates the space between sea and sky beyond the pier. Two miles long and one mile wide, the Great Orme, derives its name from the old Scandinavian Norse "sea serpent". She looms large above the town, a sheer vertical cliff face, laced and threaded with slabs of limestone and dolomite like pale-grey bones between the verdant green moss. The blunt end of the mountainous leviathan's head rises more than two hundred metres above the ineffectual lapping of the Irish Sea, and as ever, I feel insignificant and temporary in comparison to the atavistic sea serpent. The Vikings knew something of the Great Orme and the ancient power it wields. I feel as if I've drawn a strange kind of strength from it over time. And I suppose that's why I could never leave the place as they did. Never once did they look behind them. Never once did they ask me how I was coping. I wonder if they still hear the call. The Great Orme wants them back.

I press the cold glass of my phone to my lips and stare at the face of the jutting headland. For a moment, I think I see crimson red eyes burn like molten rock in the Great Orme's craggy strata. I clutch my phone tighter, fingertips turning white with the strain. I wonder if it's just me, or do all who ride the petrified back of the Great Orme dream its dark omens?

A dog bounds past me, brushing against my leg, and distracted, I divert my gaze to see it, tail wagging and nose hovering over the sand, following a trail of fishy scent. When I view the Great Orme again, the serpent's eyes have disappeared, if they were ever there, only giant, shadowy rock holding the sea at bay. I return to gazing at the sea. And not far out, in the shallows, a lone cormorant stands conspicuously on a rocky promontory, basking in the meagre rays of daylight, broad black wings spread wide in a cruciform pose. Immediately, I know there can be no going back. This is how the end starts. I feel it in the sharpening of the air on my skin, hear it in the raking caw of a raven, see it in the stoney face of the sea serpent. We are caught in its teeth now.

I press SEND –

I've sent the same message to the six of you. I'll get straight to the point – I've changed my mind... I can no longer keep our secret.

I was wrong. We were wrong. What we did, the things I made you do... were all wrong. They must now be confessed.

It's been six years since we last met at the old house, since we made our pact never to tell. We owe our victims' and their families. We must act to save our souls before it's too late.

Return to North Wales, to Llandudno, to the Great Orme, to the old house, this Saturday – 8pm. All of you.

Forever yours,

Zachary Llewellyn

Too much time,
and a deficit to come

Chapter Two

I return to the old house.

Here, the dead live with me. I hear their footsteps in the hallway, their whispers in the walls, those we murdered, urging me to confess.

Over the years, I manipulated each of my six friends, each emotionally vulnerable to some extent or other: through adverse family issues, abuses, or socio-economic conditions, all of them simply needing to feel a part of a whole. I gave them a sense of belonging, of validation, and formed a perverse safe haven. I did it because I could; recognising an authoritative leadership quality in myself early on, I imbued my own philosophy within them, and once realised as a way of living, there was no turning back – or so we thought.

Standing before the bedroom window, I watch the Irish Sea swallow the driving rain. The things we did gallop through my mind as if on a carousel, revolving but never leaving. *I am sorry. I am sorry. I am sorry…* I could say it a million times and it still wouldn't be enough. All that's left is to confess. How hard could it be?

I sense a movement behind me, and my heart-rate spikes. I turn to see the bedroom door swing slowly open. It's not that sort of door. The house is old; the door is solid wood, requiring a good push to move it. Without taking my eyes off it, and with my insides writhing, I place my rum-filled cup on the table beneath the window and stare at the doorway, waiting for something to happen, waiting for someone or something to appear.

Finally, Smokey, my loyal black Welsh terrier, enters the room, stops, lifts his head, and pads over to me, nosing his cold snout against my leg. I let out a long sigh of relief and bend to stroke his head.

'Well,' I say, crouching and nuzzling my head into his, 'it's Thursday tomorrow, and I guess we have to prepare for the arrival of our old friends. It won't be easy, little fella. They're *not* going to be happy with me.'

I wake early, before light. The long claw of fear scrapes the inside of my skull. I can feel the leaden press of the dead above me in the dark, beleaguered bones weary with their weight. It's my responsibility to release them with a simple confession.

I get up and clean the old house as dirty light is slowly wrung from the black cloth sky. Memories peck at me like frenzied birds, persistent and impossible to block. It's Thursday and a way to go until Saturday. I must occupy myself with the simultaneously abundant yet meagre time I have remaining.

My friends will need to eat, so I decide to go to the supermarket. I choose to walk even though it's raining, because I can still taste the rum on my tongue, and worry there's too much in my blood-stream to drive, but my thoughts run more freely, forging connections, making plans.

For all the calm logic I'm known for, I'm consumed by a dreadful doubt. I know I've done the right thing, the human thing, but loneliness can betray a person. How is it, I think, some people are capable of moving on, never to look behind them, content to live in the present and face the future without even a glance over their shoulder at the past? I'm not one of them. Each of us has accountability, a responsibility to each other, even to the dead. Especially to the dead.

At eight in the morning, I have the supermarket to myself. I'm cold, clammy, and drenched, but I don't mind. It feels good to feel. Before long, we'll all be punished by the ritual boredom of prison.

Returning home, my hands are scored red from carrying the shopping bags, clothes a soaked second skin. The cold more than penetrates. It has decamped and settled within my tired body, an uneasy chill floating through my blood. The old house, my house, the house where we decided to end it, to never see one another again, seems to strain with the weight of knowing, creaking and groaning as if a dying man.

I stack the fridge and the cupboards with the shopping. It's only fair they're well-fed. Full bellies will be required if we are to have the strength to commit to doing the right thing. I spend Thursday drifting around the old house, tidying, although it seems futile; everything is old and frayed. I wince. If my mother were alive, she wouldn't be best pleased. I miss her. Just as I miss my father.

I've let the day bleed away. Smokey is asleep in his basket. I can hear him breathing. As for me, sleep continues to be a hard-won battle and, as it edges nearer, so too the dread. Buffeted by the wind, my bedroom window rattles in its blistered, wooden frame, a cold draught licking at my face. The curtains remain open; I need to know the real world exists, that it's out there, the moon pushing and pulling at the sea, the Great Orme watching over us, as it always has. I need to feel something other than the sly caress of the ghosts, hear something other than the brittle creaking of their fingers before I sleep.

Broken biscuits and a smashed skull

Chapter Three

It's Friday, they'll be here tomorrow. It's still raining. I swill down some leftover rum, appreciative of the warming fire in my belly. I need it. It dampens the pain a little, and will help me get through until tomorrow. I need to be ready for them. I know it's wrong, and my wife, Orla, would reprimand me immediately if she were here. But of course, she will be soon, because she's one of the six.

Smokey twitches in his basket, dreaming. The wiry terrier is twelve now, his once charcoal black fur meshed with a shimmer of silvery grey. He's slow and sleeps often, reluctant to leave the house. I don't suppose he has long left. Hard to believe he was a little too enthusiastic for the family that had him. No one wanted him. He would have been put down if I hadn't taken him in. People can be so cruel.

The old house is like me. It continues to creak with the strain of standing, the unrelenting battle against the elements taking their toll. My reflection in the window is cast in double, distorted and ugly. Unruly jet-black hair jutting out at irregular angles, pale, drawn face and thin lips. Orla would be disappointed, but then I always felt she was disappointed by me. I will venture out again today, get a haircut, treat myself to a shave. Hell, I'll even buy some new clothes. Despite everything, I must present myself as in control, especially faced with what's to come.

My phone vibrates in the back pocket of my jeans with an incoming call. I retrieve it and my heart beats quicker at the sight of the image on the screen – Harrison. Almost unrecognisable, once as tall and skinny as a lamp post, his profile picture is now of a shaven-headed, muscle-bound beast. I should have contacted them sooner, much sooner. I groan, realising this is a video call.

I hold the phone out before me and accept the call. He's in an empty gym, floor-to-ceiling mirrors behind him. Harrison was the tallest of our gang and lacking in confidence. 'Harrison –' I greet him, but he stops me before I can continue.

'Just don't, Zac! Have you lost your mind? Your message is crazy! Listen, you wouldn't recognise me now. I'm a different man. I've moved on. You should too!'

I drag a chair back from the kitchen table and sit. I know I've got my work cut out to persuade them.

'Harrison, I know it's been a long time–'

'Fucking right, it has. Six years, to be precise!'

'I know. My message is bound to have stirred up long forgotten memories–'

'The old man,' Harrison interrupts. 'He deserved what he got. That's the point. That's the whole fucking point!'

Harrison splits open a small white rectangular paper packet and pours the powdery contents into a tall glass of water, turning into something that looks like fizzy milk. He raises the glass and his eyes hover above the rim as he swirls the frothing liquid within.

'Why?' he says, softer this time. 'I'm confused.'

I pinch my eyes shut with my free hand. 'The old man, Harrison. He didn't deserve it. He didn't deserve to die. Yeah, of course, he was a mean shit. He should have been locked up for it… but to do what we did… that was–'

'*We?*' Harrison exclaims, the blue veins in his thick neck bulging. '*You* weren't there! *You* didn't do it! *You* didn't kill the old man! It was the rest of us! You can't lay this bullshit on us now. Not now! Not after all this time!'

Harrison is fired up. It's to be expected. But I didn't expect this heavy-weight, assertive version of him. I need to let him talk if I'm going to persuade him to confess. I need to understand him as he is now. I wait.

'I remember it as if only yesterday,' he says, frowning while turning from the camera. 'We pressed the old man down on his filthy kitchen floor until he choked and became silent. He was cruel, Zac. What we did was fair. We loved that dog, it loved us.'

Harrison's biceps are twitching, crinkled blue veins bulging, and I swear they might tear with the strain. He swigs the entire contents of the glass. Wiping his lips on the back of his hand, he gazes at my digital upper half.

'I wonder, Harrison,' I say, trying not to be distracted by the new shape and size of the skinny man I previously knew, 'if the old man did what he did because he was ill, not of sound mind? Perhaps, what he did was a call for help?'

'Come off it. That's not how we do things. He was sick, alright. Sick in the head. We dealt with him. We took care of him in the best possible way. Besides, there's no going back, no undoing what's been done. You know that. Besides, it wasn't only the old man we killed that day, it was the boy too.'

I nod my head. 'I'll never forget... I'll never forgive us.'

'Just hold on there, Zac,' Harrison says, jabbing his significant finger at the screen. 'I'll say it again... You weren't there when we killed the old man. Let me tell you how it went down. While you waited outside, I pinned the old man to his filthy kitchen floor by his elbows with my knees. I covered his mouth with my hand to stifle his yelps. To this day, I can feel the shape of his crinkly-paper skin underneath my hands.'

Harrison is clenching and unclenching his fist.

'We hadn't questioned you. We followed your instructions. The old man was cruel. He deserved what he got. Costas made the first cut, just a small nick, only released a dribble of blood. Sian, her hair dyed that stupid green colour, was next. She surprised me, slashed his other wrist multiple times until she scored a deep groove. She was careful too, covering the incision with her gloved hands to prevent the spray from going everywhere. We were all wearing gloves on your insistence. Tomasz went next, ripping the blade along the old man's thigh to his knee, mustard coloured corduroy trousers turning a wet burgundy, a pool of blood gathering beneath him. Orla cut his other thigh… huh,' he laughs. 'Back then I would never have thought the two of you would get married.'

'Me neither,' I say unsmiling. 'That's the beauty of it. Lives unravel in a myriad of ways… we should let them.'

Harrison snorts. 'Yeah right! Not for the old man. We cut the cruel bastard down before he could do any more damage.' Inhaling deeply, he scrapes his fingernails backwards over his shaven head. 'I can still smell Jessie's rose-scented perfume as she leaned into me and slit the old man's neck. All the while,' he says, returning his gaze to the phone once again, 'I held the old man's head clamped to my knees and covered his mouth with my hand. I felt everything, Zac. I felt each spasm, every filthy choking wheeze. The stink of shit and piss. I remember leaning over him, gazing upside down into his grey eyes. I wanted to see his pain, wanted to see justice served. We all did, right?'

I want to tell him that was *then*, and this is *now*. We were wrong. But shaking his head, he continues. 'Outside, you took the knife and inspected us for blood. You made us take our gloves off and give them to you, stuffing them into an orange plastic bag, "Save the planet" and a picture of a dolphin on the side of it. Funny, the things you remember. You took our coats, anything with blood on, and stuffed them in the bag.

"Remember what he did to Biscuits," you said. You went on to say the old man deserved to die, that we had righted a wrong. You told us, should anyone ask, we had been playing in Happy Valley Gardens, hanging out together. You told us it was going to be fine; no one would know any better. Then you told us to leave.

'You and I helped the others over the fence before scrambling over it ourselves. The others were quick to run, and that's when you and I realised we weren't alone. Someone was watching us.

A boy, younger than us. The little fucker was in the wrong place at the wrong time. I can see him now, clear as crystal, blond cropped hair and wearing a pristine, red, Welsh rugby shirt, staring at us from the other side of the road, one foot on the ground, the other high up on a pedal, weight poised to push his bike off. You and I exchanged a glance. I remember, you smiled. I was shocked. Back then, you scared me. I wondered how long the boy had been there, how much he'd seen and heard. He swung his bike around and started off up the road, bike lurching from side to side as he strained to gain momentum.

"Stop him," you said.

'I remember looking at you for one second, one second to know you meant it; of course you meant it. I charged after the boy. To be honest, Zac, sometimes I wonder what would have happened if I hadn't caught up with him, if he had escaped and told on us. It was close, perhaps only centimetres or seconds in it. Makes you think though, doesn't it?'

I cover my mouth as if to stop something from falling out, and to let Harrison keep talking.

'Sprinting flat out, I flung myself at him, catching the flapping hem of his coat, enough to disrupt his balance, the bike skidding from underneath him, and he rolled against a broken section of concrete kerb. Half my size, he stared up at me like a frightened rabbit. I picked up a chunk of the concrete kerb – it was so heavy I had to use both hands.

The thing is… he hadn't done anything wrong. I might not have done it. I might have run away, but you told me, "Make sure he doesn't tell," you said.

'I did what you told me to do, what had to be done. It was terrible, but I don't regret killing the boy. God only knows what would have happened to us if I hadn't.'

Finally finished, Harrison purses his lips and stares at me. I nod my head as if understanding, but I never intended for him to kill the boy – only to prevent him from telling on us.

The Great Orme

With the digital distance between us, there is little chance of persuading Harrison to confess there and then.

'I'm sorry,' I say, and I mean it. I've ruined his life and the others' lives along with it. Why hadn't anyone reined me in? I would have stopped if only someone had confronted me. God, I'm so, so sorry. 'Harrison, like I said in my message, I need to see you. We have to work this out. It can only happen face to face.'

Harrison bangs his empty glass on the table and shakes his head. 'Zac, sometimes it feels like the whole world is against you.' He turns the glass in slow, even circles on the surface of the table. 'Well, that's completely wrong. It's *always* against you.' He observes me, eyes burning, like he's pouring all the feeling he has from them. 'I can't give you what you want. I have a girlfriend.' His voice has raised a pitch. He's stressed or nervous or both. 'She's smart. Perhaps as smart as you, Zac. I can't lose her. I won't.' He pushes the glass across the table until out of my sight. 'I guess you'll realise soon enough.'

The phone screen cuts to my own full image as Harrison hangs up. I flip the phone over on the table and look up, my attention caught by a shape, something small, black, and ragged, that sweeps in front of the kitchen window and disappears in an instant, most likely a crow barrelling toward some sort of object it fancies.

Seeing and speaking to Harrison has me worried, a little scared, too. What if I can't persuade him? If I can't persuade them?

I go to the dining-room and stare out of the window at the sea. I have spent a lifetime staring at the sea, hypnotised by its will, possessed by its power, its brutality. But it's as nothing compared to the Great Orme. Its shadowed cliffs dominate the sea and they dominate me. It's as if they are waiting for something to happen, waiting for something to crush.

'Jesus Christ, Smokey. How did it get to this? What kind of monster was I?' I ask, pinching my eyes, a ball of anxiety sloshing around inside my stomach. Half asleep, Smokey cocks an ear at the sound of my voice, and he rolls on his back, waiting for belly rubs. 'I need to keep busy,' I say, crouching to give him what he wants. Tears slide down my face. 'You're a good boy, Smokey,' I say through snotty breaths. 'I'm sorry for what I've done and I'm sorry for all that's to come.' An abrupt knock at the front door interrupts us.

I peer through the dining-room window. I can't see who's at the door because of the porch commanding the entrance, but my eyes follow the steps down the path and to the rusted gate hanging off its hinges. Parked up on the kerb, a police car.

The window
through which I
must see the world

Chapter Four

I stare at the policewoman, and she stares back at me. I've opened the door only as far as necessary, the edge of the door splitting me down the middle.

'Good morning,' she says brightly. 'Have you got a moment?'

The answer is no. 'Yes, of course.'

Her hair is pinned up beneath a standard issue black "bowler" hat, but stray strands of fine blonde hair have fallen loose to touch her shoulders. She sweeps them away, deftly tucking them behind her ear before tilting her head sideways and narrowing her sharp green eyes. I think she's recognised me.

'Sergeant Zachary Llewellyn?'

I smile and the guilt burns. Nothing burns like guilt. Whatever it is she's here for, I don't need it, not now. 'I've taken a couple of weeks off... y'know, a few things to put right.'

She breaks into a clean, wide smile. 'I thought so. I knew I recognised you.'

Still gripping the edge of the door with one hand, as if she might charge it at any moment, I try to think, and then I remember. 'Erm... it's Helen isn't it... Helen –'

'Starling. Yes.'

'How's it going? You've been with us, what? Three, four weeks now?'

'Four,' she replies, beaming, raising her fingertips to her chin. She's thinking, analysing.

She glances past me, trying to see beyond me into the corridor. Damn. Too keen for my liking.

The Great Orme

'So, what's with the visit? Anything exciting?' I want her to get to the point and leave.

'Oh, of course,' she says, her demeanour immediately serious. 'I'm sorry. There was an incident in town last night. An elderly man was attacked in his home, on Clonmel Street, and although it's not official yet…' She leans forward conspiratorially. 'He's dead. Murdered.'

Murders are relatively rare in Llandudno. I should know. 'What happened?'

'It's terrible, actually,' she says, feeling for the radio in her chest pocket. 'Someone broke in to his house, cut him up… he bled to death.'

The dark memory of my youth, our first murder, flares to the forefront of my mind, turning my blood hot. 'Why?' I ask, the question partially directed at myself.

She shakes her head. 'God only knows. Barbaric, isn't it?' The bulk of the yellow reflective jacket and body armour under her coat ensure she commands a certain presence, but no more so than her determined gaze. 'The murderer slit the poor man's wrists… his thighs.' She presses the heels of her hands together and gazes away. 'His neck.'

My heart plunges through my stomach. Behind her, stood at the gate, I see the cracked and toothless face of the old man from my past, Biscuits' owner. Without a sound, he laughs at me, raising a bony finger to hold his oversized sunglasses in place. With his other hand he points at the ground before him, where lies the severed head of his Labrador, Biscuits. Suddenly, he stops laughing. His forehead wrinkles as if serious, lips tighten, and they tremble. Tears roll from beneath his sunglasses, navigating deep-grooved contours in his cheeks. He stares toward my neighbour's house. I open the door and lean forward, almost doubled over to peer around the porch, but no one's there, and when I look back, he's gone too.

'Zachary… Zachary?'

Helen's voice slides through the darkness of my mind, bringing light, and I'm grateful. Strangely, I find her presence reassuring. I soften my grip on the door. 'I'm sorry, thought I saw someone. Have you apprehended anyone? Any suspects?'

'Not yet. Still mopping up. Literally. Nothing much by way of clues, either. The poor guy lived alone, in his late seventies. I can't imagine what he did to deserve that.'

'Does anyone deserve that?' I ask. A genuine question, and one to which at one time my answer would have been *yes*.

She gives me a pointed look. I detect an inner confidence behind her fresh-faced appearance. 'My guess is it's going to be a case for forensics,' she says, ignoring my question. 'The office is collecting video surveillance, but other than that, we are doing the rounds. And hoping someone has seen something unusual that might help. And so, here I am.'

'Well, Helen, I'm afraid I've absolutely nothing to report. I popped out to the supermarket early this morning, but I didn't notice anyone acting suspicious. In fact, I barely noticed anyone. It was pouring down.'

She nods. 'No. That's fine. I'll make a few more random calls, then call it a day. My shift is nearly done. Thanks, Zac. I'm still settling in, trying to get used to the new force and Llandudno, to be honest. This case is nasty, isn't it? It's horrible to think there are people in this town capable of such a thing.'

In the space of a few minutes, she's gone from referring to me by my job title and full name to just *Zac*. It's not a problem. I suppose she's being friendly. I think we're done, but as I wish her good luck and set myself to close the door, she glances up at me, eyes narrowed again. 'It's bizarre. The elderly man was discovered lying flat on his back in the kitchen… biscuits placed over his body.'

'Biscuits?' I say, while my mind shifts up three gears. 'Are you certain?'

'Yes. Seven, to be exact.'

'Seven,' I repeat. My old friends and I are seven. Seven murderers. My saliva suddenly tastes metallic and I feel queasy.

The Great Orme

I roll my tongue and lick the back of my teeth in what I hope is an innocuous fashion, raising an eyebrow to affect a modest display of puzzlement for the police officer. 'Well,' I say. 'I'm sure we'll do our best to catch the perpetrator,' and checking my watch, I wish her well, desperate for her to leave.

The radio stuck to the chest of her high-vis jacket buzzes. 'I'm sure we will,' she says, green eyes needle-sharp. 'Sorry to have disturbed you on your time off. I'll leave you to it.'

As soon as the door is shut, I collapse against it, heart racing and perspiring like I've run a fast mile. The dread within me is gathering. I'm a police Sergeant, and I don't believe in coincidences. Seven biscuits for seven murderers. One of the six has taken exception to my message, and they've left a diabolical warning on my doorstep. Why couldn't they wait until tomorrow, listen to reason? That's yet another murder I'm in some way responsible for. I gather myself, straighten up. I need to stay calm. It will all be over in the next couple of days. I need to stay in control.

Smokey trots up to me but stops rigid as a noise like a chair dragged over floorboards comes from upstairs. I tense, lifting my head and stifling my breath. The house is old, with creaking floorboards and a heating system that groans on a whim, but this sounded different, loud and deliberate. I stalk toward the base of the carpeted staircase and stare up into the gloom. Ears and eyes straining for sound or movement, but there's nothing other than the background noise that's the heave and sigh of the old house.

Relaxing a little, the unmistakable slow, drawn-out sound of something being dragged over floorboards returns. Smokey barks, short tail stiff and pointed, his gaze fixed up the stairway. I imagine a shadow moves among the other shadows at the top of the stairs. I reach for the landing light-switch on the wall and flick it on.

As the shadows recede, the bright yellow glow from the landing ceiling light reveals washed-out teal-coloured walls and a Dyson vacuum cleaner at the top of the stairs. Pleading Smokey to be quiet, I place a hand on the intricately carved oak swirl at the base of the handrail. As I ascend the steps, my sweaty palm sticks and bumps along the handrail. Smokey follows close behind, growling.

After checking the five bedrooms, even looking under the beds and in the cupboards, I find no one, and no signs of intrusion. Sitting on the edge of my bed, I rub my face furiously with both hands that I might invoke some inner steel to cope with what's to come. I can't afford to be suggestible or easily manipulated. I know what my friends are capable of. Smokey curls up in his basket, satisfied like me, that the house has settled. I sit up straight, and as ever, my gaze is drawn toward the window. I get up and go to it to observe the sea. But it's not the sea that captures my attention this time. It's the smeared lines scored on the glass panes. I angle my head so the dingy morning light catches the marks, defining them more clearly, and a fresh wave of oily queasiness drenches my gut. I see the smeared lines are letters, drawn by someone's finger in the fine layer of dirt and dust.

Top left pane: YOU

Top right pane: WILL

Bottom left pane: NOT

Bottom right pane: CONFESS

Transfixed, I stare at the words, hardly believing my eyes. I hear a noise, a short, sharp clunk from somewhere else in the house. Smokey stirs in his basket, suddenly alert and growling. I pick him up and step into the hallway, looking along its length. No movement. All doors to the bedrooms now closed by me, only the bathroom door at the end of the hall was wide open. I thought I had closed it, but I can't be sure. I put Smokey on the floor. 'Go on, boy,' I say, my voice barely a whisper. I point toward the bathroom. 'Go find.'

Smokey patters along the hall, sniffing at each door, but he's too slow, too old and impatient. I'm a grown man, for Christ's sake, a police Sergeant. Taking a deep breath, I stride along the hall, opening each door and glancing quickly within. Entering the bathroom, I notice shower gel upturned on the side of the bath and the cherry red liquid dribbling down the smooth pearl-white inner contour. I put it upright. The shower gel isn't mine. Mine is green and in the corner of the room within the shower cubicle, untouched.

Smokey trudges behind me as I make my way across the landing toward my bedroom, the old floorboards occasionally creaking beneath my feet.

In my bedroom, I study the words on the window in the hope they might reveal a clue as to their author. Other than me, Smokey, and the ghosts that live with me, the house is empty. There is, of course, another explanation, one which I'm not prepared to countenance – that I'm delusional. But I'm not. I'm not mad. People have died. They've been murdered because of me. I slide my fingers back and forth over each of the panes where the words instructing me not to confess are, and rub them clear, the glass cold and damp to the touch. It's possible I wrote the words. More than that, I think; it's highly probable. Anxious and tired, my mind is playing tricks. *Get a grip.* I'm more certain than ever we must confess. I cannot continue like this. I can't shake the feeling, the revelation of the murder of the old man in Clonmel Street, and its similarities to our killing all those years ago. It's unnerving. I'm not one for coincidences. An ache fills me, spreads from the back of my head into my eyes. I've started something, and I don't know where it's going.

Cut here

Chapter Five

I slip away from the old house, leaving Smokey behind, and all the lights on, as if their glow might cast a much-needed beacon of hope. The memory of that night six years ago, when we all met at the old house is at the forefront of my mind. That night we agreed never to meet again. We agreed to bury our crimes. We promised never to tell. I'm about to break the promise. God, they'll hate me for it.

The cold bites hard, no mercy offered. It pierces my skin and sinks its teeth into my bones. Although a pitiful concrete-grey January sky, the air beneath has an eerie metallic shimmer, like there's a build-up of one element or another, set to explode at any moment. I tread from tarmac to slatted pier walkway, my breath escaping my body in a trail of white, sparkling mist that snakes swiftly upwards. Like its belly has been sliced open, the morning sky breaks open, releasing a swirl of snow-flakes that stick to everything but the sea. The Great Orme watching over me. I arrive at the end of the pier and lean on the handrail to watch the birds riding the gentle ebb and flow of cream-frothed waves. An annoyed gull screeches, skimming over my head, and I remember the people we killed.

I used to think anyone was capable of killing. We are nature's supreme killing machines. Anyone can grab a kitchen knife – plunge it in, twist it; drive a car at a victim; smash a skull to pieces with a heavy stone. It's just a decision, like any other. Except most people don't, they won't, they can't, even with someone they hate. Once we give in to animal instinct, we lose our humanity, and we become barbaric, ugly creatures undeserving of our self-proclaimed intellect. I understand that

The Great Orme

now, even though it's too late.

Not everyone we killed was bad, but nevertheless, we decided we had the moral authority and the power. I wonder about the nature of human wickedness, how easily the truth can be obscured by the smallest denial, the weakest evasion. How quickly evil becomes acceptable, justified, until it's just a way of living. There is always a price though, and it's now. I'm shocked at how my posturing, my imagined self-importance and my delusions have crumbled. It's like someone has switched the lights on and I can see the strands that connect us: my friends, our victims, their families, me.

Something tugs hard on my hood, jolting me back, and I land sprawling on the pier's wooden-slatted floor. Senses switched to high alert; I scurry to my feet. Spinning around, arms raised, ready to fight, but I see only hardy locals wrapped in monochromatic layers, milling about. A kind old couple ask me if I'm okay, while everyone else avoids me like I might be mad.

Shaken and questioning my sanity, I leave the pier to make my way along Glan Y Mor Parade. The flat sea lies to my left and Llandudno town centre beyond the long line of tall Victorian sea-front hotels to my right. I notice yellow-vested policemen congregated at the top of Clonmel Street. A group of busybodies are talking to them, nosey locals and a journalist or two, no doubt enquiring after the details of the old man's murder. Pulling my hood up and trudging through the flurry of gently sticking snow-flakes, I tell myself Saturday can't come soon enough. I arrive at Benito's Barbers on Mostyn Avenue. Sian used to work there. Sian wouldn't hurt a fly, not really. I can't wait to see her tomorrow.

I can barely see inside because of the heat misting the windows, and the doorbell jingles as I open the door. 'The usual, Benito,' I say, before correcting myself, 'wait… to hell with it, close and sharp on the sides and back, and electrified and wild on top. Give me a shave as well.'

'No problem, my friend,' he says, deftly taking my coat and spinning a black leatherette chair around for me to sit in. He produces a lathering stick and slaps thick white shaving cream efficiently over my neck and face, almost up to my eyeballs. 'Special occasion?'

I brace, gripping the arms of the chair tighter as he scrapes the cold steel blade down my skin in rapid staccato movements. 'Just a few friends coming to stay,' I say through clenched teeth, terrified to move my jaw and sounding like a rookie ventriloquist.

'Nice. Anyone we know?' he says, wiping the blade on the towel hanging from his waist.

'Well, yes, actually. Do you remember Sian Bevan?'

He stops mid-wipe. 'Sian Bevan? Little Sian Bevan. My apprentice?'

I nod, the soapy cream leaks between my lips.

'Well, well, well,' he says, bending once more, elbows sticking out above his head as he attacks my neck with the blade. 'That explains why she's here.'

'What?' I push out an arm awkwardly through the cape to stop him.

Benito stands straight and strokes his bushy grey moustache with his fingers. 'Yes, my friend. She's bleached her hair – short and spiky, it looks fantastic! She and her partner – a beautiful girl called Fatima, I think, popped in to see me this morning. Infatuated with each other, I'd say. They were clinging to one another for dear life.'

I find out little else from Benito. Sian had better not bring her partner tomorrow – I can do without further complicating our hellish situation.

London to Kashmir

Chapter Six

Hair cut and moulded with a ladle's worth of product, I give Benito a five-hundred-pound tip. At first, he refuses, but I insist. I won't need it – prison comes all expenses paid. Stumbling outside, hair set like a carefully constructed birds' nest; an early era Robert Smith from *The Cure*.

The backdrop sounds of traffic, gulls and kids shrieking seem to be amplified as if the snow, like acoustical glue, lifts those sounds and deadens all others. Sian has arrived early and I wonder why. Her aunt and cousins still live in Llandudno, and I wonder if she's visiting them, but then I remember she hated them as they hated her. They couldn't contain their contempt at her sexuality, and she couldn't contain her contempt at their contempt. So much so that growing up, Sian spent more time in my home than her own. Time moves on and people change. Perhaps she intended to introduce Fatima to them – but I doubted it. Something turns in the fire-pit of my heart, charred embers that carry into my throat. I can't help but think maybe she killed the old man in Clonmel Street, some sort of sick warning for me. But no, not Sian. I know her and she wouldn't.

A car sweeps past, beeping its horn, making me jump. I swivel to look, but all I see through the snowfall are its blurred red tail lights as it turns the corner at the top of the road. I find myself outside *NORTH Menswear*, staring through the window, where under warm-yellow spotlights, headless mannequins pose confidently, hands on their hips, draped in designer clothes. I've never been in this store before, always feeling a little intimidated by its exclusivity, and preferring the anonymity of a chain store or internet shopping. Today, I feel different. I'm prepared to spend, and I feel like I need human interaction.

The smiling assistant tells me his name – Dylan. He asks me about my day, to which I respond with standard answers. I feel frustrated at myself that I feel on guard, even now, when all is lost. Dylan is relaxed and engaging, long, dark hair continually flopping over his face, so he has to hold it back. He tells me where he lives and how he loves Llandudno, but he wants to move to an English city where there's a bit more drama. He seems such a nice guy, although what do I know? Being a policeman makes one cynical – I've seen too many supposedly *decent* people turn out to be monsters.

I tell him I want to smarten up a bit, and up to the challenge, he retrieves some items and lays them out on the counter.

I end up choosing a pair of designer black jeans, black boots, and a salmon pink shirt. I slide my bank card inside my wallet, but a sharp cracking sound startles us. I drop my wallet and spin around. A spiralled crack is at the centre of the previously clear storefront window.

I rush outside. A young boy, a teenager, saunters toward me along the pavement, hood up, head down, staring at his phone.

'You!' I say, pulling him by his hood and pushing him up against a wall. His phone slips from his hand.

'Get off!' he yells. 'You've made me drop my phone.'

'Did you smash the window?'

'What window?'

'This one,' I say, pointing at the cracked glass.

'No.'

I loosen my grip. 'Did you see who did?'

'No.'

We glare at each other, defiance in our eyes. I let go. 'I'm sorry,' I say, picking up his phone and handing it to him. 'Did you even hear it crack?'

He reaches up to his ears and pulls out tiny black buds. 'No,

I was listening to music.'

He pushes them back in, pulls his hood up and walks away, all exaggerated swagger.

A mother pushing a pram, a toddler wearing bright yellow wellies and stamping his footprints in the snow while holding on to the frame of the pram, head toward me. Further along the street, a middle-aged couple, arms linked, tread carefully along the other side of the road. An elderly woman, walking stick in one hand, snow-coated umbrella in the other, comes from the opposite direction. None of them are suspects as far as I can tell.

In front of the store, Dylan is examining something in his hands. I join him. He's holding a small toy car and a doll, both barely touched by snow. I take them from him. The car is a small, metal, silver matchbox thing, doors that open, and that's about it. The doll has a sad expression on her brown face, but it's the letters scrawled above its round, staring eyes in red ink that make my heart flip and my stomach plummet. 'Choreji,' I read aloud, touching the letters with my thumb. The ink is still wet. On the doll's stiff white dress, some more scrawl in red-ink: *Let me rest*.

I see the face of the poor girl involved in Orla's hit-and-run incident. The image used on websites, in newspapers and on television in the days and weeks after the incident. Orla and I accepted there was no other option than for us to break up, the sight of one another a constant reminder of the horror we'd inflicted. We let everyone believe our marriage had failed because we'd "grown apart", our split a mutual decision that we were moving on. Only our five closest friends knew the terrible truth, as we knew theirs.

The memory of that awful night and how Orla had described her part in it, hits like a bullet to the brain:

The Great Orme

'Go on, one more won't kill you,' insisted one of Orla's glamorous colleagues, replacing her empty glass with a full glass of festive punch. 'You deserve it. Anyone who can market a cookbook by that dirty, old letch, like you did, absolutely deserves it! And it is our Christmas party, after all!'

Not normally a heavy drinker, Orla shrugged. 'One last drink. What harm can it do?'

I laughed at her and told her she would pay for it tomorrow.

Although it was Orla's office Christmas party, I'd invited Jessie, anything to give her some respite and get her away from her druggie boyfriend. Jessie was one of us. One of the secret seven. I'd had to persuade Jessie to come along, and it was only at the last minute she had agreed, and it was fairly obvious: her hair was wild, all irregular loose springs; she hadn't put on make-up; she wore a baggy tracksuit top and trousers; and she wore dirty white store-brand trainers. Despite that, I thought she looked amazing – a natural beauty – she was a poke in the eye to the plastic corporate marketing types swanning around.

When Jessie went to a restroom, Orla took me to one side and explained in no uncertain words it was embarrassing for her. She was on the fast track to success with Cherish Foods Limited, and at twenty-three years old, their youngest ever Marketing Director. She did not need Jessie showing up in the state she was, "like some fucking waif from the streets". I told Orla that Jessie needed our support, that she was having a rough time. "Fine, she can have it, just not in front of the hippest fucking colleagues in the food industry. For Christ's sake," Orla said. "She's a fucking mess, a fucking sore on fucking society."

We heard a cough from behind and turned to see Jessie. It was clear from the mortified expression on her face she'd been stood there the entire time. Even though Orla was tipsy, I saw massive remorse in her eyes, that she wanted the ground to swallow her up. But some words cannot be unsaid, and I too was mortified. Jessie nodded, some kind of understanding, and left us. Orla regarded me with her trademark black mascara'd eyes stretched wide, seeking some kind of redemption, desperate for me to explain that Jessie never heard her cruel words. I couldn't. Orla turned and walked away. I supposed to find Jessie.

I made polite noises for ten or twenty minutes with various people who probably felt sorry for me, standing by myself. Although to be truthful, Orla's friends' patter never registered with me on any level, and I was only there because she wanted me to be. I made an excuse and walked out on to the terrace where I tried calling Orla, but she didn't pick up. We'd agreed she would drive to the party, and I would drive back, so Orla could drink. From the elevated position of the terrace, I should have been able to see her Mercedes parked up at the side of the kerb. It was gone.

Later on, Orla told me she didn't know where she was headed, that she drove, her vision only a little hazy, following a river of red taillights. She couldn't answer my calls because she felt too ashamed to talk to me. She thought she would lose me, that I would leave her for being a dumbass. It quickly dawned on her she shouldn't be driving after consuming alcohol, so she'd left the traffic and turned down a quiet side road to park up. She hoped she'd over-reacted, that Jessie would have seen how drunk she was. She hoped she could make it up to her, give her money, even if her toe-rag of a boyfriend would end up stealing it from her.

The dull thump of the collision frightened Orla half to death. She slammed the brakes and peered through the windscreen at the empty tree-lined road. Thinking something was wrong with the car, she clambered out and edged alongside the vehicle, a hand pressed to the metal to steady herself. As she cleared the bonnet to view the front, she gagged as if she'd been shot in the stomach. She stared at that which was caught in the glare of her headlights. A little, black-haired girl lay flat and motionless on the tarmac. Only her upper torso and head visible. The rest of her body underneath the car.

Orla's mind and body went into lock-down, unable to move, think, or act. The girl's lifeless eyes stared up at Orla, beaded hair strung out around her lifeless face like a halo. Eventually, Orla moved around the girl, stepping through small puddles and staggering to the other side of the car. It suddenly struck Orla that the puddles weren't pooled water, but pools of glistening, red blood. The girl's blood.

Next to the girl lay a teddy bear. Orla lowered herself, picked it up in the hope the girl would ask for it. Orla reached out and pressed a shaking hand on the girl's chest, feeling for a heartbeat, and then over her mouth for a breath. Finding neither, Orla fell against the car's bonnet, gasping for breath. If she knew how, she would have laid down and swapped places with the girl, given her life that the girl might live instead.

After a minute, Orla straightened, and surveying the silent street, saw it was empty, not a soul to be seen. The houses were set back from the road, hidden behind the tall trees. What to do? What to do? In a panicked stupor, Orla got back in the car and did what she always did when she went too far – she called me.

At first, I was angry, not letting her speak, demanding to know why she had taken the car, how irresponsible she was, that she could have killed someone. I soon stopped when, through muffled sobs, she told me she had.

I remember instantly switching to hyper focus, my thoughts a multi-strobed stream of solutions. I told Orla to put the car's satnav on and to confirm her location. I told her to leave immediately. Through stifled sobs and incoherent mumblings, she refused. Twenty minutes later I disembarked from a cab just around the corner from her, found the longest driveway of a nearby house, and entered. As soon as the cab was out of sight, I returned to the street and, keeping to the shadows at the edge, turned into the street where Orla and the dead girl would be.

I will never forget the sight of the poor girl as long as I live: brown eyes staring up into the mist and beyond – just a little girl, but dead.

I'd shut out all feelings, blocking them at the source, my fear all too real. If released, I wouldn't be Zachary Llewellyn. I would be someone else. What I didn't realise until too late was the someone else was a better person. Cool and controlled, I told Orla there was nothing she could do for the girl, and the only thing left to do was to save herself, to save the life that remained. I drove us away, leaving the girl alone under a fuzzy, yellow moon, with no one to see her safely to the next life. Beside me, Orla gripped the dead girl's teddy bear in her lap.

Orla insisted on me dropping her at a police station, but I refused, insisting it wouldn't help, it wouldn't bring Choreji, the little girl's name as we discovered later through news feeds, back from the dead, and though they might think so, I presumed it wouldn't alleviate the family's pain – nothing could.

And so, I left Orla again, returning to the old house. But, as Orla told me, I left the remains behind. I always did. But that's not strictly true. Choreji lives with me, her perfect little face indelibly imprinted on my mind.

I try to run, but immediately bump into Dylan. He stares at me, my wallet held up in his outreached hand. 'Are you okay?'

The fallen snow is scuffed and scraped in every direction, a slurred mash of grey twisted footprints. Across the road, a woman stands in the doorway of Maisie's Chocolate Shop, the still strafing snow forming a veil between us. I wipe the name from the dolls face and hand it back to Dylan along with the car. I cross the road. The woman asks me what happened, having heard the window crack. From within the recess of the shop, someone else loiters, listening, being nosey. Dylan is standing outside the store, all floppy fringe and angular lankiness, and still holding the doll and car. The ice-cream shop next to North's is closed, and the café next to that on the corner of the street is set with tables on the pavement outside, all empty. People pass by, squinting against the snow.

Shaken up, I return to Dylan and take my shopping bag. I tell him to call the police, not that they'll do anything – it's hardly the crime of the century, purely an insurance matter. I hurry home. I feel like walls are closing in on me. I expected the opposite; this weekend is supposed to be a release.

The garden gate to my house is closed. It's never closed. Although the gate is small, it's heavy and drags, its top hinge having broken away from the post. Until now, the bottom of the gate has always been entwined in the long grass at the side of the path. The strange thing is the fine layer of snow covering the path to the door is without footprints. Whoever shut the gate did it soon after I left the house.

Placing the smart brown-paper bag with my new clothes in on the ground, I lift and heave the gate open inwards, dropping it back in the dent in the long grass.

I scan the street to see if anyone is watching me, but I don't see a soul, just a still, snow-white hush. I turn to face the house, half expecting to see a hooded figure staring at me from one of its windows. I can feel my heart hammering as I ascend the five small steps to the porch.

Although frozen to the bone, my fingers feel sticky with perspiration as I turn the key and open the door. Smokey doesn't bark, and he doesn't come.

Something is wrong… something is wrong… something is wrong… the words play on an endless loop inside my head. Smokey always greets me, albeit slowly and with nothing more than a gentle nuzzle, before returning to his basket these days. 'Smokey,' I call, 'come on, boy.'

Standing still in the hallway, I wait for his quiet bark, the slow patter of his feet. Instead, there's a different kind of noise, a hollow bang. I stiffen, alert. A rustling sound follows. I think it came from the kitchen at the end of the hallway, but the door to it is shut. I can't remember shutting it. I always leave it open, but now I'm not sure. Maybe this one time I closed it.

My thudding heart twists in my chest. I walk the length of the hallway, normal pace, normal gait, all the while the rustling from the kitchen getting louder. Taking a second, enough for a deep breath, I swing open the door.

Smokey is standing beside the kitchen table, a guilty look in his eyes. Scattered all around him, biscuits. He's uncertain. Knowing he's been naughty, he waddles up to me, guilt evident in his lowered head, nose to the red and white tiles. He expects a harsh word from me. Instead, I crouch and scratch his ears and ask him how he got the biscuits. He leans against my legs and looks up at me as if to say he would tell me if he could.

The thing is, I don't buy biscuits, never have. I pick up the bright red wrapper from the floor. Perhaps I did buy them and forgot about them, but I can't help thinking of the old man's dog, and I can't help but think someone else has been in the house.

I test the back door leading from the kitchen to the backyard, and to my relief it's locked. There's a strange, sickly-sweet odour in the air. I can taste it on my tongue. Although highly unlikely, I wonder if Smokey has done a horrible shit somewhere. I wander around the kitchen table, before stopping sharply at the sight of the white porcelain sink, stained raspberry red with blood. Enormous curved horns protrude from a woolly, white head laying on its side, a sickly, yellow alien eye with black-slitted, rectangular pupil stares up at me. A blue-tinged tongue hangs limply between thick, yellow teeth - the severed head of one of the Great Orme's Kashmiri goats.

I glance away, scanning the kitchen as if there might be more amputated body parts to discover. Smokey looks up at me forlornly. Oh, if only my boy could talk.

Sweating, and swallowing the vomit seeping up into my mouth, I grab some tea-towels and lifting the still-warm goat's head, deposit it in a heavy-duty plastic refuse bag. After dropping it in the black bin in the yard, I conduct yet another search of the house. I can't call the police. I am the police. Besides, I know this has everything to do with the messages I've sent. The magnitude of their impact dawns on me. I've not just invited six old friends back to the old house, but six killers. The years apart have diluted their dependency on me. I must convince them to see sense: I know I can, I know I will; I know I must. But how? One of them has gone rogue, one of them has killed the old man in Clonmel Street and

The Great Orme

now they've somehow gotten inside my house and dumped a fucking goat's head in my sink. I used to be so sure of myself, now I find myself asking, *what if I can't convince them?*

I clean up the sink, and clean up myself. Once showered and changed into my new clothes, I decide coffee laced with a splash of rum will calm me, or at the very least oil the cogs in my brain.

The old house creaks and the pipes stutter with the effort of pushing hot water around to heat the place, and me cradled within it. I stare out through the dining room window. In the far distance, I see the Great Orme, the imperious headland holding its head up high and surveying such futile creatures as we. A terrible sense of dread washes through me like there's needles in my blood. I've started something. Something that's going to get worse before it gets better. And yet, I know I have done the right thing. I decide to write everything down. I think it'll help me make some sense of it all. It will be our confession. It's the very least I can do.

I move to the study, the sea barely visible in the distance through the blurry snow, just a horizontal artery of grey. More than anything else, I'll miss the sea, its depth and changing moods. But we deserve the prison cell. We killed, we murdered, we caused pain. What were we thinking? Why did none of them stand up to me? I wonder if we are the children of the Great Orme, our blood and bones merely ink and pens for the sea serpent to write its history? I need to confess and soon. I keep blinking, hoping I'll wake up and things will be different. I roll up my shirt sleeve, running my fingers over the black-inked tattoo on the underside of my forearm, the sea serpent, snake-like, eyes inked red as if on fire. The tattoo each of us got, intended as our constant reminder, both of our eternal connection, and of our promise to never tell a soul what we had done.

Using my phone, I check Sian's social media pages. No updates since Thursday. Prior to then, her posts are all humorous, seemingly happy. She's here already. I wonder what she's doing and hope the answer isn't that she's hacking goats' heads.

I scan through the others' social media pages. I've been tracking them for years, checking for signs of weakness and finding none. How ironic it's me that has caved in first. Even Costas's social media has no updates. My phone buzzes with an alert – a message from Orla.

Hi Zach. It's been a while but thx for your sweet message. Fuck you if you think we are going to confess. Take care and see you soon.
Your loving wife, Orla xxx

My heart flips.

I leave the phone to one side. I will write. There is no other release, and I fear for what I might do if I don't. I slide out the top drawer of my desk, take the notebook and put pen to paper. Immediately I'm lost, detached from time, lost in that thing they call the *flow*. Our story will be documented.

A couple of hours later, I find my *flow* interrupted.

'You left me to die.'

At the sound of the child's voice, I drop the pen and lurch from the chair, sending it crashing into the wall. None of it matters – a girl, as real as I, stands before me.

The girl shakes her head, long, black beaded hair swaying about her neck. She raises her arm, fingers wriggling, reaching for me. Her deep brown eyes are swollen with sadness, and one side of her face is smeared with shining wet, sticky blood.

'Choreji…' My voice is cracked. It's the little girl Orla drove into. She's wearing the same Disney top she died in, a defiant princess punching the air. Choreji's dark skin is sickly and gaunt, her face and form stained with the bark and earth from which she has been dredged. My heart pounding, I do what my brain tells me not to do, and move closer. Stopping before the poor girl, I reach out, hands trembling with the need to console, the need to ask forgiveness.

'Teddy bear,' Choreji says, balling up her hand into a fist. 'Give me my Teddy.'

Orla has it. She took it from the scene. She kept it.

'Give it,' she says, her voice harsher and her face contorting in anger.

'I don't have it,' I manage, but it's as if my mouth is stuffed with dirt.

The girl lowers her eyes, disappointed. She turns away from me. Where the back of her head should be, instead, there is an enormous gaping hole where her skull has caved in. Glistening, wet sinewy blood drips from it, her white top drenched pink. 'It's mine. I love it,' she says, her voice sweet and fluid once more. 'Make your wife give it to me. Please.'

With her back to me and head bowed, Choreji collapses. I stagger backwards, almost tripping over myself and crashing against the white wall, cold and alone. Nothing but the smell of dank earth left behind to prove she had been there. I hold on to nothing. Choreji's gone.

I was shattered

by your eyes

Chapter Seven

The grandfather clock in the lounge sounds twelve dull chimes, signalling the switch from Friday morning to Friday afternoon. I check the locks on every window in the house, draw the bolt back and forth across the back door, and check the front door fully locks when closed. I'm missing a clue, something that can reveal how the intruder gained access. I've a feeling I'm being watched. It's a familiar feeling – I live with ghosts. This is something else. I know someone has been in the house. They left the goat's head for me, and I'm scared of what they'll do next. I'm scared the old house will become my coffin.

A knock at the door makes me jump. I gaze through the dining-room window first, just in time to see a taxicab churning up virgin snow, a trail of brown slush left in its wake. One of the six has arrived early. Taking a moment to compose myself, I open the door.

'For fuck's sake, Zac. Are you going to let me in or what? It's fucking freezing out here!'

'Beetle eyes,' I mutter, as my wife shoves past, dragging a shiny pink suitcase after her. 'You're early.'

'Yeah, I'm fucking early, Zac. One of us needs to stop you before this gets out of hand.'

I take a side-sweep glance along the street before closing the door.

It's been six years since Orla and I have seen each other in the flesh. We stand in the hallway, gaping at one another. Forever majestically gothic, she's head to toe in black, a wide red belt her only concession to the light. I notice she's still wearing her wedding ring. I'm not. Before I know what's happening, she comes at me, wrapping her arms around my midriff and nestling her head against my chest. I hold her tightly, resting my chin on top of her head, breathing in her zingy scent. I could stay like that forever. It's all I want.

'Zac, why are you so stupid?' she mutters finally, and I'm immediately reassured. I love her. I always will. Even our treachery cannot erase what we have. We kiss and, upon breaking away, she stares up at me. 'Zac, what the fuck do you think you are playing at? You can't tell anyone what we've done. It's suicide. What's to be gained by giving ourselves up? Please… tell me your message is some sort of stupid ruse for something else?'

Breathing in her familiar perfume, a zingy orange tang to it, I stare down at her face. Heavy black eye shadow and thick liner surround her eyes, long eyelashes flickering like beetle legs.

'I'm so sorry, Beetle-eyes.' I bite my lip and sigh. 'I've been mad. How can we not confess? You, me, the others… we're killers.'

The whites of her eyes disappear behind the smudged blackness. Finally, she emits a soft groan, and raises both hands either side of her head, cupping her cheek bones, strands of jet-black hair pulled taut against her pale skin. I'm reminded of the Edvard Munch painting, *The Scream*.

Smokey appears, wagging his tail furiously; he hasn't forgotten her.

Lowering her hands, some kind of composure regained, she glances at him but ignores him. I'm offended. Even after all this time, he still loves her, as I do.

I take her coat and we go into the lounge and sit next to each other on the sofa. Orla sits stiff and upright, clearly worried.

'How have you been?' I ask, but she ignores my mundane attempt at breaking the deadlock, and turns the focus on me.

'You look so tired, haunted. This *place* looks so tired. You've let you and it slide.' She strokes the sofa's brown cracked leather. She's right. I have let things slide. The old house is tawdry and mean, a relic… I feel it has assimilated me and made me the same.

'It's not important…' I say, but she cuts me short.

'Why, Zac?' She turns her face to mine, gazing up at me. 'Why now?'

I struggle for the words, the words that have been so clear to me, the resounding logic that has gradually manifested and led me to this point. Orla doesn't relent, refusing to avert her eyes, demanding a response from me, one which we both know she deserves.

'Guilt,' I say finally, lowering my gaze to my interlaced fingers. 'Fear perhaps, but mostly because it's fair… because it's the *right thing* to do.'

I glance up to observe her reaction. She stares at me, eyes stretched wide, a minuscule shake of the head. She thinks I'm insane.

'It's difficult to explain…'

'Boy, do you need to explain,' she says, eyebrows raised.

'It's a feeling–'

She erupts, standing up and flinging her bag across the room, metal adornments on it clanking against the mirror hanging above the fireplace. I rise to my feet and we both stare at ourselves reflected in the newly cracked glass.

'How fucking dare you?' she screams, at the mirror, at me. 'A fucking feeling! Is that it? You want us all locked up for the rest of our lives, for the sake of your fucking feeling?'

Her head is thrust forward, cat-like, normally snow-white face scorched pink with anger, spittle on her lips.

'It's the right thing. This time, it is the right thing to do.' My voice is subdued and unrelenting; this is my first test, and no matter how hard this gets I must persist.

'Don't you see?' she says, her tone softening, pleading almost. 'There are consequences to your decision that are unknown. It's not just us who are affected, it's…' she hesitates, grimacing. 'Others… innocent people are affected too.' She blows out hard. 'I'm sorry. I'm just saying the world doesn't revolve around you, Zac. You aren't God. Why can't you let things be? Let people find their own way through? Why do you always have to manipulate everyone?'

Orla's words carry weight, they always did. She may be right. Perhaps I must suffer, waste away in a pool of my guilt until I die – but it's not that simple. I've seen Choreji in the old house, and real or not, I've seen the other ghosts. Those we killed returned to demand justice. Now, my purpose is to deliver them justice.

'For fuck's sake, Zac! I'm still your fucking wife!'

Orla shakes her head, throwing her hands in the air in despair. 'Six fucking years without a single word from you, and then you send me a generic fucking message! Do you have any idea how that made me feel? Why now, Zac? Why, after six fucking years?'

There's nothing I can say that will explain or eradicate Orla's anguish. My blood, bones and soul are screaming at me to relent, to change my mind.

'I still love you,' she says, taking a deep breath and smoothing her hair down. 'I've always loved you and I always will. You know that. But there's not a day goes by where I don't think about Choreji, the life she might have lived. Every day I think about the pain her family suffers, their torment of knowing I exist, but not knowing who I am, where I am, that I'm free. But I'm not free. I also live with the guilt, the torment. For fuck's sake, her family appeared on TV, pleading for their daughter's killer to give themselves up. They were in tears, their hearts and lives shattered. I was ready to give myself up, but you made me understand the way it had to be. All seven of us knew too much of each other. We had to go our separate ways. It made sense. We had to forge lives without the constant reminder…'

Three stealthy knocks reverberate on the front door. Orla and I both bristle. We hold one another's gaze within the mirror until finally she takes a deep breath. 'You'd better get the door,' she says, turning away from the mirror and from me.

It's the police officer again. She's out of uniform, wearing red jeans and a padded, purple coat, strands of blonde hair poking out from beneath a snow-smattered, red bobble-hat.

'Helen,' I say, firmly gripping the door, 'is everything alright?'

'Sorry, I just finished my shift. I rent a place along Abbey Road, moved in a few weeks ago. I was kind of passing and I thought you might be interested. It… it's not good, I'm afraid. There's been another murder.'

My heart rate spikes. 'What? Another?'

She nods, releasing a sigh. I'm suddenly mindful she's new to the area, new to the job, her resilience yet to be hardened to the cruelty humans inflict on one another. Yet there's something about her I find intriguing, an underlying vitality that contrasts wildly with the old cold in my rotten bones.

'A murder?' Orla squeezes alongside me, so I have to let go of the door.

Helen responds with a brief nod.

'Come on in,' Orla says, exchanging a worried glance with me.

I notice Helen noticing the cracked mirror on the wall and Orla's upended handbag beneath it on the floor, but she says nothing. She takes up a seat in one of the leather armchairs, leaning forward, knees touching, and hands clasped on top of them.

Orla offers Helen a drink and tells me to make it. I return from the kitchen, a cup of tea each for them, while I take a sip of coffee infused with a substantial dose of rum.

'Orla says you've lived here all of your life, in this house,' Helen says, raising the cup to her mouth.

'Yes, I've never been able to leave… it was my mother's,' I reply, sitting next to Orla on the sofa. 'Orla and I have been separated some time now. In fact, this is the first time we've seen each other since…' Orla's beetle eyes enlarge. 'Well, in six years.'

'I'm sorry,' Helen says. 'I don't mean to intrude.'

'Not at all.'

'I should leave,' Helen says, a kindly smile on her face and putting her cup down. 'You told me earlier you have some things to "put right".'

'No, really…' I begin, but Orla interrupts.

'So, tell me, since when did Llandudno become Wales's murder capital?'

I glance from one woman to the other.

'Helen told me about the old man murdered on Clonmel Street,' Orla says. 'Absolutely awful.'

The Great Orme

Helen's eyes rove around the room, even up at the ceiling. She's taking it all in, tea in one hand and fiddling with the bobble on the end of her hat with the other. She needed to talk to someone, that's why she stopped by, but like all good cops, she can't help but observe, taking mental notes.

'A boy, they've taken him to hospital but, well, it was brutal.' She fixes us both with a look, held long enough to gauge our reactions, to read our facial micro-expressions. Such a key skill for a cop. I doubt though, she's seen into the window of my soul, and sympathise with her if she has. She takes a sip of tea, clearly deciding she's staying. 'It happened at the foot of the tramway, outside the chip shop.'

The Tram station is down the road and around the corner from the house.

'Go on,' Orla says, keen to know the details.

Helen nods. 'The boy was dragged from his bike.' She pauses until I make eye-contact with her. 'His attacker smashed the boy's skull in using a rock.'

I open my mouth, but nothing comes out. I can't look at Orla, but I can feel her eyes like lasers burning into my head. I picture Harrison, all those years ago, a chunk of jagged concrete in hand, smashing it into the poor boy's head – the unfortunate witness to our flight from the old man's house. I roll my eyes, trying to clear the sickening memory.

'Are you okay?'

Helen's face stares back at me, brow furrowed with concern.

'It doesn't get any easier,' I half-lie, because it does. You grow numb, you deal with the facts, disregard the people, their feelings. You have to. It's the only way to cope. But, and this is something I've learned recently, it catches up with you. All the deaths, the evil, the pain, it catches up with you, it smothers you, it eats you up from within. It gets you in the end.

I stand, pressing my temples with thumb and forefinger. 'When?'

'About eleven this morning.'

'Why?'

'Too early to say.'

'Suspects?'

'No idea.'

'Clues?'

'Strange, really. Just words etched in the snow beside the boy.'

'What words?'

'Only a couple,' she says. She stops pulling at the bobble on her hat and fixes her unblinking gaze on me. 'Don't confess.'

The old house groans, a loud creak from above, and we all look around uneasily. I feel a small cold hand slide into mine and glance at Orla, but she has both hands wrapped around her cup. I jump up, shaking my hand and spilling my coffee.

'I'm sorry,' I say, rubbing my wet fingers down my new black jeans. Goose-bumps run up my arms.

I sit again, my brain racing with the new information.

Helen recommences pulling at the bobble attached to the hat. 'The killer scraped crosses in the snow on either side of the boy.'

I shake my head.

'Like crucifixes, I suppose,' she adds.

Crucifixes. Crap. It must be Costas.

Orla reaches out and squeezes my hand, her hand warmer, softer than whatever had touched it seconds ago.

'Any ideas?' Helen asks me.

'No,' I reply promptly. 'Will the boy make it?'

Orla's hand grips mine tighter.

'He was a mess.' Helen coils her finger around the base of the bobble and squeezes. 'I can't see him lasting long.'

'Are you okay, Zac?' Helen asks, setting her tea on the coffee table.

'Yes, I–'

'Truth is, it's a difficult time for us,' intervenes Orla. 'Zac and I are at something of a crossroads.'

Helen nods as if understanding. Apologising, puts her cup down and insists she's taken too much of our time. Especially, she says, bearing in mind that after six years, me and Orla must have so much to catch up on. She tells us she's not working the weekend, that she's glad as she could do with a couple of days off to relax. She puts on her bobble-hat and coat and thanks me for the tea. At the door she apologises again for relaying the awful news, especially while I'm on leave. I wave off her apology and thank her. I mean it. She's given me much to mull over. I feel sorry for her and say she's welcome to call around anytime. I wonder what she'll think when she learns of our confession, whether she'll think she noticed anything suspicious about us this afternoon.

Orla takes herself upstairs. Even though we are in the same house, and even though I love her, it seems there is a wasteland littered with unspoken truths that neither of us can bear to traverse. It dawns on me Orla may be as haunted as me. I'm even more convinced confessing is the only route to some kind of peace.

In the kitchen, I take a gulp of rum, straight from the bottle this time.

A shadow looms at the kitchen doorway. It spooks me until I realise it's Orla. Even after all the years that have passed, she's still able to cast a scathing glare at me for drinking from the bottle.

'I need it,' I say by way of excuse. I tell her about the day's events, and she ends up having a tumbler of rum for herself.

'Zac,' she says, her voice firm and measured. 'You're making everything worse.' She's sat at one end of the kitchen table, and me at the other. I smooth the grain of the oak, searching deep into its pattern, Orla's voice rattling around my head. 'Two more people dead. Because of you. Because of your messages. I'm not sure confessing is the cure you think.'

I dig my fingernails into the woodgrain, tugging at it. I tell her about the message left on the bedroom window, the attack on me at the pier, the doll daubed with Choreji's name at the clothes store, and finally, the goat's head in the sink.

'Holy shit,' she whispers, picking up her glass and downing the contents. 'How much of a hint do you need, Zac? How many more people have to die?'

I slap the table. 'It's not my fault one of them is killing!'

Startled, Smokey slinks away from my feet.

'But Zac, honey, it's the fucking consequence...'

'No, Orla!' I stand up, taking a deep breath, staring down into her coal-black eyes. 'I will not be blackmailed. For the sakes of our victims, their families, and for us, we have to do the right thing. We think we have moved on, we haven't! The dead live with me! They are here! And they demand justice. They deserve justice! We... you, me and the others. We have no choice but to confess!'

Orla stares back at me impassively, eyes only slightly widened by my sudden show of emotion. It's not normal, I've surprised myself, but I find it strangely re-affirming, and I wish I had given way to feeling rather than controlled action more often. Who knows what it might have prevented?

A thought suddenly occurs to me. It makes my skin creep. 'Orla, when did you arrive in Llandudno? Did you come straight here?'

'For fuck's sake, Zac,' she says, shaking her head but not looking up.

'Tell me,' I insist. 'When *did* you get here?'

Orla places both hands flat on the table, pressed as if about to stand, but she doesn't. Finally, she raises her gaze, her eyes blackened with syrupy mascara tears. 'I got a cab here, straight from the train station.'

Crocodile tears or not? I don't know. I recall seeing the cab pulling away from the house, but... well, the truth is, she stabbed an old man. She left a little girl for dead. She's a killer.

I get up and walk around the table, wrap my arms around her shoulders, but this time she bristles at my touch, the love between us a pained, neglected, twisted creature.

'Just answer me one question, Zac,' she says, smudging her tears into blackened circles around her eyes. 'Truthfully.'

'When would I do differently?' I ask.

She shrugs. 'There's something I need to ask you.'

My stomach tenses.

'Did you cheat on me with Jessie?'

An indecent descent

Chapter Eight

Her question stuns me. For all that has happened and all that we have done, I was not expecting it, and suddenly it feels like the most important question in the world. I draw breath and retreat to the kitchen sink, staring out of the window. The overgrown yard is draped by a thin blanket of snow, metal slatted garden table overturned, bubbles of brown wet rust clinging on for dear life.

'Yes.'

My back to her, I hear a whimper, a stifled sob.

'When?'

I turn to face her, struggling to find the words, my tongue suddenly swollen and dry. 'Just a kiss,' I manage eventually, before adding, 'that's all,' and knowing it sounds trite when it's everything in the world.

'When?' she repeats, head raised and her face hard like a stone-white mask.

My words come out jumbled. 'The day... Choreji... the day of the accident.'

The stone cracks, mascara tears released like streaming black wells of ink. 'No,' she gasps.

'After you left, Jessie reappeared. She was upset. You had called her "a fucking mess, a fucking sore on fucking society". I consoled her, hugged her, and she kissed me... we kissed. That's all. Nothing more.'

She nods as if accepting, but I've misread her.

'You bastard!' she says, spittle flying from her mouth. 'Of all days on God's earth, you chose that fucking day?'

'She was drunk, Orla.'

'And you? You were sober. So why?'

'I don't know why and can't explain why.' I bow my head. 'It was one second… just one second.'

She slams the table with her fist. 'I should leave right now!' Her face is set hard again, teeth clenched.

I rub my forehead, a vain attempt to stimulate thought and reason. 'You saw Jessie. She was intoxicated with the same red punch concoction you were drinking — God knows what was in it. She pulled my head in to hers and kissed me. Honestly, as soon as my brain engaged, I pulled away. That's all. Nothing before that and nothing since.'

'Hold up,' Orla says, mirroring me and rubbing her forehead. 'People… my colleagues, will have seen it. No one has mentioned it. Oh my God! I'm a fool – everyone's laughing at me!'

'No, Orla! That's not true. It was on the balcony, no one else there. No one saw.'

'Are you sure? Because, Zac, I don't think you can be!'

'I'm sorry. So sorry,' I say, reaching out to tighten a tap that doesn't need tightening. 'I love you, and only you. That's it. All these things we've done. Everything we know. You are the only one I can truly trust. I'm being honest… finally.

Orla grunts and takes a deep breath. Her blood-red lips part as if to say something, but nothing comes. I desperately want to reach out to her, but I'm scared. I'm scared she'll push me away.

'Oh, Zac,' she sighs, shaking her head in slow despondent arcs. 'What's wrong with you? Why do you destroy everything you touch?'

It's a great question. I don't have the answer.

She buries her head face down in her arms on the table and mumbles incoherently. I don't know what she's on about. I stare at the pale-blue-tiled kitchen wall, the once white grooves in-between the tiles eaten up by encroaching black mould. The spotlights in the ceiling are reflected on the tiles, and in the reflections, I see the faces of our victims. Exhumed and rotten, their grim, granite eyes staring back at me, accusing, demanding.

I drag my gaze away. Orla has her head still buried in her arms. I should reach out, explain further, beg forgiveness, and not confess to the murders – but I can't. Instead, I walk away, leaving the kitchen for the sanctuary of the study.

I write. It's hard, my mind is fogged. All I can do is to document my perspective. It's all I have, all any of us has. Anyone who ends up reading this confession will hate me. It's okay. I hate myself more.

Time passes unnoticed and I suddenly sense someone standing in the doorway – Orla, of course. She's holding a brown teddy bear to her chest. It's *the* teddy bear – Choreji's.

'Zac,' she says, her voice soft and thoughtful. 'There is another world, you know? Separate from the Great Orme.'

'What?' I say, dropping my pen, slightly bemused.

'We could run away. Just you and me. We could start a new life, new jobs… raise a family,' she says, her chin lowered, eyes gazing up at me, either pleading or hopeful. I know she knows I can't. I can't break the chains of the Great Orme.

I thrust the back of my head against the back-rest of the chair. 'It's impossible. Look at me. I'm as good as a ghost now. Anyway, what kind of father would I be? How could I look my child in the eyes and expect their trust? After what I've done. After what we've done. I don't deserve to be a father.'

'Is there anything I can say to change your mind? Anything at all?'

A core of me insists I take her hand and run. To chance it. To put love first. But I can't. I can't forget. And neither can she.

I shake my head mournfully. 'No.'

A single slow nod signifies her acceptance.

She stares down at the tattered little teddy bear in her arms. As if summoned, Choreji appears, stumbling and wailing, trampling over the crumbling icy-wet tarmac she died on, the cold, damp air from that tragic night now in the room with us.

Smokey barks, his body stiff, eyes focussed on Choreji. The

The Great Orme

young girl's brown eyes are fixed on Orla, on her teddy bear.

'Orla, give her the bear,' I say, but my brain is syrupy, and the world seems to spin faster and faster.

'Give Choreji the bear,' I repeat.

But Orla doesn't seem to realise what's happening. Her eyes shift uneasily from me to the rest of the room, searching each corner.

The pressure, the force of feeling Choreji is projecting, is too much. It's choking me, sucking the air from within my lungs.

As I'm on the verge of collapsing, something in Orla clicks and, still standing in the doorway, she holds out the skinny brown bear and stares at it. I can't breathe. Choreji reaches out to take the teddy. But she doesn't take *it*. She lifts a paler copy of the bear, holding it up high above her head, her face an explosion of light. I hear children's laughter; I see richly coloured flowers, a sky of blue and gold.

Finally, I can breathe. I swallow great gushing swathes of air. It takes a minute, and all the while Orla stares at me, open-mouthed and wide-eyed, teddy clutched to her chest once more.

'She didn't take it.'

I blink back tears. 'She didn't need to. It was the gesture she needed. It's a start. It's why we have to confess. The gesture, good, kind, right, is all we have left to give.'

Orla caresses the teddy bear's head, black nail-varnished fingernails pulling at the scruffy brown fibres. Seeing the notebook on my desk, she takes it and opens it without asking, flicking through the pages. I worry I've revealed too much, that it might alter her perception, dissuade her entirely from confessing. She stops at the pages I've written about the night Choreji died. It's those pages that make her turn away, perhaps too painful to be gazed upon. She tosses the book back onto the desk and leaves the room.

I stalk the downstairs rooms, wondering at my sanity. *Did I really see Choreji?* I'm desperate for Saturday evening to arrive. The old house is full of draughts that turn into whispers which follow me from room to room. They enter my head like corkscrew screams demanding their stories be told. I've got to get away from the old house for a bit. I'm suffocating and I need to clear my head.

I find Orla in the Study, like a female version of me; sat at my desk, staring ahead, out of the window and toward the sea. 'Let's go for a walk,' I suggest.

'Sure,' she says after a long pause. 'That'll fucking sort everything, won't it?'

On the ground, brilliant white snow is tinged grey in places, already on its way to slush. The road is devoid of traffic. It's that sort of day. We hurry, the ascent up the Great Orme as familiar to us as the contours of our own faces.

Navigating the steep, winding road, we talk little, until, pausing for breath at a gate that would lead us off the road, Orla asks, 'What if someone needed you? Would that change your mind?'

I sigh, a plume of white mist escaping my mouth. 'No one needs me, Orla. They mustn't. Least of all you. Look what I've done to you, to us, all of us.'

Within the hour we are raised on the Sea Serpent's head, at the top of the Great Orme where the cold wind is king. It stings our faces and its icy fingers tug at our clothes, seeking out skin to touch. The Great Orme's hulking two-mile mass of limestone grassland is dusted with a smattering of snow, sheep and, of course, Kashmiri goats. Our breathing is quick, the blood flows fast through our bodies as we walk. Orla remains silent, distant. Unsurprisingly, in these conditions, humans are few.

'I love this place,' I say, talking as much to myself as to Orla, as we meander past jagged rocks of white limestone and grey dolomite, rich seams of copper ore bleeding through them like blood, evidence of the old copper mines.

'It's in me, a part of me, a needle to my vein I can't do without. Even when we were kids and we came up here to play, it made me feel like anything was possible, like I could achieve anything. Here, high above it all, it felt like I could touch the sky, and it still does. The Vikings were right to name it the Great Orme, the "Great Sea Serpent", the way its ancient head rises out of the sea to dominate. Hell – it's over three-hundred million years old. It's seen and knows far more than us.'

I touch my face with freezing hands, feeling it's still there. 'We've been lucky to live here, Orla. There is nowhere else I'd rather be.'

I stop. 'Orla?'

'I don't think I can do it,' she says, raising a hand to cover her mouth as if something might spill from it.

I'm not sure who moves first, but we embrace, holding each other like when we were young, both of us clinging on to the other, never wanting to release. For all of Orla's drive and ambition, and my decay and decline, I understand we're eternally connected, two sides of the same coin.

Eventually, Orla pulls back and, still holding my hands, gazes at me, her beetle eyes black swollen lakes. 'You know, after we all met up for the last time at the old house, I returned to London, to work, but a few months in, I discovered…'

The wind sweeps around us, holding us up like we are the only people in the world.

'What did you discover?' I ask, cupping the side of her face.

She holds my gaze like she's in a trance, not a flicker in her eyes.

'Nothing,' she says, looking down. 'I took some time off work… six months or so… depression.'

My legs feel heavy, and my heart sinks, the weight of gravity suddenly too much, like I've crash-landed on the Great Orme.

'Why–'

'I love you,' she interrupts. 'I will always love you, Zachary Llewellyn. No matter what is to come. Remember that, please.'

It feels like I'm punishing her, and I don't want to. I want to explain, but she seals my mouth with her lips and we kiss.

She pulls back. 'Let's go to Church.'

St. Tudno's Church, little more than a stone-built cottage, is surrounded by closely knitted graves, leaning stone crosses and coffins sculpted with Celtic patterns. Sad-faced stone angels stare mournfully out to sea. Next to the church, an ancient white stone lectern faces inland. On the days in the summer, when the weather is kind enough, the vicar still preaches to the faithful in the open air. When we were very young, we'd take turns addressing a pretend congregation, damning them to hell for the most minor of misdemeanours. I wonder if that's how it all started; me preaching like some kind of crazed self-righteous religious fanatic to the others.

Orla has disappeared. My heart races with anxiety as I spin around searching for her. She emerges from behind a giant kneeling angel statue. She's untied her hair and the jet-black strands squirm wildly about her head. She looks amazing, perfect, a medusa that could command the Sea Serpent. The urge to change my mind and live a life with this beautiful woman spins up from my stomach and attempts to batter my brain into submission.

She smiles at me, but it's a strange smile, a far-away smile, one that makes me uneasy. 'Let's go inside.'

The space within isn't much bigger than my dining room. A round stained-glass window on the north wall and a series of narrow Victorian windows on the East and West walls provide the light. I find the little church oppressive, its stone cold and unforgiving. I can feel my heart pounding, hear the gush of my blood rushing through my head. Perhaps the old place knows who I am and what I've done. I wipe my dry lips with the back of my hand, tasting the salt blown in from the sea on my skin. The soles of Orla's wet shoes squeak sharply on the stone tiles as she makes her way along the aisle. I follow close behind, passing austere wooden benches jammed close together on either side.

Orla stops at the altar. I observe the painted tablets set in the wall behind the altar, etched in Welsh with the Lord's Prayer, Creed and Ten Commandments. High above the altar, the ancient plaque of the stigmata, four golden limbs protruding from a golden heart, all daubed with red splodges,

The Great Orme

representative of the five wounds Jesus received when he was crucified. I silently ask God for forgiveness, although I'm convinced I'm undeserving.

Orla kneels, placing dark-red flowers she has taken from somewhere at the foot of the altar. 'For you, Choreji,' she whispers. 'Forgive me. I'm so, so, so sorry.'

She says something else, but I only catch the word "Jericho", but I can't understand why. *Then Jericho* were an ancient nineteen-eighties band, and their hit song – "Big Area", is *our* song. The lyrics spin through my head, and I almost crash to my knees at how appropriate they are for where we find ourselves. Anyone who doesn't feel for certain kinds of music isn't really human.

I feel the walls closing in. I need to get out. I stride toward the doorway, the wooden benches on either side like jagged teeth trying to snap at me. Outside, among the graves smattered with patches of snow, I pull out my phone in case I have any new messages, but there aren't any. I've forgotten the phone signal on the Orme is patchy at best. If there are any messages, they'll have to wait. Something ice-cold slithers into my free hand. I glimpse down to see Choreji, her hand in my hand, her face specked with spit and blood, and clutching her teddy tightly to chest, her dead gaze fixed on me.

Her mouth opens, and a never-ending train of black butterflies batter their way out, enveloping my head, wing-tips scraping my face like icy razor-blades, metallic wings clicking in my ears like gnashing teeth. Pulling my hand from hers, I recoil, swiping furiously at the dense black cloud. I can't see and I can't breathe. The centre of my chest throbs. I become swallowed by the clicking blackness.

Someone is pulling my sleeve, dragging me to my feet. The black butterflies have disappeared as if they were never there. Choreji has gone too, and Orla is leaning back, pulling at my arm. I rub my eyes and let myself be pulled to my feet. I'm convinced Choreji knows everything. She'll hang around until I've confessed to everything.

Orla and I end up at the edge of Orme, where we stand in silence, above us the sky a flat grey apart from a trail of thin white clouds like broken bones. In the distance, I observe the murky outline of the two bridges that connect mainland Wales to the island of Anglesey.

'So that's all there is. We are killers. There's no saving us,' Orla says, staring over the edge into the depths of the Irish Sea. 'I guess you are right, Zac.' Her voice is strangely calm, soothing even. She advances nearer the edge. 'I lost myself when we killed the old man. Then, when I killed Choreji –' Her words drift away, too quiet to be heard.

I gaze out at the distant smudges of winter birds bobbing on the waves, and again the dream snags – one of me and Orla leaving this place, running and keeping on running, the two of us burning our rope to its end. A raven darts up from beneath the cliff edge, and I backpedal, nearly tripping over. Flailing, heavy and ragged, the bird fights the buffeting wind, before tumbling away beneath the edge and out of sight, only its harsh grating croak revealing of its presence below the cliffs.

'I can't help anyone, now. I can't be of any use. Not even…' Orla's words fade again, into the sound of the slow-breaking waves below, the chirring wind, and the raking croak of the raven.

'Orla?'

She never looked so small, drowned in my padded green coat, like a little child. Something small drops from her hand, and flutters to the ground. It snags on a clump of grass poking up from a patch of snow. The shape of her stance changes, almost imperceptibly, but the invisible cord we share snaps tight. My saliva suddenly turns harsh and metallic.

'Orla?' I repeat, but the sound coming from my mouth rolls out stiff and slow, while Orla's movements are sharp and agile.

She propels herself forward, dangerously near the cliff edge, then beyond, long black hair flailing wildly, and she's still striding as she leaves the land.

All the lee
and the loney

Chapter Nine

I scramble as close to the edge as I dare, frantically scanning the rocks that meet the sea way below.

I stagger, the ground seeming to pitch, to become an incline, as if the sea serpent is thrashing its head that it might cast me off into the sea along with Orla. Doubled over and crumpled like a piece of paper and fighting for breath, I call out my wife's name, my voice alien sounding, a mutilated thing.

Suddenly I see her, a tiny speck of emerald amid the distant rocks that lead into the sea. She doesn't move. The near-vertical cliff face is a smooth, uneven surface with protruding rocks and crevices that jut out from the side of the cliff from top to bottom. I'm shaking. My legs won't work. I can taste rising vomit. I feel lightheaded, my brain a fog. Help, I need help, but the headland is a universe of its own with only me in it. I take-in a deep breath and yell her name again, hoping it might rouse her. There's only one way down from here, and I'm sorely tempted. My phone falls from my pocket. I grapple for it, my fingers clawing the snow and snagging on a small square of red knitted wool. Realising it's what had fallen from Orla before she jumped, I pocket it. A quick glance at my phone reveals what I already know – no signal.

The King's Head pub next to the Llandudno Tram Station at the foot of the Great Orme is full of locals. I'm sitting on a stool in the corner at the bar. Two men in smart, black waistcoats sit on a bench near a steamed-up window, strumming their guitars and singing folk songs. They are good, well-rehearsed, but I can barely see them over the heads of the early Friday evening throng heralding the arrival of another weekend. Having already

The Great Orme

drunk a pint of dark real ale, I order a neat rum and gulp it, knowing the best I can hope for is the alcoholic medicine will steady my nerves, and even if it doesn't, what does it matter? My wife has just died, having taken her own life, and it's my fault. I stare at my phone, so as to avoid eye-contact with anyone. I remember Orla and I talking about our deaths and our funerals on a semi-drunken night years ago. I was concerned about my carbon footprint and leaned toward cremation. Orla insisted we were obliged to donate our organs to any who needed them. She even wanted for us to leave our corpses to a bunch of medical students to probe in the name of the greater good. We laughed about the aspects of us that would give the students cause for concern. We'd assumed death was a long way off and waiting to meet us when we were together and old.

A polite ripple of applause causes me to look up, and I see the grey, bearded chin of one of the musicians, his arm held high, holding a pint in acknowledgement to those who are clapping. It's been two long hours since I found the young couple at the top of the Great Orme. They thought I was crazy when I nearly wrenched the phone from the boy's hand. But he came good for me, found the coast guard number and thankfully, finding a weak phone reception, he did as I asked and told them a body had been seen among the rocks on the north side of the Orme. It had taken me an hour to find the couple, and the helicopter took about an hour to get mobilised – too long. I was almost in the pub before I heard it. It'll be all over the local news sites soon.

My hands are still trembling. It feels as though all eyes are on me; sneering, accusing, condemnation and hatred writ large in every expression. I feel like standing up and screaming at them all, confessing there and then. But I must wait. I must do the decent thing and inform my friends first. It's the least I can do before their lives and their freedoms are taken. Out of the corner of my eye, I think I see Orla, bundled up in my green coat. I catch my breath as she smiles, deep red mouth and black beetle eyes vivid and beautiful, then in an instant her face crumples, skin gives way to a cracked and bloody skull. She's gone in a blink, but the image remains. The Great Orme is breaking me up bit by bit. It's eating my heart.

I rub my eyes, scraping them to force the image from my mind. It truly is the end for us now. Once they've identified her, they'll trace her journey to Llandudno and then, well then Helen, the new police officer, will know. They'll think it murder; they'll think I pushed her – successful businesswoman killed by estranged husband. If there's one thing I've learned in my time as a cop, is that we like it clean, we make the jigsaw pieces fit. Even when they don't, society would fall apart if we didn't. *Guilty or Not Guilty.* There is no in between.

The musicians announce their next song: A folk song called The Cruel Mother. Their gruff voices bleed over melancholic guitar chords:

She took out her reaping knife – all the lee and the loney
There she took those fine babes' lives – down by the greenwood sidey-o
She wiped the blade against her shoe – all the lee and the loney
The more she rubbed, the redder it grew – down by the greenwood sidey-o

Even among people, I'm alone. Everything I hear, see or do, takes on a significance beyond that of the normal. A lanky young barman wearing his hair in a ponytail approaches me, three short glasses held in a triangle formation between his hands.

He has to shout to be heard over the music. 'Excuse me. Are you Zac?'

I eye him suspiciously but nod, and he places three neat rums on the bar before me.

'I didn't order them,' I say matter-of-factly.

Placing both hands on the bar and leaning in toward me, he says, 'Someone left a piece of paper on the bar, a twenty-pound note beside it.' He pushes a folded piece of A4 paper toward me across the varnished oak bar-top. Unfolding and holding it flat on the bar, I read the message written in neat uppercase blue ink.

Three rums for the miserable-looking bastard sat at the end of the bar. He's had a murderous day. His name is Zac.

'Who was it?' I ask straight away.

The barman raises his eyebrows, lips pursed tightly together, and wipes the bar with one swift flick of a towel. 'Not a clue.'

His attention is promptly snared by customers pressed up against the bar, waiting to be served. I leave the drinks and squeeze my way past the people at the bar, checking each face in case I recognise one of tomorrow's visitors. I end up scouring the entire pub for my old friends, but see none of them. Holding the pub door open to let someone in, I take one last look over my shoulder, desperate to identify a killer in the crowd, but I'm the only killer I know of.

It's an uneasy walk home. A fine and freezing drizzle has slid off the sea, sticking like a spider's web to my hair and face. I tread carefully. The snow turned to slippery grey slush.

Orla's dead. Orla's dead. Orla's dead. The words run through my mind like an endless train. I stumble past merry people and their merry conversations, until exhausted, I arrive at the old house. I wish my mother was there to welcome me home, but even she chose death over me. I have no one. Orla was right – I destroy everything I touch.

Shutting the front door behind me, I remember at least I have Smokey, and I do love the old rascal. He's the one constant in my life. I call his name, my voice rattling through the stillness of the old house. 'Smokey,' I command. 'Here boy.'

A faint whine leeches from upstairs, and instantly I know he's in pain. I rush up the steps, taking them two at a time, shouting his name over and over, his whining getting louder. I stop on the landing, momentarily determining where the awful sound is coming from. Finally, I burst into my bedroom and stop as if I have slammed into a brick wall.

Smokey is hanging from the ceiling, trussed by his neck with cable wire to the light, his rear legs dangling beneath him, twitching. I jump up on my bed and grab hold of his body, lifting him up, taking his weight and fumbling furiously to detach the cable from the light fitting. Smokey untethered, we both drop in a heap on the bed, and I gather him in my arms. His deep brown eyes are cracked with blood-red fissures, and above his collar his grey-black fur is parted, exposing a dark purple line where the cable dug in. He licks my hand and I nuzzle my face into his fur and thank God he's survived.

After checking Smokey over and soothing him with gentle caresses and soft words, I conclude he's okay. He'll be sore a while, not to mention traumatised, but whoever did this to him has failed.

Smokey in my arms, tears streaming down my cheeks, I wander through the old house checking for someone or signs of a break-in. I grab a knife from the kitchen drawer, even though I'm not scared… people don't scare me, it's the ghosts I fear. You can deal with people; you can't deal with ghosts.

I need to see the others; do as I've always done - make them see sense. But this time, common sense, and not the twisted interpretation of sense that led me wearing horns and carrying a spear, through fiery Hell.

I turn on all the lights in the rooms, opening the cupboards, checking under the beds, the bathroom, pulling back curtains. All the windows are shut tight, and the back door is locked and bolted. Returning to the kitchen, I'm struck by a thought, an explanation. The others have a key to the front door. Of course they do. My mother gave them out when we were teenagers; the old house was an open house; my friends welcome to come and go as they pleased. My mum thought the place was too big for the two of us and she enjoyed the additional company, especially since the death of my father. One of them still has their key and has used it to get in. One of them is trying to scare me, to stop me from confessing.

The Great Orme

Feeling disconnected, as if things aren't real, I stand before my bedroom window, coffee in hand, staring into the settled darkness, the Irish Sea, the hypnotic chinks of light that come and go. I think of Orla; of the others, and see dark clouds battling for dominance. The cloak of darkness rolling toward me, sky and sea converging, my head full to bursting with the noise of thunder and crashing waves. A thick, long tail lashes out, and the sea serpent's jaws open wide until that's all I can see, bone-white pointed teeth visible, and eyes glowing red. I snap the curtains shut.

Even Smokey whimpers. Something we don't understand is in the Great Orme, and in the old house, and perhaps in me. I don't know what to do. Everyone around me is dying.

How can I sleep? I sink into the worn armchair in the library at the back of the old house overlooking the backyard. I've made myself a sandwich, but I'm not hungry. I eat it anyway. I'm going to need all of my strength to get through tomorrow. *One more day*, I tell myself. One more day to get through, and then I can give up. Hell can have me.

The chair used to be my father's favourite, and so I draw on the memory of him, anything other than trying to understand what was happening.

I remember being four years old, my father handing me my first football, a light-weight plastic thing, with an orange and black hexagon pattern printed on it. My mother yelled at him, telling him he didn't need to drink every night. I couldn't have been more pleased with the gift. I didn't understand why my mother was so mean to him. My father kissed me on top of my head before attempting to kiss my mother, but she had turned away.

'I won't be late. I'll only have a couple tonight.' He always said that, but he always stayed until chucking out time and, according to my mother, always rolled in late and drunk. Apart from that night, because that night he never returned at all.

I remember her howling. I remember the way the sound

made me feel. The way it scorched my ears and burrowed deep into my innards. I remember sitting up in bed, blanket pulled up to my chin and chewing its edge. I remember creeping downstairs; my mother needed me. I remember poking my head around the corner of the library door, seeing my mother doubled over on her hands and knees as if she'd been shot in the stomach. Shuffling their feet uncomfortably, two policemen, their backs to me, stood over her. A ball of fire spun in the pit of my stomach, anger... why didn't they do anything to help? I ran to her and threw my arms around her neck. I wanted to help her, but her cries of despair rang out like it was the end of the world. For her it was, and perhaps for me too.

My father had been killed. And, from then on, the days became heavier. My mother lived only for me, and I felt guilty because of it. I gradually learned that a fight between two men had started at the pub. My father intervened in an attempt to break it up. One of the men turned on my father and punched him, a fatal blow sending him crashing to the slate-tiled floor upon which he cracked his head. He was rushed to Llandudno General Hospital, where he was pronounced dead on arrival.

My father knew the man who landed the fatal blow. We all did. He was famous, in Llandudno at least. During the summer months, he ran a Punch and Judy show on the Pier. Turned out he had already served a sentence of a couple of months in prison for burglary. The law hadn't dealt with him appropriately, and since then, nor have I, unable even to look him in the eye. The problem is, he's changed. He served six years for killing my father. Since then, he's run a hospice in town for the homeless. He does great work, often in the local news, having set up those in need in clean and safe accommodation, or else he's turned around drug addicts' lives, giving them opportunities and hope. I see him occasionally, and I know he sees me. We never speak, never hold one another's gaze for more than a split second. I feel he wants to say something to me, but I don't care for it. I can't bring myself to think about it. It reminds me I'm not in control.

I realise now, from that moment, my mother changed from the considerate and caring woman that would help anyone in need, to someone who fiercely protected her own, railing at people for the merest of offences. I don't like to project my upbringing or my environment as excuses for what I did or who I am… but… but I have to accept, it may have a bearing.

Smokey is curled up in my lap. He stirs, ears erect and alert to something somewhere. I stroke the poor thing's belly and hope he'll recover from the trauma. I know I'll never recover from the trauma of losing Orla. All I have left is the ability to document what we did. That is all I have to give. And so, compelled to write, I lift Smokey and place him carefully on the floor. He barks and even wags his tail. My heart goes out to him. I love that boy.

After giving Smokey a treat to chew on, I go into the study and sit at my desk. I need to transfer my notes onto my computer, but something in me declines. I slide my laptop off the edge of the desk so it lands with a thud on the floor. Digital words are so easily tossed into the abyss, content comprised of zeros and ones. I need to continue to scratch the words with ink. They must bleed on to paper. The physical connection seems necessary, now more than ever.

The night and the old house come alive. The central heating has kicked on, loud, hammering noises coming from the water tank in the loft and the pipes hidden in the walls. It sounds like a truck full of crates is being unloaded upstairs. It's never sounded as bad as this. Even the old house is breathing its last dying breaths. I get up and run up the stairs, in case it's not the central heating. I switch on the lights and find everything as I left it, as Orla and I left it. The sound has stopped. All I can do is write, and write what I think I know, so I write these words now, before it's too late, before the Great Orme takes us all.

I find the flowing daub of blue ink on white paper cathartic, my words held up by faint green lines. I wish I'd done it sooner.

A thought occurs to me and I stop suddenly, curse, and drop the pen like it's caught flame. I reach for my coat, draped over the back of the chair, pull out the note the barman gave me, and unfold it. It can't be, but I know it is. The note is a page from my notebook: the hue of the paper, the faint green lines, even the density of the blue ink is the same.

A divine death

Chapter Ten

Biting my lip, I stand the notebook up on its edge and thumb the pages until my fingernail catches an undulation near its spine. I lay the book flat on the desk, and open it where my fingernail holds. Where the pages are bound, I'm not surprised to see the rough edge of a torn-out page, but I am surprised to see a crude sketch of a hangman's noose and a simple smiley dog-face drawn in the leftover margin.

Smokey barks, stands rigid, ears pointed. I shut the book, check my watch. It's eleven-thirty.

Smokey barks again. Growls.

Two knocks at the front door, flat, slow. I shush Smokey and steel myself. Perhaps it's the police. Perhaps they found Orla, linked her back to me already. I'm not ready to confess yet. I have to explain to the others first. I prepare to obfuscate and lie.

I open the door. It's not the police. It's a vicar, and not just any vicar, it's Costas.

There's a moment, no more than two seconds, but indeterminably long, just staring at one another. Costas' skin appears less taut, his hairline more receded, but his dark-brown hair is still carefully crafted, wavy and swept back off his forehead with glossy product, and his warm brown eyes still magnified behind black-framed glasses, but it's the perfectly white clerical collar around his neck that defines who he is these days.

We embrace, and it feels good. With Orla gone, I'm sorely tempted to turn Costas around and head to the police station there and then, but I know an end is coming, our confession almost ready.

The Great Orme

I usher him inside, and watch Smokey scoot away, and wonder why.

In the hallway, I take his jacket and relieve him of his suitcase. With giant, firm hands, he takes me by the shoulders and holds me at arms-length. It's as if nothing has changed, six years merely a scratch on the skin of the Great Orme. He's a big man, well over six feet tall. He raises his eyebrows so they poke over the top of his glasses, and he even manages a smile of a sort, generous and warm. 'Zac,' he says, his voice a rich baritone and smooth metre, 'we are *not* confessing.'

The warmth I feel at seeing my old friend suddenly dissipates, replaced by the harsh chill of purpose. I feel my bones soften with doubt, the sheer weight of carrying my body too much. What if these people have moved on? What if time has eroded my influence? I half expected this, but the reality of it momentarily stuns me. 'Costas, *you* of all of them, you with your faith, you must understand? We must be honest. We must confess.'

He removes his hands. 'What good will it do, Zac? Too much time has passed. We'd only be raking over old coals, causing even more hurt, more despair.'

'Because it's the right thing,' I say. 'Morally, it's the right thing to do.'

'I'm not sure, Zac. We're not in control and never were. We don't have to be. *You* don't have to be.' He runs thick fingers through his hair and sighs. 'God is.'

'Costas,' I say, my voice raising a pitch. 'Don't you see? This is Hell. *We* are living in Hell. The Devil is in control here, and we have to stop it.'

Costas falls back against the hall wall as if pushed. He removes his glasses and rubs his eyes. 'Zac,' he says, pushing his glasses back on. 'It's you. You have to let it go. Move on. You aren't the judge. Let God be the judge.'

'Costas,' I say, my voice back on a plain and even keel. 'You… We… killed a little girl. Chloe. We killed her.'

Sat in the Lounge, I pass Costas a glass of rum.

'Move away from here, this town, this old house. It's poisoning you,' he says, swirling the amber liquid in his glass while staring at it. 'Start again, someplace new. Do good! Throw yourself into charitable works. That's the way forward!' He slugs back half of the contents of the glass and wipes his lips. 'Do good!' he says again, nearly spitting with the force of expelling the two words from his lips.

The big man leaves me saddened, but I understand his position. I will persuade him. I must. I must persuade all of them. I always did.

'It's not as easy as that,' I say. 'We both know it. It's time for us to face up to what we did. Time for us to be held accountable.'

'You are always so sure, aren't you?' he says. 'Not everything's binary, Zac. There are degrees in all we see and do. The line is graduated. Only God can say where the limit is. What good will our confessing do?'

I stare at his crisp white dog-collar. He notices and touches it self-consciously, pushing his glasses up his nose. Rocking back his head, he finishes the rum in one gulp. 'You understand,' he says, staring at the empty glass in his hand. 'You'd be condemning us, all of us? All lives effectively over, our families destroyed, all the good we have left to do, never to be done. You realise this, don't you?'

I top up his glass and notice Orla's handbag on the sofa beside him. My heart rate accelerates. What do I say if he asks about it? Costas breathes in noisily, the bag tips slightly, resting against his leg. He picks it up and moves it along the sofa. He's miles away, contemplating the situation he finds himself in.

'One of us is still killing,' I tell him.

He meets my gaze. 'What?'

I tell him about the old man, how he was murdered, the biscuits left behind on his body. I tell him about the young boy, the brutal attack to his head. He listens intently, breathing heavily, nodding thoughtfully. I'm irritated. I expected more from him, but he seems worn and distant. I tell him about the doll and car left for me in town, the Kashmiri goat head in the sink, the note left for me in the pub, Smokey strung to the bedroom light. For some reason, I don't tell him about Orla, and I don't reveal Sian is in town.

I get up and stare into the cracked mirror on the wall. My reflection stares back at me, pink shirt, pale face, choppy jet-black hair – I think I'm a reflection staring at a reflection. I ask Costas when he arrived in Llandudno and how he got here.

'My car is parked outside. I came straight here.' He doesn't say anymore. I turn to face him. He's slumped forward, elbows on his knees, glass held limply in his hand and head lolling forward.

I sit and wait.

'You had me worried, Zac… since receiving your message. I couldn't wait until tomorrow. Had to come sooner. I have to change your mind.'

Costas cocks his head and gazes at me. His glasses slip down his nose. 'Zac, I'm so tired,' he says, pushing them up. 'I think I need to sleep. It's been a long journey and…' He puts his empty glass on the carpet and lays his hands flat on his knees, palms facing upward, clenching and unclenching his fists.

I lean forward in my seat. 'The marks on your hand. How did you get them?'

His hands stiffen. He stares down at his palms faced up, at the faint red streaks scored across one of them. 'Them, they're nothing.' He turns them over and rubs them on his knees. 'The weight of my suitcase, I guess. Brought more than I need.'

I think of Smokey strung up to my bedroom light; the cord tied around his neck. I imagine Costas hauling Smokey up, the strain of the cord in his hand. 'Do you still have a door key?'

He and I exchange a glance. A fleeting moment of suspicion between us.

'I've no idea what happened to that.'

My brain hurts, and I am tired. I show him to his room. 'How is Jules?' I ask, standing in the doorway.

'She's good. In fact, she's the best. I love her more than anything. I can't go to prison, Zac. I can't leave her. We need each other, we depend on each other for our sanity.' He unzips the lid of his smart, brown suitcase, flipping the lid up and backwards. A pocket-sized antique wooden crucifix fixed with a bronze Christ lies on top of neatly folded clothes. He takes a small sideways step, which obscures most of my view of the case. I think of the crosses drawn in the snow next to the little boy's body the police officer told me about.

'I made arrangements to cover me in my absence. Mine is not the sort of job you can easily drop at such short notice. I rang the Bishop. I could tell he was peeved. There are two funerals on Saturday and the usual services on Sunday to cover, but I guess it's his problem now. And Jules, bless her, she was very understanding. I told her I needed to come back, back to Llandudno, back to the Great Orme, back to you. I told everyone an old friend has taken ill and I must visit, and to be fair, that is the truth.' He throws me a glance which I read as sympathetic, but I can't be sure.

'Costas.' My voice carries a force enough to stop him as he's unpacking. He sees the concern in my face, walks right up to me, stopping barely arms-length away. 'Can I trust you?' I ask.

He closes his eyes and grimaces as if in pain. 'I don't know if I can trust myself. Ultimately though, well, I trust we'll do the right thing in the end. We'll consider things carefully, all of us. I'm sure of it.'

I nod, appreciative of his honesty. He is a good man. He returns to attend to his suitcase.

'As I was packing to come here, Jules told me to "be careful".' He is bent over the suitcase and fidgeting with its contents. 'In the few years we've been married, Jules has been such a supportive wife. I mean, it can't be easy being married to a Vicar, let alone being married to me.' He chuckles to himself. 'The thing is, her conviction in God and the afterlife is a force more vehement than my own, and it's never faltered. She is properly beautiful, far too good for me. Everyone knows I'm punching above my weight. I love her. Jules must not know what I did to that poor girl. She must never know. She must never discover

The Great Orme

about the murder of the old man, the other murders. I worry about what it would do to her.'

Costas is on a roll. He needs to release, and I let him. This is the start of his confession.

'The thing is Zac; I'm held in such high regard by all in the Parish. I try to persuade myself that a life dedicated to God is worthy reparation for my crimes, and all the work I've done for good causes the same. But –'

He throws me a sideways glance, and I nod in encouragement for him to continue.

'The little girl we killed – Chloe, well... six months later, her mother killed herself. She never recovered from her loss, forever distraught she never said goodbye to Chloe. Zac,' he says, removing his glasses then replacing them, 'we effectively killed two people, daughter and mother.'

He picks up a Stephen King novel from the suitcase and taps it against the palm of his hand and stares at the blank wall.

'I think I'm going mad, Zac. Chloe's mother haunts me. As real as this book in my hand, I've seen her.' He stops tapping the book and places it carefully on the bedside table. 'Her long blonde hair always soaked with perspiration and stuck to her face. *"You took my daughter too soon,"* she says. *"You didn't let me say goodbye."*

I press my forehead hard against the edge of the doorway as if the pressure can dull the image in my head, but it doesn't, it just makes it burn more vividly: Chloe's bright smiling face, a beaming force of youthful energy, an image that was posted on the internet after she died.

Costas lowers the suitcase lid and moves protectively in front of it.

'I'm sorry,' I say. 'Go on, please.'

Costas shakes head. 'She cries. Chloe's mother always cries. I want her to stop, Zac. I need her to stop crying.'

I stand up straight and fiddle with the cuffs on my new shirt. 'Tell me how it happened. Tell me exactly how it played out from your perspective.'

Costas regards me, confused, forehead scrunched up. He takes a deep breath, lowers himself to sit on the edge of the bed, and removes his glasses.

'I'd not long been ordained. Chloe was twelve years old. Her family were members of my parish. And they trusted me. They had faith in God and in me. Chloe was terminally ill. She had a highly malignant osteosarcoma and had been through multiple courses of chemotherapy and radiation therapy, as well as four surgical restrictions. They'd recently discovered a hemopneumothorax in her right lung. All curative options had been exhausted. She had two weeks to live, if she was lucky.

Chloe's parents had requested my presence at her hospital bedside, as if my prayers could save her or at the very least see her safely on to the next life.'

Costas pinches his eyes. I won't let him relent. He needs to tell it how it was, and I need to hear it so I can write it down. 'Carry on.'

He sniffs, dabs his eyes with the heels of his hands, and continues: 'Her parents looked like zombies. They hadn't slept for God knows how long. I told them to go home, to get some rest. I told them I would keep her safe. They trusted me, Zac. They trusted me!'

I nod my acknowledgement, and it's all I can do to stop from bursting into tears myself. The story is terrible, but I want its telling to hurt us both. I want it to drive a stake right through us. We deserve far worse.

'She and I were alone in her hospital room, the lights low. I took her hand in mine, her glassy-blue eyes staring up at me, her skin yellow, drawn, older than her years, ravaged by that cruel illness. Her forehead was shiny with sweat and what was left of her wispy blonde hair stuck to it...'

Costas gasps in a lungful of air to regulate his breathing. 'She still managed a smile,' he croaks, turning his head away so I can't see him dab at the tears.

I want to surrender there and then. I want to hand myself in and let justice take its course, but I know it never really can – nothing can atone for what we have done, and nothing can release the well of horror I carry with me daily – and nor should it.

'She was little more than a skeleton,' Costas continues, glasses in his hand and the other covering his eyes. 'A skeleton under the blanket, muscles wasted away to nothing. God damn, I prayed. I pressed her hand in mine and gazed deep into her eyes… sad, beautiful blue oceans. She suddenly started gasping for air, as if the room had been expunged and I kept it all for myself, her body jolting spasms I had seen before and recognised as the onset of death. I needed to talk to someone, someone more tangible than God, so I called the next best thing – I called you.'

I remember the call vividly – who could forget a call like that? Costas was in tears. I could barely hear him through muffled sobs. I've spent long days and nights since then wondering why I hesitated, what right I had to do so. 'Go on,' I say to Costas.

'You answered straight away,' he said, his eyes glistening with suspended tears. 'You listened carefully, like you are now, as I poured my heart out, dropping the shield of the cloth as I can only do with you. On Chloe's bedside table was a small square red emergency button. I told you I was going to press it. You told me to wait, that it was over for her. What right had you to say that?'

None, was my answer. None whatsoever.

'I waited… perhaps one minute, you and I in silence, but the sound of Chloe frenziedly gasping for air, deafening. I released her hand and opened the door, searching up and down the corridor for a nurse or doctor. But it was late and whatever staff remained were nowhere to be seen. I stepped back in the room and closed the door and reached for the button, but Chloe's arm shot out and grabbed my wrist, preventing me from pressing it.'

Tears are streaming down my friend's face. 'We interfered,' he says through thick trembling lips. This time, Costas breaks. He doubles over and falls to the floor, crumpled like a huge black flag. I rush over to him and sit him up, his back leaning against the side of the bed.

'When we killed the old man, it was different. He had been cruel. He had lived his life. But Chloe…' he sobs.

He takes his time, stretching his legs out along the floor and gasping for control of his breathing. 'In no time at all, she'd gone. Free. All the while, I recited verses from Philippians:

"For to me to live is Christ, and to die is gain… for I am in a strait betwixt two, having a desire to depart, and to be with Christ; which is far better…"'

I watch Costas fumble with his stiff clerical collar – the pure white band, the outward symbol of his holy calling. I suspect it feels tighter than it used to, like it's choking him.

I leave Costas' bedroom for my own. In my bed, Smokey curls up next to me, foregoing his basket for the first time since he was a puppy. He's scared, and rightly so after his experience today.

I'm scared, scared of what we did. And fear what's to come. I have my notebook with me – It's time to confess about Costas, and about Chloe, and Chloe's mother.

Tomorrow is the big day and, if Costas' reaction is anything to go by, I've got my work cut out to convince the others to confess, but I have to believe the weight, the burden of what we did, is too much for any of us to bear, because simply – it is.

I place the book and pen on the bedside table and turn off the light. Tonight, I've drawn the curtains, as if they might be a protective barrier to all that is to come. In the darkness, they appear to float, glowing eerily, the sea behind them, shifting and reflecting what light there is. I turn my head to one side, listening. Something is scratching. Smokey's ears are pricked up, and he's trembling. The scratching sounds like it's coming from behind the curtains. A bird, I tell myself. A bird moving about on the eaves, maybe a pigeon, or a gull. I'm about to get up, but the sound stops. Not conscious enough to get out of bed, just awake enough to register the sound coming and going, I fall into some kind of sleep.

Orla's absence is eating me alive. She drifts into my dreams. I see her falling from a hundred different angles, and each time I chase after her and each time I'm too late. She dies over and over again, and so do I. My heart shattered and broken, like her body on the rocks below. Semi-conscious, I twist and turn in my bed. I can hear the tide advance and return, an uneasy rhythm with my own breath, the sea gradually claiming Orla for its own.

I wake. It's dark. The sound of the sea still reverberates in my ears. I sit upright, arms outstretched, groping for Smokey. He's beside me, his body wedged into mine. Still caught in a half-sleep, I hear another noise, a faint knocking sound. Smokey raises his head; a low growl rumbles and vibrates in his belly. It must be Costas, I tell myself. It must be, although my mind is imagining Orla, body misshapen and bedraggled in seaweed, the knocking the sound of her bumping over the rocks as the sea sucks her toward its depths. The knocking sound disappears as she is swallowed entirely and only the relentless sound of the sea's waves breaking persists.

Startled, I abruptly sit up, eyes wide open, the sound of running, splashing water still present, but external to my head. I blink and rub my face to be sure I'm fully awake. The sound isn't going away. I turn the blanket back and pick up yesterday's clothes from the floor and hurriedly dress. Strange as it is, I breathe a sigh of relief, recognising it's only the sound of the running bath I can hear. I glance at my phone on the bedside table for the time: 5:30 a.m.

Costas' bedroom door is shut. I stride purposefully toward the bathroom at the end of the hall, the noise of pouring water and the heave of the old pipes magnifying as I approach. The bathroom door is shut, so I knock. No response. I knock again, louder this time. Nothing. I try the door handle. It's unlocked.

On opening the door, I find water spilling from the bath and soaking the floor-tiles. I switch on the light, and barefooted, splash through the water, quickly reaching for the taps, turning both off. I notice immediately the overflow hole in the bath is blocked, stuffed with a flannel.

'Zac?'

My heart leaps and I swing around to see Costas in t-shirt and shorts. His huge frame fills the doorway, his eyes scrunched up, unused to the light. He's just woken up.

'Bit early for a bath?' he says, surveying the floor, bemused.

We stare at one another, minds turning over. Finally, raising a hand to his chin, Costas says what we are both thinking. 'So, if you didn't run the bath, and neither did I, who the hell did?'

Levelling the lies

Chapter Eleven

We search the house, Smokey, with his nose to the floor. I stupidly yell, 'Hello?' as if whoever is doing this to me might take that as their cue to appear. Nothing. Again.

I take photos with my phone because, well, because that's what people do, although I'm not sure an overflowing bath counts as evidence for anything other than dementia or a leaky tap. I'm determined not to cave in so easily. My time is nearly up. I only have to get through the weekend.

I drain the bath and throw down a bunch of towels to absorb the water. At six in the morning, Costas and I stand in the kitchen, dressed, shaved, and ready for the big day.

Orla's absence is a source of pain in my chest. I feel as if a hole has been drilled through my sternum through which my heart bleeds. I try to imagine with time I'll develop some sort of ice-like clot to stem the painful bleed, but in reality, I know it's a wound that is impossible to heal. I've lost my father, my mother, and now my wife prematurely. Orla was right, *I destroy everything I touch*.

I offer Costas a coffee and pick up the kettle, reaching out a hand to turn on the tap. I freeze. The sink is filled with murky red water, something floating on its scummy surface. I pick out a tiny wooden doll, about three inches high, a wooden artist's manakin. I turn it over in my fingers and notice a scrawl in fine black ink on its back– "Arianwen", and the imaginary hole drilled into my heart throbs just that little bit more.

'You okay?'

Holding the doll out before me as if it will explain, I turn to face Costas. 'It's my mother,' I say.

Costas' brow creases. 'Your mother? Arianwen?'

'This figure represents my mother, she… it was floating in the sink.' I show him my mother's name scrawled on its back.

Costas shakes his head in disbelief.

'I am creeped out,' I say. 'Someone is entering my home to taunt me. And they are doing it with ease, me and Smokey oblivious.'

I feel like I'm dead, a ghost. None of it is *really* happening. But it is. It is.

'You know,' Costas says, peering at me over the rim of his glasses. 'You never discussed what happened to your mother.'

I drag a chair back from the kitchen table. 'I got in from a late shift. The house was quiet and still, which was unusual. My mother always stayed up waiting for me, tea and toast ready to go. She worried about me, about the job. Smokey wasn't there to greet me, so I knew something wasn't right. I wondered if she had fallen asleep on the sofa in the lounge. That happened occasionally, but all I found was an empty brandy bottle and glass on the coffee table. Unlike my father, my mother didn't drink. Thinking she had gone to bed and was asleep, probably not feeling well, taken Smokey with her, I checked in her bedroom, but she wasn't there either.'

Elbows pressed into the kitchen table, Costas fiddles with his glasses, fingers shaking. I push down the plunger on the cafetière. 'I found her in the bath, Costas. Smokey flat out on the tiles, not a wag or a look of acknowledgement for me – he knew what she'd done.'

Costas shakes his head. 'God have mercy.'

I cover my face with my hands as if it will block out the image, but all I can see is her, slipped down in the bath, her face bobbing gently in her own blood, eyes closed, dead. 'The water was bright red, her arms cut to ribbons.'

Blindly, I reach forward to lift the cafetière, and now my own hands trembling, am unable to do so.

Before I know it, Costas' huge arms are wrapped around me,

containing me, and I'm sobbing for the death of my mother, and for the death of Orla, for the unfairness of it all. Life is neither fair nor unfair, that's what I thought, that's why I took control, to make it fairer somehow, but it hasn't worked out, it hasn't helped. I move uneasily and Costas releases me. I manage to pour, adding milk and sugar to Costas' coffee, I explain that perhaps the death of my father and my mother, had propelled me into taking control, to exacting fairness, justice, in a world where it didn't exist. But there's no light at the end of the tunnel. I've only made the world worse and the tunnel only gets darker.

Costas informs me only God can exact real justice.

'You may be right,' I say, wiping my wet eyes. 'Killing also kills the killer. It dehumanises them. Us. Look what it's done to me. It's time to confess, Costas. For God's sake, your sake, for mine, for all of us… It's time.'

Pacing the kitchen and eyeing me carefully, he sips his coffee. We hold one another's gaze, old friends comfortable in doing so, despite the circumstances. He stops still at the centre of the room, rocks his head back, and groans. All I can see is his wide chin above the stiff white clerical collar.

He speaks words at the ceiling, with the calmness and surety of one well practiced in reciting them. 'For when I kept silent, my bones wasted away through my groaning all day long. For day and night, your hand was heavy upon me.'

He lowers his head, his gaze reconnected to mine. 'Psalm thirty-two, verses three to four.'

'Sounds like you need to confess,' I say. 'Relieve the weight of *his* hand a little?'

I never expected him or the others to thank for me for this decision. Why would they? It spells the end for us all. We'll be removed from society, the others separated from those they love. Now Orla is gone. I have no one, just Smokey, and I can't bear to think about what might happen to him.

Costas stares at me as if my words have drifted right past

him without connecting. 'You understand, don't you?' I ask. 'Especially you.'

This time he nods, but his face is ashen, drained of all colour, and he's flicking his tongue out, licking his lips nervously. His mind is racing with the worry about the consequences of our decision. And rightly so.

Despite the warning signs closing in on me, having Costas with me in the old house has renewed my confidence a little. I don't know which one of the other four is angry at me, angry enough to kill again, but I will not be put off. I need to tell Costas about Orla, but decide to wait, to tell all of them together. They loved her too. The tragedy of her death must make them see, make them understand.

The water in the sink had been dyed red with the contents of a bottle of tomato sauce, the empty bottle in the bin. Costas pushes me to one side, leans over the sink and vomits. He heaves and wretches, mumbled apologies in between. I grab a tea towel from a drawer, thrust it at him, grab another, turn on the tap and wipe around the sink again.

'I'm so sorry,' he says when he's done. 'I don't know…' He's unable to finish his words, pulling at his collar like it's a noose around his neck.

I sit him at the table and fill a glass with water.

'It's harder still for me, you realise?'

'Why?' I hold out the glass of water.

Hunched over the table, he takes it and shakes his head. 'Think about it, Zac. A Vicar confessing to murder. I'll be vilified, painted as some evil creature, but worst of all, they'll assume Jules knew. They'll dig and open up her past.'

There's a pause while I wait for him to continue until, finally, I lose patience. 'Her past?'

He sips at the water, glancing nervously at me out of the corner of his eyes. 'It's not been easy for Jules. Sometimes people have to draw a line and move on, however hard it may be.'

'Just how difficult was it for Jules... before she drew the line?' I draw a chair back and sit, legs stretched out, arms crossed.

'You don't understand. I'm scared of her... her reaction.'

'What do you mean?'

His fists are clenched, his eyes glazed with tears that don't fall. 'She won't stand for it. She's the force behind me and has built the life we have.'

'I still don't understand. She's a good woman. You both have your faith, isn't that enough?'

'She's a fighter, Zac. If I know her like I think I do, she won't let me go without a fight.'

'What does she know? Have you told her, Costas, about the murders?'

'Perhaps, I...'

'Perhaps?' I interrupt. 'Either you have or you haven't. Which is it?'

'I don't know. On Sunday nights we would drink – a lot – our escape from the weight of everyone else's troubles. I may have inferred something or other, although I am sure I never told her about Chloe and her mother.'

He pushes back in his chair, looking over my shoulder like he's seen a ghost.

'I can see her mother right now. She's stood behind you, a knife in her hand.'

An icy draught slices across the back of my neck. I jolt forward in my chair, swivelling around to look behind me, braced to do something, although I'm not sure what. No one is there, yet something has changed. I can feel it in the air, and I believe Costas. Of course I do. Somehow, Chloe's mother is here. She's with us; watching, waiting, urging us to do the right thing.

'She follows me everywhere,' he says. 'I always thought ghosts were rooted to places. Turns out they can be rooted to people too.'

I stand, unable to relax.

'It's fine, she disappeared as you turned around – trying to

The Great Orme

make me seem crazy.'

I wonder how many people see ghosts but never tell anyone. Why would they when it's impossible to prove?

'Just how far would Jules go?' I ask.

My phone buzzes loudly, vibrating in my jeans pocket. We both stiffen. Hardly anyone calls me. I take my phone and read the display: "Unknown Number".

'Hello,' I say tentatively, clamping the phone to my ear.

There's a click, and an upbeat automated female voice plays: 'Good morning, Zac. I am the Leveller, and I saw you kill Orla.' There's a pause, then she continues. 'If you don't want to die, don't confess. It's that simple.'

The message clicks off and the phone connection severs.

Costas stares at me expectantly, face etched with concern. 'What's wrong?'

'Someone threatened to kill me if I confess.'

I don't tell him that whoever it is, was on the Great Orme earlier, that they saw Orla fall. From a distance, perhaps it appeared as if I'd pushed her. It's possible. How can I persuade any of them to confess if they think I've killed Orla? What am I doing? Everything is getting worse.

'Huh? What?' Costas is on edge, impatient to know more.

'An automated message,' I say. 'Whoever it was said they were *The Leveller*.'

Costas pulls the wooden crucifix from an internal pocket within his blazer, clutching it tightly. 'God forgive us,' he says through gritted teeth.

'What are you going to do?' His eyes flicker behind his glasses. He's aching for me to change my mind. To make it like it was before. It's too late for that.

It's my turn to feel sick. 'I'm going to confess,' I say.

He lowers the crucifix.

Smokey trudges into the kitchen from wherever he's been, probably snoozing, and, taking a wide arc to avoid Costas, he settles at my feet. I trust Costas, but I trust Smokey more.

I leave Costas alone, telling him I need to clear my thoughts, that I need to write. Smokey follows me to the study. Sitting at my desk, I open the draw and take out the notebook. For a time, I become lost in doodling a sea monster on its hard, green cover. Trapped within its coiled tail, I sketch Orla, then Costas, and so committed, I feel I must draw all of them, Sian, Tomasz, Harrison, and Jessie. I sketch myself over the top of the sea monster. Outside, the wind buffets the windowpane, rattling it in its worn wooden frame as if raging at me for all I've done. Orla's body must have been found, unless the sea had taken her, but I doubt it. The rocks will have held on to her, I think, but nothing is certain. There's nothing on the news sites yet. We'll see.

Smokey, asleep at my feet, stirs and growls. I stop writing, holding the nib of the pen to the page, and take in my loyal friend. 'Hey Smo–'

A large hand rests on my shoulder and I twist around in my chair. Costas stands over me, staring down at the notebook. I immediately place a hand over the top of it.

He says nothing and I ask nothing. If he's read any part of what I wrote about Orla's fall to her death, he doesn't show it.

'I didn't try to hang Smokey. I'm not responsible for any of the evil that's happening now.'

I nod, appreciative of his directness.

'It'll be good to see Orla later,' he adds. 'She'll know what to do.'

My stomach muscles tense. I make clear and direct eye contact with Costas to see if he flinches, that he might avert his eyes suggesting deceit, but he doesn't. In fact, he holds my gaze, and I wonder if he's testing me. I end up averting my eyes.

That's the way to do it

Chapter Twelve

We're not hungry, but decide to go out for lunch anyway. It could be our last meal out, a sobering thought. Smokey with us, too fearful to leave him in the old house after what happened to him last night. It's a slow descent into town, where the snow is all but gone, washed away by the overnight rain. The sky hangs low and heavy, draped in a seamless canvas of muted grey and silver. I glance over my shoulder at the Great Orme, stone meeting sky appearing as if the edge of the world. The primordial reptilian creature's spine rises in jagged peaks, flanks slant downwards like scales, fleeting moments of light sparkle like glints in the serpent's eye. This land is alive. Nobody can convince me differently.

Llandudno's streets are mine, or so it feels. I know them so well, but today I see them, and the people that use them, differently. People scurry past like ants, all with some place they've come from and some place to go, each of them caught up in trivia, oblivious to the two killers and a dog that they pass by. Well, most people.

Someone stops us. Helen. The new police officer, off duty, removes her red bobble hat and tussles her golden blonde hair. 'Hi Zac. How's it going? Left Orla at home?'

Costas coughs, wheezing as if he's having an asthma attack. 'Are you okay?' Helen asks, her brow furrowed with concern.

'Yes, yes, I'm fine,' he replies, thumping his chest to clear it.

I try to smile, gesturing from one to the other. 'Police Officer, Helen Starling, meet Vicar, Costas Benedict.' Costas automatically strikes out a huge hand, swamping Helen's in his.

'We are going for some lunch. Fancy joining us?' I ask. Orla's body hasn't yet been discovered. She would know if it had. 'We'll see Orla later.' One last lie. It's acceptable, I think, buys me the time I need.

'Oh… well, only if I'm not intruding. That would be lovely. Thank you.' She bends and fusses over Smokey. He likes her. I like her.

We end up at my favourite café, The Rabbit Hole. I figure if this is going to be my last paid-for meal, this is where I want it. As its name suggests, the café is set beneath ground level, and we descend the steps to it. We sit at a table against a white wall a handwritten blood-red quote from *Alice in Wonderland* painted on it – "Begin at the beginning and go on till you come to the end, then stop".

Costas and I notice one another reading it and exchange a quick glance, both knowing we've reached the end. It's time for us to stop.

Smokey gets a bowl of water and a treat to chew on from the waiter. Helen's voice is rich and direct. She smiles a lot, and I can sense a keen intelligence behind her eyes. She looks from me to Costas when we speak, contemplating our every word.

She's grateful for our company, and I wonder if there's a loneliness she feels. At times we hold one another's gaze a moment longer than is necessary. The copper in me kicks in, and I wonder if she suspects something, if our bumping into one another is not merely by chance. It's the sort of thing I might have done when I cared more. I raise my guard, conscious not to reveal too much, just in case, but I'm not hugely worried - the whole world will know about me, Costas and all the others in a matter of days.

She's inquisitive, asking lots of questions: how me and Costas know each other, about his family, our plans for the weekend.

I see no point in lying, so I tell her we're having a reunion. Some old friends are visiting. Next to me, Costas mops his brow with a handkerchief, only chipping in occasionally to confirm what I've already said. The waiter brings our food. Helen has linguine, Costas a cheeseburger and fries. I have vegan pancakes coated in a raspberry coulis, banana and chocolate. I have declined to eat flesh for many years for one reason or another.

I raise the subject of the recent murders, asking if there have been any further developments.

'I guess you would know more than me, being more senior?' she replies. 'Has anyone been in touch with you about them?'

It's a good call. The murders are major news for a place like Llandudno. She should expect me to be in the know, even if I'm on leave. 'I've been busy,' I say, before devouring a huge piece of syrupy pancake. 'Preparing for my guests.'

'So, you won't have heard there's been another death?'

Costas drops his burger, melted cheese, meat and bun separate, splattering on the white tablecloth. 'Sorry,' he mumbles, scraping up the mess with a knife.

I hand him a paper napkin as calmly as my own nerves will allow. My heart clangs as if a ball-bearing is bouncing around inside its metal cage. I'm sure everyone can hear it. *They've discovered Orla.* I adopt what I hope is a normal tone, and ask, 'Surely not *another* one?'

Helen lays her hands flat on the table, pausing before speaking. 'Possibly.'

She observes the other diners. Ever popular, the café is crammed with day-trippers and locals alike. Families and couples stand at the door in their coats, waiting for tables to become free so they can be seated. I scan their faces in fearful anticipation of seeing one of my old friends, wondering which of them is threatening me, attempting to prevent me from confessing. I wonder if they would actually try to kill me. My skin prickles, cold, and I shudder at the thought. Smokey notices and gives a short bark. I lower a hand and pat his head to reassure him. I never expected this. Sure, I knew most, if not all of them, would resist; of course they would, but these people aren't stupid. They will come around to my way of thinking. But despite my good sense and best intentions, a creeping sensation carves its way through my bloodstream - I don't know the others as well as I thought. They are killers. What have I done? I've invited six murderers to the old house. I've made things worse. Even more people are being murdered. I consider confessing right away. I could tell Helen outright and that would be that. But it's impossible. Despite the distance between us, I still love my friends and I owe them an explanation first.

'Apparently a man *fell* from the pier during the night,' Helen says, her voice lowered and her eyes focussed unblinkingly on me and Costas. 'He drowned. His body washed up in the early hours, found by a dog walker.'

'Do you have a suspect?' The words leave my lips before I can stop them.

Helen angles her head ever so slightly, her eyes fixed on mine. 'Not yet.'

'Jesus, this place is going to Hell,' I reply with a wave of my fork. 'Do we know who he is?' I pop another piece of pancake in my mouth, but the appetite I didn't have already has entirely disappeared.

She leans forward on her elbows. 'Apparently,' she whispers. 'It was the guy who managed the Homeless Shelter here in town – Yestyn, I can't remember his surname.'

Her words strike like ice into my heart. I see his face, the face of the stocky man who killed my father; bald head, nervous blue eyes hidden behind round glasses, and grey-stubbled chin. A fatigue washes through me, this news has drained any remaining energy I had.

In a moment, I discover myself slid down my chair. Costas has gripped under my arms. It hurts, but I can't respond. There's a commotion as waiters and customers rush to my aid, their voices distant, muffled. Costas is laughing, standing me up straight, clapping me on the back. My lungs fill with air and my head clears. Strength suddenly returned. 'I'm fine,' I say, pushing him away, although I'm not, the man who killed my father has just died, and that on top of losing Orla, along with everything else that's happened has led to an intensity of feeling I can't explain, one that's been locked up inside of me for so long, and it just became too much. I don't know if I can get through this.

Costas promptly settles the bill and we leave, stepping outside and up the steps, onto Trinity Square. For once, I'm glad for the crisp, cold air of January.

Costas and Helen ask me if I'm sure I'm okay, and Helen suggests we get a taxi back to my house. I insist I'm fine. I pick up Smokey and walk, headed toward Mostyn Street, which I know will be busy with people. I want to see people. I want to be among people. This is freedom.

'What do you think brought that on?' Helen asks.

'Yestyn killed my father.'

Both appear astonished. Costas knew the man. All six of them did. 'Good Lord, Zac! Of course!' he says. 'I'm so sorry.'

'He was a good man in the end,' I say. 'He took care of vulnerable people, organised charity fundraisers. But I still hated him, the old him, him and his fucking Punch and Judy show. Me and Dad used to sit on the tarmac by the pier watching it, my dad laughing even more than me.'

'I'm told he'd written a note.' Helen's voice sounds apologetic. 'He had a bottle tied around his neck… some printed words in it.'

'What?' I say, stopping. 'What words?'

Helen meets my gaze. 'For the sakes of the *old house* and all those in it, I deserved to die.'

I screw up my face. 'What?'

All three of us know he didn't kill himself, and there's only one old house as far as me and Costas are concerned. I wonder if either I, Costas or even Orla referred to it as such in our conversations with Helen. The knot in my stomach tightens. A darkness is coming for me, and it seems there's nothing I can do to stop it.

I set Smokey down and walk on while Helen and Costas talk, but I don't hear them, all I can think of is Yestyn and Orla.

'This is where the old man was murdered on Thursday night,' Helen reminds me as we turn right on to Clonmel Street.

I wonder how we ended up there, reasoning either coincidence or a part of my subconscious at work. Then I remember, I don't believe in coincidences, the police force is trained not to.

The old man's house is a peach-coloured four-storey terraced building, pastel yellow and pink guest houses set either side. Its forecourt is spacious, a patio garden, low walls and borders packed with well-tended plants. At the front door stands a policeman. Recognising me, he walks up the path to join us.

'Hey, Zac!' He bends to pat Smokey. 'The old man had a dog,' he tells us. 'Golden lab, beautiful. The killer beat the crap out of her. Poor thing's traumatised. Hope someone takes her in.'

We attempt to discover if Sammy has any more leads, but he doesn't know anything. 'No one saw anything, so I guess as usual we'll be reliant on CCTV. Although there was none in the house so we'll be dependent on any others. I can't imagine they'll find anything.'

'What's the old man's name?' I ask, fearing to pull the thread in case it and I unravel.

'Joshua,' says Sammy, one hand on his radio.

Across the road a group of teenagers on bikes laugh, only swear words discernible in their garbled chatter, otherwise its couples and neighbours stood facing the house, the magnetism of murder attracting them. I search all the faces, just in case.

A couple of white police vans are parked up along the pavement. An officer emerges from one of them to join us. It's Lewis. Like Sammy, he's wearing a stab-proof vest. Hell, even the police are scared.

Lewis smiles, lips pursed as he approaches us. 'Afternoon,' he says, acknowledging me and Helen, and nodding at Costas. He must be wondering what we're doing with a Vicar in tow. 'Poor old Josh Pinkney. What did he ever do to anyone to deserve this?'

'Josh Pinkney,' I repeat. 'As in the old headmaster of Ysgol John Bright secondary school?'

'That's right,' Lewis says.

'Mr. Pinkney, he was our Headmaster,' I say, turning to Costas.

'Good Lord. Not him too?' Costas replies, taking a deep

breath and holding his glasses on his face as if they might fall off with the news.

'He had it in for us. Thought we were a bad bunch. Do you remember?'

Costas nods. 'Would you believe it?' he mutters.

Lewis knows little more than Sammy. After some small talk we leave, emerging from the street into the wide-open expanse where land meets sea. Dark clouds amass on the horizon, but still, being the weekend, the road is jammed with parked cars, tourists and dog walkers wrapped and zipped up to protect from the bitterly cold breeze gusting in from sea. I can't help but let my eyes follow the coastline down to the pier, the place Yestyn *fell* to his death from hours earlier, and then to the Great Orme itself, where, barely twenty-four hours ago from my wife fell to her death. I am born of Llandudno's dominating landmark, any strength I draw, taken from the ancient rock. It's in my blood, it's in my bones. I'm at the mercy of the Great Orme.

Costas grips me by my wrist, and once again I'm alive to his and Helen's presence.

Helen makes her excuses and leaves us on the South Parade opposite the Pier. There's a calmness in her walk, and I get the feeling she knows we are watching her as the space between us grows wider until she disappears. I'll never see her again. After this weekend I'll never see anyone I know again.

'Are you okay, Zac?' Costas asks me, knowing full well I'm anything but. The others will be arriving in a few hours. I'll be face to face with someone who is still killing, and I have to stop them, then I have to make them confess – all of them.

Marmalade spread

Chapter Thirteen

Two o'clock in the afternoon. Only me and Smokey in the old house as far as I'm aware. Costas wanted some time alone before the others arrive, *to collect his thoughts*. I left him at the Pier.

Four people dead within two days. My fault? Indirectly, yes. I invited the killers back. One of them is out of control. Whoever the Leveller is, I have to stop them, make them see reason. Tonight, the truth will out, and tomorrow we'll be in handcuffs.

I'm sat at my desk in the study, pen in hand, book open before me, dark breaking waves crashing through my thoughts, dousing them with dread. I feel compelled to write. I wish I started writing earlier in life. It's like constructing a mirror, one that reflects new angles of reality, a way of tilting both oneself and the universe so we can see things previously hidden from view.

An hour in, a high-pitched moan drifts through the ceiling. I drop the pen to listen. It's nothing new. Sometimes I think the house is constructed of actual moans and groans rather than bricks and mortar, but the sound takes on a deeper significance now. Everything seems to be closing in. I search for a weapon, something to protect myself.

I consider a lampshade, a vase, an iron, all ridiculous as weapons. I wonder how I ever survived as a policeman. The moan continues. My brain tells me it's the old house's antiquated water pipes squealing, but my heart is convinced otherwise, it's as if the sound is interspersed by gasps for breath.

The moan increases in volume, veering into a shrill squeal, then stops as abruptly as it started. Poised, I wait, my eyes locked on the window, the sea beyond, all my energy given to listening, but the sound has gone and all that remains is the standard hum and creak, the old house once more reduced to slow despairing sighs and pained murmurs. There's an itch in my blood – I have to check upstairs. Smokey is up there. I steel myself and switch on the landing light before ascending, fearing the worst for my loyal pal even though I know nothing can have happened to him while I'm here.

In my bedroom, Smokey lays still in his basket – too still. I approach him, my heart pounding, wondering if the Leveller has finally got to him. I lean over him and am relieved to see the rise and fall of his curled-up body deep in sleep, the walk having worn him out, poor thing. I leave him and perform the ritual of checking every room, the acrid taste of fear wet on my tongue. I check the bathroom, all clear. I work my way through the other bedrooms, prepared and ready for my guests, until finally I check in on Costas' room. His bed is unmade, closed suitcase on top. He isn't back yet. He's taking his time. I wonder why he came early. I slide his suitcase toward me, but pull too far and it topples off the bed, contents spilling out onto the carpet. I curse under my breath, righting the case and picking up his clothes, carefully placing them back inside the suitcase. I realise it doesn't look good, that he will suspect I've been snooping, but then I think that's the least of my worries, and in a moment, I'm proven right. It *is* the least of my worries. I can't believe my eyes at what I see tumble from within a folded t-shirt and clunk to the floor.

I pick up and stare at the object in my hand: a gun. An actual real-life gun. I sit on the edge of the bed, turning the pocket-sized black metal weapon over in my hands. *Why? Why has Costas brought this with him? Why does he, of all people, even have such a thing?*

My brain races to determine his rationale – perhaps it's for protection, perhaps he's afraid of me. I have never considered any of them could be afraid of me. The thought makes *me* afraid. People respond irrationally through fear, this I know, the urge to protect, either themselves or others, overwhelms, cool clear logic shrouded by base animal instinct.

I wrap the gun in the t-shirt once more, knowing he will realise I've rummaged through the case and discovered it. If he trusted me before, he certainly won't now. I make up his bed and as I put the suitcase back; I hear the distinctive rattle of a key in the front door followed by the twist of the handle. I tense. Costas said he doesn't have a key.

A crawling dryness fills my mouth. Stirred from his slumber, Smokey barks. I can hear the door scraping stiffly over the worn beige welcome mat.

I reach for the suitcase and fumble for the t-shirt with the gun wrapped in it, with all that has happened in the last day or two I figure I may need it. I meet Smokey on the landing, and suddenly he's off, bounding down the stairs, tail wagging furiously.

Half-way down the stairs, I see who it is.

'Harrison,' I exclaim. Suddenly I'm terrified. Terrified of what this day and evening will bring. Harrison laughs, a giddy, high-pitched shriek which tears a vacuum in the atmosphere. He's taken his coat off and his black t-shirt appears merely as another layer of skin wrapped around his muscle-bound torso.

He smiles wide, whitened teeth glistening in the gloom of the hallway. 'Zac, are you going to shoot me?'

We sit at either end of the kitchen table, the gun flat on the table between us. I can't take my eyes off him, he's massive, in impeccable shape, worth two of me, far removed from the raw-boned stick figure of our youth. White-framed sunglasses are propped on his black, smooth-shaven head. He scratches his jutting chin. 'Where'd you get that fucking gun? Don't tell me you're losing it? I love you man... but I need to know what's going through your mind.'

'It belongs to Costas. He's here. He's out walking.'

'Costas?' he squeals, slapping his hand on the table. 'Our Costas?'

I nod. 'The one and only.'

'Jesus fucking Christ. Perhaps there's more to the old sandal creeper than I thought!'

The super-size Harrison makes me feel nervous. I know what he's capable of. The sequence of him as a kid, hammering relentlessly with the kerb-stone at the poor boy's head plays like some awful social media clip in my brain.

I offer him coffee. He accepts. 'You've still got a key to the old house?' I say, my back turned to him while I fill the kettle and thinking to myself if he were to pick up the gun and shoot, I wouldn't stand a chance. This is the way my mind is working, and it scares me. I try to think of all the times I've felt this way and remember I'm still here.

I pluck two mugs; mine, a touristy grey mug with a linocut black and yellow image of the Great Orme looming high over a thrashing sea, and a plain white mug, from an open shelf above the counter. Harrison was always quiet, self-conscious, a lover of history, of war and battleships. And yet now... I know he's changed, not just physically, but in his manner, his thinking, his confidence. I can sense it in the way he's moving. Fluid. Deliberate. I heap coffee into the cafetière, feeling the weight of his gaze on the back of my neck. He's biding his time.

'Black for me.'

'Sure.'

'Make it strong please, man. It's been a long drive. I need a boost.' His voice is relaxed and friendly, as if nothing has changed, as if it's a normal day, two friends having coffee at the weekend.

I set the cups and cafetière filled with boiled water on the table next to the gun.

He watches diligently, his head cocked to one side. I've always had the upper hand on my friends, an unspoken deference from them with me being their leader. Tonight will test that premise, a lot of time has passed between us. I wonder if people can really change, and looking at the man of steel before me, transformed from the skinny kid who couldn't maintain eye contact for more than a second, I decide they can.

I sit at the opposite end of the table. Harrison, perfect fake white teeth, smiles. 'Zac, can I still trust you?'

'One hundred per cent,' I reply, and I mean it. 'I've only ever been honest. Even when we killed, it was done from a position of honesty, albeit tragically mis-placed.'

He laughs, the same strangulated sound as before, like an asphyxiated goose, he never used to laugh like that, fake. 'That's the problem, Zac!' he says. 'Honesty! It'll be the death of us!'

I take a sip of coffee, it's stronger than I normally like, but that's no bad thing, I'll need my wits about me.

'Trust is an entirely different beast to honesty,' he says, scratching his immaculately stubbled chin. 'I need to be able to trust you. Trust you when you tell me you *wouldn't* confess, because you *are* going to tell me that aren't you Zac?'

'You can trust me, Harrison,' I say, setting my mug on the table. 'And you can trust that I *am* going to confess.'

He jumps to his feet, flips the solid-wood chair around, lifts it high above his head and brings it crashing to the floor, smashing it so the backrest detaches completely from the seat.

For a moment, all air seems sucked from the room. I can't take my eyes off him. He's stood, frozen, hunched over, staring at the splintered wood in his hands, thick veins in his neck, pulsating. A sudden jerk, and he pulls apart the chair, so he holds a single chair-leg, a weapon. He straightens and turns to face me. Then, like a light has been switched on, his features change, rage replaced by calm. Of course, that's the thing that scares me about Harrison, it always has, his capacity for violence, his eagerness to mete it out.

'The dead are dead, Zac,' he says, breathing hard. 'Confessing won't change that.' He points the chair-leg at me. 'Anyway, I won't let you.'

He waves the chair-leg and forces a smile. 'What will it take?'

My tongue feels welded to the roof of my mouth.

'Careful consideration and no small amount of intellect.' The words are neither mine nor his. Shocked, both Harrison and I turn to see Costas stood in the kitchen doorway.

The old house is a place of shadows, and the spotlights in the kitchen ceiling don't illuminate the doorway as they do the rest of the room. Costas steps into the light but I'm already on my feet and I've snatched the gun from the table, pointing it at Harrison and then at Costas and back again at Harrison.

Costas, ignoring his gun in my hand, thrusts out his own hand toward Harrison. 'Good Lord, haven't you've grown?'

Harrison regards the chair-leg in his hand as if it arrived by teleportation. He drops it and clasps Costas' hand, beaming smile returned.

I wonder at them; they are polar opposites, Costas open and gentle, Harrison, closed and despite his newfound confident persona, afraid.

Costas strides toward me and takes his weapon. 'I suspect you're wondering where a small parish vicar gets a gun?'

'I'll tell you, shall I?' Costas continues, as he weighs the thing lying flat in his hand. 'It's my wife's. It belongs to Jules.'

'Why on earth would she have a gun?' I ask.

'Why indeed?' He leans over the sink, gazing into the courtyard through the window. 'She thought I didn't know about it. It was hidden in her underwear drawer of all places. I suppose she thought I'd never look there.'

Harrison snorts, covering his mouth.

Unmoved, Costas continues. 'I knew this weekend would be difficult and... well, Jules would do anything for me. Let's just say I thought it safer to take it.'

'You thought a gun would be safer here in a house full of *murderers* than in a vicarage?' Harrison's words come across as scornful, but his point carries weight, it's what we are, I'm so ashamed.

Costas presses himself up against the sink. 'She's a killer too,' he says.

Harrison and I regard one another, our faces slack with shared disbelief.

'What are you saying, Costas?' I ask.

'Jules killed her own mother; shot her. With this gun.'

Costas turns the object over in his hand, the gleam of the yellow spotlights reflected in the shiny black metal.

'She's the same as us,' he says, turning around and gazing at the tiled floor. 'Her mother abused her and her sisters for years. Unimaginable horror, I can't bring myself to tell you.' He shakes his head, pinching his eyes together under his glasses. 'She still has nightmares.' He pulls at the white clerical collar around his neck as is his habit. 'Just a teenager, Jules killed her mother to protect herself and her sisters. Of course, you guys will understand?'

After a slight delay, Harrison responds. 'Of course, we do.' He glares at me, 'Don't we, Zac?'

In my pocket, I feel for the red square patch of wool Orla dropped, squeezing and rubbing the tightly knitted mesh between my fingers. I've no idea what relevance the material has, I can only assume it meant something to her, something important, something I'll never discover. I realise too late, I was blinkered; I let her down; she needed me more than I knew; she wasn't the hard-hearted go-getter I thought she was. Orla had accepted that confession was the right thing to do but she couldn't face it. She threw herself from the Great Orme instead.

'Earth calling Zac!' Harrison's voice snaps me out of my head and into the room.

I raise my hand while I consider the question – Jules killed her mother to protect her sisters. Do I understand?

'I understand,' I say, rubbing underneath my eye with my finger. Costas smiles appreciatively. He's a good guy, and it pains me to tell him the truth, but that's why we are gathering. 'Although it was wrong of her to do so,' I add.

Costas' smile drops and Harrison curses, kicking out aimlessly at the broken chair pieces before him.

Costas hangs his head. 'Chloe died because you made me hesitate.'

'I'm sorry Costas. It was wrong. I was wrong. And now...' I

The Great Orme

sigh, a sigh that hurts my chest such is my depth of feeling.

'And now, all that's left is to ask for forgiveness. We have to confess.'

Harrison drags another chair from the table, scraping it roughly over the tiles. He sits dramatically, folding his arms across his significant chest. 'Let's see what Orla has to say on the subject, eh? She'll tell you straight, for sure.'

My heart swells painfully. Smokey appears, trundles toward Harrison and lies at his feet, nestling against his legs, eyes half-closed, content.

'Harrison,' I say, watching him dangle an arm to caress Smokey, intrigued that killers are not the one dimensional monsters most people would perceive them to be. Killers can show affection, and they can love too. *Shit, it's a complex world*, I think to myself. 'Have you killed again, since the old man and the kid?'

The pristine white smile returns to his face. I wait, stiff as a tree.

A sharp explosion shatters the peace, and I'm involuntary flung to the floor. Out of the corner of my eye I see Harrison falling from his chair too. I roll over, landing flat on my back and peer through raised arms at Costas. He's holding the gun outstretched in his hands, pointed upwards. Above him the ceiling is cracked, a bullet-hole punched through the yellowing plasterboard.

Harrison and I get to our feet. Harrison takes the gun from Costas. 'Jesus Christ! You could have killed someone!'

The irony isn't wasted on any of us. I sweep up the detritus on the floor, wondering if things can get any worse. There's a knock at the door.

I open it to find Rose, my neighbour, the lovely old lady from next door, stood before me.

She waves her walking stick around as she speaks. 'Oh, hello Zac. Did you hear an explosion? Scared the life out of me. I was worried for you. Are you okay?'

Rose is ancient, tiny, and remarkable. Sharp as a fox. She has lived in the house next door for as long as I can remember. Her husband disappeared years ago, and I mean disappeared. I was twelve years old. The old man went out to buy a tin of paint and never came back. Nowadays Rose volunteers in a charity shop in town during the week, on a Sunday she plays the organ at Christ Church, just off Abbey Road. She exudes an energy and mental acuity that is bereft in many much younger people.

Despite everything, I smile, she's been ever-present, a rock to my sea of pain. I explain that a cupboard fell over. Rose nods while pulling a face that says *bullshit*. She's almost falling over to see past me along the hallway.

She holds green-rimmed spectacles in place on her nose with finger and thumb. 'It looks as if you've company.'

I look over my shoulder to see Harrison right behind me, practically blocking the entire hallway off with his broad bulk.

'How are you, Rose?' he asks, not unkindly.

With a sigh, I move to the side to afford Rose a better view of Frankenstein's monster.

Leaning forward, and still gripping her specs, Rose examines my old friend, and as I'm about to give up on her and make our excuses, she thrusts the rubber tip of her walking stick at Harrison.

'It's you. Isn't it?' she says. 'Henry… Harry. No, it's Harrison, isn't it?'

'You remember me?' Harrison says, a daft and genuine grin on his face.

'You may have grown a bit, but yes, I jolly well remember you. You're the fucker that killed my Marmalade!'

I roll my eyes. I remember it well. The scream in the middle of the night. Mum running next door in her dressing gown. From my bedroom window, I watched as my mother, with one hand gripping Harrison's skinny arm, pulled the knife from the cat's body staked to the trunk of the cherry tree in Rose's front garden. And all because the poor moggy had peed on his sports kit he'd left lying in my front garden earlier that sunny day.

He rubs his shaven head. 'I'm sorry,' he mumbles hopelessly, smile crashed by the rebuke.

The Great Orme

I whisper at him to disappear, before cajoling Rose back home. 'He thinks he's got away with it doesn't he?' she tells me rather than asks me. I can feel her whole body shaking with rage as I help her up the slope toward her front door. 'I'll tell you this… he has *not* got away with it. Not by any stretch of the imagination. He'll get his comeuppance soon enough. You mark my words.'

She's left her front-door ajar. I push it open wide and see her inside but she's not yet calmed. 'It was a long time ago,' I tell her.

'It doesn't matter!' she reprimands. 'He killed my beautiful Marmalade. We didn't have kids. We had her.'

I make a cup of tea and sit her in her armchair. She takes my wrist as I pass her tea, her grip stronger than I expect. 'Do you remember when you were little, and you used to come around here to see Marmalade? You were such a little thing, always such a good boy, not like that loopy lump, Harrison. I'm not surprised you joined the police force. You were destined to make a difference in the world, especially after what happened to your father… then later on, after what happened to your mother… I'm amazed you turned out so well!'

Rose takes her tea. 'I'm sorry,' she says, glassy blue eyes staring straight at me over the rim of the mug, and perhaps straight through me. 'They say that over time, feelings of loss and grief tend to become less intense, and that you begin to find a way to live with them. It's a God damn awful lie. Maybe it's true, if your loved one has seen out their time and dies of natural causes. But anything else, well, it leaves a burning ball of anger inside you. As far as I'm concerned, that ball of anger has to be unleashed eventually, or it'll end up killing you.'

Is she right, I wonder? Does one injustice inevitably lead to another? Treat someone cruelly and usually they will do the same? No. That's the road to Hell, and I should know. The only way I can salvage any glimmer of light from the cesspit of self-loathing I occupy is by confessing. Once all others have arrived,

I will make them see sense. I have to.

I return to the old house to discover another early arrival – Sian.

In the corner of the lounge, the grandfather clock made by my father clangs waveringly. The clock will outlive me. We wait for the chimes to dissipate, all the while Sian and another woman stare at me, evaluating.

'Six o'clock. You're early,' I say, sounding unnecessarily unwelcome.

No sock, only buskin

Chapter Fourteen

It breaks. A sound I love. Sian's good-natured throaty laughter cracks and dances around the room - so warm, so generous. I suspect even the old house, with its draughts and ghosts, will find it hard to resist. I can't help but smile, swept up as I am in a world that was never meant to be, and one from which I must escape. Sian fizzes with energy, blonde cropped hair, silver spiral ear-rings, pierced nose, deep cobalt-blue eyes wide and clear, full enough of life for two. Six years have hardly touched her, at least not on the outside, it seems.

A shield seems to have dropped, and we finally embrace. Her positive energy is contagious and I feel better for it. She's the most transparent of all of us. She'll understand why we have to confess.

I fight the urge to tell her Orla is dead. It must wait until all are present. It won't be long.

Costas appears at the door, a glass of wine in each hand. 'Ladies?'

Behind him, Harrison's bulky shape manifests within the gloom of the hall. Sian's jaw drops and she blinks rapidly, watching on as Harrison manoeuvres around Costas, joining us in the Lounge.

'What the f..? Where has my skinny boy gone?' she all but bursts.

'Come on,' he says, holding hulking arms open wide. The two of them embrace, and it seems to me, such is their difference in size, they could be two separate species.

Sian reaches up and caresses his chin. 'What have you done with the old Harrison? If it wasn't for your peanut-shaped head, I wouldn't recognise you!' She cackles, grabbing his arm and squeezing a bicep.

The Great Orme

I notice the small black sea monster tattoo, on the underside of his forearm shift, making it appear as if the monster is alive and riding the single wave etched beneath it. We all have the same tattoo. A graphic reminder of our pact never to tell.

'I swear you are wearing a bodysuit and the real Harrison is gonna step out of it any second!'

She leaves him and skips to Costas, a kiss on the cheek and a whisper in his ear as she takes the drinks. Almost imperceptible, but something in her whisper casts a flicker of an uneasy shadow on the Vicar's face. I wonder if I may have imagined it. Sian returns to the other woman and hands her a glass of wine.

We men stand and wait like posts while the two women kiss – a purposeful and powerful display of togetherness. Finished, Sian rounds on us. 'Gentlemen,' she says. 'Fatima, my wife.'

Previously content to observe from the sideline, Fatima, dazzling in a body-hugging shiny emerald dress, steps forward and I can tell immediately she enjoys the attention, a calm confidence about her. Although only a little taller than Sian, she stands erect, a distinct presence. Holding her wine glass out before her, one hand on her hip, lazy mocha eyes aimed directly at me, she speaks, every word clipped and sharp. 'It's great to finally meet you. I know how important you are to Sian. She loves you. She'd do anything for you.' Her eyes linger on mine for longer than is necessary before she turns her attention to Harrison and Costas. She raises her glass at them and they do the same back as if hypnotised. 'There's no need to worry. Sian has told me all about you. Absolutely everything.'

I stiffen, and I sense Harrison and Costas do as well.

'Sian?' Harrison asks.

'It's true,' she says, clutching the wine glass tight to her chest. 'I had to. I should've before and I absolutely had to on receiving your message. I trust Fats with my life. And you should trust her with yours too.'

'No offence, Sian, Fatima,' Harrison bleats, throwing a hand in the air. 'But I don't. Not with mine. Why should I? Remember our promise of six years ago?' he says, tapping his tattoo. 'Our commitment to one another? The more people that know, the more likely we are to be caught. This isn't just a secret, it's our lifeline.'

'Um... excuse me,' Fatima says, waving sarcastically at Harrison. 'I thought the whole point of your convening was to agree to share your little secret... to confess?'

Harrison rubs the top of his smooth head, muscles bulging unnaturally as he does so. 'No. I think you'll find Zac has some inner doubts, and we are here to reassure him. You agree don't you, Costas?'

Costas fiddles with his white clergy collar, Adam's apple bobbing as he swallows before responding. 'It's difficult,' he manages eventually. 'There's a lot to consider. Many lives will be impacted. I think...'

His phone sounds - a rousing three-second discord of Hallelujah. He takes it from his trouser-pocket and adjust his glasses, pushing them up his nose as we look on. He listens to the message before lowering his phone in slow motion, a loose-lipped expression on his face. 'A message,' he says blankly, his gaze finally settling on me. 'It's from your friend, Zac. It's from *the Leveller*.'

My heart spins. 'What's the message?'

Costas shakes his head, raising a hand to his mouth, afraid to speak.

'Go on,' I gently urge, my heart fast and my blood hot.

'It was an automated voice. It said... *Confess and I'll kill Jules.*'

Outside, car tyres screech on tarmac and the roar of an engine disappears into winter's early evening darkness.

'Hmmm... bit of a quandary, huh?' Fatima turns away from us, and peers in the mirror, tucking her long and glossy brunette hair behind her ears. 'You need a new mirror.'

'He needs more than a new mirror,' adds Harrison. 'He needs to remember our promise!'

'Okay you guys,' Fatima says, spinning around to face us. 'Let's not beat around the bush. What a freakin' mess! What did you

The Great Orme

expect? You *are* all murderers. This is a freakin' viper's nest!'

'Well, Fats!' Harrison says, reaching around to the back pocket of his jeans and producing the gun, a bright and wide smile on his face. 'Better hope you don't get bitten.'

I eye him as I would a snarling Alsatian. The sound of the wind and the rain, heaving and pushing at the window, jangle my already shredded nerves. I'm cocooned in the old house with these people who are almost as near to the edge as me. I'm watching them closely, trying to decipher their behaviour so I can resolve the situation and get the outcome needed.

'Wait a minute. Who is *the Leveller*?' Fatima asks, her eyes wide and inquisitive, and completely non-plussed by the sight of the gun. While waiting for an answer, she strides toward Harrison, and we watch in amazement as she casually takes the gun from him, shaking her head as if disappointed by the actions of a naughty child.

Sian joins her wife, grabbing her gun-toting arm. 'Looks like we are gonna have to sort these boys out!'

Turning to Harrison she demands, 'what are you thinking? Are you insane? Has all that muscle filled your head and squeezed out your brain?'

Costas has moved to Harrison's side, and he puts an arm around his shoulders, which seems to calm the giant a little.

Fatima sips from her drink, and places the glass on the coffee table, before nonchalantly turning the gun over in her hands, examining it. She caresses the trigger, testing it.

Fatima is a new dynamic to our group and I can't fathom if her bravado is genuine or a mask. In any case, I wonder if I can use it to my advantage.

'Please, Fatima. Give the gun to Costas,' I tell her. 'It's his.'

She stops, cocks her head and observes me coolly. 'You no longer control your old friends, and you certainly don't control me. Perhaps this Leveller person has the right idea? Perhaps you are better off keeping your promise?

'Listen Fatima,' I say, unsettled by her bravado. 'I don't think you understand what you are getting embroiled in. The best thing you can do, and I say this because I love Sian, is to leave, and leave now. For your own good.'

I glance at Sian, hoping I carry some of the old sway.

She is unable to meet mine nor Fatima's gaze, her cobalt blue eyes fixed firmly on the floor.

'Sheesh Sian, you never told me he was so freakin' dramatic,' Fatima says, shaking her head and placing the gun on the mantlepiece beneath the mirror.

Sian puffs out her cheeks. 'A lot has happened in six years, Zac. Fatima deserves to be a part of this process, just as much as I do. It affects her as much as it does me.' Then her voice softer, quieter, and perhaps a little fearful she asks, 'Who is the Leveller?'

As if the evening can't become even more theatrical, a distant thunder rumbles, its vibration tangible in my bones.

Costas rubs his face, both hands sliding back and forth under his glasses. Also feeling the pressure, Harrison pulls at his t-shirt and lets it ping back to create a draught. Sian lets go of Fatima's hand and clasps her own hands together, twisting her fingers back and forth.

'I am actually scared now,' she says. 'We are only waiting for Jessie, Tomasz and Orla to arrive, and I'll tell you now, there's no way any of them are going to confess.'

'We don't know who the Leveller is,' Costas states. 'But whoever it is, they threatened Zac too, threatened to kill him if he confesses.' Costas chest rises and falls rapidly, and his face carries a new glistening sheen of sweat. 'If it's none of us, then by default it has to be one of the others?'

It's time for me to exert some authority, time to take control. I tell them about the recent murders, about the attack on Smokey, the crazy warnings left for me, but still, as much as I know I should, I can't bring myself to tell them about Orla. I will wait until the other two arrive.

The Great Orme

Sian excuses herself and leaves the room. As soon as she's gone, Fatima is on the offensive once more. 'Just a minute,' Fatima confronts me. 'Looking from the outside in as I am… How do we know you aren't the Leveller? After all, you instigated each and every murder. You are the damn Godfather of all of this. How do we know this isn't some freakin' elaborate plan to get us to turn on each other so we do confess?'

'She has a point, Zac,' Harrison adds, nodding.

'Seriously?' I say, turning on Harrison. 'I've brought you all here to do exactly the opposite. I want to stop the killing, end it. Once and for all.'

Fatima laughs. 'It's not going so well, is it? I mean, for God's sake, Zac, I pity your poor wife. From what I understand, you've kept her distant for six years. God only knows what damage you've done to her.'

I'm immediately taken aback by her bringing Orla into the conversation. What has that got to do with her? I fire straight back. 'Fatima, have you killed anyone? Do you understand the unbearable pain we've inflicted? You think that's okay?'

There's a force to my words that comes from deep within, and I'm reassured I'm doing the right thing. I wipe my brow. 'We have destroyed people's lives. They can't sleep. Why should we?'

Fatima stays tight-lipped, eyes locked on mine until finally she averts her gaze and her shoulders sag a little.

I walk to the window and pull back the curtain, seeking the solace of the big sea, but it's already dark outside, and the horizon is feint through the rain-streaked glass.

I let the curtain fall back and turn to face the others.

Fatima sweeps her long hair behind her neck, and I notice a softening of her eyes. Perhaps the brutal reality of our situation has hit home. She turns away to hide her vulnerability, but I can see her face in the mirror, and from where I'm standing, the longest crack in it runs vertically, dissecting her head in two. She really does love Sian, and she doesn't want to lose her.

I realise how hard this must be for her, and how brave she is, to enter this "viper's nest". She's put herself in the line of fire. She's got attitude and although it's a little mis-placed, I think I understand her. If only I can persuade her that to save Sian, she has to let her go.

Sian appears in the doorway to the lounge, fingers pressed to her pale face.

Fatima starts toward her, but Sian holds up a hand to stop her. Her lips are trembling, her fists clenched. 'Fats, what if Zac is right?' she says, her voice earnest. 'What if it's time for us to confess?'

Lightning strikes, a brilliant burst of light at the window that makes everything in the room appear vivid, stark shadows cast on the floors and walls. The accompanying thunder breaks, and sounds like it's far off, prowling in from the sea. There'll be more to come.

'The Leveller,' Costas mumbles, his face pallid and drawn. 'He… or she, is still killing. They've killed the old man, the boy, perhaps even your father's killer, and now… now they are threatening to kill you and Jules. Zac, we've got to stop whoever it is.'

'We will,' I reply, with a surety that surprises even myself.

'We will,' says Harrison, although both he and I know our methods are incompatible.

'I had my hair cut yesterday… at Benito's,' I say, attempting to tease out information, and looking pointedly at the two women.

Fatima laughs. 'Oh Benito! He's such a cutie, isn't he? I want to take him home with us. Sian wanted to say hello for old times' sakes, didn't you?' she asks, tilting her head and running her fingers through her hair.

'I love that guy,' Sian agrees. Then, as if understanding what I'm after, adds, 'We stayed at a B&B last night. We didn't want to impose on you any earlier than necessary.'

I nod, crazy thoughts spiralling around my head. 'Kept yourself busy?'

'Yes,' Sian replies sarcastically. 'But too busy to go about a

The Great Orme

murdering spree,' she adds, shaking her head. 'If that's what you were thinking.'

'I honestly don't know what to think anymore,' I reply. In an attempt to dispel a fragment of the impending doom, I rub my hands together and add, 'Jessie and Tomasz should be here soon.'

'And Orla,' adds Harrison, which is as good as an uppercut to my chin for my positivity. 'So, let's not jump to any conclusions just yet.'

Jump. Does he know what happened to Orla or am I being paranoid? Could he be the Leveller? Costas pats him on the back and nods his head. Sian sighs out loud. Fatima turns to face herself in the mirror again. The messages from the Leveller have all been automated, pre-recorded. Any one of them could be the Leveller, I think to myself.

Sian eyes me, dagger-like gaze. Her pale face has tinged pink. She excuses herself, leaving the room. Fatima makes to follow her, but I block her, standing in the doorway. 'Please, Fatima. Let me speak to her.'

Fatima rolls her eyes. 'Fine, I'll hang with the boys. I'm sure we've lots to talk about.'

As I'm leaving, she calls out, 'I can't wait to meet your wife, Zac. I'm sure we'll have lots to talk about as well.'

Zombie lovers

Chapter Fifteen

I let Smokey through the doorway before shutting the door to the lounge. Stood in the darkness of the hallway, the muffled chimes of the grandfather clock sound from the lounge. Seven o'clock. Jessie and Tomasz will arrive soon. Both are sensible people. They'll understand. They have to. I switch on the hallway light, but Smokey is already padding along the hall to the closed study door and sniffing at it.

I knock, wait, and enter the room.

Sian is sitting at my desk, facing the door. On seeing me, the tears roll. I rush to embrace her, enveloping her like she's the last person on Earth. It's all I can do not to cry with her, for Orla, for all those we killed, for our own wasted lives.

I wait until Sian's sobs subside and release her. She rubs her eyes with the backs of her hands to dry them. I sit on the corner of the desk. 'It's gonna be hard,' I tell her. 'But when you think about it, you know it's the right thing to do. What we did... It was evil.'

Sian smiles disconsolately, tossing her head back and ruffling her cropped bleached-blond hair. 'And perhaps I'm the worst. After all, I've killed more people than any of us.'

It's true. Little Sian lives with more ghosts than any of us, except perhaps for me. I live with them all.

'You told Fatima... everything?'

She nods. 'I had to. I needed to.' She clasps her hands together in her lap and stares at them. 'There's not a day doesn't go by I don't think about what we did, what I did. Zac, when you love someone, you share everything.'

'So, tell me about it,' I say, wishing I could be as vulnerable as her. 'Tell me how you told her.' I feel guilty asking, but I'll need all the information I can get for our confession. I glance at the desk drawer that houses my notebook and notice it's not fully shut. Did I leave it like that?

'Zac, I had to tell Fats. One day, when I got in from work, my feet and back killing me as usual – I've had it with cutting hair for a living… I just opened up, released it all. It was either that or go insane. Fats, ever supportive, opened a bottle of white wine, while I took off my coat. We sat at the kitchen table, then she asked me how my day had been.

I told her it had been murder. Then I broke down in tears.

Fats told me it couldn't have been as bad as her day. She passed me her phone and in the photo on her screen she looked like the un–dead - freshly dug out of the grave, blue-tinged skin, bald apart from a few straggly strands of hair, torn clothes, and blood – her face splattered with blood.'

'What the…?' I exclaim, alarmed.

Sian manages a smile. 'Fats is an actress. They had her hanging around in a zombie get up, just to do a thirty-second take… and it was fucking freezing! They had her crawl across the dirt as if she'd emerged from a smoking fire.'

I wince at the mention of fire, but I don't think she notices. I let her continue.

'When will I get a break?' she asked me, a question I've heard a thousand times before. *Hundreds of acting classes and thousands of pounds for that!* She won't give up, Zac. No one deserves a break more than her. She's ten years older than me, and thirty years wiser.'

'I'm not so sure, Sian,' I say. 'You are wiser than you think. You lead with your heart, and despite all of this, you'll end up doing what's right.'

'Yeah, well, as she was telling me about the zombie stuff, that's when my phone buzzed. I'd received your message to come here.'

Something in the study catches my eye. A flash of movement.

Sian extends her arm across her chest like she's about to crash a car. I thought I saw a fire, faces screaming to be set free, and I think Sian did too.

We glance at each other nervously, each of us afraid to admit what we saw.

Sian draws a deep breath and continues. 'As soon as I saw the message was from you, my heart flipped, and all I could hear was their screams, and all I could see was the fire, the all-consuming fire.

Whatever it is, Fats said. *It can't be so bad, can it?*

You told us to tell no one. No matter what. But I took the risk, Zac. She deserves to know. I should have told her before – she's my wife.'

Sian stifles a sob. 'Everything changed from that moment on. She and I can never be the same. As for you, Zac. You always stared at the sea, and I wonder if you've been staring at it so long it's drowned you deep inside and ended up washing away all feeling.'

It's a shrewd observation from Sian. Perhaps even true at one time, but not now. Now, the dam has burst and I'm consumed by feeling.

'So, I told her, Zac. I told her about all seven of us, what each of us has done. I told her about Biscuits and the old man, the young boy, about Harrison, Jessie, Orla, Costas, and Tomasz. Zac, I told her about you, your control of us, your manipulation of us, how you used the murder of the old man and the boy to control us. I told her about your warped sense of justice. It's only now I realise, you brainwashed us. Too late. We can't change a thing.'

I'm taken aback. Sian blames me entirely for everything. All I can do is listen to her.

'She knows that six years ago, you summoned us to here, where we learned about one another's terrible deeds, those you directed as if we had no other choice, as if they were the right things to do, normal things.

And, of course, I told her what I did, what you told me to do.'

Sian stares straight ahead, electric blue eyes like diodes, and as if in a trance like state, I know she's about to replay the entire episode for me.

The Great Orme

'I was the last to leave Llandudno, last to leave you, Zac. And where do those who are lost go? London. I had hoped to leave behind the guilt of our murder of the old man and the boy. I found a job easily enough. A smart barber in Richmond. I got friendly with another barber who worked there - an arrogant bastard, but funny with it. We became close, just friends, of course. His name was Kenzo, he had two gold front teeth, drove a high-end Tesla, always had cash to spare. I often joked he must have robbed a bank. He definitely didn't get the money from cutting hair. One day after work, we went for drinks. My curiosity got the better of me and I asked him where he got his cash – I mean, Richmond tips were fairly generous, certainly compared to Llandudno standards, but like I say, cutting hair didn't come close to explaining his wealth. Kenzo took me back to his house, a beautiful Grade II listed building in the nicest part of town.

I asked him how he could afford such a place, all high ceilings, expensive-looking soft furnishings and modern art on the walls, lots of lit candles, and the air full of the dodgy stuff smoked by its occupants.'

Sian wrinkles her nose as if she can smell the scent, and I notice Smokey has his snout pointed up in the air, sniffing. I can smell it too, the distinctive harsh chemical and woody taint of weed. Unperturbed, Sian continues, reliving the memory, wrapping me up in it:

'Kenzo told me he helped people. But the way he said it, the smirk on his face, well, I was ready to leave right away. But then three men and two women entered the room. They talked in a foreign language. Kenzo ignored them, pouring us both large vodkas instead. One of the women called Kenzo over. Money was exchanged. Huge wads of cash. After they finished and the others left, I asked Kenzo directly where they got the money from. Topping up our glasses, he told me they looked after people, desperate people, those who wanted to live in England – at any price. He talked about nationalities, fees, and revenue as if it was a proper business, as if it was normal. I felt slightly drunk, and dizzy with smoke, but none of what he said felt right to me.

I told him straight that he was trafficking people. I hoped he would deny it, and offer a plausible explanation. But instead, he laughed, deep, throaty roars of laughter. I can see him now, like he's here in the room with us.'

A spark ignites before the window. At first, I think it's lightning, but the spark is a flame, flickering blue, yellow and red. Sian reaches out for me and I grasp her hand. Smokey is on all fours, tail erect, growling. The flame explodes into a ball of white light, and within, a skeletal face, charred and black, two gold front teeth exposed within its seized grin. The grin cracks, the teeth and jaw shatter to nothing, but not before a handful of words, sad, desperate and rasping, tumble out – 'You killed my children.'

Smokey stops growling and lies down. Sian and I look from the window to one another, unable to speak. Sian withdraws her hand from mine and presses the heels of her hands into her eyes and lets out what can only be described as a whimper. I reach for her shoulder but she shrugs me off, lowering her hands and continues what she has to say until it is said. She needs to, and I wonder if Kenzo needs to hear it too.

'Kenzo leaned in toward me, thick lips wet, breath stained with vodka and smoke. I could see the pores in his skin, the yellow tinge in the whites of his eyes.

You British and your privilege, he spat, his strange accent suddenly clipped and harsh. *If you'd seen half the things I have, you'd be like me. Worse!*

He glugged back his drink and threw the empty glass at the wall. Both glass and my nerves shattered at the same time. I thought I knew him. You think you know people, what they are thinking and how they feel, but… He asked me to join them, told me it was good money, told me to think *very* carefully.

He took me roughly by the chin… gripped my neck with his other hand… told me he always liked me… a lot. He leaned in to my face, but the door to the lounge opened and, like a pack of foxes, the others slipped silently into the room, sly glances cast at me. One of the men had a gun, buffing it with his sleeve.

Kenzo laughed. I removed his hands from me and slapped him, hard. I heard the gun click as it was cocked. I feared there was no way out. To buy time, I asked him to tell me more. He laughed again, telling me they owned more than a hundred people. All of whom, if they worked hard enough, would eventually make enough money to buy their freedom. He told me it was a lot of people and a lot of risk, that they had to keep them under complete control, that only two things worked with such people – fear and discipline.

The others seemed agitated, talking in murmurs to one another at the back of the room. He tried to justify what they did, explaining that the people they owned, got a roof over their heads, food in their mouths – usually.

He told me they ran a brothel on York Street, where most of the women worked, and some of the men. I asked him if they are forced to do what they do. He grinned. *They pay their dues*. He went on to tell me that once they became too used up; they got moved on to the packaging factory on West Street, so they could continue to pay their debt.

I told him straight, Zac. *It's abuse. It's slavery*, I said.

He told me, *no*, that the people were immigrants, desperate for an opportunity, a new life in England. That it was better than their alternative.

I found it hard to believe. He shrugged and asked if it was a problem for me.

I was terrified. It felt like I was in a movie, one with a bad ending, so I tried to give the impression I was tough and unfazed, it was my only way through, and I told him it was more of a problem for them than for me. He laughed at that, the explosive laugh I used to love and now hated.

Work with us, he said, an order, not a question.

I lied and told him I was up for it.

Kenzo nodded to the others as if to say I told you so. The man with the gun tucked it inside his jacket. Kenzo stood, arms wide. I had to play along, so I stood and hugged him. I needed help. There was only one person in my entire world, one person I knew who could help in a situation like that.'

Sian reaches out and squeezes my hand, a haunted smile on her face.

'More vodka was consumed, as if we were celebrating. I restricted my intake as much as is possible. At two in the morning, I explained I needed to go home. Kenzo warned me to be careful. He'd not been careful, and didn't know me as well as he thought he did. He'd taken a big risk. I was a murderer.

He fumbled in the pocket of his jeans, eventually producing a key and giving it to me.

I was puzzled, and it must have shown.

He told me I'd need to be there often from now on. He even suggested I could share his bed if I wanted. He said *that*, even though he knew all about me.

I felt the glare of the others watching as I took the key. I just wanted to be away. Acting, I told him and the others I wouldn't tell a soul. Kenzo told me that tomorrow evening they'd take me to the other house, introduce me to the *little* people. The thought made me shudder, but I rubbed my hands as if in anticipation. I wondered what it was about me, that Kenzo thought I was capable of such things, that he could trust me.

He told me I'd never regret it. He took a scarf from a hook on the wall and wrapped it around my neck. *It's cold out there. You be careful.*

I found myself thanking him and the others as if they've done me a huge favour, and I was gone, outside and forcing myself to walk at normal speed and not run, but inwardly my heart was hammering, fuelled by fear.

I don't know why, but I ended up on York Street, stood outside the house where the supposed *little* people resided. It seemed ordinary apart from an industrial looking and wide gun-metal grey door. The windows were dark and the bins in the front garden were overflowing with rubbish.

I sensed I was being watched. It took me a while, but the light from a nearby streetlamp helped me pick out the whites of someone's eyes, peering down at me from the smallest window on the top floor.

It was the face of a girl, no more than eleven or twelve years old, nose pressed against the glass. She suddenly disappeared, but as I was about to give up and turn away, she reappeared, this time with a piece of paper pressed against the glass. I strained to read what was written on it, but it quickly became clear. Four elongated letters reached from top to bottom of the page.'

Sian spells out the letters for me, as if she's seeing the sign for the first time – 'H E L P.'

I scrape my forehead with my fingertips.

'Then the sign disappeared and so did she.

My phone pinged. An alert informed me I was being tracked by an anonymous connection established half an hour previously. It had to be someone from the house.

I was terrified. I thought they were coming after me, that they'd kidnap me and shoot me. I called you, Zac. You were the only one I could turn to.

You spoke to me as if we had spoken only yesterday, no surprise or alarm in your tone at the lateness of the call or as I explained what had happened and where I was.

I insisted I go to the police, but you suggested it was dangerous, that I'd be intercepted. You told me they would be on to me, and they couldn't and wouldn't take risks – that I was in serious danger. You told me Kenzo and his friends were scum. You told me they'd have friends, dangerous friends, that they'd come for me. You told me to power down my phone and go back to Kenzo's. You told me what I needed to do, what I had to do. You told me I had to up the ante. That I had to scare them more than they scared me.

Kenzo's house was in darkness. I stood at the door and waited, half expecting it to burst open, but it didn't. Whoever was monitoring my location must have fallen asleep. I thought of the girl in the window, her call for help. She was so young – I didn't want to imagine what she was being put through. So, I pushed the key into the lock, the loudest sound, sure someone would have heard. I twisted the key and, with a gentle push, opened the door inward.

The hallway was thick with gloom and the marshmallow scent of marijuana. How on earth did you convince me to return to the lion's den, I wonder? In my head I cursed you, but I was in way over my head and well, I trusted you.

Leaving the front door ajar, I entered the hallway and poked my head around the lounge door, half-expecting to see Kenzo asleep on the sofa, but he wasn't and the room was empty. Next to an extinguished candle on a bookshelf was the box of matches. The sound of my striking one and the subsequent flare of flame sounded to me like a firework ripping through the atmosphere. I was convinced the whole house must wake up, and I stood motionless, expecting the creak of floorboards from above and the stampede of lions down the stairs.

Incredibly, there was no movement, and no sound, so I transferred the flame from match to the candle. Trying not to think, I lit all the candles in the room before returning to the bookshelf. I picked out a book at random, one I'll always remember – And Then There Were None, Agatha Christie.'

Sian lets out an anguished groan before continuing.

'I turned the candle flame on the pages and let them burn before tearing the pages and stuffing them among the books on the shelf. I applied the candle to some of the other books.

I set flame to cushions, curtains, anything that would burn. In the hallway, I positioned a table under the smoke alarm attached to the ceiling. Your instructions were clear in my mind and I followed them precisely, standing on the table and disconnecting the wire from the battery alarm. I threw Kenzo's scarf on the bottom of the stairs and lit it. There were a bunch of coats hanging on hooks by the door, so I threw them in a heap around the scarf, which was already spitting flames.

Pulling up the neck of my jumper, I covered my mouth to filter out the smoke. I pushed the door to the lounge open wide. I closed the front door quietly behind me, only a small click as the latch caught. Head down, I walked away and phoned Kenzo like you told me to. But he didn't answer. A little way along the street, I heard a scream ripple through the stillness of the night. It stopped me dead in my tracks. I didn't want to, but compelled by some macabre curiosity, I turned around. I was shocked by how quickly the flames had taken to the house. The windows lit up in a blaze of orange fury. Screams as sharp as razor blades sliced through the sound of popping and crackling flames. I called you and you urged me back to the house, to rouse them, but I knew it was already too late. I hugged the shadows all the way home.

When I got home, I sat, alone and in the dark, cold to the bone and brooding, a monster. I turned my phone on again and it immediately vibrated – you calling me. I hit decline.'

'I'm sorry, Sian,' I croak, my mouth pressed to the top of her head. 'I'm so, so sorry.'

She pulls back and kisses me on the cheek. 'I think we all are,' she says, nodding as if asserting the truth for herself as well. Hurrying, she gets up and tells me she needs a little time to compose herself. She leaves and I hear her footsteps ascending the stairs. I take out my journal, my heart a weight I simply cannot carry for much longer. I write these words while they are fresh in my mind. Despite everything, our confession is progressing. We will have a record of events, a record that will damn us to some kind of justice. We mustn't complain. Orla's, Costas', Harrison's and now Sian's vengeful acts documented, and ready for judgement to be issued. Tomasz and Jessie's are yet to be recorded, but I'll have the details soon enough. It's all barely believable. A mess. Who can help us? No one. Let prison have us. It's the least we deserve.

A knock at the door. I make sure I'm first to greet either Tomasz or Jessie – it's neither.

A man, dressed smartly head to toe in black, stares back at me, similar age, similar height to me but with a premature grey streak running through his wavy shoulder length hair. On seeing me, he switches on a smile, but his pupils have narrowed. I'm immediately wary.

'Zac? Zachary Llewellyn?'

I respond with the slightest of nods, giving the man little encouragement. I haven't time for this.

'My name is Jorge. I'm Tomasz's partner. Is he here yet?'

This isn't supposed to be a party. Couples aren't invited. I've not made myself clear enough. I look beyond him. A slick lime-green Tesla is parked up half on the road, half on the pavement alongside some other cars.

'He won't be expecting me,' Jorge says, rubbing his hands together for warmth, 'but neither were you I guess.'

'Correct,' I say matter-of-factly. 'So, what exactly are you doing here?'

The man pauses for a moment, taking the time to choose his words. 'I want to keep him safe.'

I glance up and down the street, telling myself it will be over soon. 'You'd better come in.'

The others stop talking as we enter the lounge. 'Everyone,' I say abruptly. 'This is Jorge. Tomasz's partner.'

His introduction is met with stony silence. Finally, Harrison pipes up. 'You invited him?'

'No, I did not,' I reply tersely.

'Jesus f–' Harrison starts, before I interrupt.

'So, tell us Jorge, how did you end up here?'

Our new arrival holds his hands up defensively. 'I read the message you sent him, Zac. I read all his messages.'

I hear Harrison curse under his breath.

'Look, I'm not just his partner, I'm also his agent. I take care

The Great Orme

of his... our business.'

He takes his car key fob from his pocket and fiddles with it, regarding each of us with quick, darting eyes.

'All a bit dramatic, isn't it? A secret? Victims? A confession? It can't be that bad, can it?'

Each of us looks to the other but say nothing.

'What was it? Did you rip people off, take their life's savings or something?'

No one speaks.

'You're all alive, right? No one's died. I'm here only because I love Tomasz, and I'm worried for him. He left without a word. I don't know if you guys are aware, but Tomasz is... well, he's prone to psychological setbacks. You have to tell me what you've done. I can help him. I can help you. We can't have any of this, whatever it is, leaking out to the press. They'd murder him.'

Tomasz's depression troubles are not well documented. Of course they wouldn't be. He and Jorge feed the media and the public a slick diet of fulfilled football happiness to maintain his superstar market value.

Although Jorge has entered forbidden territory, I shrug my shoulders and invite him to sit on the sofa. 'Let's just say we took some things too far. Tomasz included. We have a situation even Tomasz's millions can't fix.'

Tight-lipped and chest puffed out, Harrison fixes me with a hard stare. He doesn't want to tell. He still wants to keep our secret.

'It's not yet eight o'clock,' I say, looking at my watch. 'Every one of you is early. There's time enough for Tomasz to arrive. Jessie too.'

'And Orla,' Harrison adds, one eyebrow raised. 'She's coming too, right? Shit, we need her, man.'

'I invited all of you,' is the best I can manage.

Another rumble of thunder rattles the windowpane and my nerves with it. Louder this time; the storm is creeping in off the sea. Before long we'll all be in the eye of the storm in more ways than one. My throat feels like it's clogged with something. I can barely breathe. I need to do something. I've got to remain fluid. 'You must be hungry?' I say, clapping my hands together. 'I bought food, nothing fancy, just some stuff you can help yourselves to.'

The response is less than enthusiastic, but even murderers have to eat. I shut the kitchen door behind me and bend over, both hands flat on the table, not thinking I'm going to be sick exactly, but to stop the whirring sensation, the feeling the Great Orme is shifting beneath my feet. I need to concentrate to keep my balance. I can't let things get any worse than they already are.

I can't believe Orla's gone. It's one thing to be apart from someone you love, but to know they no longer exist brings with it a crushing futility. Worse, it's my fault. All of it. I try for excuses – I had pushed Orla away, not through animosity, but through love. I wanted her to have all she wanted, for her to realise her ambitions, career, travel, to achieve all she was eminently capable of. I wanted none of those things, or so I had told myself. It suddenly dawns on me. I needed her. I needed a little at least of some of those things, something to care about other than feeding the sea serpent. All I had needed was a push toward those things. I didn't need them in the same quantity as Orla, and perhaps Orla didn't need so many of them as she thought she wanted. Maybe, between us, we could have found a happy middle. Isn't that what life's all about? I scrape the oak table surface with my fingernails, pulling and scratching the grain. I love Orla. I need Orla. I always did. Now, it's too late.

Somehow pulling myself together, I open the fridge, pulling out the ready-made platters of food. Lost in thought, I don't notice the kitchen door open and I only realise someone is present when I feel the soft touch of their hand on the small of my back. I almost drop the plates.

'Sian?'

Her wine glass is topped up. She stares bleakly at the hole in the roof. 'Your world is falling down around you, Zac. You're collapsing ours too.' She plucks an olive from a plate and pops it in her mouth.

The Great Orme

It's all my fault, and I tell her so, walking back and forth between the fridge and the table, putting out a selection of foods – pitta bread, humous, olives, cheeses, and cakes, the occasion feeling more and more like a funeral party. I want desperately to tell her about Orla, but still, I can't – not yet. I need to win them over first. Once they discover Orla's dead, they'll blame me, and I will have lost. Our victims and their families condemned; the truth forever hidden.

I ask Sian about Fatima, both interested and keen to divert the conversation away from the inevitable until all are present. She tells me Fatima will stand by her no matter what, and knowing that gives her the strength she thinks she needs.

An explosion turns us to stone. It's muffled, but by now I know instantly what it is. Gunshot. It sounded like it came from the lounge.

I throw myself through the kitchen doorway, closely followed by Sian, and we nearly collide into Harrison and Jorge stood outside the lounge, having just come through the front door with holdalls, the expressions on their faces equally puzzled as mine. The lounge door is closed. My heart-rate accelerating, I press the handle, push the door open and enter the room.

Behind me, Sian's cry strikes like a crack of a whip against the side of my head.

Costas is backing away from the fireplace, away from Fatima, unable to unlock his gaze from Sian's wife sprawled face-down on the carpet, next to her, the gun.

Sian pushes past me. 'Fats,' she pleads, descending on her wife and throwing herself over the woman.

My stomach contracts, a hot rising swell of vomit forces its way into my mouth. I swallow it back. Me, Harrison and Jorge encroach closer, hardly daring to breathe, but we stop sharply as Sian springs up and hits Costas with a right upper-cut to the jaw. The Vicar drops like a black flag; I suspect more in shock than from the force of the blow. Before any of us can react, she picks up the gun and stands over him. 'You bastard,' her face is red, and she's crying. 'You've killed Fats. You've killed her!'

I can barely breathe. This is a mistake. It has to be. It's impossible. Costas hasn't killed Fatima. He wouldn't.

Costas pushes up on his elbows, mouth slack. 'N…No,' he stutters. 'She attacked me. She attacked me, Sian.'

I take a step toward Sian, but she swings around, arms outstretched, both hands glued to the gun. 'He's killed Fats,' she whimpers, the gun pointed at me.

Costas sits up, but Sian spins quickly, sending him sprawling once again with a sharp kick to the face. She directs the gun on him.

'No, Sian!' My words sound calm, controlled, although I feel anything but.

'Don't you dare, Zac!' She screeches. 'Don't you fucking dare. You made us what we are. You gave us the capability. You created us. Look what you've done to us! You've destroyed us! You got Fats killed!'

Her arms are shaking. She's going to shoot him and there's nothing I can do.

'Sian, stop!'

The voice is new to the room. One I recognise. In the doorway stands a statuesque fair-haired figure clutching his ear pods in his fist, the tiniest, tinny sound of slurred beats and fast rapping occupying the second of silence.

'Tomasz!' exclaims Jorge.

Tomasz's eyes are fixed on Sian. 'Please Sian, don't. Costas is one of us,' he urges, his voice ever quiet and understated. 'We need to look after each other. Now, more than ever.'

Sian actually smiles. I think she's lost her mind. I wouldn't blame her. I think we all have to some extent. She fires the weapon.

Goal hanger

Chapter Sixteen

Costas screams, short and sharp, but it's only the jaded spruce sideboard before the bay window that has incurred damage. As I should expect, Tomasz is quick. He dashes across the room, and before any of us knows what's going on, he's grabbed the gun from Sian, and she's dropped, depleted, into his arms.

'What the hell is going on?' he says, holding her up. 'Have you all lost your minds? And Jorge, what are you doing here?'

Without waiting for a reply, he regards the body on the floor. 'And who... who is she?'

A commotion ensues where my lounge feels like it's become a platform at London Euston train station. Jorge rushes to Tomasz and the two exchange words, but I'm not listening. Harrison and I rush to Sian, but she pushes us all away and crouches over her wife, tilting her over on her side. Her chest, and the emerald dress covering it, soaked through with wet ruby blood. Sian feels for a heartbeat and, finding none, lifts her bloodied hands to her face. We watch while she lowers her head to Fatima's mouth, listening for breath. Sian's face stretches in silent anguish, telling us all we need to know. Fatima is dead.

I try to intervene, but Sian actually growls at me like a protective wolf, not letting me near her deceased partner. I don't know what to think. I don't know what to do. I feel as if my head has burst into flames.

Harrison has Costas pinned to the floor and is gripping him by the throat. 'What the fuck are you playing at?'

Costas' face has turned purple, blue veins in his neck set to burst through his skin, flecks of white spit on his lips, choking. I touch Harrison's shoulder. 'Stop,' I command. Incredibly, he does, but not without a derisory look over his shoulder at me first.

Minus the expletive, I ask Costas the same question as Harrison.

He takes his time, drawing himself to a sitting position and rubbing his neck while seeming to wait for his breathing to regulate. His crucifix has fallen from inside the pocket of his blazer. I bend to pick it up and give it to him.

'She attacked me,' he says, holding the crucifix out between me and him as if I were a demon.

'Why?'

'I only told her that maybe you were right, Zac. I told her just maybe we *have* to confess. That God might possibly forgive us.'

He's sweating, and he seems to have aged, creases and shadows in his face where there were none before. Unable to hold my gaze, his eyes shift uneasily. I can't help but question if he's telling the truth.

'And she attacked you for it? With the gun?'

He nods. 'She picked it up from the mantelpiece and pressed it against my stomach.' He rubs his slightly rotund stomach as if to reinforce what he's saying. 'I panicked and grabbed her hand, but she resisted and then…' He stares at the crucifix, turning it to face him and rubbing his thumb on the on the brass figure of Christ. 'And then the gun fired.'

Like a springing cat, Sian leaps at him, punching and scratching. 'Liar,' she screams, tearing into him with everything she's got. She's quickly drained of energy and by the time both me and Harrison take hold of her, she's stopped. Sobbing, she pulls her arms free from us and stands defeated before Costas. 'You are twice the size of her and ten times stronger. You only had to take the gun from her. That's all you had to do…'

She doubles over as if it is her who's been shot.

'Sian. I'm sorry,' Costas mumbles. 'It was an accident. It was her. She pulled the trigger, not me.'

Sian straightens, touches her eyes to dry them, but I don't see tears, only rage. Then, suddenly, she's impassive. Silent. Expressionless.

Both wind and rain slap at the window. It feels as if the old house has been swept up and carried off in a tornado, like the house in the Wizard of Oz.

Tomasz is visibly trembling, and Jorge mumbles something about taking him off to a room upstairs for some privacy. I sit on the sofa, hands clasped together, staring into space.

Taking a wide berth around Sian, Costas disappears to his room to see to his scratches, cuts and bruises, and perhaps his conscience.

Harrison lets go of Sian.

'Take her upstairs, please,' asks Sian.

Harrison dutifully obliges, lifting her, and Sian leaning close in to Fatima and touching her face, the two of them take her body upstairs. Harrison soon returns. I try to say something to him, but without looking at me, he holds up his hand to silence me and tells me he's hungry. We get some food from the kitchen and return to the lounge. Tomasz and Jorge appear, arms draped around one another as if either one were to let go, the other would drop in a heap. I pour drinks without asking what anyone wants, and hand each of them a glass filled with red wine. We collapse into the leather chairs, Tomasz and Jorge on the sofa, me and Harrison in the two armchairs. Smokey trundles over to Harrison and settles at his feet.

'What the hell is happening here, Zac?' Tomasz asks, his voice barely a degree above normal volume, and holding up his long floppy blond fringe, his trembling apparently abated.

I take a mouthful of wine and swish it around in my mouth before swallowing, but it tastes like cold metal, like I imagine blood would taste. I force it down, lean forward and set the glass on the coffee table – I can't drink any more of it. It's feeding my crisis, both existential and real. 'Well,' I say, rubbing my sweaty palms on my jeans, 'first and foremost, there's a dead woman in my house – our beautiful friend's wife. Shot by our righteous Vicar. And secondly, as if that wasn't enough – our little secret has gotten other people killed in the last day or two.' I hold Tomasz's gaze searching for an acknowledgement of the Hellscape we inhabit.

'You really believe we should give up everything?' Tomasz says, glancing at Jorge. 'I'm not sure. We are talking about a lifetime in prison, right?'

I nod my head.

Tomasz laughs, his face full of fear. 'I'm at the peak of my career. Just imagine what the media would do to me, to my friends. Why now? Why?'

'We should never be in this position,' I tell him impatiently. 'We should never have allowed any of it to happen!'

'Fucking hell!' Harrison states loudly, his voice gone to that high pitch when he's nervous, and both hands gripping the arms of the leather armchair. 'We are where we are! Let's deal with the fucking problem! We need to work out what we are going do with the body upstairs!'

'The body has a name, Fatima!' I tell him, feeling my blood boiling. 'This is the whole fucking problem! All of this. It's about people. Human beings. Loved ones. We can't dispose of them like they're fucking rubbish!'

'No,' replies Tomasz as quick as a flash. He's not even considered what I've said. 'That's exactly what we do. We come up with a plan, dispose of the body. We can leave here and get on with our lives. We should keep our secret like we said we would.' Tomasz is softly spoken as usual, as unassuming a celebrity as you could imagine. 'Until I read your message, I was just about coping. I'd just had a good training session. I didn't even feel my hamstring pulling. I think there's a decent chance I'll be selected for the game on Wednesday, and I need to be playing, to be scoring. I'm twenty-nine now and the younger players are like wolves, nipping at my heels, praying I'll get injured. I'm a role model, Zac. I do charity work. I visit dying children. I raise money for hospitals. We can't confess. It wouldn't be fair on all the people I help.'

Although we have to listen carefully to pick up his words, I can sense his confession coming, and while I know what he did, I need the details so I can write them down later, so they can be formalised, so they can help the victim's family in some way. However gruesome Bart was, his family weren't – they deserve the truth. I hate to do it, but I ask Tomasz why he thinks we had to do what we did to Bart.

'Are you serious?' he asks, eyes darting from me to Jorge, and back to me again. 'You know what that creep did to me!'

It's worked. 'Remind us, Tomasz,' I implore. 'Remind us why it was deserved and how we gave him what he deserved.'

Tomasz continually has to hold his fringe off his forehead to prevent it getting in his eyes. I wish he'd wear his Alice band like he does when he's playing football. He stares at the coffee table as his memory starts to play and he recounts what happened all those years ago in the hope it may persuade me not to confess. 'I was only sixteen. Bart insisted I stay behind after training. He thought my gait was stiff and wondered if there was a problem. He wanted to check me over. He made me take kit off, all of it. Of course, I was apprehensive, but I didn't doubt him. He'd been the physio at the club for years, a big man. You wouldn't mess with him, not at that age, anyway.'

Tomasz's voice trembles. Jorge grasps the top of his partner's arm like he might stop a collapse.

'I was laid on the physio table. Bart picked up some lubricant and turned out the light.

All I could hear was his breathing coming faster and faster. I complained, but he told me to be quiet or it would hurt more.' Jorge shifts closer to Tomasz on the sofa and wraps a protective arm around his shoulders.

'Imagine how I felt,' Tomasz continues. 'The pain, the bleeding, the humiliation, the shame… the disgust I felt at myself. It happened more than once. Maybe to other kids as well. I hated myself. I hated Bart. I confided in you, Zac. I trusted you.'

Tomasz glances up at me. 'I trust you now to keep our promise. Your promise.'

I purse my lips. 'What did we do to him?'

He returns his gaze to the coffee table. 'I remember laughing when you told me, *Ultimately, everyone who dies, dies of heart failure.* Never a truer thing said.

We left it late, the same week I gained my first cap for Wales. I did as you instructed. I visited him late at night, around two in the morning. Older and weaker, Bart welcomed me in, apprehensive but with a glint of excitement in his eyes behind those wire-framed spectacles of his.

I can picture him now at the doorstep. *Well, well, well, Tomasz Trueman! It's been a while,'* Tomasz imitates in a pretty good Cardiff accent. 'His hallway stunk of damp and rotting vegetables. He was wearing only grey boxer shorts and a navy-blue Adidas t-shirt. He told me how well I'd done for myself before ushering me into his lounge. He said I was a celebrity, and how proud he was of me. He even said he liked to think his small contribution helped me up the ladder.'

Tomasz visibly shudders, every part of him vibrating – an uncoordinated spasm, and although it only lasts a second, it reveals the imprint of the trauma left behind.

'I swear, my heart beat faster and harder than it ever did on a football pitch,' he continues, the fingertips of one hand digging into his thigh. 'Our roles were reversed. I'd grown, and he seemed to have shrunk, in his sixties and in poor shape. His lounge was all beige and frayed, just like him. Everywhere, framed and signed photos of boys and men in football kit. I saw my own young face among them, a smile for the camera, my sixteen-year-old smiling face betraying nothing of my fear, my guilt. And stood next to me, Bart, track-suited, arm around my shoulders.'

Jorge inhales loud and deep, as if he's preparing to inflate a balloon. He and Tomasz gaze into one another's eyes, their bond evidently strong. He lets out his breath and continues.

'Seeing a pen on his sideboard, I pulled our photo from behind the glass and signed it - "Dear Bart," I wrote, "I owe you. Hold your head high."'

Tomasz considers each of us, no satisfaction on his face, just a haunted, little boy lost kind of expression.

No harm done, eh? he said. *Just a wee bit of fun between two consenting men. Experimenting… perfectly normal, everyone does.*

'I retrieved a chair from his dining room and placed it in the middle of the room. Leaving the chair where it was, I stood before him, man to man, and told him how what he had done to me still affected me – the fear, the anxiety, the depression, the mess of a man I had become because of him. I did my best to explain it to him, that he might understand he had almost driven me to take my own life.'

Tomasz eyeballs me, his lips quivering, eyes blinking fast to hold back the tears. 'The rapist laughed at me,' he says.

The two men squeeze hands, their knuckles turning white.

'He said I was being ridiculous, that I enjoyed it, that it was me who enticed him. I told him I was too scared to stop him, that he had threatened to tell everyone, that it would be the end of me.

He told me I was a coward, that I should *get over it*. He didn't stop there, he went on and on about how lucky I was, about all the things he did for me, about how he had prepared me to be the star I was today. He told me I was pathetic, ungrateful. He wouldn't shut up, so I shut him up. I put my hand over his blubbery mouth, suffocating him, but stopping short of blackout.

All I had wanted was to see remorse in his face, to hear a few genuine words of regret.'

Tomasz shakes his head, eyes burrowing into mine. 'If he had, I may have relented. But he was like a robot, incapable of empathy. *They were different times*, he told me, as if everyone abused young boys back then. He told me I was a dirty queer, a freak. He told me to get out and hope he didn't tell the world about my filthy little secret. He said one call from him to the media would destroy my world.

I felt sick, he smelled of vinegar, the same as before, the memories all too vivid and the sensations too raw. He struggled, spitting at me, but he'd let himself go, too flabby, no muscle. His spectacles slipped down, hanging from the cord around his neck, and his greasy-brown, thinning hair was sticking up as if he's had an electric shock. I stared into his eyes, searching for understanding, something, anything that may have pulled us from the brink of your instructions.'

I nod my head, wishing too that Bart had shown some remorse. I want to say I thought he would – that I never guessed he wouldn't. I turn away from Tomasz's haunted and accusing stare. My eyes focus on Harrison's plate which is full to overflowing with chicken wings, cheese balls and a single tiny tomato. He hardly dares to look away for fear of something toppling from it. Although I don't feel like it, I force myself to eat a sandwich to appease my mind's insistent nagging that I need the fuel. I must stay alert. 'Go on,' I mumble, my mouth full.

'He told me it was my word against his, that I didn't want to throw it all away, wreck my career by embarrassing myself, that I'd lose my sponsorships. He said I had no evidence, that he'd done nothing wrong.

I told him he'd raped me, not once, not twice, but countless times. I told him I still felt the pain, the terrible sensation, the tearing, the bleeding, the loneliness of keeping the abuse secret. The public think I'm distant and unemotional, they've no idea. So many times, I drove to the M6, stopped at a bridge, got out of the car and leaned over the rails, prepared to throw myself into the fast lane. If it wasn't for you, I would've jumped. Zac, each time you talked me out of it. You saved my life... Perhaps it's time for me to save yours.'

The back of my throat constricts as if there's a snake trying to force its way out. I feel so much for Tomasz, but what he did, we need to hear it all. 'Tell us how you ended it?' I ask.

'Bart had his chance, but he'd given me nothing, no remorse, no guilt. I did as you said. While holding him in a headlock, I took the tights from my jacket: 100 Denier - Thick - Opaque, tore open the packets and tied two pairs together and stuffed a third in his mouth. I used the other three pairs to tie his wrists together behind his back before tying the others around his neck. The ceiling was high, an upturned brass light-fitting at its centre.

I was only doing as you instructed, Zac.'

I bite my bottom lip, my mind spinning. I was convinced Bart would relent under the pressure. If Tomasz had called me, I would have stopped him – I would have pulled him back from the brink.

'You had told me Bart was a bad apple, that he could have committed many more indecent crimes, perhaps still would. You reminded me of his weak heart, two heart attacks already, a third was always going to be inevitable with his lifestyle.

Still holding him in a headlock, a hand over his mouth, I got another chair from the dining room and positioned it next to the one in the lounge. It was awkward, and he wriggled like hell, but I managed to lift him on to the chair under the light fitting. I told him to save it for a few minutes when it would be of more use, make the ending quicker for him. He was shaking his head, grunting snot, all desperate muffled sounds. I got up on the chair beside him and tied the loose end of the tights to the light fitting. His t-shirt was sopping wet with sweat, it dripped down his bright red face. He was suffering, and I was glad.

Your plan was perfect. I stepped down from the chair and left him in position. He tried to bend forward, clutching his chest, but the noose simply tightened around his neck. I turned my back on him and placed my chair neatly back under the dining table. I returned to see him shaking violently, heart attack in full swing. To be sure, I lifted his feet from the chair and tipped it over. I released him and stepped back. He hung suspended like a soaked sack of stones, feet swaying above the overturned chair, blood vessels in his eyes, strained to bursting.

It didn't take long; a few pathetic kicks and his breathing and heart became still. 'So, there it is,' Tomasz states, gazing at each of us present. 'The monster committed suicide, as far as anyone knows. And that's how we'll leave it, right?'

This is the most pitiful gathering of friends that ever existed. The heartbeat of the house, the grandfather clock chimes eight o'clock. It's a sound that barely used to register with me, one that now slides under my skin and screams an urgency that tells me time is almost up.

A knock at the door. Thank God. Bang on time, Jessie has arrived.

A rose among thorns

Chapter Seventeen

'Rose?' I'm holding the door open but blocking her way in and trying not to roll my eyes to avoid showing my disappointment that it's not Jessie on my doorstep.

Rose stares out from a tightly drawn hood, her grey-white face cracked with deep channels as if she herself has been hewn from the limestone of the Great Orme. The hem of her bright red coat flaps around her legs, and the rain hammers at her in diagonal lines such is the strength of the wind. She seems as if an elderly little red riding hood. I suddenly become fearful for her safety, housing a pack of wolves as I am.

She waves her walking stick at me. 'I heard that explosion again. Another cupboard fallen over?' Her tone is sharp, mocking, and demanding of respect.

She raises a cloth to her glasses and dabs at the lenses, ineffectually trying to clear the raindrops. The cloth is actually wool, a square of red wool... mine... Orla's.

'Where'd you get that?' I ask. 'It's Or... It's mine,' I correct myself quickly.

She holds the material out before her. 'You dropped it when you took me home earlier. Here, have it back. It smells lovely. Clementines... Perfume. You could do with a good woman. I always thought it such a shame when you and Orla split up. But then, she always knew her mind that one – she never took any prisoners.'

I take the soft wool, suddenly the most precious of things, and before I realise what's happening, Rose has stepped over the threshold, brushing past me, muttering to herself. My brain clicks and whirrs into action. 'Rose,' I call after her. It's impossible to believe I was ever in control of any situation. I'm certainly not in control of this one.

Forgoing the protection of the porch from the blustering rain, I step outside and walk up to the open gate. The rain slashing at me through the dark; I inspect the street for anyone crazy enough to be out in the cruel night. Of course, it's just me. I'm the only crazy one.

I suppose no one else heard the gunshot. The other house neighbouring mine is empty, for sale. It seems to me we live in an age where people ignore a potential gunshot in their own street but get worked up about a random act of violence in the U.S. they've seen on the internet thousands of miles away. I feel a little of the old Zac resurface. The one who would run into the street, discover the source of the shot, the one who would exact justice. The problem was I always went too far. I shudder at the thought… I shake away the feeling or perhaps only subdue it. The street is quiet, only Rose has heard the gunshot. The sound hasn't travelled any further. Anyway, people are cocooned in their homes, sheltered, warm, and looking at the world through glass screens instead of doing something about the injustices, the corruption, our burning the world until there's nothing left to breathe. Beyond the houses opposite, the craggy land breaks, descending downwards, until swallowed by the sea… just as Orla was.

Back inside, I discover Rose sat in the lounge, coat off and a cup of tea balanced on her knees. Only Costas is in the room with her. He peered at me; his face ridden with something like guilt. I don't know how he'll ever recover from this. I don't know how any of us will.

'Well, well, well,' Rose intones. 'Zachary Llewellyn, you never mentioned Costas was coming! Really! And a Vicar now! And such a handsome one! We have to look after him. It's all too easy to forget Vicars are people just like us, making it up as they go along, the same capacity in them as us to do terrible things.

Don't worry though, I'll keep an eye on him. We'll make sure this one stays on the straight and narrow.'

She winks at him and gulps on her tea, her wispy grey hair stuck flat to her head from wearing her hood up. 'You and Zachary used to be out on the road at the front of my house kicking that football from morning to night, drove my Heddwyn to despair.' She sighs. 'Poor man, he never deserved what he got, not at all.'

She smiles, and her eyes look faraway, tinged with watery sadness. 'Every time that ball came into our garden, it was always Costas who came and knocked on our door to ask if he could get it back. Always so polite, a lovely child. Zachary, you never used to ask for it back. Oh, good Lord, no. You always had him doing your dirty work for you.'

'Rose,' I say, sitting next to her on the sofa, scrutinising the still full mug in her hand. 'It's getting late now. You should be settled next door. A storm is coming.'

Rose frowns. 'Nonsense! It seems to me things are just getting interesting. Costas was telling me that as well as him and Harrison, some more of your old friends are here, and more to come!'

I fix Costas with a hard stare. He turns away, unable to hold eye contact.

'Oh, I can't wait to see Jessie and Orla. Two girls with bags of attitude. You don't mind if I hang on until they arrive, do you, Zachary?'

Lightning strikes. We all gaze at the bay window, momentarily drawn by an inverted world, outside flooded with light and within cast in darkness. Rose starts chatting but I don't hear what she's saying, because a shadow flits across the window, as if pulling quickly away out of sight. It could have been anything at all. I suppose it could have been a speck of dust in my eye or a reflection from within the old house. And yet, I'm sure it wasn't. It was someone. Watching us.

Stifled laughter forces me back to the activity within the room.

The Great Orme

Tomasz and Jorge, arm in arm appear and walk around the back of the sofa, still snorting with laughter at something Rose is saying. How can they? Costas just killed someone. The body is upstairs. Thunder rumbles closer now, rattling the bones of the old house.

Still nagged by the thought we are being watched through the window, I make an excuse and leave the lounge. I'm a policeman, trained to investigate. Opening the front door, I step beyond the cover of the porch into the icy rain once more. It drills at my face, although not nearly hard enough.

There's no one to be seen. I step onto the sodden grass and walk over to the lounge window. Years without soap has left the glass grimy. Someone has drawn something in the grease on the pane nearest to the door, and on closer inspection I can see it's a squiggle – a wavy line with a circle at one end. In the circle are two dots – eyes. Although rudimentary, there's no doubt in my mind it's the sea serpent, the wavy line beneath – the sea. I instinctively touch my forearm, where under my shirt, as for all my old friends, the same character is depicted in the form of a tattoo – the sea serpent, the Great Orme.

I rub the crude image from the window, and through the cleared glass I see Costas, his back to me, arms raised, gesticulating. Facing me, Rose seems to be clutching her cardigan, pulling it up her neck with one hand and violently thrusting out her walking stick at him. I rush inside.

The lounge falls silent as I enter. Costas is holding his glasses in his hand before him as if punching the air with them. His face is wet with tears. He holds my gaze. Deep brown eyes tunnels to who knows where. He relents, dropping his arm, closing his eyes and shaking his head.

'I think it's fair to say we are all up to speed,' Tomasz says, drumming his fingers on the back of the sofa as if he's informing me of a trivial matter. It jars. The central heating groans from within the walls, the old house doesn't like it and I don't like it.

'Stop it!' I shout. Then, seeing the looks on their faces, taken aback, I apologise. Tomasz takes a deep breath and lets out a long sigh while drawing the zip of his sports jersey to his chin. Over his shoulder, I see Jorge, his pale face entirely stoic.

'Something has got to give,' Tomasz says, face tilted at an angle and his voice gentle, tired. He switches his gaze to Rose, who's now standing at the centre of the room, leaning on her walking stick.

'You are the famous footballer, aren't you?' Harrison bleats. 'You should be anticipating your next move. What are your tactics? Defend or attack?'

Tomasz pulls his sports jersey collar over his chin and bites the zip in his teeth.

Rose peers at him over her glasses at Tomasz. 'You grew up in the children's home. What's it called? Blodwells?'

Tomasz nods.

'Well, you're a survivor, and I, for one, am proud of you.'

She takes up a seat on the sofa and commands Tomasz to sit next to her. They reminisce about the old days. Rose even demonstrates some insight about his successful football career. She's been tracking his progress. I invite Jorge to take a seat next to them. I feel for him. He must be terrified at the situation he finds himself in. He appears thoughtful, carrying himself with a surety and a calmness that belies the situation he's found himself in. I wonder what he's thinking.

Costas sidles up to me. 'It's not the end of the world. What's happened?' he whispers. 'We can sort this out. Can't we?'

I fix him with a stare, wondering what he's really asking, what he really wants me to say? Should I say "let's forget it, let's leave all of this behind and move on as if nothing has happened." Is that what he wants? The thing is, I love Costas. I do think what happened with Fatima was a tragic accident. 'We'll do what's right, Costas. It's about time.'

It's long past eight, and I'm worried about Jessie. She's late. Perhaps she's decided not to come. A pretty young woman, she was probably the kindest of all of us. I remember the kiss we shared on that fateful night all those years ago and guilt punches me in the stomach. I want Orla back. I don't know how, but I'm holding the grieving at bay. I simply must hold the mourning tsunami that is about sweep me away until tomorrow when all this will be done.

'How's Sian?' I ask.

Harrison nods at me to follow, and we leave the lounge, and together, he and I go to my mother's bedroom. Sian is sitting on the edge of the double bed, Fatima laid in the middle, face down, arms limp by her side. On seeing us enter the room, Sian turns away and leans over the body in the bed and begins caressing her dead wife's hair.

Harrison leans his hulking frame against the wardrobe. He gives me a disparaging glare, shaking his head as if to suggest it's all my fault. He's probably right. If it wasn't for me, Fatima wouldn't be dead. Orla wouldn't be dead. None of them would be dead. I couldn't hate myself more.

We remain respectfully quiet for a while, our gazes averted from the carer and the dead. Tomasz appears behind me. I move to allow him entry through the doorway. He's taken off his sports top to reveal a baggy red t-shirt that belies his athletic frame. Harrison pushes off from the wardrobe and puts a taciturn arm around the footballer. Side by side, Harrison's cool brown skin, and Tomasz's ruddy pink. I see the two boys I grew up with, and how they've changed into powerful, strong creatures.

Tomasz squeezes Harrison affectionately around the waist before making his way to the foot of the bed. He ruffles his slick, fair hair, turning it into something resembling a discarded bale of straw. The room is silent apart from the external noises of howling wind, incessant rain, periodic thunder, and the eternal creaking resistance of the old house's beams and joints. I can only hope both I and the old house can withstand the storm to come.

The silence within is as thick and as uncomfortable as you would expect with having a corpse in the room. My eyes are fixed on Tomasz. On the football pitch Tomasz is a notorious poacher, grabbing the majority of his goals through instinctive anticipation, arriving in the six-yard box and meeting the ball before anyone else even realises what's happening.

I thought I knew Tomasz, as I thought I knew the others, but I'm not sure I know myself anymore.

'Instead of coming here, I thought I might kill myself today,' he says matter-of-factly.

Even Sian, in her grief, gasps.

'What? Why?' I ask, appalled.

He sighs. 'I see Bart, and I see the old man every day. It's like they live inside my head. Even so, I decided it's better to live and fight for happiness than to die and let misery win.'

He lowers his head despondently. Fringe flopped forward, hiding his eyes.

Harrison props himself up against the wardrobe again and snorts. 'Tommy boy is right! Zac, take note!'

Sian throws a curt look at Harrison and he holds an apologetic hand up in acknowledgment and continues. 'We need to focus. We need to persuade Zac from throwing us off the fucking cliff…'

'Enough!' I say, glaring at Harrison. I'm convinced he knows about Orla falling from the Great Orme.

Harrison sniggers at me like a schoolkid, pacing the room, rubbing his bald head back and forth. 'Tomasz, let me tell you one thing. You killed a child abuser. You removed an evil from the surface of the planet. You prevented that sick fucker from abusing others! A job well done, I'd say!'

'There are other means that result in the same effect,' I say.

Harrison actually stamps the floor in anger like a little kid. 'Zac! Look what you are doing to these people. You've got to stop!'

I pick up a small pair of nail scissors from my mother's dressing table, easing them open and closed. 'Once we believed murder was justified, it didn't feel like murder. It became something else. Something logical and acceptable. That's when the trouble started. That's when we became capable of killing again and again.'

I regard Harrison. I peer over at Fatima's prone body, partially obscured by Sian, who understandably appears not to want to let go of her wife. Finally, I gaze at Tomasz, this guy won't let me down, it's not possible. 'Tomasz,' I say. 'I can't live with the guilt, and I can't live with the ghosts. There's only one way out. You must see that?'

Harrison sets both hands on his hips and stares at me, his face an explosion of rage. The veins in his thick neck seem to pulse, and his scalp glistens with beads of sweat.

'Fucking crap,' he spits, marching up to me, swinging his arms and flexing his chest. He grabs me by my shirt and hauls me up so only the front rubber edges of my Doc Martens' remain in contact with the carpet. Tomasz and Sian shout at him, but he ignores them.

'This can't go on. You arrogant shit! Can't you see? You are only making things worse?' His nostrils are flared, and he's breathing hard. I can't believe for an instant I actually contemplate stabbing him with the scissors.

'Let him go.'

It's Jorge.

Still holding onto me, Harrison looks over his shoulder to the doorway.

Jorge enters the bedroom, seemingly calm and unfazed by the drama before him. 'Let him go, Harrison. We need to be astute… smart. It's the only way we are going to get through this.'

They are wise words, and apply no matter our inclination to confess or not to confess. Harrison puffs out his cheeks, letting go of me, and shaking his head.

Tomasz touches Harrison's shoulder as he passes, a conciliatory act that seems not to have any visible impact on him. Jorge meets Tomasz at the foot of the bed, kisses him on the cheek, before walking to the bedside and bending to whisper something in Sian's ear.

She responds with a simple nod, an acknowledgment. He leaves her and returns to Tomasz's side.

Jorge is a steadying and rational influence. I hope I can count on his support.

A difficult silence is broken unexpectedly.

'Excuse me.'

Rose is stood in the doorway. 'I don't mean to disturb you, but there's someone at the door. Should I open it?'

'Can't Costas get it?' I ask, straightening my shirt.

'He left about ten minutes ago. Said he needed to get something.'

We all regard one another, puzzled expressions on our faces.

'Oh dear.' Rose waggles her walking stick in the direction of the bed and Fatima.

'We're all tired, Rose,' I say, walking up to her to obscure her view. 'Come on, let's open the door to our guest. It'll be Jessie, you remember her?'

Before Rose can respond, Harrison cuts in sharply. 'How do you know it's Jessie and not Orla?'

Because Orla's dead, I think to myself.

I leave his question unanswered. Heaven knows how I'm going to explain Orla's death to them, but I'll have to tell them imminently.

Assisting Rose down the stairs, I wonder what she saw, what she heard, and where Costas has gone.

The sight of Jessie on the doorstep clutching a pale blue, flower-patterned holdall is as good a tonic as I can get right now. She pulls her hood down, and a shock of glossy black curls bounce out from underneath, framing her face. Despite myself, the memory of our illicit kiss at Orla's corporate Christmas party plunges into my thoughts but not for long as she gives a quick, tight smile before swinging a punch like a golf club at my head. 'You bastard.'

Ecstasy in

drowned sorrows

Chapter Eighteen

I pull away just in time to deflect the full force of the blow, her small fist glancing off my jaw. I reach for the doorframe to steady myself in preparation for a follow up punch.

'How dare you drag me here! To this place!'

She is shaking with the force of her words. 'I've made a new life, Zac. I will *not* have you ruin this one too!'

I see deep burning hatred in her eyes. Why would I have expected anything else I wonder? I rub my chin. 'Good to see you too.'

'Haven't we suffered enough? After all, we've been through,' she says, weaponizing every word.

Jessie is loyal and kind. It was her loyalty and kindness to her boyfriend that nearly ended up killing her. Thanks to my intervention, it ended up killing him.

She seems oblivious to the cold driving wind and rain, the persistent rumbling thunder overhead, and she holds her ground, her laser-like gaze continuing to burn through me.

'Despite the literal attempt to knock some sense into me, it is good to see you,' I say flatly. 'Let's get you inside.'

Her face finally softens, and she rolls her eyes. 'Just wait until I see Orla. Between us, we'll put you right.'

A number of cars are parked up outside, and I assume one of them is hers. I reach for her holdall and beckon her inside, thinking to myself I must have been crazy to invite them all back – how the hell am I going to persuade them to confess and give up the lives they've created for themselves?

We all congregate in the lounge, even Sian. And despite her initial anger, Jessie gives everyone a hug. Even I eventually get one.

The Great Orme

Jessie and Harrison make only the slightest eye contact and I wonder what has passed between them, other than the ice-cold fact she killed his brother.

I'm concerned about Rose, and put an arm around her, suggesting she heads home. Unbelievably, she refuses, shoving me away. The old authority I used to possess diminished further still. She takes a seat on the sofa while suggesting we "young ones" could benefit from her sage advice.

I wonder how we cannot confess: Rose and Jorge are embroiled to some extent, Sian's wife is lying dead on my mother's bed, Orla is lying dead at the foot of the Orme's cliffs or swept out to sea, a wave of other murders all about us, an unknown murderer threatening us should we confess, and the ghosts of the dead all about demanding we do this one right thing.

'So, two questions,' says Jessie, to a timely ripple of far-off thunder.

'Question one: Jorge and Rose,' she says looking from Jorge, who's standing legs crossed and with his arms folded, to Rose, sharp pale-blue eyes peering inquisitively through the lenses of her green-framed glasses, 'how much do you know?'

Jorge responds first: 'Enough to know, we are all in very deep trouble.'

Rose nods in agreement. 'I wasn't born yesterday, young lady… very far from it. I've learned a thing or two in my time. One of which is, knowing a criminal when I meet them, and it seems to me this house is crawling with them.'

Jessie shakes her head in disbelief before fixing her gaze on me and raising her eyebrows questioningly.

'You should leave now,' I say, addressing Jorge and Rose. 'Both of you. You're already witnesses, and I don't want you to be implicated further–'

'No,' they reply in unison.

'Fill us in, Zac,' Jorge says, uncrossing his arms and sweeping his carefully curated wavy brown locks away from his face with both hands. 'You are right – Rose and I are already incriminated.

It would kind of be nice to know everything, even if only for our own protection.'

I weigh up his request before concluding these two will know everything soon enough, and anyway, this time tomorrow, we'll all be held at the police station, our lives as we know them, effectively over. I tell them about each and every murder, all apart from Jessie's boyfriend, which I invite Jessie to tell herself – I'll need to write the depressing details down later.

After I summarise the tragedy of the deaths, I ask Jessie to explain what we did to her boyfriend.

'Seriously?' she asks. 'Now?'

'It's as good a time as any,' I say, in the knowledge we have little time left. People need to know what happened, how it happened, and why it happened.'

She takes the glass of red wine thanks him, and gulps a mouthful. She holds the glass pressed to her chest, eyeballing me like I'm a predator and she's the prey. 'Fine, I guess it'll fill the time before Orla arrives.'

I rub my face as if it might wake me from this nightmare or at least get the desperately needed blood moving to my brain.

'I have a family now, Zac. One I love with all of my heart. I'll live with what I did, as we all must, but they must never know. Never.'

No, I say to myself. They will know. That is the price we have to pay.

Jessie sighs, takes another gulp of wine, her dark eyes seem to soften a little, and she begins: 'The kids were arguing in the back of the car, and my husband was driving, moaning about the kids, and that was when I noticed I had a message from you.' She glares at me.

'Six years suddenly felt like six minutes. The memory so vivid, so painful, your message was a time machine I don't want.'

Staring down at her glass, Jessie swirls the wine, so the liquid skirts dangerously close to the rim.

'What I did to Ollie… for your benefit Jorge, Rose… Ollie is…

was, Harrison's younger brother. And also, the love of my life.'

I take a sideways glance at Harrison, who is sitting, his head in his hands and staring hard at the floor. Rose and Jorge nod their understanding, both unflappable – and that makes me nervous. They should be running miles from here.

'I was twenty-one. Ollie two years younger. We were living in Cardiff, a tiny apartment near the Bay. Ollie had one hand on the door handle. *I'm only going to see the guys*, he said, laughing at me. *I'm finished with that stuff. Trust me, I am*, he said.'

Jessie has scrunches up her eyes as if she's about to receive a blow to the face. The memory is still painful for her. All I want to do is hug her, protect her, but it's too late.

'I tried to pull him away from the door. I pleaded, begged him, a mess, tears streaking down my face… again.'

Everyone in the room is either stood motionless or on the edge of their seat.

'He pushed me off him, punched me in the face and when I was on the floor, he kicked me in the stomach so I was winded. While I lay there, curled on the floor sobbing, he told me he loved me. I was scared because I knew I couldn't save him; all of my love couldn't save him.'

Jessie wipes a single tear away from her cheek with her free hand and takes a sip of wine. Pursing her lips, she breathes out long and slow. Calmed, she continues: 'I took the biscuit tin from the high shelf in the kitchen cupboard. In it, pills, old and new, lots of them, for all kinds of things. I opened every single bottle and packet, emptying the lot of them into a brown plastic bowl. I plunged my hand in, swirling the contents around. I poured myself a glass of water, truly believing it was the only way out. Then…' She hesitates, regarding me like I've just landed on the planet. 'Then I wondered what you would do, Zac. I wondered what you would do if you were me. So, I called you.

You immediately calmed me, your cold, calculating logic, exactly what I thought I needed. I thanked you and hung up. I did as you instructed – I ran Ollie a bath and waited.

Ollie returned; a smile as wide as a hyena's. He wrapped his arms around me and told me he loved me, that he was sorry he punched and kicked me, that he'd been agitated but would soon be okay. In one hand, he clutched a dirty cloth bag. Of course, he'd been to see his dealer. I had reached rock bottom. I had nothing left, nothing to give. I felt so worn… depleted, empty. He kissed the scar on my forehead – a reminder that he was unafraid to wield a knife to prevent me from stopping him from using. He went into the kitchen to put the kettle on. It was the signal, that innocuous act was always the beginning of my re-occurring nightmare.

But this time, the nightmare was going to have a different ending. Instead of putting up a fight and being beaten half to death I did as you'd instructed. I led him to the bathroom, and without mention of the bowlful of pills in the kitchen, he brought the kettle with him.

I cried while I undressed him, but he didn't care. He had what he loved, what he needed in the bag. Clutching the bag close to his chest, he stepped into the bath, craving eyes and broken face someplace else, a million miles from me. I sat on the toilet seat and talked to him, asked him to stop, but he didn't even respond, only washing his arm, eyes fixed on the prize. He reached into the filthy green bag and began the ritual.'

Harrison sobs, turns it into a cough, but nonetheless it's a sob. He still has his head in his hands, his fingertips slide further up his face – stretching upwards the corners of his eyes.

'Something I'd watched Ollie do a hundred times over… Ollie carefully warmed the silver spoon from underneath with a cigarette lighter, the sticky black tar within glistening and softening to a muddy brown colour. He added a drop of the boiled water from the kettle and, from grease-smeared bottles, added a drop of lemon juice and vinegar to dissolve the heroin.

Taking a clean needle and uncapping it, he dipped the tip

into the drug and drew it slowly up. He tapped the upwardly pointed needle to rid it of air bubbles. Satisfied, he balanced the needle in the soap dish on the side of the bath and took his trusty tourniquet from the bag – two old condoms tied together. Defeated, I watched the man I'd lost my job for, lost my family for, lost my dignity for, given up life for. I'd left Ollie before… twice. And each time he'd found me. Threatened to kill either himself or me unless I went with him. He would've too. And through it all, I still loved him, but you had convinced me you were right; something needed to change, something drastic. It was either him or me, you said… and you were right.

He rolled the tourniquet up his arm, already opening and closing his fist to pump up the vein, any that weren't collapsed from the years of abuse. He aimed the needle in the direction of the blood flow, toward the heart, and pierced a sorry looking vein. His face creased with concentration, he pushed the plunger in, only pausing when he saw his blood in the needle so he knew it was right. He released the tourniquet and steadily injected.'

Jessie reaches up and her fingers trembling and twists a black spiral of her hair.

'I felt so old and drained, a real zombie,' she says, before blinking away the tears threatening to fall. 'Ollie had tipped his head to the side, facing me, tiny unseeing pupils, his breath shallow and slow – he'd gone. I kissed his cheek, pale, cool skin flushed pink. For the last time, I told him I loved him. At that point, I called you again, like you told me.'

Harrison coughs again, a strangled clearing of his throat. *There had to have been another way*, I think. Something that could have prevented a murder.

'Zac, I told you Ollie wasn't functioning, too drowsy, too hazy. You told me to run the tap some more, and if I thought it best, to ease him under the water, to hold him there. You told me to close my eyes. I heard gurgling.'

The room stops as if caught in time's cool amber. No one moves, until finally, Jessie wipes away a solitary tear. 'I still think you were right, Zac. And I truly believe you saved my life that night.'

I'm desperate to correct her, to tell her otherwise, that there must have been a middle-ground, but the words are stuck. I wonder why a binary point of view is always easier to take than the considered rationale that navigates a sensible path through.

Jessie leans forward and places her wine glass on the table. 'I killed him,' she says, her bottom lip quivering. 'I killed the man I loved.'

'Jessie,' I say, releasing words that are the wrong ones. 'I... I was wrong. I'm sorry. There were other ways. You could have stayed with me...' My words are pathetic.

'You don't get to say that,' she replies, her words stern, teacher-like. 'Not now! Not ever!'

I understand – but know she's wrong. Even though I'm inarticulate I do get to say it, because it's true. I should have had her stay with me. I should have looked after her. I should have kept Ollie away from her. That should have been the answer, and not the one I gave her.

Harrison gets to his feet, striding around the room like a caged beast. 'Look Jessie, if you hadn't killed him... I would have. For fuck's sake, why didn't you tell me about the beatings?'

'Precisely because you would have killed him,' she replies matter-of-factly.

Then, she adds, 'You knew he had been abused?'

'Okay, okay,' Harrison cuts over her, evidently not keen to discuss it further. 'So,' he says impatiently, 'You had another question?'

Jessie reaches for the wine glass. 'Yes. Where are Orla and Costas?'

All eyes settle on me. Even the old house seems to hold its breath in anticipation of my response.

'Costas has gone for a walk, apparently,' I say.

Jessie pulls a face. 'In this?' She points at the window being lashed with diagonal splashes of rain. 'That's insane. You don't just go for *a walk* in this sort of weather. He's gone *somewhere*... and he's up to *something*!'

The Great Orme

She's right. My heart sinks. Please Lord, I pray, don't let Costas be the *Leveller*.

'How about Orla?' Jessie adds. 'It's not like her to be late.'

I can both see and feel the gleam of Harrison's smile break open at the corner of my vision. He knows something is amiss, and it gives him pleasure.

'Orla won't be coming,' I say. 'She… she can't.'

'Oh Zac, my boy,' Harrison says. 'You are beginning to worry me… and I'm not naturally a worrier.'

'Well, perhaps that's part of your problem,' I mutter.

He's on me in a flash, grabbing me in a headlock.

'It's all your fault!' His voice is ramped up like a nervous whinnying horse. 'You can't just decide to end it! It might fucking surprise you there are a few more fucking opinions in this room as well as yours!'

The others quickly crowd around and it's Jorge's voice I can hear telling everyone to calm, to be reasonable. Gradually Harrison's iron arm relaxes and I'm able to slide from his hold.

'Listen Harrison,' I say, catching my breath. 'Perhaps you are right. Perhaps it *is* all my fault, but I have not committed one murder, not one single murder. I have not stuck the knife in, pushed someone under, lit the flame, crashed the car, strung someone up, waited while a girl dies or…' I take a deep breath, 'smashed a young kid's skull to bits!'

The others visibly stiffen, affronted by the facts and distracted from Orla's whereabouts. I wait a few seconds to gain control of my breath then I tell them directly: 'But yes, I am accountable. Yes, I have violated the law. And yes, I too am the perpetrator of these crimes, but we all have responsibility, each of us. Each of us owe it to the dead *and* the living to confess. And so, you *must* understand… we will confess.'

The sound of my heart pounding rings in my ears, and I'm convinced Harrison is set to attack me again, but a thought jumps out at me. 'Who's got the gun?' I ask.

My question unnerves them, yet each of them can only shrug or shake their heads.

'Gun?' Jessie says, eyes nervously sweeping the room for the weapon. 'You have a gun?'

'It was on the mantelpiece beneath the mirror, wasn't it?' I ask, looking around at everyone for confirmation. No one answers, they only look questioningly from one to another.

'Costas must have it,' Harrison suggests, his bicep flexing as he rubs his arm.

'I'm concerned for his safety. For his sanity,' I say. 'We need to find him,' I add, heading for the lounge doorway.

'I'm staying here.'

I stop at the doorway and look back at Harrison.

'It's pissing down out there. We'll get soaked,' he whines. 'Anyhow, he could be anywhere.'

'Look,' I say, fixing Harrison with a hard stare. 'I believe one of us is the *Leveller*. One of us is killing. It must stop. We have to stop them. We need everyone together again, so we can sort this out, once and for all.'

'Hold on,' begins Harrison, but Jorge cuts in…

'Zac's right,' he says, his tone calm, his gaze steady and unblinking, oozing calm authority. Letting go of Tomasz's hand, he moves comfortably between me and Harrison. 'I suggest we do as Zac says. We need to be careful. We don't need more *mishaps*. Let's find Costas, and like Zac says, sort out this mess once and for all.'

Sian makes her way forward. 'Agreed.'

I'm pleased to see she has found her voice, and though ashen-faced, her blue-eyes at least seem to be back to the here and now.

I suggest we split up. 'He can't have got far. He only left, what? Maybe half an hour ago?'

There's some back and forth while people retrieve their coats from bags or cars. When done, I pair Harrison with Jessie, to their obvious but unspoken annoyance. Naturally Jorge and

Tomasz go together. Me, Sian and Rose watch as the two groups head off in opposite directions into the thunder-filled night.

I turn to my neighbour. 'Rose. It's best you stay out of this. Trust me. You don't need this at your time of life. Let me take you home.'

'It's too late for that,' she says, shuffling out of the doorway into the unyielding rain. She waves her walking stick high above her head. 'Besides, I've an idea where we can find your vicar.'

Sian shrugs her shoulders and follows. I curse under my breath as we follow the elderly lady down the path and turn right towards town. The relentless rain doesn't give up, few but the most fool-hardy are out and about on this wet and freezing Saturday night. Through rain-blurred eyes I'm acutely aware of the sea serpent's steep and rocky prominence, vast chasms of solid black rock set against the dark nothingness of the sky watching us as we three children of the Great Orme, drain like spiders in a sink into the plughole that is town.

'Where are you taking us, Rose?' I have my arms wrapped around the two women, as much for my comfort as for theirs. The rain drips from our hoods. I can't help but marvel at Rose. Beneath her sodden coat I can barely feel her form, and when I can, it's all bone. I *know* there's another energy in us other than the physical, and Rose has copious amounts of it. I can only admire her.

'Where else would a man of the cloth go when in need?' she asks, waving her walking stick in front of her. She barely seems to need it, her gait and pace constant without it.

'A church?' says Sian.

'I would certainly think so,' she says, and cackles. 'Whether it's to worship God or the Devil, is another question. Anyway, what's the difference?'

'The nearest Church is Christ Church,' I say, wiping my brow clear of dripping rain.

Rose points her stick into the pouring rain like she's trying to thread it through the raindrops. 'That's right. My church!'

'Let me take you home,' I insist. 'You'll catch your death of a cold in this.'

'I've been in worse situations than this, my dear,' she replies unwaveringly. 'Much worse.'

How? I wonder. What could possibly be worse than this situation?

It doesn't take long before we turn off Old Road onto Abbey Road and next to Marks and Spencer's is Christ Church. The nineteenth century church is gorgeously gothic – pointed arches, intricate stained-glass windows, but with a severed spire, destroyed by a storm a few decades ago.

Rose prods the arched wooden door with her stick, the cobalt blue colour still vivid in the dark. 'The door should be open.'

I push it, and it groans as it opens inwards. All of us glad to get out of the incessant rain, we enter the church.

Cold and dripping wet, we stand in awe for a moment, taking in the wide-open silence of the holy place. An involuntary shudder ripples down my spine as if an ice-cold finger has scraped along it. It gets me moving and we creep forward silently and respectfully, reverence demanded by the vast capsule of old stone. No living soul to be seen, it seems Rose was wrong. Costas isn't here.

We stop at the top of the aisle; the knave is flooded with the gentle rainbow radiance of the arched stained-glass window beyond the pulpit. I open my mouth to suggest we leave but before I emit a word, a scream, short, sharp and guttural, shatters the silence.

Sian grabs my arm and yelps. Rose instinctively brandishes her stick before her as a weapon. The scream, like a sudden sharp press of the church organ, reverberates around the sheer walls and disappears as quickly as it came, sucked up by the high vaulted ceiling. It's impossible to tell from where it came. A tension spreads behind my face, like a hand pressing its fingers against the inside of my skull, searching for a way out.

'Who's there?' I ask, my normally steady voice, weak and reedy, gobbled up before it reaches the opposite end of the church.

The strained silence returns, thick and cloying. Someone

else is in the church, either scared or trying to scare us. I leave Sian and Rose, putting my cold hands to my lips to check I'm not a ghost, that all of this is really happening. I glance back at the two women stood beneath the pulpit, solemn faces watching me as I prowl along the aisle.

The church seems to quiver like a dying man, its bones brittle and its breath rasping. Dead, rotten faces with black soulless eyes, freshly dredged from the mud they were buried in, glance up from their hymn books to observe me as I pass. My heart slams back and forth, punching my chest to sound an alarm, one to run, to escape. The congregation are singing, if it could be called such, the guttural screech of the word 'Jericho,' over and over, until my head is filled with the rambunctious sound and I fear it might explode. 'Stop!' I yell with all the force I can muster. At once, the congregation's jaws snap from their skulls – a splintered cracking sound like that of a tree trunk torn vertically in half, and the congregation disintegrates and disappears into dust, gone. Rose and Sian scream. I swivel around, looking back along the aisle toward them, where they're standing with their backs to me.

'I'm coming,' I shout out, running along the aisle.

Sian and Rose stand motionless, staring at the round stained-glass window high up in the wall. It has been smashed. All around them on the raised wooden-panelled floor, glass fragments lay scattered. Among the broken glass, lies a metal golden cross. I pick up the crucifix, it's solid and heavy. Through the smashed window, nothing other than darkness pours in from outside.

There's a small card tied to the cross, a beige coloured gift-tag. I read the uppercase scrawl out loud:

'There is but one God. Confess only to him and no one else.'

I put the tag in my pocket without the others seeing, knowing the tag only indicts Costas further. We leave the church, shaken and wary. The rain has eased slightly but the wind whips with snake-like ferocity, snapping at anything and everything as we trudge back to the old house.

On entering my street, I notice my bedroom light is on. It definitely wasn't on when we left. Eyes narrowed against the wind, I'm certain I can see a shadow behind the drawn curtains… someone in my room.

Despite the freezing conditions, I make Sian and Rose wait while I head toward the house alone. For a moment I envisage Fatima risen from the dead, desperate to be reunited with Sian, and so, with a head full of ghosts and my heart chugging heavily like an old and dirty diesel engine, I glance over my shoulder, half expecting the rotten-boned Christ Church congregation to be chasing me up the hill.

Nobody and somebody
at the same time

Chapter Nineteen

I knock at my own front door, hoping the courtesy begets a normal response – the night can't get any worse, I tell myself hopefully. There has to be someone inside and this time they can't disappear without a trace.

I don't hear anything from within, not even a bark from Smokey. *God, I hope he's alright*. My fingers wet and frozen, I fiddle for my key in my pocket, and I think I hear the sound of muffled footsteps on the carpeted stairs. I wait, but no one comes. I raise the key to the lock but before it makes contact, the door, stiff and swollen with the rain, is tugged open from within.

Costas stands before me; ample frame filling the doorway, Smokey next to him, his short tail wagging in a blur at seeing me.

'Where the hell have you been? We were worried. We've all been searching for you.' I sound like a concerned and angry parent.

He blinks rapidly, as if returning from a deep concentration. 'Nowhere really… I just needed some time on my own, thinking time. Where is everyone?'

'Looking for you, you dullard!'

He's clutching a piece of paper in his hand.

'What were you doing in my bedroom?'

'I've not been in your bedroom.'

'Don't lie to me, Costas. You of all people.'

'I'm not,' he says flatly. He seems tired, his warm and friendly persona battered by the events of the weekend. Understandably so, I think.

'Honestly, I've not been upstairs since I got back.'

Still stood on my own doorstep like I'm an unwelcome guest

at my own house, I observe the Vicar stood before me, a man I thought I could trust.

'What's that?' I ask, nodding toward the piece of paper in his hand and forcing him backwards into the hallway as I enter.

He observes the piece of paper like it has just landed in his hand. 'Ah, yes,' he says, adjusting his glasses, and peering over the top of them at me. 'Very strange. Your printer stirred into life… and this popped out of it.'

He hands me the page, a photo. The image is taken from above, looking down on rocks, the sea lapping at them, and in among them a distant green-coated person staring up the cliff-face at the camera. Black hair and beetle-eyes, it's Orla. Alive!

My heart surges hot with hope. I grab Costas's sleeve. 'Did you take this photo?'

'Of course not,' he replies abruptly. 'What's going on, Zac? What's happened to Orla?'

'How long have you been back?' I snap, ignoring his question.

'No more than five minutes.'

'And you've been downstairs the entire time?'

'That's right. I've been sat in the kitchen.'

My heart is thudding fast – I'm thinking of Orla, and yet I have to deal with the situation at hand. Ridiculous as it may seem, it crosses my mind the someone I saw at the bedroom window may be Orla. 'Costas, someone else is in here. I saw them from outside, at the bedroom window.'

'It's impossible, Zac,' he says, pulling his arm from my grasp. 'I would have heard them? Although…'

'Although what?'

'Well, when I got back Smokey was locked out, in the back garden. You didn't leave him there?'

I curse and push past him. 'Are you serious? In this weather? Go and get Sian and Rose, they are at the bottom of the street. Wait, how did you get in? You told me you didn't have a key.'

He nods his head, feeling his chest pocket on his blazer. 'That's right. I borrowed Harrison's. He left it on the kitchen table.'

'Get the others,' I say. 'I'll check upstairs.'

I shut the door after him so there's no escape for whoever is hiding.

'Where are you?' I yell from the hallway, raging at the intruder. 'Show yourself, Leveller!'

I wait, the terse scrape of my quick breath all I can hear. Unable to wait more than a few seconds, I burst into life. I tear around the downstairs rooms first, throwing cushions, opening cupboards and checking behind doors – I will not let whoever it is escape this time. The kitchen door is bolted from within, the walled back garden still and empty.

Good, whoever it is will be trapped upstairs. I flick the landing light on, and grabbing the banister, haul myself up the stairs. The long landing, teal-painted walls, once clear and fresh, now dull and tawdry, stretches all the way to the bathroom at the end, empty. My bedroom is nearest, and in darkness. I push the door inwards, reaching in to flick the light-switch on. The room appears empty, my bed still unmade. I check in the cupboard, even under the bed. The light was definitely on and I'm convinced I saw someone. I walk up to the window and peer at Costas, Rose and Sian entering through the gateway into the front garden. A chill scrapes down my spine – the curtains had been closed; the silhouetted figure I saw stood behind them.

I wonder if it's the old house, perhaps the ghosts within, mocking me, making me mad. It's possible I think to myself. Maybe I've exhausted any logic I once had, maybe I'm confused, seeing things that aren't real.

Something stirs in the doorway, my heart jolts, but it's only Smokey. I breathe a sigh of relief. 'If only you could talk.'

Yet to check the other bedrooms, I only get as far as the next, my mother's, where Fatima is laying on the bed, except she doesn't. She isn't there. The blankets on the bed are crumpled, patchy with blood stains, but her body is gone.

Rooted to the spot, my chest heaves, my eyes swivelling in my head, looking for something that might reveal what is going on. Two standalone cupboards are open, my mother's clothes within, as we left them. The dressing table coated in dust, set with her perfumes and makeup, remains untouched as it has for years. I'm reflected in the oval mirror at its centre – wet hair stuck to my scalp, my face pale and translucent, eyes dark with circles. I seem as if a ghost.

I need to think. I'm not crazy and I'm not a ghost – not yet. Someone has moved Fatima's body. Costas? If not him, then who? And where? And why?

The room's navy-blue carpet is still smeared with dark red spots – bloodstains from when Fatima was carried in to the room. As far as I can tell, nothing else is out of place. I check all the other rooms but no one, living or dead is present. Downstairs, I hear the front door open, followed by the alternating voices of Costas, Rose and Sian. *Christ, what do I say to Sian?*

While I'm thinking, the others arrive, a barrage of angry questions hurled at Costas.

We amass in the dining room, sat around the huge oval table made from solid English oak, eight of the ten chairs around it are taken up by each of us. Everyone has a drink, mostly alcohol of one sort or another. Only Rose doesn't, preferring coffee and keeping her wits about her. The room smells of damp, everyone still in their wet clothes and the towels I brought down with me are strewn about, either on the table, across the backs of chairs or in Rose and Tomasz's case, draped around their shoulders. The mood is agitated, people's nerves have been shredded by the events so far. I dread announcing the latest news, it may tip some of them over the edge, Sian especially.

I place the photo of Orla face-down on the table. 'Everyone… listen to me,' I say, clenching my jaw and waiting. 'You won't believe what I have to tell you… I'm not even sure I do.'

They all become quiet, exasperation writ large on so many

of their faces. I wonder how much more these people need to suffer before they acquiesce and confess.

I don't embellish the hard cold fact, stating it as it is. 'Fatima has disappeared,' I tell them. 'She's gone.'

My words are met with expressions of incredulity, it seems no one was expecting this particular announcement.

Naturally all gazes turn to Sian. It seems my words have taken a moment to sink in for her.

'Disappeared?' she asks, her eyes roving about the room as if Fatima might be hiding among us.

'Without a trace,' I say, shaking my head to express my own disbelief.

Sian stands suddenly, bursting up from her seat as if the neurons in her brain have only just started firing. She slams her hand on the table, her eyes wild and alive, incandescent with rage, the old energy returned. 'She's dead! She can't disappear!' she all but screeches at me as if it's my doing, as if I'm stupid or worse, lying.

I quickly explain I saw someone in my bedroom as we approached the house, that I discovered Costas having not long arrived back at the house, his finding Smokey locked out, the light on and then off in my bedroom, the curtains opened, and finally, the empty bed in my mother's room, Fatima gone.

I've barely finished before Sian rushes from the room, followed closely by Tomasz and Jessie, leaving the rest of us sat in silence. We can hear the three of them moving about above us, muffled cries of anguish from Sian.

I don't know what's going on, and I don't know what to say, but my heart is thumping, it's pounding and set to burst with that tiny fragment of deceit that we call hope. Orla may still be alive.

Sian and the other two soon return, Sian held up by them lest she collapses. I would wish none of this on her. She is a light, a flame to which people are drawn.

It's Tomasz who breaks the silence, directing attention back to me, his voice both quiet and clear. 'What else is there?' he

The Great Orme

asks. 'There's something else you need to tell us. You seem… energised somehow.'

I wonder if my usually stoic expression has given way to something more easily readable as I reach forward and drag the piece of paper toward me.

'Jesus Christ, Zac. Spit it out!' demands Harrison, banging his empty glass on the table. Knowing what he's capable of, I'm getting concerned for Harrison, his temper seems to be reaching boiling point at increasing frequencies.

Flipping the page over, I slide it along the table, past the empty seat next to me, towards Jessie who has left Sian and is sat and leaning back with her hands pressed to her face. She too, is distraught and peers through her fingers at the page.

She slides her hands down her face so the tips of her fingers cling to the edge of her jaw.

The photo is grainy, and presumably with the photo having been taking at maximum zoom the image is slightly pixellated. 'Orla?' she says, leaning forward to inspect the photo. 'It's Orla! But where is she? She seems to be in trouble!' Jessie lifts her eyes to the ceiling in thought before firing off more questions at me. 'What's this all about? Is Orla alright, Zac? Who took this photo? And when?'

I slump back in my chair, and rock my head backwards, staring up at the ceiling. 'It was taken yesterday afternoon… after Orla fell from the Great Orme.'

As I expect, my words are fuel to a fire of questions which are thrown at me leaden with anger and disbelief.

I explain we went for a walk up the Great Orme, Orla having surprised me by arriving early, yesterday. And, knowing it doesn't look good for me, I tell them she literally ran off the cliff… and fell. I know they are bound to assume I pushed her off. I can hardly believe she jumped, why should they?

'You pushed her off,' Harrison bleats, the first to say what everyone's thinking. 'You pushed your own wife off the fucking

Great Orme!'

'Wait!' I shout, clutching the edge of the table. 'Everyone. Wait!'

'I know what it looks like,' I say, trying to appeal to any vestiges of compassion they may have. 'I think she became overwhelmed with what she'd done... and with what is yet to come when we confess. I should have seen it coming, but I never expected Orla...'

I don't know what to say. I am at fault. How can one person be so hopeless, I wonder? But despite my stark ineptitude, there is a glimmer of hope, one I'm desperate to share with the others: 'The point is, she's still alive!' I hold up the photo. 'Someone has hacked my printer; they sent that photo to it. I thought Orla was dead, but she's not! This photo proves it! She's crawling about the rocks.'

I flap the page in Costas' direction. 'The photo was printed while Costas was here – while we were out searching for him.'

Costas takes his turn to field a barrage of questions he hasn't any answers for. The knowledge that Orla's alive has my hands trembling. My blood is heating under my skin and my chest is heaving.

'What the fuck is wrong with you, Zac?' Harrison has left his seat leaning over me. He snatches the printed page from me, examining it while holding it up for all to see, as if evidence in a court of law. 'Did you kill her? Did you kill Orla?' he demands, his voice escalating to that high pitch that is a sure sign of imminent danger.

'Really?' I reply, 'Orla... my wife? I'd take my own life before I'd take hers.' My voice wavers, and I take a deep breath to try to slow my racing heart. 'I saw her body beneath the cliff, among the rocks. I thought she was dead. I thought...'

I was wrong. Orla wasn't dead. And I left her... I gave up on her. 'I should have found a way down there,' I tell them. 'Someone else may have done exactly that – that someone being the *Leveller*. They were on the Great Orme with us.' I scan the faces of my house guests and the uninvited. They stare back at me, their faces as if strangers, it's as if they are watching me play out a drama on tv, as if our experience isn't universal, that their experience is in some way detached – that they can turn the tv off and walk away, go back to their real lives. How wrong they are.

'What did she ever do to deserve you?' Harrison tosses the picture across the table. 'Apart from love you more than anyone on this fucking planet.'

The old Zac would have a logic ready to share as a response, this Zac has none.

'That's enough.' Jessie cuts in, my surprising defender. She splays her hands on the table, raising her fingers slightly to examine her orange painted fingernails. 'Zac hasn't killed anyone. Ever. We did. We are the only ones to blame. We shouldn't have listened to him.'

Jorge quiet until now, raps the table with his knuckles, drawing everyone's attention. 'Anyone mind if I give an outsider's perspective?'

Tomasz sits Sian in a chair and moves to Jorge's side. Everyone waits for Jorge to continue, while he pushes up the sleeves of his round-necked black jumper. He's dressed like an extra in this tragedy, but I get the feeling his part is bound to become more significant. 'Someone in this room is the Leveller. Someone here is manipulating all of us, and I wonder, I just wonder, if it's you.' Jorge speaks with the easy eloquence of a man used to being listened to, persuasive and convincing with every word uttered.

I lower and shake my head. 'No, Jorge. I…'

'Hear me out,' he says, maintaining his focus on me. '*You* are the orchestrator of all of this, am I right?'

I don't like the way this is headed.

'Perhaps you invited all of your *old friends* back here that you might incriminate them, that you might save yourself?'

'What?' I'm bemused.

'Maybe you are worried one of your friends will break, that they'll confess. So why not invite them back to the old house,' he says, eyebrows raised and something resembling a smirk on his face. 'Tease out the ones that might confess, and finish them off, one by one. Surely you can see we have to wonder if you might be the Leveller, trying to save your own skin?'

All the hope I had in Jorge has disappeared. He's clutching at straws, and for reasons I can't fathom, he's trying to indict me. 'We'll see, won't we? This time tomorrow, I will have confessed. We will have confessed. It will all be over.' I get to my feet, casting my gaze around those assembled, desperate to shine some kind of light in the all-consuming darkness. 'I love these people. They are family. We *have* to confess? We do it for our victims… and now that includes Fatima too. Let me tell you this,' I say, leaning in. 'Whoever it is among you, playing at being the Leveller, it's time to stop. It's time to stop before anyone else gets killed, because that's the way this thing is headed, and I don't think anyone here is ready to die.'

'You were right, Tomasz,' Jorge responds, thoughtfully placing a fingertip to his chin. 'This man is self-centred. He doesn't have any close family like the rest of us, and he has no one else to consider but himself. His outlook is completely different to anyone else's here. He's not taken that into account at all.'

'Wrong!' I state, my patience with this stranger all but gone. 'I have my wife. I have Orla.'

'Hmmm… that woman you haven't bothered with for six years? That woman you abandoned in her darkest hour? That woman that *fell* from the Great Orme? Yes, I can see you must truly love her.'

A smirk appears on his face, and I'm ready to punch his lights out. 'You know nothing of us, and it would be dangerous to assume you do,' I warn him.

'Is that a threat? Should I be concerned? Are you going to get someone to do your dirty work? Should I be concerned for my life?'

It's all I can do not to race around the table and shake him. He is purposely antagonising me and making the situation even worse than it already is. I wonder if it's possible he's the Leveller.

Harrison, who has been prowling around the table throughout the exchange, stops behind Costas, who is still seated. He places a hand on Costas' shoulder. 'Costas, man. What the fucking hell is going on? You brought a gun here. You killed Fatima. You found the photo of Orla. And you disappeared for some *me time*. It's not a great look if I'm honest. You'd better not be the *Leveller*?'

Costas twists his neck to gaze at the supersized killer. 'Of course I'm not. This is… all so terrible. I'm struggling to cope to be absolutely honest. Forgive me.'

Harrison squeezes Costas' shoulder. 'We can all do without this kind of stress. We shouldn't even be here,' he says, casting an accusing glance at me.

Costas ruffles his thick brown hair. 'I needed a little solitude and prayer. I went to church.'

'Which one?' I ask, ready to call him out him if he says Christ Church.

'Gloddaeth United Church, for what it's worth. I needed time alone with God.'

So, assuming he's not lying, Rose was right, we just got the wrong church is all. Although, the *Leveller* was on the same route as us. Rose catches me looking at her.

'May I say something?' she asks.

Poor Rose, I think. She's too old for this kind of crap. It'll finish her off.

She places her walking stick flat on the table top with a click, and stands. 'As awful as all of this is, based on what I've heard and indeed my own bitter experiences, in my humble opinion, I'd recommend you do not confess.'

I groan within.

She pauses, chin held high, observing us all with calm conviction. 'As weird as all of this is, and I do feel truly conflicted, but…' She clears her throat, raising her hand to her mouth before continuing. 'I sort of get it. I think we need to move on, what's done is done. We did what felt right at the time. And now, well yesterday's gone. It doesn't exist. Only now, and all being well, the future, are all that exist. Take care of the ones that are left, the ones you love, while you can.'

'What's the "we" all about, Rose?' I ask, both bemused and frustrated. She shouldn't be here.

Her eyes well up, and behind the lens of her glasses a single tear trickles down her lined face. 'I know what it's like to be pushed to violence… to exact revenge.' She angles her head, her face held in a grimace of irrefutable pain. 'I killed a man.' She turns her gaze on Costas. 'I killed a Vicar.'

The atmosphere in the room already taught, tightens further.

'Why, Rose?' Jessie asks, and I'm not sure I want to hear the answer.

Rose removes her glasses and folds them neatly, face up on the table. Her gaze turns to the corner of the room, but she's not looking at anything. She's time-travelled, she's seeing and feeling whatever happened at some point in the past. She opens her mouth to speak, but it seems the words are stuck. Finally, she manages to force them out. 'He raped me. The Vicar. He raped me. I was only seventeen.' She covers her mouth with her hand, but too late, the words have been released.

Harrison withdraws his hand from Costas's shoulder. Our young Vicar sits up straight, hands pressed together against his lips as if in prayer, eyes locked on Rose.

Show me how you
do that trick

Chapter Twenty

A commotion ensues around Rose as people leave their seats to fuss over her. Jessie appears behind me, hands rubbing the tops of my shoulders, pulling at the fine cotton of my pink shirt. The dig of her fingers deepens harder into my flesh, working into the base of my neck, the top of my spine, her sharp fingernails scrape across my skin with each push and pull. Feeling like I'm caught in an electric beam and tingling throughout, I exhale long and slow.

'I have a family now,' she says, her voice soft, warm and soothing on my neck. 'I love them. And I must protect them. Just as you must protect Orla. Zac, you have to find her!'

She manoeuvres beside me, so we can see one another, and gently cupping my chin in her hand, she squeezes hard. 'Like, right away!'

I raise my hand and grab hers, our gazes locked together, a lifetime of knowing between us. She is right. I can't fail Orla again. If there's a chance she's alive, I must find her. 'But where?'

'Jesus Christ, are you a police officer or not? How about where you left her? How about where she is on this fucking picture?' She holds up the piece of paper with Orla staring up from base of the cliffs. 'The Great Orme, idiot! And now!'

It's a cruel winter night, and I'm grateful Harrison and Jessie insist on coming with me.

'But what about the Leveller?' Costas asks the room. 'And what about my gun? We don't know who has it?'

'Best stay alert,' I respond.

'And Fatima?' Sian asks.

We've left the others to search the house for signs of both the

The Great Orme

Leveller and Fatima. The Great Orme is an unforgiving beast at any time, steep and slippery, dotted with rocky outcrops, but on a dark and wet freezing night in late-January it's at its worst. Having spent our formative years exploring every nook and cranny of the Orme, the other two know their way just as well as me. In many ways the land is ours, and we also belong to the land. In some ways I feel it's trying to take back what was taken – us.

We decide to take the most direct route; steep, hard work. The wind's icy claws slash and stab at us, warning us away. I feel as if for all the world, the slow breathing Great Orme will rise up with us on its back and toss us into the sea.

The summit in sight, I glance up and I'm sure I see a fleeting movement, a flicker of a shadow between interspersed ribbons of melted snow. It could be anything… or anyone. I tap Jessie on the arm. 'Up there,' I say, pointing the torch we've brought with us. Jessie and Harrison scan the solid dark edge of the land against the nebulous charcoal sky. We wait but nothing shows. I drift the torchlight from side to side but there doesn't seem to be any signs of life. I envisage Orla staggering around the top of the Great Orme, bloodied and bashed, the shadows calling her one way and then another, dooming to tread the rocky expanse forever without escape. I try to calm myself; I know not to get carried away, at night everything takes on a more sinister significance, and anything seems possible.

We continue our ascent, and with every step, an irrefutable sensation penetrates my bones, something like a hum, a power that bleeds from within the ancient ground. I know what it is. I've always known. I always thought it was the elation of the elevation, the space, the perspective, the Great Orme holding me high above it all, sharing a glimpse of its enduring power, one that has existed for millions of years and one that will exist for millions after we are all gone. One thing is for certain, we are merely momentary observers of a far greater power, one that we'll never really know or understand.

Invigorated by the surreal strength pulsing through me, I pull my coat zip up against my chin and press onward and upward, crouching and using feet and hands to ascend, the effort palpable, each step demanding more effort and determination. I have to see for myself. I have to know if the Leveller's photo is a picture of trickery and if my wife's body remains laid on the rocks where I left her or if she's gone. There's been nothing in the news about a body being discovered.

Jessie slips on the sodden ground, slamming into the mud face first. Harrison grabs hold of her and lifts her up. I ask her is she's okay, but she rubs her face with her hands, unwittingly smearing the shiny wet mud across her cheeks and forehead. 'Tomorrow, I go home,' she says, 'to my family.' She's off, taking the lead, scrambling upward toward the heart of darkness.

The view begins to expand and the wind gains strength as the familiar landscape is transformed by the darkness into a dreamscape of silhouettes and shadows. Emerging from steep incline onto flatter ground, a gut-wrenching shriek tears through the stillness. It's Jessie. My heart hammers in my chest as I stagger and lift my head. A pair of malevolent, glowing eyes gleam at us from behind a jagged rock. With a nightmarish leap the spectral beast hurtles toward us, a spray of soil and snow thrown up in the air, more of the creatures following close behind. Jessie screams again, clutching hold of me and Harrison, burying herself into us. The hellish spectre of shaggy-faced creatures with massive curled horns rears up before us, electric blue eyes cut with horizontally elongated pupils staring back at us. I stab the torchlight at the beasts, and frightened, they change direction, bolting away. In the dark, three of the Great Orme's Kashmiri goats, disturbed from their slumber, twisted parodies of the gentle regal creatures I had grown to love.

I aim the torch light, bouncing around after assailants, my breath coming in huge heaves. Jessie, Harrison, and I, remain locked together, letting go of one another only when the goats have disappeared from view. Finally, still shaken, we share flustered, awkward smiles before moving on, the rain light but whipping us, our ascent over.

The surface of the Great Orme frosted with patches of snow, appears like a glacier. Lower and to our right, we see the bleak stone whiteness of little St. Tudno's Church, surrounding gravestones, weathered and ancient, jutting from the Great Orme as if its jagged teeth. The cold air hangs heavy with the scent of damp earth and sea salt. The Great Orme's unyielding strength permeates the marrow of my bones, its soul-troubled soil rising to caress and cling to me. I scrape and wipe at my face, my neck, my entire body, but it seems the soil is everywhere. It wraps around my throat, seeps into my mouth, bleeds into my lungs, and hardens my heart. As crazy as it sounds, I knew then as I had always known, the Great Orme was inside me.

'Come on, show us where Orla fell,' Jessie asks, rubbing her hands for warmth. I turn to Harrison and Jessie, their faces appearing grey and anxious, and I wonder if they feel the Great Orme's power as I do. I think it would be impossible not to. The Great Orme has shaped us, and it knows what we've done.

The three of us stand at the dizzy edge of the cliff, gazing down into the depths, where Orla would have lain. The sea laps at the rocks in swathes of froth and foam. I try to direct the torchlight over the rocks, but it barely touches, the light ineffective from such distance, all below a murky, shadowy seemingly empty space. I shout her name, but my voice is swallowed by the eternal sound of the waves breaking on the rocks. In the darkness the sound is a curious lullaby. I imagine myself stepping off the edge, the fall an enticing descent into oblivion, the purest of escapes. I wonder if Orla succumbed to the same lullaby. Part of me hopes so, because to imagine she had pre-planned her death, is too awful. My head snaps backwards, and I'm tugged away from the edge by Harrison's strong grip on my hood.

He lets go of me, his face and head shiny with a sweaty

sheen in the darkness. 'Sorry, Zac,' he says, visibly shaken. 'For a moment, I thought…'

He's unable to look me in the eye, the old nervousness returned. I wonder if he was about to push me rather than pull me back, a change of heart at the last second. I observe Jessie stood beside him, black curls poking out from the edges of her raised hood. These are two of my most beloved friends, to consider they might have it in them to kill me, terrifies me. I push away the thought.

'The cliff face is smooth,' Harrison points out. 'It kind of veers away from the top like a slide. It's possible Orla slithered down, and there's sand among those rocks at the bottom. Either Orla got rescued by the Leveller, or she got swept out to sea.'

I can't help but think her plight brings into stark relief the expression "between the devil and the deep blue sea."

'Zac.'

Jessie has to repeat my name again to get my attention. She hands me a transparent plastic A4 folder containing a single page. 'Look at this. It was tied with an elastic band just there.' She points at a nearby abandoned fence post.

I point the torch light at the folder. Scrawled on the page within, the following:

Orla is alive.
Just.
I have her.
Promise not to confess and I may let her live.
The Leveller.

I lower the folder to my side and stare at Harrison and Jessie. The relief I feel at knowing Orla is alive is more than tinged with an inner burn that the Leveller has her. *Is she safe? Where is she? What do I do? Will she survive?*

Harrison has the answer. 'It's over. Enough is enough. We

can't confess. For Orla's sake if no other.'

I nod, a hard lump in my throat. I must save Orla. And I will. A searing pain ripples through the pit of my stomach as if the Great Orme has stuffed its limey stone-cold tongue down my throat and twisted it in my gut.

Placated by my quiet acceptance, Harrison and Jessie lead me back down the Great Orme, their arms entwined with mine in our silent descent, and I can sense a feeling of solidarity toward me where previously there had been none. Their soft touch and relaxed faces say it all.

We descend deeper into the night's black embrace, and I have the feeling we are on the brink, at a point of no return, where the outcome is not mine to decide, and perhaps not theirs, it's down to the *Leveller*.

The old house, being a semi, mirrors the adjoining house: pointed arches over its windows, steeply pitched roof and jutting barge boards. The building appears to have grown organically from the ground in which its foundations are embedded. It protrudes like a snapped bone through the Great Orme's ripped skin; skeletal fragments.

Costas opens the door to us, spectacles in hand, eyes set to burst from their sockets and ringed with dark circles.

He throws a nervous glance over his shoulder. 'Helen's here,' he whispers. 'The policewoman. I think she's onto us.'

Harrison clears his throat preparing to say something but isn't quick enough.

'I told her you went to the pub,' Costas continues in hushed tones. 'It's all I could think of, but she insisted on coming in. She reckons she's discovered something you'll want to know.'

A plague of thoughts breaks out in my head. Perhaps they've found Orla, but alive or dead? Perhaps there's been another murder, the Leveller unable to stop killing. Or maybe Helen has simply worked out my connection to the murders. Maybe it's all over, any decision taken out of our hands.

'I'm sure it's all fine,' I say, not at all convinced. 'She's new to the area and keen to make friends.'

I step into the hall but Harrison grabs me by the arm, pulling me back. His voice is in my ear. 'Be careful. No funny business.'

'Maybe she's what we need,' I reply. 'Maybe we all need a little fresh focus?' I easily remove his hands from me. He bites his lip, uncertain.

Having removed our coats and hung them up to dry, we enter the lounge. Helen is in conversation with Rose, the two of them sat side by side on the sofa.

On noticing us, she touches Rose gently on the arm, pausing the conversation. 'How was the pub?' she asks immediately.

Helen's coat is draped over the back of the sofa, red bobble hat balanced on top of it. She's holding a full cup of coffee. She isn't going anywhere soon.

I won't lie. Not anymore. 'We haven't been to the pub.'

She lowers her cup and flicks a loose strand of blonde hair away from her face. 'Oh, Costas said… '

'We've been up the Great Orme.'

In the room, I feel the cord that connects us all, tighten.

'But it's so late, and the weather so awful. Why?'

Jessie appears, placing a glass in my hand. I thank her, and swirl the syrupy amber liquid around before taking a gulp, grateful for its tingling warmth. I let out a short, sharp sigh. 'Helen, my wife is missing. Orla is missing.'

Helen leans forward and places her cup on the table, her focus directed plainly at Sian, who's standing with Tomasz before the cracked mirror. 'Sian, you told me Orla had gone home?'

Sian responds quickly and quietly. 'Oh, I thought she had.'

Jorge moves between Tomasz and Sian, putting his arms around both of them. 'It's getting late. I'm sure there's a simple, plausible explanation. Orla may well *have* gone home for all we know.'

Helen gets up, her jaw clenched, thinking, calculating as she observes all in the room. I recognise a steel in her I had previously missed.

'Costas mentioned you've discovered something?' I ask, taking a sip of rum.

'Yes. The young boy,' she says, her face implacable. 'The one attacked at the funicular. It's incredible.'

'What is?' I say, my nerves raw.

'He's not dead. He's undergoing surgery as I speak. They think he's going to pull through.'

Silence seems to bloat the room. Helen keeps her head up, continuing to monitor me and everyone else for a reaction.

Tomasz raises his hands to his face, and clasping his chin, directs a question – or is it an accusation? – toward me. 'You told us his skull was smashed in?'

I nod.

Helen interjects. 'It was. It's a miracle. His bicycle helmet was found nearby, cracked all over. It seems the initial blows were dealt while he wore that. It was removed at some point, but we guess his attacker was disturbed before she could finish the job.'

'She?' Costas blurts, saying what has probably sprung in all our minds.

Helen's jaw clenches again, her only outward submission to her inner thoughts. 'Around the time of the attack,' she says, poker face unreadable. 'A witness saw a woman running in the opposite direction. Thought it odd because she wasn't in running gear. The only other thing the witness recalled was the woman had heavy, black, made-up eyes.'

I want the sky to fall in and the sea to rise and wash everything away, forever. I lock my legs stiff, to prevent the sickening that is swelling within from flooring me. All eyes are on me, but all I can see is her face. Her eyes. Orla's eyes. Beetle eyes.

Death of a vicar

Chapter Twenty-One

My heart pulses fast and hard. I try to think to avoid drowning in overwhelm. The boy was attacked yesterday between eleven and eleven-thirty a.m. First contact from the Leveller was the automated message I got this morning. Costas was with me. All other messages from the *Leveller* had come today. Orla had arrived at the old house yesterday, early afternoon. By taxi, she had said. Direct from the station, she had said.

'It's impossible,' I say, suddenly aware everyone is waiting on my response.

Helen picks up her cup. 'What's impossible, Zac?'

She knows. She met Orla. Nobody forgets Orla.

'Where is she, Zac? Where is Orla?' she asks.

A pain streaks through my brain. I press my fingertips against my forehead as if I can claw it away. A short sharp bang resounds and the mirror hanging on the wall shatters, its silver shards scattering over the mantelpiece and the hearth below. Smokey yelps and scampers, crashing into my feet, where he presses, whimpering.

Tomasz is standing behind the sofa, one trembling arm held out and pointed at the mirror, in his hand *the* gun, Costas's gun.

'Tomasz,' I beg, frozen to the spot. 'Put it down.'

'Where do we go from here?' he asks, before pointing the gun at his temple. 'Perhaps there's only one way out.'

Agile of thought and moving with practiced stealth, Rose, walking stick in hand, appears alongside Tomasz. He's some place in his head and either not aware of her or doesn't see her as a threat. She reaches up and takes the gun from him like she's taking an empty tea cup from his hand. 'The football season isn't over yet, Tomasz,' she says, a kindly smile on her face. 'Your team depends on you for goals.'

The rest of us breathe a collective sigh of relief. But it's short-lived. She doesn't lower the weapon, instead she turns and points it at us, crooked finger curled around the trigger, arm steady, appearing for all the world as if she's held one before.

'What good is it to anyone, you lot rotting in a prison cell?' she asks, translucent grey-blue eyes unblinking through her green-framed spectacles. 'Zac, these people aren't like you or me. They don't live with the ghosts of the Great Orme as we do. They have *real* lives in the *real* world. They have people who care about them. People who depend on them.'

I had never before considered my lifetime neighbour and I shared similarities – our lonely lives, our dependency on the Great Orme, perhaps even the ghosts we live with. I look at her anew, the woman with fashionable green spectacles, sensible pale-blue cardigan, smart silk paisley neck scarf, walking stick in one hand, gun in the other – deserving of more respect.

'Let me tell you,' she says, her eyes glistening, even more watery than usual. 'It doesn't matter now. At this time in my life it doesn't make any difference.' She lowers the gun, staring at it like it's burning a hole in her hand. Rasing her head, she seems to be seeing through us, to another world, another time.

'I shot him. I shot the Vicar. Dead.'

Her gun bearing hand trembles, and I'm concerned because her finger is still clasped to the trigger. 'Rose,' I say, but she's still in the other place.

'He birthed my baby. In church. Same place he raped me – behind the altar. He put the gun in my hands, held them, squeezed my hands, pressed my finger on the trigger. He made me kill my new born baby boy.'

She turns her head away sharply, as if to avoid the scene playing out in her mind. But she can't avoid it. Just as I can't avoid the memories of the murders I've instigated. There are some memories whose permanence is as physical as the bone and blood that moves us.

The tears come. Silently at first. The dam that held them back for God knows how long, finally decimated. She's snotty and gasping for air. 'I killed my baby boy,' she says, her voice a pitch higher and her face contorted with agony.

'No,' Jessie says, reaching out an arm that doesn't touch. 'You didn't do that. He did it. The Vicar did it.'

'He put my boy in a bin bag,' she continues through stifled sobs. 'Put him in with the rubbish. He told me he had done it before, to others. He said he'd do it again. "God's will" he said.'

Rose regards the gun in her hand, her fingers twitching on the handle and the trigger. 'He said if I told anyone, God would punish me. Punish me with the same gun that killed my boy.' She licks her lips where the tears and snot are collecting. 'I watched where he hid the gun. He kept it in the church. A secret door embedded in a tomb. First thing the following morning I went back. He had opened up to prep for Sunday service. He was alone. I smiled at him. Told him I understood. Then, when his back was turned, laying out Bibles at the front for a reading, I took the gun. I stood behind him. When he turned, I told him he was going to hell.' She emits a high-pitched gasp. 'Then I shot him.'

It's as if we are all turned to stone by Rose's confession. No one moves or hardly breathes.

'I wiped the gun free of my fingerprints and put it in his hands,' she continues. 'I walked up the aisle, turned around and walked back to him. I screamed. I screamed like it was the end of the world. People came… I don't remember much else.'

She blinks suddenly as if back in the room; her gaze drifting from one person to the next, tears stemmed. 'He deserved it. I dare any of you to tell me he didn't.'

Stunned, no one utters a word. Jessie embraces the old lady, two women together, consumed by grief.

'I've never told anyone,' she says, her face peering beyond Jessie's shoulder, 'not even my husband.'

'What happened to your husband?' I ask, finally finding my voice. 'All I remember is he disappeared when we were young. I remember the police at your house. My mum back and forth checking on you.'

'He left me without a word,' she says. 'Discovered soon after, living with a woman in Bangor. He didn't even have the decency to tell me. She kicked him out after a couple of months though. Anyhow, he got his comeuppance. He came back to Llandudno, not to me I might add, no I wouldn't take him back…' She hesitates, lifting her spectacles to wipe reddened eyes. 'He moved into a house nearby, not so far from the school, the one you attended.'

My stomach washes with a hot acid glaze, one that creeps up towards my chest. I can feel something awful rising.

'Even now, I can hardly believe it,' continues Rose. 'My husband, he was murdered. In his own home.'

The sickly substance gushes up my throat and nearly spills out of my mouth. I swallow it back. 'Murdered?' I ask, wiping my lips.

'Stabbed to death. Someone broke in. Heddwyn must have disturbed them, but he was so frail, he wasn't at all well. The burglar even killed his dog, a gorgeous golden lab called Biscuits.'

I was lost and then I was found, and it's still the same

Chapter Twenty-Two

I pick out the faces of my old friends - Tomasz, Sian, Harrison, Jessie and Costas. They stare back at me, expressions bleak and ghostly in the reflected light of the peacock patterned lampshades. I feel my pupils expand like a drop of ink in water. I love them all. No matter what has happened or what may happen, they feel like a part of my physical body, although increasingly it feels like those parts are being sawed off, a throb at each serrated piece of flesh. Ever reliable, the grandfather clock in the corner of the room chimes, eleven o'clock. It will all be over soon.

'Rose,' I say, hands clasped under my chin, eyes cast downward. 'It was us. We killed him. He killed Biscuits, so we killed him.'

Rose jolts her head to one side, mouth gaping. 'You... you killed my Heddwyn?'

I nod. 'We all did,' adding, 'we didn't know he was your husband.'

She clings on to Jessie as if she's just been shot and is struggling to stay standing.

'You too, Tomasz?' I fear she may collapse any moment. 'You killed my husband?'

The superstar footballer nods and averts his gaze.

'Me, Tomasz, Harrison, Costas, Jessie, Sian and Orla,' I say. 'We were fourteen years old. We loved Biscuits. On our way to school we would stop by the old man's... Heddwyn's garden. Biscuits would always be waiting for us, for the treats we brought. One morning, we saw your husband stood outside his front door, shovel in hand, and Biscuits' severed head on the floor before him. The rage we felt at the injustice was all-consuming. We decided we couldn't let him get away with it. We felt we had to take revenge, the ultimate revenge. So, we killed him.'

Ever full of surprises, Rose wipes her eyes, straightens her glasses, then, detaching from Jessie she pulls her pale blue cardigan neatly so the hem circles her waist. 'You were only children. And all of you killed Heddwyn?'

'No.'

Harrison's voice is strong and clear for once. 'It was Zac. It was always him.' He jabs a finger toward me, the action causing a rippling wave of muscles beneath his skin-tight t-shirt. 'He decided *we* should kill him. We did as he commanded. Let's be clear, none of this would have happened if it wasn't for him. None of it! All of these deaths, all of them are because of him.'

I know he's right but I can help fire back at him. 'Why did you never say "no"? Why did none of you refuse?'

'For God's sake, Zac,' Jessie intervenes, black curls bouncing about her head with the force of her words. 'We looked up to you. You were our leader. You had the courage of your convictions. You did what you said you were going to do, always. You were the coolest kid in town. We would have done anything for you. Look at you, you're a cop now. You followed through. You always had that way about you, a core of steel. People didn't mess with you. We didn't either.'

Harrison runs a hand back and forth over his smooth scalp. 'People were afraid of you, Zac… We were afraid of you.'

'You see,' Jessie says, running her hands through her curls, 'we are… *were*… in awe of you. You were charismatic, intuitive, you thrived on chaos… on crisis. We never knew if you were going to be kind-hearted or create a dangerous situation. And we,' she pauses, thrusting a pointed finger in the direction of each of our old friends, 'we were susceptible, vulnerable, each of us looking for someone to rescue us from something.' She turns back to me, wide brown eyes, infinitely sad. 'We were devoted to you.'

I breathe out hard. 'You make it sound like a cult.'

'You took us in. You cared for us. You controlled us. Perhaps it was a cult.' She rolls up a sleeve. She jabs her finger into her tattooed skin and circles it around the black-inked sea monster. 'You even branded us!'

I screw up my face. I can't believe what I'm hearing, but I know, like I must have always known, she's right. This is how it happens. This is how people do the unimaginable. We have blinkers in our brains. We do not see the whole picture; we don't even know there is more of the picture to see, or worse – we don't want to see the whole picture.

I see it now though, and that counts for something. I'm absolutely convinced of what we must do. 'I'm sorry. I'm so, so sorry for everything. I was wrong. So badly wrong, I just couldn't see it, but now I can. Too late. But we can't carry on... That way leads, well it leads to where we are now. We have to confess.'

We seem to hang, suspended in a strange spell for a moment, where no one moves or speaks. In my mind, I repeat to myself it can't get any worse. Then I remember, Helen has been sat quietly listening to every word.

I gesture with an outstretched hand towards Helen, sat implacably still on the sofa throughout. 'It seems we've just confessed.'

Without saying a word, the policewoman gets up and takes Rose to a seat on the sofa where they both sit. Helen deftly takes the gun from the elderly woman. She points it at me.

'I'll be honest... I'm a little scared right now,' she says, standing up again. She takes her time, maintaining eyes and gun on me, head held high. 'The law exists for a reason,' she says, her gaze sweeping around the room, scrutinising the others.

'It exists to protect the majority, to protect society. To keep us safe, so we don't have to protect ourselves through our own actions.' Her gaze returns to mine. 'To protect us from the likes of you.'

Helen exudes a steady confidence, a steel, but I'm unsure how deep it runs, whether it's only part of her training.

'Perhaps you should leave,' I suggest. 'For your sake more

than any other.'

'No chance,' she replies, quick as a flash. 'People are dying on our doorstep, Zac. I can't walk away. Not when I know it's to do with you.' She glances around at the others. 'All of you.'

Jessie stifles a cry, and Harrison beams like a proud parent. I can't help but wonder at their reactions, and I wonder too, what we have become, just how numb we were and what monsters we are.

'Zac,' Helen says firmly. 'You want to confess, so confess. Tell me what you have done. I want to hear all of it. I'm part of this story now. And if anyone moves to stop him,' she says, brandishing the gun at everyone, 'I'll shoot.'

To the astonishment of all looking on, I tell her. It's the truth after all, and I won't deny anyone the truth any longer. I tell her about the old man again, about Jessie's drug abuser boyfriend, Harrison's brother, how we drowned Ollie. I tell her about Tomasz's sexual abuser, and how we strangled him to the point of a heart attack. I tell her about Choreji, the little girl Orla drunkenly crashed into and killed. I describe as kids, how we had murdered the old man – Rose's husband, but it's only upon my recounting of how Harrison smashed the unfortunate little boy's head in with a lump of concrete kerb, that I detect a flicker of something in her eyes, a narrowing perhaps. Even so, Helen's grip on the gun remains steady.

Costas groans and flops, doubled over, hands on knees, as I describe how we hesitated and let Chloe, the sick child die in hospital. I finish with the fire, the fire that Sian started, the fire that killed Kenzo along with the other human traffickers.

For each death, I describe the context, our rationale, as if it might help wash the stains away, but it doesn't. They just soak deeper. All the while, Helen stands directly beneath the room's central ceiling lamp, the top of her blonde hair lit like a halo, and face cast in shade. The strange angel swallows and licks her lips, nodding as if understanding as I describe the murders, waiting until I come to a stop.

'All of which leads us to this weekend, to now,' she says before recounting the deaths that have occurred, so present and so near: The old man at Clonmel Street, stabbed, murdered in exactly the same manner as that in which we killed Rose's husband. The tin of biscuits left on his dead body, an obvious reference to our murder. Harrison bows his head as she once again describes the vicious attack on the boy at the funicular, the kid still fighting for his life in hospital. Turning back to me, she relates the death of my father's murderer, Yestyn, his apparent jump from the pier into the sea, the message in the bottle tied to his washed-up body – *For the sakes of the old house and all those in it, I deserved to die.*

I give her an account of the warnings received from the Leveller. I tell her about Orla, how she jumped from the cliff, and my bewilderment in discovering her gone, that she *may* still be alive. How I must find her before it's too late. The atmosphere in the room feels ugly, like a raw and open bloody wound infected with a sickening combination of filth and flies.

'Really! Do we forget so easily? So soon?' All eyes turn to Sian.

'My wife!' Sian's words are spat and cut with pain. 'My wife – Fatima, was shot and killed here in this room only a few hours ago – by him!' Without looking at Costas, she points an outstretched arm toward him.

Helen nods as if she's been told the weather forecast is mild and breezy. 'So, where is she?'

With a metal belying her small stature, Sian describes the *accident*, and how we found her body disappeared from my mother's room.

I notice a sharp rise and fall in Helen's chest and a brief machine-gun blink, another sliver of evidence of emotion. She licks her lips again. 'Show me.'

Sian takes her upstairs while the rest of us wait in a swamp of silence, troubled in our own thoughts.

A scream. Sian.

The Great Orme

Me, Harrison and Tomasz react as if struck by hot irons, crashing into one another as we charge out of the room and up the stairs, launching ourselves through the doorway into the cocoon of purple flowered wallpapered walls that is my mother's bedroom, where we stop dead behind Helen.

'Well, either you are lying or someone is trying to make a point, albeit slightly unorthodox,' Helen says, waving her hand at that which all of our unbelieving eyes are fixed on. Sian is crouched over the bed, and over Fatima's body. I move to step forward but Helen thrusts out an arm, preventing me getting closer. 'You should know better,' she says curtly. 'Give her space.'

'But how?' Harrison's voice comes quietly. 'It's impossible.'

I cannot believe what I am seeing. Fatima's body had disappeared and now it's returned.

Tomasz grabs me by the shoulder. 'It's the Leveller. He's here. He's in the house.'

Propelled into action, we look for evidence of where and how the body disappeared and reappeared. Tomasz calls out, pointing to a meagre trail of dried blood spots that lead to the doorway. We examine the swirling blue patterned carpeted hallway for more blood but it peters out to nothing, just a few steps outside, nothing to suggest where the body has been. I can't wait for forensics to show up, but in their absence, I rely on the old-fashioned method of using my eyes to look for clues. On hands and knees, I search underneath the bed; the carpet caked in thick dust, no blood, but there is a fresh piece of white A4 paper. I slide it out. An uppercase scrawl is written on it – in red ink:

Zac,
Stop now!
Do not confess!
*   …or you are next to die!*
With love,
The Leveller

Amid organised panic, we notify the others of our discovery and a scattered search of the house ensues. No corner is left undisturbed but, as ever, other than ourselves, we find no one and nothing out of the ordinary.

Back in the lounge, the mood is fraught.

'It's one of us,' Sian suggests, patrolling the room like a caged jaguar, and a look on her face twice as mean. 'One of us is the Leveller. There's no other explanation,' she says. 'Fatima's body was moved, hidden and returned. We are the only people in the house.'

'Perhaps you are the Leveller?' suggests Tomasz, but not entirely meaning it.

Sian halts mid-step, turning slowly to face him. She opens her mouth to reply but thinks better of it, and instead sighs deeply, shoulders slumped. Jessie is quick to defend her.

'Come on, Tomasz. Are you serious? That's just evil. The Leveller is trying to manipulate us, using *her* dead wife!'

Tomasz bows his head.

'Perhaps it's you?' Harrison asks Jessie.

'You think so?'

'You did drown the man you loved.'

Jessie stalks toward him, eyes enlarged and face set hard. 'Perhaps I should tell the rest of them about you?'

Harrison laughs, but I sense it's hollow, filled with uncertainty. 'You're a killer, Jessie, a murderer, just like the rest of us. Get over it.'

Jessie stops in front of him, body tensed, feet easing a few inches further apart. I half expect her to land a blow on him.

'You,' she says, one hand thrust up and pulling at the curls in her hair, 'went to Cardiff, before you came here.' With her other hand she jabs a finger into Harrison's muscular chest. 'You went to my home in Llanishen. I think you intended to kill me.'

Tomasz raises his hands to his face and groans.

I straighten my spine. 'Harrison?'

The Great Orme

The snide white smile is gone from his face, and he suddenly looks drawn and older, his pumped body softer.

'I couldn't kill you, Jessie,' he says, as she drops her hand. 'I thought I might, but I couldn't… even though you killed my brother. I still love you. We all do.' He rubs his hand back and forth over his smooth scalp, as he does when he's anxious. 'I had to see you. I had to know I couldn't kill you. That's all.'

'You scared my family, Harrison,' Jessie accuses. 'Ade called me – he saw you looking through the window – he described you. My husband isn't stupid, he's a lawyer. He'll be onto us. I have to get back to him, to calm him. You scared him. He mustn't find out.'

'Yeah, well, perhaps he isn't so smart,' he says, biting his lip. 'I saw him kissing another woman in your home.'

'Oh, Harrison please don't. You're a liar!'

I catch Jessie's wrist just before it flies.

'I swear it, Jessie,' Harrison says. 'No wonder he's scared.'

'It's not possible,' she says, but her wrist becomes limp and her voice trails off as if she knows Harrison is telling the truth.

Three steady knocks at the front door make everyone flinch, all looking with eyes wide from one person to the next as people do at the sound of an old-fashioned landline telephone ringing.

'Who the hell can that be at this time of night?' says Harrison, searching us all for an answer.

Always more agile than I would expect, Rose is up on her feet and already on the move, waving Harrison to one side with her stick as she passes. A dumbfounded expression on his face he duly obliges. 'You sit yourself down. I'll get it,' she says. 'Hopefully it's the Leveller… and about fucking time as well.'

I pray, I mean really pray, it's Orla.

You brood of vipers;
how will you escape the
sentence of hell?

Chapter Twenty-Three

Rose ushers a tall young woman, perhaps a little younger than me, into the room. Her hair is long and dyed red, fire-engine red. Whoever she is, I expect her to be a handful.

'Holy God!' Costas exclaims, raising both hands to his mouth before striding toward her. They embrace, she with her chin held up and turned away from him, eyeballing us. He's perspiring, beads of sweat on his forehead caught by the light of the lamps. They release and he pivots to address us. 'Everyone, my wife, Jules.'

Jules looks anything other than a Vicar's wife, glossy red lipstick, low-cut shimmering-orange top, plus oodles of swagger.

I find it difficult to hide my disappointment. I had hoped it would be Orla, somehow magically revived and well. As for each of the others, I don't know, perhaps they each had their own secret hope. In any case, I'm quick to act, walking up to Jules and introducing myself before proposing she leaves immediately, explaining there are plenty of hotels and guest houses where she can reside until we have settled our business.

'I'll do nothing of the sort,' she says, swiftly dismissing my suggestion and removing an expensive-looking tan-coloured coat. 'I've been worried about you, Costas. Something about you before you left, the look on your face. Something's wrong, isn't it? I had to come. Whatever it is, I can help. You know I can.'

The magic is gone. I used to be able to orchestrate events and people as I wanted. It used to be so natural I didn't even have to think. Now, I find it such hard work, both physically and mentally draining, and always with diminishing reward.

The Great Orme

'Right,' says Jules, forcefully clutching hold of her husband's hand and addressing all gathered together in the lounge. 'Who's going to tell me what's going on?'

I see creases and lines in Costas' face that are new, the man seems more haunted than most, his countenance increasingly filled with darkness and doubt. The man is suffering.

'Tell her,' I say to no one in particular. 'You might as well tell her everything. She'll learn soon enough, anyway.'

The tension in the room is unbearable, the energy projected by each person, a combination of distrust, desperation and fear. Shadows dance on the walls casting eerie silhouettes against the worn teal-coloured wall paper, every spoken secret clinging to the walls, the living and the dead bound together by them. I have to remove myself. I mutter an excuse and go to the study where I sit at my desk. The grandfather clock's dull chimes bleed through the walls of the old house. Midnight. It is officially Sunday. This is the day we confess. I can only pray no other lives are taken before we do so. And perhaps a life can be saved, Orla's.

The words flow easily, and again I wish I had started writing earlier in life. It's the perfect way to organise one's thoughts, it's a way through. The urge to document, to leave our mark, the most basic human instinct. Occasionally I look up from writing and gaze out at the world beyond my window. It seems so far away, the lives of others so separate, so disengaged from my own that we might as well be living on different planets. Everything we do has consequences. I wish I'd been like most other people, and considered those consequences before acting. Those people are the world's real heroes; those who see everything in the round instead of cruel black and white.

The book is up to date. I know the others hate me for what I have asked of them. Prison will provide me all the time I need to contemplate our deeds, but first I must identify and stop the Leveller. The others can't be persuaded until I do.

An idea forms, but I don't like it. It will mean subduing

honesty and playing with their emotions. It's likely they may hate me even more for it. I'll tell them all I've changed my mind. That we won't confess. I will need to observe their reactions, perhaps one of them will break cover and reveal themselves as the Leveller, and Orla will be released.

I reach for the glass of rum in front of me. Did I bring it with me or is it one I left before? I don't know; it doesn't matter. The only thing that does matter to me is that we confess, for the sake of our victims, their families, and our own souls.

Smokey and I leave the study and find the door to the lounge is shut. We wait outside. There's no need for them to shut the door, no need at all, unless… unless they are conspiring against me.

Hot dread pulses through my veins. Perhaps they are all in on this, all of them set against me, none of them are ready to confess, only interested in saving themselves. Smokey grumbles, he's wondering why I'm delaying. I decide my idea may be timed to perfection. I open the door and enter the lounge.

The room falls silent at my appearance. They are stood about in twos and threes, all with drinks in hand, half-empty bottles of wine on the mantelpiece and the coffee table. Smokey trundles up to Harrison and lays at his feet.

Helen is standing with him, the backs of their heads reflected in the few remaining reflective mirror shards behind them, making it appear as if their skulls are exploded. They are close enough that their wine glasses are nearly touching, too close. Does Helen blush? I can't be sure, but on making eye contact with me, she leans away from him. In the corner next to the bookcase, Sian. Her dead wife is upstairs, perhaps. Who knows? Such is the situation; nothing is as it seems. Sian's head is lowered, her gaze some place else. Have I lost the old Sian? Was she already lost? Either way, I ache to have her back. Jessie is stood next to her, and watching me watching her, she purses her lips. I remember the kiss of betrayal we once shared, one I'll never forgive myself for. I love Orla. I always loved Orla.

The Great Orme

My capacity for destroying everything and everyone I love is remarkable.

Jorge, Tomasz and Rose are stood before the bay window, drawn curtains patterned with pictures of blue owls, their white eyes round and wide. They peer at me, either sympathy or derision cast thick on their faces stained a dirty yellow by the lamp-light. Stood between coffee table and sofa, Costas and my new guest, his wife, Jules. They are last to turn and face me. Their faces appear strained, Costas with hands thrust in his pockets and Jules with clenched fists held at her sides.

I realise I'm holding the glass with what's left of the rum. I smile, a crocodile smile, and empty the glass in one swift gulp. 'I've made a decision,' I say, licking my lips. 'One I think you'll approve of.'

Eyes dart from side to side, checking one another for reactions, uncertain. Good. I've caught them off guard.

I make them wait, walking to the coffee table and placing my empty glass on it. 'Right. Here's the thing,' I say, straightening, taking a deep breath. 'I've changed my mind. We aren't going to confess.'

Everyone reacts so differently, nine different minds, nine different worlds. I struggle to capture their reactions, to gauge their thoughts.

'Halle-fucking-lujah!' Harrison exclaims, briefly exchanging a glance with Helen before striding toward me, arm outstretched in readiness for a shake of hands.

'Oh my God,' blurts Jessie covering her mouth and reaching out a hand for the bookcase to steady herself.

As if I've pulled a pin from him, Costas falls to his haunches, head down and rocking. Jules hauls him up and kisses him passionately on the lips. The passion isn't returned, he's too overwhelmed.

Stood between Tomasz and Jorge, Rose takes Tomasz's hand in hers and squeezes. I see him gaze down at her and smile as Harrison clasps my hand and embraces me. I hear cries of relief. Jessie and Sian flop onto the sofa and hang onto one another, heads locked together, crying.

Harrison's voice warms my ear. 'What took you so long?'

He lets go of me and proceeds to congratulate everyone in the room. I step back and watch. A bottle of bubbly appears, the cork is popped, glasses are handed out. Even Sian lets her glass get filled.

My crocodile smile crashes, the scene before me too ugly, everyone so relieved at getting away with murder. A boy is in hospital fighting for his life, perhaps Orla is too for all I know. They are the lucky ones. Someone here has murdered this very weekend, our old school headmaster in Clonmel Street, my father's accidental killer - killed, and Costas killed Sian's wife, Fatima, her dead body still here in this old house. People's lives are ending so others think they might save their own in some warped way, but this isn't warfare, we aren't protecting our land from a brutal invader, this is mass murder.

My eyes are drawn to the only person not to move, Jorge. He's still stood at the bay window, countenance unchanged, Rose and Tomasz having drifted away. He notices me looking at him and returns my gaze, unyielding, giving nothing away. Running his fingers through his glossy brown hair, he raises his glass at me, and winks. He knows I'm deceiving them.

I'll see it through, even if for a moment – I have to give this idea a chance. I need to find out who the Leveller is.

'Who is it?' I ask, unable to think of anything more subtle. 'Who is the Leveller?'

The room falls silent.

I wait. This poker game needs to play out.

It's Helen who breaks cover, striding confidently toward me. 'Zac, I'm going to report you,' she says, in the practiced assertive manner that all cops are trained in. 'All of you.'

She stops at the sofa, her green eyes seem cold and unforgiving, and I'm suddenly wary of her.

'Aren't you scared?' I ask.

She scrunches her face, puzzled.

The Great Orme

'You should be,' I say. 'I am.'

'Why?'

'We are surrounded by murderers.'

She smiles, or is it a smirk? I'm not sure.

'What about the Leveller?' I ask her. 'No one is owning up, and whoever it is, is here with us right now. They'll carry on killing. Are you good with that?'

Helen picks up her hat and coat from the sofa. 'This is police business.'

Her voice sounds different and something in the way she hesitates to leave causes me to doubt her. She's stayed too long. She's testing me. She knows I'm not sincere. She knows I will confess. I think she's trying to draw me out.

I could let it play out. I could see how far she will go. See if she leaves. See if she does report us. But I know – I know even if she did try to leave, the Leveller won't let her. She'll get hurt. I can't let that happen.

She glances at the doorway, eyes widening, pupils shrinking.

Jorge pushes the door shut with a click. He turns to face us – the gun in his hand. All eyes turn on him.

'She's lying,' Jorge points the gun at Helen. 'And he's lying,' he says, pointing it at me.

'Jorge, come on? What's this all about?' Tomasz asks, pulling the zip of his training top to his chin.

'You are out of your mind, Zac,' Jorge says, staring directly at me, a thin smile on his face. 'You and your ghosts… this whole Great Orme drama… you have no intention of keeping our secret. Tell them, Zac. Tell them I'm right.'

Relatively quiet until now, I realise Jorge has been assessing the situation, navigating a way through.

'What about Hel…' I begin but my words are cut short by an explosion. He's fired the gun.

Screams stab the air as Helen staggers backwards, colliding with the solid oak coffee table, glasses and cups on it scattering and smashing as her body slams on to the surface and rolls off onto the carpet.

Harrison rushes to Helen's aid. There's blood on her thigh.

'The Leveller,' Jorge states, his voice still firm, lamplights gleaming in his dark eyes, 'whoever that may be – is right. We won't be confessing. Why? I'll tell you. Because there's nothing to be gained by it. We only have everything to lose. Everything.'

'He's missed her, thank God,' Harrison gasps.

'Of course I missed,' Jorge responds.

'My leg – it hurts,' Helen says through a pained grimace.

'You've cut yourself, broken glass,' Harrison assures her. 'You'll be okay.'

'You could have killed her!' I shout at Jorge, my voice guttural. Nobody moves, shocked by my sudden ferocity, as am I. It's as if the moment is stopped in time and we are all nothing more than insects trapped in amber.

I let myself breathe. It takes a great effort, but I won't lose control – not now.

I kneel beside Harrison, who has his thumb and finger pressed either side of a wide shard of curved glass sticking out of Helen's thigh. I take hold of her hand. She turns her face away and presses it into the plush burgundy carpet. A small circle of blood has already permeated her jeans.

She screams. Harrison holds up the blood smeared chunk of jagged glass he's retrieved from her thigh.

'We have to stop the bleeding,' Harrison says, concern etched across his face. 'We need to get her an ambulance.' Jorge is still holding the gun, pointing it at me.

'We don't, Harrison. She'll survive.' He steps toward me, lowering the gun. 'This trigger sure is sensitive. I can see how Costas mistakenly shot Fatima.'

'Don't Jorge. Just don't,' I say wearily. 'Please, put the gun down.'

Jorge rolls his eyes. 'Why on Earth should I trust you? Why should any of us trust you? You are playing games with us. In fact, I wouldn't be at all surprised at all if *you* are the Leveller.'

There are murmurs behind me, uneasy shifting of positions as the idea formulates in their minds.

'Perhaps all of this is your alibi?' he continues, and gazing down at Helen laying prone on the floor, he adds, 'Perhaps, this policewoman is your conspirator?'

Helen groans.

'When we are done, perhaps *you* hand us over, and *you*, without blood on your hands, never having murdered a soul in your entire life, plead innocence.'

'It's an interesting theory, Jorge,' I say. 'But wrong.'

'Really? It's easy for you to confess, to rid yourself of guilt, because you never actually killed anyone. What about the rest of them?' he says waving the gun. 'Think how they feel right now. But that's the problem isn't it, Zac. You don't. You don't think how others feel. You just get them to act. You get them to do what you could never do yourself.'

His voice is flat, devoid of emotion, but, like a newsreader's, it is clear, calm and confident, therefore trustworthy. I want to shake him by the shoulders and tell him not to be so stupid. We are dangerous. We must be stopped. Why can't he see that?

But his idea is taking hold, I can feel their creeping acceptance of it, the control he's exerting, in the way people are straightening up, the way they are looking at me, a little confidence re-established in their eyes. Jorge raises his eyebrows and waves his free hand as if to say "there you go, they agree with me". I hate that I can see myself in him.

'And so…' Jorge says, his focus maintained on me, as if I am the clear and present danger in the room. 'These people are right to be wary of you. We are yet to discover what has happened to Orla. I can't imagine anyone jumping from the Great Orme, so perhaps you have finally decided to act for yourself and push her?'

He's leading them with open-ended questions, all plausible, which place doubt, or worse, *certainty* in their thinking. I can feel my blood pumping through my body, my heart pounding in my chest, my hands are hot, clammy.

Jorge looks me right in the eye, challenging me to deny his accusations, challenging me to take control. 'Convenient, isn't it?' he says. 'Orla's disappearance, I mean. Where is she, Zac? What have you done with your wife? Perhaps she is the Leveller? Perhaps the pair of you are?'

It's too much. I lunge toward him but an arm wraps around my chest, holding me back. 'Costas! Let me go!' I shout.

'It's okay, Zac,' he says, breathing hard. 'I'll take care of this.' He lets go of me and marches up to Jorge, slaps one of his giant hands on his shoulder and with the other, grabs the gun. Jorge tries to hold on, but it is immediately apparent Costas is physically stronger than I thought, and Jorge is weaker. Wrenching the gun from Jorge's grasp, and having humiliated him, Costas turns on us, waving the gun at everyone. 'What is wrong with us? Where is our humanity? Our conscience?' He clears his throat. 'Zac, you were right. We must confess!'

'Costas!' Jules snaps, her voice severe, reprimanding. 'What do you think you're doing?'

'No Jules,' he responds firmly, and then softer, 'I'm sorry, but it's the only way. Of course it's the only way. There is no other way.'

Behind his glasses, his eyes are rimmed red and glisten. From within his blazer pocket, he retrieves the small wooden crucifix adorned with the bronze Christ. 'It's time. It's pastime, actually. I, for one, cannot continue with this self-inflicted torture. We can't continue to pretend none of this has happened. This isn't life. Look at us. We are turning mad. The madness, it's contagious.' He gazes down upon the crucifix, rubbing the bronze Christ with his thumb. 'Matthew, twenty-three, thirty-three.' His voice shaking, he recites to us:

'You serpents. You brood of vipers; how will you escape the sentence of hell?'

None of us have time to react as Jorge's fist swings from out wide and drives into Costas's cheekbone. My old friend crashes to the floor.

Dreaming in orange

Chapter Twenty-Four

I move quickly and, like a murderous game of pass the parcel, it's my turn to grab the gun. Jules rushes past me to help her husband to his feet, while reprimanding him for his stupidity. He's seems either dazed or lost. Out of the corner of my eye I can see him looking around at the others as if he's just landed on the back of the Great Orme, the strange and deadly beast taking him on a journey neither he nor the rest of us want.

Jorge attempts to snatch the gun back from me, but years of police training kick in and, without thinking, I have him in a headlock and the gun pressed to his temple.

I manoeuvre behind him, letting him stand up straight but still holding him tight and close, my arm fast around his neck. He pulls at my arm to free himself. He's surprisingly feeble, and it's easy for me to hold him. I lean in, pressing the side of my face against his. His skin is soft, and he smells clean like strawberries.

Jorge relents, lowering his arms, his body becoming slack in my grip. I release him, pushing him clear of me. Dressed all in black, long, thin, pointed face, calculating eyes, and his chin-length wavy hair ruffled, he stumbles towards Tomasz, but holds off his lover's attentions, turning around to confront me.

'Don't worry, Tom. It's fine. Like me, Zac has never killed anyone, nor will he. He gets others to commit murder so they can take the rap for him.'

He's right. For all the deaths I've orchestrated, I cannot kill anyone myself. I've been a leader from the back, urging on the troops at the front.

'Except for Orla,' he adds. 'The coward tried to kill his own wife.'

The Great Orme

I lower the gun, and for once I don't over-think. I lunge at Jorge and land a swift punch in his midriff. He sinks to the floor, doubled over, clutching his stomach, gasping for breath.

'This old house is my home. While you are here, you'll show a little respect.'

Tomasz glares at me but I ignore him and turn my attention to Helen. Other than Harrison, only Rose has gone to her aid, kneeling at her side and stroking her hair. I'm disappointed with the others. The broken glass tore deep into her thigh and it's bleeding profusely. 'Helen needs our help,' I say to them. 'We need to stem the bleeding.'

Helen has vomited, and Harrison is wiping her lips clean with his thumb. Then, reaching under her, he hoists her up onto the sofa. With great care, he proceeds to prop up her injured leg with a cushion to the sound of Helen grunting through clenched teeth.

'I know a little bit about these things,' Jessie says, leaning over the back of the sofa. 'It looks worse than it is. You'll be fine.'

'She's fucking bleeding her leg off,' Harrison replies. 'How can you say she'll be fine?'

I leave the room and return, first-aid box in hand, eyes fixed on the young policewoman. She sees me and groans, closing her eyes.

Harrison takes the plastic green box from me and opens it. 'We need to clean the wound.' He reaches for the waist of her jeans and fumbles to undo her button and unzip them.

'What do you think you are doing?' I say, placing a hand on his shoulder.

He twists his neck to observe me, but he can't hold my gaze for long, eyes flitting in every direction, and I can almost hear his mind whirring.

'Here,' Jessie says taking the box from him. 'You leave the room.' She opens the lid of the box. 'I'll remove her trousers, clean the wound and bandage her up.' She thumbs through the box and picks out the packet of paracetamol. 'I'll give her four of these. She's in good hands. Now, boys – go!'

She, Sian, Rose and also Jules, the latest addition to the vipers' nest, stay in the lounge while the rest of us converge in the kitchen, Jorge included. I still have the gun.

Against my better judgement, more drinks are poured for everyone, wine for them and rum for me. No one sits, we all find some place to lean against. Each time I genuinely think it can't get any worse, it does. I think everyone is falling apart. The only thing I know for certain is in a few hours, one way or another, this will all be over. I pray no one else dies first.

Tomasz pushes himself away from the fridge he's leaning against, and the Great Orme fridge-magnet fixed to it swings precariously at an angle. He walks over to Jorge, taking his hands. 'Are you okay?'

Jorge sighs. 'I just want this to end.'

Tomasz pulls Jorge toward him and the two men collapse into one another.

'Jorge,' I say as Tomasz's lover breaks their embrace. 'Tell me honestly, are you the Leveller?'

He sighs again and shakes his head. 'No. Are you?'

I shake my head. 'No.'

Regardless of our stupidity, time marches on, signalled by the muted chimes of the grandfather clock from the lounge. One a.m.

'Perhaps it's Helen,' Jorge suggests with a shrug.

'Come off it,' I say. 'What has she got to do with any of this?'

'I don't know,' he replies. 'You tell me.'

He holds my gaze, eyebrows raised waiting for an answer.

'She's new to the area,' I say, doubting my justification. There's definitely something strange about Helen. 'Lonely and looking to get to know people.'

'How long have you known her?'

'She joined the force a few weeks ago. I only met her for the first time on Friday morning…'

'Hold on!' Jorge waves his hand dismissively in the air. 'You only met her Friday? As in – the day before yesterday?'

The Great Orme

'Yes, but…'

'Come on, Zac. I know you police chums stick together, but in all seriousness, there's something amiss here. She's not just befriended you. She's targeted you!'

He rolls his eyes. I feel stupid. 'She visited again on Friday afternoon, when Orla had arrived?' he asks.

I nod.

'And then you and Costas happened to *bump* into her Saturday lunchtime in town? Ate lunch with her?'

Jorge has an excellent memory and an eye for detail. He'd make a good cop.

'And she comes again! Saturday evening! What do you think, Zac? After all, *you* are the cop.'

His dark eyes are wide, cool black, but impassioned at the same time.

'Perhaps she's just doing her job, Jorge,' I say, not convinced I'm right.

'Sure,' he says, laughing. 'Why didn't she bring the whole fucking force with her? Unless she works alone. Works alone perhaps maybe because she *is* the Leveller?'

'Guys, come on,' Harrison says, taking a sip at a glass of red wine and wincing, the drink not to his liking. 'Let's keep this close to home. She's not the Leveller. She has nothing to do with this.'

'Okay then, Big Boy! Perhaps you're the Leveller?' Jorge states, fixing Harrison with an accusatory stare.

Jorge seems to be firing accusations randomly now, and I wonder if he's not as smart as I gave him credit for, maybe he's more desperate than smart, and that could be worse for me.

'Not a chance,' Harrison laughs, resting an arm awkwardly on top of the cooker. 'Although, as you are considering anyone here could be the Leveller, it turns out Rose has a dark bit of history, perhaps she's our Leveller?' He laughs again, but as usual with him, it's uneasy.

'Shit guys,' Tomasz says, grabbing hold of a chair backrest. 'At this rate, we'll have Smokey down as a suspect.'

Costas stares up at the hole in the ceiling he caused by shooting at it. 'Heaven help us.'

'One thing I do know,' Jorge says, ignoring the Vicar's plea. 'Whoever it is, they are right. We must not confess.'

'I disagree.' Costas lowers his head and removes his glasses.

I thank God for Costas.

'We must trust to God,' he says, a flicker of a fire returned to his eyes. He clasps his hands together in front of his chest, fingers tightly interlocked. 'We should confess and leave the natural course of events to play out.'

'No way.' Harrison accidently knocks a saucepan on the cooker making it clang as he pushes himself away. 'Costas, you do know what they do to child killers in prison don't you?'

Costas mouth drops like he's about to vomit. Taking a gulp, he regains some composure. 'She was suffering, Harrison. Chloe was dying. I pray, for you and for me, for all of us, that the good Lord shows us mercy.'

Harrison looks flabbergasted, as if Costas has just walked over and slapped him. I see Harrison's fingers curl into fists as he turns to face Costas, taking a step toward him.

I slam my glass down and move between them, gun in hand. I see the two men as boys, as they were so many years ago, playing and laughing. It's my fault. It's all my fault they are the men they are today – murderers, both.

'You are not listening,' Harrison snaps, reaching past me to put his wine glass on the table. 'I will *not* give up my freedom.'

I wonder at the man I used to know, pencil thin and anxious, now carved like a bronze god, muscles and veins twitching and rippling with each hot breath.

'By trying to contain... this, we are making things worse,' Costas insists, bringing his hands to his face, the tips of his fingers brought together in a prayer-like gesture. He stares at

The Great Orme

the tiled kitchen wall like he sees something on it. 'This isn't freedom.' He closes his eyes. 'Far from it.'

'Fools,' mutters Jorge.

Harrison grunts in agreement. 'He's a holy fool,' he says, glancing at Costas. 'The worst kind.'

'Tomasz,' I say, considering the footballer's remoteness, his silence. 'What do you think? What should we do?'

The footballer's chin is tucked into the funnel collar of his red sports jersey. I think if he could, he'd bury it completely so he wouldn't have to deal with any of this. He sweeps his long blond fringe off his forehead. 'Guys, I don't know… I just don't know. It feels like we are damned if we do and damned if we don't.'

The footballer pinches the bridge of his nose with forefinger and thumb. 'To be absolutely honest, I'm so tired. I suspect we all are. It's been a long day. Too much has happened, too much to think clearly. Why don't we get some rest? See what the morning brings, and perhaps… perhaps things might be clearer?'

He's right. Everyone is tired and emotional; the alcohol hasn't helped. Tomasz holds some sway, more than he realises. When the quiet man speaks, we listen.

Back in the lounge, the women have managed to stem Helen's bleeding, but she's pale and exhausted, in need of rest. Harrison and I carry her upstairs. I forgo my room, and we deposit her in my bed where she seems to fall asleep immediately. We can't help but check on Fatima in my mother's room and strange as it is, we are relieved to see she's still there.

Rose refuses to go home, claiming to be too scared to leave, which I find odd, one might think it scarier to stay in a house full of murderers, but then I suppose she's a murderer herself. I get to thinking who in the old house isn't a murderer – just Jorge, Jules and Helen. An alarm goes off in my head - I correct myself, remembering what Costas told me and Harrison about Jules, how she had killed her own mother. I groan inwardly, she couldn't be the Leveller, could she? It's possible I suppose.

Perhaps she's trying to save Costas.

Harrison offers up the room at the back of the house I had intended for him, insisting Rose sleeps there instead. She doesn't thank him.

Costas and Jules shut themselves away, and we hear their raised voices through the walls, not enough to decipher their words but enough to understand they are arguing.

Sian and Jessie share a bedroom, as do Tomasz and Jorge. Downstairs, I turn the heating up, and the old pipes grumble discontentedly with the additional effort required of them.

Harrison takes the sofa in the lounge and I scatter a few cushions in the study for me and Smokey.

I spend an hour writing, documenting the events of the night, tuned in to the sound of the steady scrape of pen on paper. Here it is, our record of what happened, as far as I know, anyway. I wonder if it should be mandatory for all criminals to write with their own hand, confessions expressed with thought, feeling and context, and thus we should better understand the human condition.

My middle finger bears a bright-red pressure mark from my tight grip on the pen. I stare at the space on the page and wonder what words will be there tomorrow. There was a time I think I would have known, but I would have been wrong; no one truly knows what tomorrow brings. We like to think we are in control. We are not.

Finished, I close the book. In the distance, the far-away sea is a pool of black ink lurching from side to side under an angry dark sky. I think of Orla, where she might be, the fear she must be feeling. I am consumed by helplessness and hopelessness. The old house is full, yet I've never felt more alone.

I settle down on the cushions laid out on the floor as a makeshift bed, Smokey wedged against me, and out for the count within seconds. Even in the half-death of sleep, I find no consolation, the dead, unable to rest, dredged from the deep black soil they were buried in, lean in close to me, their whispers no longer distant but nagging, nearby things, their stilted breaths, their rasping murmurs, their desperate groans all the louder because they know I hear them.

I reach out, half-asleep, half-awake in the darkness, clawing the air, try to push the sound away. But it's as if I've offered it some encouragement, and the stifled noises grow louder, become more urgent. There's more though… through the decayed odour of rotten death, a fresher, faint oily citrus scent.

'Stop!'

My own voice sounds alien, dis-embodied. I'm fully awake now. I clasp my hands to my ears in the unrealistic hope the ghosts will go away.

Click.

Smokey stirs. I feel his fur bristle. He stands. Rigid. Alert.

He growls.

The sound of grunting, struggling breath comes again. Not mine and not his.

He leaves my side.

I hear him snorting and sniffing excitedly, pawing at something.

The window hangs as if suspended in the darkness; the rain has stopped and the dark skies are clear. Pale slices of winter moonlight shine through the window, patterning the furniture, the floor, and the body lying before the door.

I jolt upright, arms locked straight and hands pressed flat to the floor, there's an ever so slight zesty tang of orange hanging in the air.

Smokey whines sympathetically, nudging at the body with his nose, licking its face. He knows who it is. Suddenly, I know too; the perfume, Black Citrus. It's her. It's my wife! It's Orla!

God looks down from heaven on the human race to see if there is one who is wise, one who seeks God

- psalm 53:2

Chapter Twenty-Five

It's her... It's her... It's her. The words punch like a hammer-drill in my head. Closer now, I hear her muted gasps, she's struggling to breathe.

I stand and hit the light-switch with my fist. Orla, lit up in yellow, beetle eyes half-closed against the harsh glare of the electric light, has ankles, knees, arms, and mouth, all bound with wide grey tape. She's still wearing my quilted emerald coat. Her black jeans and Doc Martens boots are caked with dried mud. Her long black hair is a gnarled twisted helmet about her head.

I swallow hard and I feel like a door in my heart has opened releasing a cage full of birds. She winces as I peel the tape from her mouth. Released, she spits as if poisoned, gagging and heaving. Something tumbles from her mouth. She sucks in air like the life-giving elixir that it is, chest heaving rapidly up and down. The jettisoned thing glistens with her saliva on the threadbare beige carpet, its hard black and shiny body, still, dead. It's an insect... a beetle. I lean over and stare at my wife, smeared coal-black eye make-up melted and merged with streaked cherry-red lipstick, her face pocked with raw cuts and bruises.

I stroke her hair with the tips of my fingers as if checking she's real and not another ghost in a world full of them. 'Are you okay?'

Her lips only tremble in response, and her eyes flicker, still adjusting to the brightness of the light. I want to pick her up and run away. I want to go now, immediately. I want to hide from whoever is doing this to me, to us. Why did I ever let the love of my life go in the first place?

The Great Orme

She opens her mouth to speak, but is unable to, and instead she glares down at the tape binding her arms. I respond by tearing it away and doing the same on her ankles and knees.

'Fuck's sake,' she says hoarsely, as I help her to sit up. 'Drink.'

I look around, and seeing only a barely-filled glass of rum on my desk, I pass it to her. She rolls her eyes disparagingly, but downs it anyway. She is stronger than she knows.

Holding my hand, I get her to stand, I want to see if she's suffered any damage, if she's in pain. She holds herself up, scanning her body, checking for herself it's in one piece.

'Are you hurt?' I ask.

She lifts her gaze to mine. We hold eye-contact for a split-second before collapsing in a tight embrace, Smokey pushing between our legs.

'I'm sorry,' I say, and I mean it. I've let her down badly. I promise myself I will never do so again. The grandfather clock chimes, muted from the lounge. It's five in the morning.

Sat at the kitchen table, she sips at a pint-glass of water and nibbles on four slices of buttered toast. Smokey waits patiently at her feet, licking his nose in anticipation of a crust.

'I wanted to die,' she says, lowering a ripped piece of toast for Smokey.

I nod, my eyes burning with tears that will not fall. 'I won't let you. I've been a fool. I won't let it happen.'

Her shoulders sag. She sighs. My heart breaks.

'Yeah, well, I couldn't even do that properly,' she says, rubbing her wrists still marked red from the tape that had bound them together.

I lean across the table, taking her hand in mine, our fingers meshed together, holding on to one another. 'I thought you were dead. After you jumped, I saw you lying at the bottom of the cliff. I just assumed…'

'Me too,' she says, taking a bite out of her toast. 'I kind of rolled and tumbled, you know how it banks out from the top… until I reached the bottom. I must have banged my head. I guess I was unconscious. I don't know how long after... but I managed to stand up. I thought I saw you at the top of the cliff – it wasn't you. I don't know who it was... just a vague silhouette. I think I collapsed again. When I came around, all was dark, and I was wrapped head to toe in a blanket, alone in a bedroom, nothing but the bed and an old set of drawers in it, a burning candle providing the light. The window was boarded up and the room, thick with dust, was locked from the outside. On top of the drawers, a glass of water and seven painkillers, each with one of our names written on the foil, all seven of us.'

She emits something sounding like a whimper before drawing a deep breath and sipping on the water.

'Do you have any idea who it was who found you... who took you back to where ever it was?'

She shakes her head, rubbing her forehead. 'To be honest, I think I've been drugged. I still feel groggy.'

'And you've no idea how you got here, I guess?'

'I'm sorry, Zac. I feel useless. I don't know a thing.'

Orla appears close to tears. It's hardly surprising, she's traumatised and will be for a long time yet. Perhaps forever.

She reaches across the table and squeezes my hand. 'What is happening? I'm scared. I'm really, really scared.'

The pit of my stomach burns, the feeling we are closer to the end, closer to knowing, is terrifying. I summarise for her everything that has happened since I last saw her... since she jumped to her intended death. She listens intently, a gently whispered 'fuck' at intervals. When I'm done, she seems sad, far away. I ask her what she's thinking.

'You are still decided?' she asks, fixing her gaze on me with her beetle eyes.

'What?'

'You are still determined to confess?'

I hardly know how to reply, because I know it will break her heart again, and it will leave us where we were – at the edge of the Great Orme, staring down into the abyss. I can only be honest. It's all I have left. 'It's the only way through. For you and for me. For them too, although they don't know it, but they will. Costas appears to have come around to it, and Tomasz is on the brink. Let's make them see sense. Let's do the *right* thing, Orla. There can't be anything more important can there?'

She smiles, tight-lipped and sad, unclasping her fingers from mine and retracting her hand. One single tear spills and runs the length of her cheek. She catches it at her chin, dabbing it away. 'Who do you love most in the whole world?'

'You, always you.' The words escape without hesitation.

Orla stares at the floor in silence. She's holding her breath. She releases it, and the tears flow unchecked. I feel her pain and I catch my breath to prevent the choke at the back my throat from exploding.

'There isn't a day that goes by I don't think of Choreji and…', she glances up at me, holding my gaze. I can feel her searching me, her eyes boring into mine, looking for something I can't give her. 'She haunts me. Every year that passes, I think of what she might look like now, what she might be doing if she were still alive. The life she might have led. Imagine we had a child, Zac. Imagine it had been her. How would that make you feel?'

She waits for my reply but I find it difficult. How can I know how it would feel? I guess that's my issue – I can't know. To lose my parents in the way I did was awful, but to lose your child, I can't imagine. I just can't.

Her breath wavers as she speaks. 'I wonder, every day I wonder, what if you hadn't made us kill the old man? That single decision, its significance, the lives that hinged on that choice made in a blink of an eye. The way that choice defined not only our lives thereafter but the lives and deaths of so many others. Forever.'

'Orla…'

'If you think I haven't already been punished Zac, you'd be wrong.' She presses her fingers against her forehead. 'It's all up here – my life sentence began the day we killed the old man. It's just got worse after. It never stops. Never.'

She dangles a hand and lets Smokey lick it.

'I'm sorry,' I say, the words made for when it's too late. For when the damage has already been done.

She inhales deeply through her nose, and exhales through her mouth, her shoulders sagging. 'If you want me to confess, I'll do it,' she says, picking up a crust from her plate and feeding it to Smokey. 'If that's what it takes... I'll do it. I just hope that...' she pauses, blinks slow, takes another deep breath and continues, 'I pray she understands.'

My hand is still on the tabletop where she left it. She reaches out and squeezes it. It means everything.

'She?' I ask. 'You mean Choreji?'

Orla stares at me, her thoughts elsewhere. 'We've lost so much. More than you know... more than you know,' she repeats, lifting her head and shutting her eyes tight. 'I just hope whoever or whatever's looking down on us, can see us for what we are, for the love we hold, that we aren't the beasts that many might imagine. That we have –'

I stand violently, scraping back the chair so it topples over noisily behind me. Smokey yelps, and startled, Orla's eyes flash open wide, and she gets to her feet too. 'What's wrong?' she asks, reaching out for me. 'Apart from everything.'

'Orla! Shit! That's it! Oh my God!'

'What?'

'Of course! Why has it taken me so long to realise?! You've nailed it! It's the Leveller! The Leveller is looking down on us!'

I'm gone, through the kitchen door and thundering up the stairs taking two steps at a time.

The only way is up

Chapter Twenty-Six

Orla has followed me up the stairs, emerging onto the landing and running into me in the middle of the hallway. 'What the fuck is going on?' she shrieks.

The commotion wakes the old house and its inhabitants, and one by one the doors to the bedrooms open, old friends and more recent acquaintances appearing in the hallway. On seeing Orla, all appear momentarily stunned, then, one by one they rush her, firing questions and offering embraces. I don't have time for any of it, my attention is focussed elsewhere, directed at the ceiling, at the square loft hatch directly above me.

Harrison's nasal whine rings out from the top of the stairs as he swings himself around to face us all. 'Orla! What the... What's going on?'

'Get me a chair,' I say, ignoring him. 'Someone, get me a chair, quick.'

Tomasz springs into action, dragging a wooden desk chair from his room. Without taking my eyes off the hatch, I place the chair to the side of the hatch before standing on it. Although I haven't used it in years, the silver lever in the middle of the ceiling's loft-panel pulls out easily.

'Watch out,' I say to the killers gathered below me. The panel retreats, a soft whirring sound, and the sectioned loft ladder tips down in front of me. I jump off the chair. Moving it to one side, I grip a cold aluminium rung, damp with dust, and releasing the catch at the side of it so the ladder extends to its full three sections, I watch as it touches the floor at a diagonal.

Sian grabs my arm, concern etched on her pale face. 'What's going on?'

The Great Orme

'Look,' I say, pointing at the coving on one side of the hatch.

'Blood,' she states, cobalt eyes like ice, gazing upwards at the tiny spots of red smeared along the edge of the coving.

I place a foot on the bottom rung of the ladder, and before I ascend, Orla is beside me, one hand clutching hold of my arm, the other clasping Sian's hand. The two women appear fraught, Orla still wearing the mud-caked clothes she fell to her near-death in, and Sian, visibly shaken by all that's happened and happening, her face creased with new lines that make her appear ten years older than she is. I don't want to leave either of them, afraid for them. The assembled killers surrounding me may hide the Leveller in plain sight, but I'm convinced the Leveller has been in the loft, hiding Fatima there and bringing her out again in order to scare us into submission.

Harrison helps Helen limp toward us. She seems wide-eyed and alert, colour returned to her face. I'm glad. She doesn't deserve any of this. Then I remember, I don't know her at all, and I wonder why she has waited? Why hasn't she already alerted the police? There's a dead woman in the old house.

Jorge's voice rings clear, snapping the tension and gaining the attention. 'Orla. Nice to finally meet you. I'm Jorge, Tomasz's partner. How did you get here?'

He's stood in the doorway to his and Tomasz's bedroom, deadly serious expression set on his face, and dressed, much like me, all in black. It seems everyone is dressed, all set for the early morning as if ready to turn up an event of some kind. Tomasz is stood behind Jorge, arms wrapped around his lover, clinging on to him like he's a life raft.

Orla hesitates to answer, perhaps wary of the new face. I reply for her. 'Someone rescued her from the rocks. Saved her life. They left her in the study while I lay asleep.'

'Anyone we know?' Jorge asks, dryly.

This time Orla and I answer at the same time, but with different answers. She says she doesn't know, while I confirm it's the Leveller, it has to be.

'Of course,' Jorge says, voice steady, commanding, sarcastic. 'Did you jump off the Great Orme, Orla?' he asks. 'Or were you pushed?'

Everyone waits for her reply, even the ghosts, who are stacked along the landing, either burned, drowned, blue from suffocation, skull-cracked and bleeding, or bodies sliced to ribbons. They sense an end coming as do I. I only wish I knew what it was and how to influence it. I squeeze the rung of the ladder to ensure I stay upright and to prevent myself from fainting. Why does no one else see them?

'I jumped,' Orla replies. 'Of course I did.' Then realising the insinuation in Jorge's question, she lets go of my arm and presses her hands to the sides of head. 'You didn't think Zac pushed me?'

'We can believe you, right?' Jorge asks her, his voice thick with cynicism. 'You don't look so badly injured to me. Perhaps you lay still among the rocks to give Zac the impression you were dead. Then you got up and walked away, just as you walked away after you killed the little girl, whatshername… Choreji? You left her for dead.'

Choreji is pushing past the other ghosts, her head dangling at an odd angle, wet ruby blood glistening where the back of her skull is caved in.

'I wanted to die,' Orla says looking past the others, and I know she sees Choreji; her eyes are stretched wide and staring. 'The guilt… I couldn't live with the guilt. Not on my own. I'm so sorry, Choreji.'

My heart collapses in on itself at the cruelty I've inflicted on the person I love most in the world.

Tears are streaming down Choreji's face, crying for a girl who died so many years before, crying for herself.

I tear my eyes from her to Jorge, furious with him, but also the others. 'I'm resorting to begging you. Please, which of you is the Leveller?'

I make a point of examining each of them, but all I get in return are jutting lower lips, shakes of the head and blank stares. I've lost any control I once had over them. The Leveller is in control. I am being manipulated and there's nothing I can do about it.

'We should all confess,' Orla says, letting go of me and Sian and glaring at all gathered. 'Whoever of you is the Leveller… You've lost your fucking mind. Even if you got away with all of this, the killing will never stop. We have to stop this fucking craziness, it can't go on, we can't go on like this… not if we ever cared about one another! Let's do the right thing – just for once!'

No one moves or says a word, just the sound of terse breaths, and the clunk of the central heating firing up. The ghosts have disappeared if they were ever there, and Costas makes a move towards Orla but Jules won't let go of his hand, so he stays put. His face is stricken, a morbid grimace clear to see. I think he saw them; I think he saw Chloe, the little girl he left to die, right here on the landing. I'm still holding the ladder, one foot on the lowest rung. 'It's okay Orla, we'll find out who it is soon… very soon.' I gaze up at the gaping square hole above me. I feel suddenly sick, a black cloud bumping around inside my head. What if none of them are the Leveller? What if, scared out of their wits, one of them has told someone else, someone who's now trying to protect them? Someone scared enough to want to stop me before I do any more damage? Someone scared enough to kill others, scared enough to kill me?

I look over my shoulder at the people I've collected here in the old house. Anxious, bold and indifferent eyes observe one another as if in a poker game. I hope for a subconscious flash of emotion, a telling blink, excessive fidgeting, something, anything that might give me a clue.

'Be careful, Zac,' Sian says, and as if reading my mind, 'the clues are up there… perhaps the Leveller is up there.'

I can feel hot sick bubbling up. I could be about to enter the Leveller's lair. One more death. Mine.

'Wait a second!'

Jessie, in skimpy shorts and a vest, skips along the hall and disappears down the stairs. She returns quickly. 'Here,' she says, handing me my rubberised Black & Decker torch. Orla and Jessie exchange a glance that seems to speak something unspoken – a quiet acknowledgement of the events at Orla's Christmas party all those years ago.

I nod my thanks, I'm not thinking straight, of course I'll need a torch. I climb the ladder and enter the darkness of the loft for the first time since my mother died. A damp, cold draught permeates my clothes and settles on my skin making me shudder. I switch on the torch but the light is weak, the batteries need replacing; the darkness seems to sense it's more powerful than the light, tracking and constraining it. Sian, Harrison and I used the torch when we went up the Great Orme. I think it has had some more use between then and now. I hear Smokey bark from below. He's anxious too.

Old boxes and suitcases are heaped here, there and everywhere, unevenly balanced on the spongy yellow insulation covering the floorboards. I move among them, holding the light low so its reach touches the floor. I suppose I'm looking for something out of place, a clue, and although it takes a while, when I find it, it shakes me to the core.

At the left-hand side of the loft, the wooden boards that separate my loft from the adjoining loft of the supposedly empty house next door are smashed through, leaving a gaping hole. Other than Rose in the detached house on one side of me, it seems the Leveller may be my neighbour in the house joined to mine.

I step through the hole, hardly needing to duck, such is the scale of the damage. A musty tinge to the air and an acrid taste like soured apples on my lips, the neighbours' loft is even colder and damper than mine. Piles of old magazines and cardboard boxes full of old and broken things are piled to the sides having been pushed aside leaving the way to the exit clear, the dust on the exposed floorboards scuffed. All is quiet, and the cold permeates through to my bones.

I edge toward the neighbouring house's square hatch set in the floor in the same place as mine, my innards seething like there's a thousand writhing mini sea serpents desperate to escape. I stop

The Great Orme

at its edge, shining the meagre light on it. At its centre, a square card, a picture. I lean over, it's a photograph that I'm obliged to pick up. It's a photo of someone sleeping. Me.

The inside of my cheek is turning raw where I'm biting it. I examine myself in the photo, lying on the cushions in the study, Smokey pressed into me, eyes open, haunted. The photo was taken only a few hours ago, and by someone known to Smokey, else he would have barked. The Leveller *is* one of them.

They've used my camera. I have a Fuji Neo instant camera I bought in town just weeks ago – I thought it might capture the ghosts I saw – except it didn't, same as my phone didn't. The Leveller is taunting me – always one step ahead. I flick the catch holding the loft door in place and it drops, swinging on its hinges. I sit at the edge of the hole, legs dangling, no ladder here but beneath me a shabby leather dining chair all set to receive me. I wait for a moment, and lower myself.

The hall is gloomy, the window at one end splayed with the skeletal shining fingers of the morning light clawing at the glass. Standing still on the chair, I listen. The silence is immense. It feels as though the house is listening to my thoughts. Of course, this house is part of my house – the old house, it's the same building, it belongs to the same ground; it belongs to the Great Orme – to the Sea Serpent. Something cold swipes at my neck, but when I scan around, there's nothing there.

I feel queasy, sick with dizziness. It's like I can feel the Earth's rotation and I'm out of step, out of time with it. I fall, crashing to the floor, face pressed to a carpet sticky with the residue of bugs. My throat feels like a rusty exhaust. I think I hear laughter, a thin cynical giggle, drifting, gloating. Moving stiffly, I slide my hands along the carpet and push myself upright. Outside, a car rumbles down the hill, the glance of its headlights momentarily bending the fingers of light at the window. I take a deep breath but the atmosphere is thick with dust, damp and decay. I must push the darkness from my mind. I must think. I must be rational – lives are at stake, including my own.

The layout of the landing is a mirror of the old house,

although more dilapidated, more oppressive. I check each of the rooms along the landing, all of them completely empty, devoid of furniture. All of them, except for the one before the bathroom at the end, furthest from the stairs. The light within is on, its glow apparent beneath the closed door.

I press the handle. The door is unlocked so I open it, the sprung hinge pushing back at me. Within, a naked bulb hangs from the centre of the ceiling, a sad yellow glow colouring the bare walls. Holding the weighted door open I observe on the far side of the room, a single bed, a set of drawers beside it and a boarded-up window beyond. I realise it has to be the room where Orla was kept.

The bed is unmade. A piece of paper lies on top of it. I strain to see what it is. I take a step into the room, afraid to let go of the door in case it swings shut, and I get locked in. The paper is a handwritten note. I know it's meant for me. I have to enter the room.

I glance up and down the hallway and toward the top of the stairs in case someone is lurking, and taking a deep breath, I run to the bed, snatch the paper, and run back to the door, only just catching it before it swings shut. My hand trembling, I read the words written in red ink:

Zachary Llewellyn,
Time's up.
No more chances.
No more warnings.
Stop now.
Don't confess!
Your life depends on it.
Orla's life depends on it.
Your loving neighbour,
The Leveller

A surge of hot blood swamps my head. I crumple the paper in my fist just as, from behind, a hand settles on my shoulder.

There is poison in
the fang of a serpent

Chapter Twenty-Seven

'Tomasz!'

Tomasz squeezes and releases my shoulder. 'Is everything okay?'

I stare at his face, nervous small round eyes peer out from beneath his long blond fringe.

He clears his throat. 'Orla's been through a lot.'

'What do you mean?'

He twists his mouth. 'I can't say it's definitely her, but y'know, she was prepared to die rather than confess… perhaps that's still the case… perhaps she intends taking you to the grave with her this time.'

'Are you saying Orla dragged herself back from the bottom of the cliff and holed herself up in here? That she's been doing these crazy things to scare me? That she killed the old man, she killed the man who killed my father, attacked the boy too?'

Tomasz scratches his head. 'The boy… well, Helen said a woman with eye make-up like Orla's was seen leaving the scene of the crime. I don't know, Zac. It has to be one of us, and she loves you so much. You broke her heart when you split up, perhaps more than you care to realise. Unrequited love… it can turn someone…'

I try to get my head around the implications of what Tomasz has suggested, but he's way off. 'The photo of her gazing up from the cliff… she didn't take that, someone else did.'

'Possibly, but remember, Orla works in marketing, it's easy to mock up something like that using AI. She's an expert at it.'

There's a loud thump. Someone else has arrived on the landing. Harrison's bulk appears behind Tomasz. 'Everything alright?'

'What do you think?' I reply, raising my eyebrows and glaring

The Great Orme

at him hard. 'Look at this.' I straighten out the crumpled piece of paper in my hand and hold it out for the two of them to read.

'Dead simple,' Harrison says scrutinising the writing. 'You'd be a fool to confess, wouldn't you?'

'I need your help,' I say, a grinding sensation in the pit of my stomach. 'We've got to stop this. Now. Before anyone else gets hurt. You must see where we are headed unless we do something to stop it?'

Harrison's eyes widen. 'The Leveller, whoever it is, will kill you. You don't stand a chance. You don't know who it is. When they come for you, you won't see them. It'll be too late. There's only one way to stop them. You know what you must do.'

I clench my teeth before responding. 'What should I do, Harrison?' I say finally. 'People. Real. People. They died because of us!'

His mouth is twisted into an odd little smile, perhaps it's just his way.

I thought I knew them so well, but I don't even know myself anymore. It seems we left those three boys behind the night we killed the old man. I used to pride myself on being able to read people, what I saw in the eyes and the corners of mouths, their breathing. 'What do you think, Tomasz?' I ask, giving up on Harrison. 'What should I do?'

'It seems it's all or nothing,' he replies, his shoulders slumping and shaking his head. 'The stakes are way beyond high. I think you need to let us live and be with the people we love.'

I nod, it's a fair if unworkable interpretation of our situation. 'Harrison,' I say, turning my focus back on him. 'That poor boy you bludgeoned to death is buried on top of the Great Orme, in St. Tudno's cemetery. Occasionally, I still see his parents at his graveside when I'm up there. Fresh flowers, always. Even after all these years.' I regard Tomasz, fixedly. 'They can't be with the person they love.'

I feel as much as see Harrison's glare on me, he's annoyed but also pained. He moves away and together, the three of us search the house, but it's a squalid shell, the old neighbours having moved out most of their furniture over a year ago, leaving behind a place for damp and age to encroach. Only that which wasn't worth taking: a few old chairs, chipped cups, and other unremarkable items left behind. The place is dilapidated and depressing and requires a lot of work, it's not a wonder it hasn't sold.

Strewn on the floor downstairs, we discover chocolate wrappers, brands I have in my house. There's even a cushion taken from my mother's room, and the cutlery on the kitchen counter is mine.

Tomasz calls me into the empty lounge. He holds out a cheap plastic orange football, photos taped to it, nodding at me to take it.

The first photo I see is of an old man… Josh Pinkney - our old Headmaster. He's lying face-up on a white-tiled floor, his body lit by a bright light, biscuits strewn over him. Dark pools of blood have formed – perhaps were still forming when the photo was taken. Of course, it's the copy-cat killing at Clonmel Street. The blood oozing from the poor man's neck, wrists and thighs reflects the artificial light but not as much as his wide-open eyes do. They are staring at the camera – staring at his murderer.

I feel sick but nonetheless my eyes flick to another photo taped to the ball, it's of a young boy, his head streaked red with blood in stark contrast to the bright white snow he's lying in. I spin the ball to see yet another photo, this time a close-up shot of the man I should despise more than any other, the man who had literally punched the life out of my father. Yestyn, tiny hooded eyes behind wire-framed round glasses, stubbled face and bald head staring back at me, the way his face is stretched screams alarm, the pier railing and black sea glinting behind him. I hate it, but can't deny the feeling – a pang of sympathy.

I emit a subconscious moan. The next photo I see is of me.

It appears zoomed in, as if taken from a distance, therefore a little blurry, but there's no doubt – my back to the photographer, I'm opening the door to North Menswear store.

'Easy tiger!' Harrison says as I turn and accidentally bump

into him. 'Looks like the Leveller has a hobby!'

I roll my eyes and shake my head. I toss the ball to him. 'This belong to you?'

He stares down at the ball, turning it over, his face all furrowed concern and despondency. He stops and looks at me then back at the ball, turning it so I can see the black printed word – CHELSEA. 'Not likely,' he says tossing it back at me. 'But...'

'But what?' I ask, my patience about to snap.

'Well, doesn't Orla live in Chelsea?'

'Shit!' Harrison exclaims. 'You're right, Tomasz. She does!'

I take the amateur sleuths with me and we leave by the front door, returning to my house. Jorge's face is a picture of bemusement as he opens the door to us. I push past him, thrusting the ball at him.

'A clue!' he announces to those gathered as we enter the lounge.

'Well done, Sherlock,' I say. 'But what does it tell us?'

Immediately Harrison points out the Chelsea connection. Orla appears affronted by the inference and flatly denies she's the Leveller. The debate swings around to why the photos are stuck on a football. Theories are exchanged based on Tomasz being framed or threatened, but no one is giving any ground.

I observe them all and I honestly don't know which is the Leveller. It's not Orla. It mustn't be. Arguments start, people are tired and emotional. I am too. The Leveller is ramping up the fear. I need ten minutes to get my head together. I mumble something about getting changed and head up the stairs. I feel dirty, I need a shower. I need to be clean, even if for a minute.

The water runs cold for a few seconds before warming up as the hot water pipes clunk into action. Head tilted back, and with eyes shut tight, I stand submerged in watery isolation, the drum of the droplets on the plastic floor and the whir of the bathroom fan drowning out all other noise. I try to collect my thoughts. The Leveller is male. Has to be. To carry Orla back from the edge of the Great Orme, then to lift and carry her from the loft, just as he did for Fatima. But as is usual, my thoughts soon give way to memories, stained at the edges, and floating like razor blades within my head. Fractured, distorted images give way to faces, pleading dead faces. We killed them. My heart feels old. My heart feels cold.

Something makes my blood itch. I open my eyes. Turning toward the steamed-up shower door, I can see someone stood on the other side.

My heart leaps. An arm reaches forward, and the door is drawn back.

'Orla,' I gasp through streaming water. She is naked.

She enters the shower, closing the door behind her.

We hold on to one another, entwined, possibly for the last time, a flicker of innocence, of happiness, of falling down crying. Through the blur of spraying water, she stares up at me, beetle eyes gone, washed away. We are as we were when we entered this world. We cling to one another, to dead dreams. All the love, all the love I have to give to her, useless, because I've left it too late.

An hour later, collected in the dining room, Orla and I are dressed, washed and clean, but facing the glare of the condemned.

Through the window, the old sun has risen again, continuing to throw us spinning around and around as it always has, our wet little rock merely one of a billion trillion in a never-ending universe. Even the sun seems tired, the light it affords us is bleak, painting all in sepia. Everyone is seated and serious, each cradling a mug filled with coffee or tea. This is it. Our time is up. I see Orla at the far end of the table, a seat left for me next to her. I make my way through the brooding silence, head up, gaze steady; I need to portray confidence. Their heads remain bowed as if at a funeral party.

'I found this note next door,' I tell them, taking the crumpled piece of paper from my pocket and unfolding it.

I drag the empty chair away from the table and sit, taking

a sip from the mug of coffee left for me. I pull a face, it's too strong, but at least it'll keep me alert. Composing myself, I read out the note from the Leveller, my "*loving neighbour*", urging me, or threatening me rather, for the last time not to confess.

I toss the paper on the table. At the far end of the table, holding hands, Costas and Jules gaze at one another, thoughts unspoken. Could it be the pair of them I wonder? Two murderers, unprepared to give up the lives they have worked for... killed for. Next to them, on my left as I consider my elderly neighbour, Rose, her walking stick on the table, placed before her as if a weapon. We killed her husband. She killed a vicar. Given the right (or wrong) circumstances, who isn't capable of murder, I wonder? She slurps her tea, licking her lips, moist glassy-blue eyes peering over the green-rimmed frames of her specs at me. Does she care that, under questioning by the police, one of us is bound to let slip her crime? She'll be accountable still, even after all this time. Perhaps she's like me, unable to live with the guilt, the ghosts. Perhaps our dilemmas have brought her own to the fore. I still can't get over the fact the old man we killed was her husband.

I switch my view to the other side of the table, to Sian. I instinctively offer up a smile, don't ask me why or what it's for – compassion, empathy, sympathy, perhaps all three, I don't know. But she responds with her own half-smile, one that is flat, crushed, filled with sadness, one which breaks my heart. She runs pale, long fingers through her spiky, bleached hair. It's not the Sian I know, and perhaps never will be again, but I can probably say the same for all of us. Yet she was always so full of life, more vibrant and colourful than any of us. And now, now the love of her life lays murdered here in the old house, body upstairs.

Beside Sian, Jessie lifts her head, sharp, small, brown eyes defiantly hiding a world of pain. I love her, a protective love. I only ever wanted to keep her safe, the intolerable mental abuse she suffered at the hands of Harrison's brother, Ollie, the ordeal of destruction dealt by him, by the drugs, too much for her. There is a far-away look in her eyes, perhaps to Ollie, her one true love, the one she killed. I wonder if he took her soul with him after she drowned him. He took everything else. Perhaps she's thinking of her family? The safe world she's built, the one I'm about to smash to pieces. The one she's desperate to maintain even though her husband may be having an affair.

Toward the far end of the table, Jorge and Tomasz, hands tightly clasped, flesh white and pink where they are squeezing – it seems we are all clinging on to that which we love the most at this time, perhaps mindful it could be the last. Tomasz, always so sullen, so quiet, hard to read, coughs, politely covering his mouth, and sweeps his long blond fringe back from his forehead as is his habit. Such a nice guy, sensitive, and so deserving of the fame and fortune his talented feet have brought him – the fortune I am about to destroy, the infamy I am about to bring. His will be the most public shame – *Superstar footballer is a double murderer!* He will get absolutely caned. And as for Jorge, caught up in this mess, I know little, but his life will also be turned upside down. He'll lose Tomasz, he'll lose the life he's become accustomed to. He's watching me watching him, poker-faced, cool, calculating, but his actions reveal his fear. He may not have shot Helen, just missed her, but he took the risk and pulled the trigger. That alone suggests a dark capability within.

Beside me is Harrison, and next to him I see Helen's long blonde hair fallen forward, her head down. I'm certain her being here isn't a coincidence. Why implicate herself? She seems preoccupied, fiddling with the strapping on her leg. What does she want from all of this? Why is she here?

Harrison drums his fingers on the table, twitchy and impatient as ever. 'Jer-i-cho,' he says, lowering his torso to the tabletop and peering under the page which is tilted up on a crease at its centre. I reach out to pick it up but he's quicker, snatching it away.

'Jericho,' he says again, louder and pointing at the back of the page, holding it up for all to see.

Toward a corner, in the same red ink as used on the front, the word *Jericho*, doodled in block letters, then scribbled over. Has the Leveller written it? Could it be a clue?

I take the page from Harrison, ignoring his look of objection. 'Does this mean anything to any of you?'

I wait, holding out the page while taking a couple of sips of the coffee. It makes me wince, I'm fussy about my coffee, and this one really is incredibly strong. Hard as I try, in observing their responses, their mannerisms, I don't detect a slip of the mask from any of them. Each look from one to another, quiet murmurs exchanged, eyebrows raised, shrugging or shaking their heads. Finally, Orla stands, but frustrated, I stand too, toss the page on the table and lean forward pressing both hands flat on the tabletop. An ache is swelling in my brain, it's developing a jagged edge, becoming a fierce pain.

'Enough–', but I struggle to continue as a dizziness swills through me and I drop an elbow to the table to support me. Next to me, Orla grabs my arm, beetle eyes, lips smeared with cherry-red lipstick, and bruises dampened by stark white makeup. I'm staring as the colours collide, her face taking on the look of a cheap and grotesque clown.

'Zac?' She says, clown face stretched with concern, and sliding her arm around my waist. 'Are you okay?'

Taking a deep breath, I nod, pushing her away. Confused, she places my coffee mug in my hand. I take another sip of the stuff in the hope it perks me up.

'For fucks sake!' Orla shouts at everyone, hands clamped either side of her head, fingers splayed wide. She looks like the Edvard Munch *Scream* painting. 'This has to stop! We'll all end up either mad or dead!'

I hang my head, staring at the table. I can feel Orla's force, her energy returning, not wholly, but beginning, and I'm glad, so glad. I'm not sure I can do this on my own.

She slams her fist on the table, and it seems to me the thud of the impact is delayed coming a second after contact. I close my eyes, except doing so triggers a deeper darkness, so I open them again quickly. I take a deep breath. The air is thick with tension. People are momentarily intimidated by Orla. No one dares move.

'What are we? Fucking ghosts?' Orla demands. 'For fucks sake, are we that far gone, we can't see sense? We are all as guilty as hell! Zac didn't make you kill. None of us *had* to kill. Each of us *chose* to kill. Now we must *choose* to stop. The Leveller. Has. To. Stop!'

'Then stop.'

All eyes land on Jorge.

'You heard me,' he says, standing up. 'Orla, why don't you stop killing.'

He and Orla hold one another's gaze. As I think Orla is about to give it to him with both barrels, she sits, deflated, exhausted. She's not at full strength yet, of course she isn't. But Jorge isn't done with her. 'A woman with heavy black eye makeup was witnessed running from the funicular, from the boy? Was that you, Orla? Did you smash the boy's head in and leave him for dead?'

'No, I fucking didn't,' she replies as quick as a shot. She leans back in her chair, sighing out loud.

'Jorge,' I say, trying to set my cup down, but it's as if the table's a moving target, and I slosh a little over the lip of the mug. 'I don't really know you… but I know I don't like you…'

Tomasz sits up straight. 'Hold on a minute, Zac, that's not fair. Jorge and Helen are the only ones among us who haven't killed…'

'That's not true.' Helen lays her hands flat on the table as if presenting her playing cards, playing her hand, and I suspect that is kind of what she's about to do. 'I killed someone.'

'No, Helen,' Harrison blurts, but she raises her hand, halting him. She winces as she adjusts her leg under the table. 'It's true. I killed someone. I murdered them. She was in custody. In a cell. She had killed her niece, but that wasn't it, she had abused her… horrifically.'

The Great Orme

I feel and hear Harrison's chest inflate as he prepares to say something again, but she flashes a glance that stops him. My mouth and throat are parched. I take another sip of coffee – it tastes peculiar.

'During a night shift, I went to her cell. I tore her bedsheet and hooked it through the ventilation grill high up on the wall. I tied the other end around her neck and hoisted her up. It's the most common prison suicide practice. She deserved it. No doubt about it. Pure evil.'

Even though we are used to murder, all are bereft of voice at Helen's admission. We do not know this woman, and she has confessed a murder to us. She's killed someone – murdered them, not in self-defence, but in cold blood. She's like the rest of us. I'm astounded. Why would she confess to us? Why is she here? Why am I a magnet for murderers?

Jorge – who else? – breaks the impasse. 'Jesus Christ,' he bristles. 'What about little old Smokey? We shouldn't be at all surprised to hear he's mauled someone to death? That would leave me as the only one yet to kill.'

The queasiness is getting worse, my skin is perspiring, and all the while Jorge's expression is becoming darker, sinister, cartoon-like.

All around the table, vague mutterings, queries and denials, and all the while my throat burns. I raise my hand to my neck, opening and closing my mouth, which feels dry and furry. I lick my lips, but they feel numb, a heavy metallic taste on them. I swallow the acrid taste but it clashes with something else rising up to meet it. I feel giddy like I've just stepped off a rollercoaster, like my body has forgotten how to coordinate movement, the room and the faces in it swirling about me. I must focus. I try to fix my gaze on the table, on *my* mug. I notice the coffee in it has a blueish-grey tinge.

I projectile vomit, copious amounts of grey lumpy puke splash over the table. To the muffled sounds of shouting and scraping of chair-legs, I feel myself slide to the floor.

I think I'm drowning. My face is wet, my hair damp. I push up, gulping greedily on stuffy air and thrashing like a wild animal, but the sea washes over me and strong hands push me back down. Then I see it coming, the screaming blackness, eyes of fire, the sea serpent, the Great Orme. My forearm shoots out across my face to protect myself, scratching at the darkness swamping me, but the beast glides closer and closer, the serpent's head thrashing wildly, lips peeling back into its ears, a ripped-open face of fangs. The terror lunges at me and I feel the full force of its strike across my face, and I sink, falling into an endless pit of darkness. A tearing screeching pierces my ears. I can feel my flesh, blood and bones pressed against what feels like cold hard rock, but it's not, it's fossil-like reptilian skin. The sea serpent stretches and twists its neck, glowering over its vast body at me. I'm riding on the beast's back. The serpent roars, a rolling wave of sound broken from the depths of hell, then it bucks and I'm flying upwards, erect and gasping for air.

I'm on my feet, staggering, concerned voices clash, hands touch my body from everywhere. I push them away, aware I'm back in the dining room, the killers stood around me.

The dizziness and the sickness have passed, my head is clearing. I reach for my mug, my mug. The mug I always use, depicted on it, the image of the Great Orme – jutting black headland risen from the sea, the land depicted as a ferocious sea serpent, blazing red eyes. 'The sea serpent,' I say softly. A girl's voice I don't recognise swishes through my head: Get away, get away and leave this place.

But I can't. Here lies my heart. Even if it's breaking my bones, it's home. Home, sweet home.

I have too many old mugs and cups, all stacked on the dresser in the kitchen, but I always drink from this one. Someone has noticed and they've poisoned my coffee. I tilt the mug, peering at its contents, still two-thirds full, a bluey-silver-grey tint to it. I breathe in its aroma, a metallic, peppery tang.

'Zac, what happened?' Orla tugs my elbow, her voice fraught with concern. 'Are you okay?'

The Great Orme

'Someone tried to poison me.' I hand her the mug.

There's some bustle as the others take turns inspecting its contents, then inspecting the contents of their own mugs, and for the first time in ages, I laugh. They are uncertain, seeing shades of blue and smelling aromas that might or might not exist. Harrison hands me a glass of water. I thank him, downing it in one gulp. My tongue and lips still tingle.

'It's fortunate you vomited,' Helen says. She's stood next to Harrison. 'You probably cleared most of whatever it is from your system.'

'I hope so,' I say, wiping my lips on the back of my hand. 'So,' I state loudly. 'Who made the coffee?'

Jorge appears through the doorway, a bowl of soapy water in his hands. He places it on the table and starts to scrub away my vomit.

'We did.'

All eyes turn to Sian. Diminutive yet powerful, she reaches out and clasps Jessie's arm. 'Me and Jessie made the coffee. We used some Lazy Sunday ground coffee you keep in the fridge.'

'Honestly guys,' Jessie says, taking hold of the backrest of the chair in front of her. 'We didn't do anything.'

Sian's grip on Jessie's arm tightens. Jessie stares at me, eyes like muddy pools, and I wonder to what extent she will fight for a life, one designed to rid herself of the torment of the past.

'Well, someone did,' I say, rubbing my forehead vigorously. 'Someone here poisoned my coffee. If it wasn't either of you, then you must have seen something, either while you were making it or afterwards? Did anyone help you bring the cups in?'

'Jesus Christ,' Harrison says, dragging his hand down the velvet textured wallpaper adorning the wall he's propped against, the rich teal paper scored with fine gold sprigs was my mother's last upgrade to the house before she died. 'Jorge and I helped them. We brought the drinks in,' he says, his voice broken into frustrated and familiar high-pitched falsetto. He moves in front of the window, at the other end of the room, the white morning light backlighting him as a dark, crooked figure. For a moment he reminds me of Bela Lugosi from those old black and white horror films. I shudder at the thought.

Jorge straightens, cloth in one hand, holding his lower back with the other. 'You may not like me, and well, to be honest, I don't like you, but it certainly wasn't me that poisoned your damn coffee.' He continues wiping up my vomit.

'Just know this,' says Orla, fire returned to her belly. 'Whichever one of you did do it, well, you'll have to go through me before you get to Zac.'

Tomasz's pale face burns red, all pent-up emotion. He strides around the table, touching poor old Rose on her shoulder as he passes, she clutches hold of her walking stick lying flat on the table as if preparing to physically defend herself. Tomasz stops behind Costas and places a hand on Jules's shoulder sat next to him.

Costas reaches for his glasses, holds them on his nose, in disarray, uncertain how to respond.

'Julia… Jules,' Tomasz says. 'You shot and murdered your mother – your own mother. I am correct, aren't I? Harrison?'

Harrison groans, grasping his bald head with one hand and digging his fingernails in to his scalp, clawing backwards. I can see the tracks of the lines left behind in his skin.

Tomasz addresses Costas with mounting confidence, his pupils dilated and staring. 'It's true, isn't it?'

Costas removes his glasses and looks pensively at Jules. She holds his gaze for a microsecond, long enough for me to read into the damage done to their relationship because of the Vicar's transgression.

Jules removes Tomasz's hand from her shoulder as if it's a filthy rag. 'How dare you?' she says, standing and facing Tomasz squarely, as tall as him and more confident. 'You don't really know anything of me, so don't presume to. I'm not your Leveller.' She pauses before stating, 'However, I do have some sympathy with his – or her – cause.'

My already brittle heart strains that bit more, another fissure. I wonder how much a heart can take before it gives up completely. I should have seen this coming. Faced with life imprisonment, people will fight hard, anything to avoid their lives as they know them, ending. They are terrified. All are keeping their own counsel, all on edge, scared to breathe, scared to blink for fear of crashing toward a confession or crashing toward a killing.

Jules flips her gaze from Tomasz, facing inward toward the rest of the room. 'Nothing of me, of my life, is prone toward that which is not directly in line with the wishes of our Lord. Yes, I've made mistakes, but who here hasn't? Anyway,' she says, finding Costas' hand and squeezing it with her own. 'Forgiveness is everything.'

She proceeds to quote the Bible, 'Mathew 6:12, 14-15,' she says, before reciting:

'For if you forgive others their trespasses, your heavenly father will also forgive you, but if you do not forgive others their trespasses, neither will your Father forgive your trespasses.'

She smooths her ruler-straight red hair, a strange composure on her face replete with clinical make-up and stiff jawline, giving the air of someone not to be messed with. 'Each of us has so much to lose,' she says. 'We need to move on. We need to forgive one another. Leave it to the Good Lord to evaluate why we did what we did, let Him gauge the extent of our regret.'

'Wait!' Costas has found his voice, and he too, gets to his feet. 'Jules isn't the Leveller! Do you remember, Zac? The message? The phone message I got from the Leveller.' He turns to face his wife. 'The Leveller said…' his voice and excitement trail off noticeably, so I finish his sentence for him.

'Jules would be killed if we confessed.'

The married couple stare at one another, and a new fissure splinters my heart.

'So,' I say, turning the focus back to Jorge, an implacable expression on his face. 'It seems you *are* the only non-murderer here? The only one of us who might walk away from all of this? Go ahead, spoil it, tell me I'm wrong, tell me you're a killer too.'

Jules steps away from the table, pushing Tomasz aside. Jorge scratches his clean-shaven neck, pulling at the neckline of his jumper – the only sign he's feeling pressure. He makes his way toward the bay window, looking out from the dark house to a sky that glows like a grey diamond. He turns to face us, the edges of his form blurred by the cold grey light from behind. 'Sorry to disappoint, but I'm not a killer. And, Zac, technically, neither are you. I still think you are playing us for fools.'

'Go on,' I say, wishing for him not to go on, wishing he had never set foot in the old house.

'You've been distant from every single murder scene. Your link to all the murders is tenuous to say the least. You've only ever suggested to these people what they might do. Something you can easily deny. *You*, Zachary Llewellyn, are not a murderer.'

He pauses, nodding in agreement with himself. Before anyone else can say something, he adds, 'You, out of all of us, have the least to lose.'

His words hang in the air like smoke, and I wish I could clear them away, but he's right, I have never, hands-on murdered anyone – but I am culpable, as their leader, the one who gave the orders.

'Quite why you are so desperate to condemn your friends by confessing today, is a complete mystery,' Jorge says, tugging at the frayed green curtains, lip curled in disdain.

'He's not confessing today, or any day.'

While Jorge has been talking Jules has moved. She's beside Orla, and she's pointing the gun, her gun, at the back of my wife's head.

Defence versus attack

Chapter Twenty-Eight

'Do you know how hard it's been to build this life?'

'Jules?' Costas pleads, pressing the palms of his hands together as if praying.

'No Costas! I've seen hell and I'm not going back there. I'm not, and I won't let you go there either.'

Jules's skin at the top of her chest has turned red and patchy. Orla stares at me, beetle eyes wide and set to burst from her face. *Do something*, they urge.

'You don't think we went too far?' I ask Jules. 'Costas… we… took precious days of life from poor Chloe. We robbed her family. Even one day of life more – just imagine what that would have been worth to her family; Orla and I left poor Choreji, dead, her family never knowing who killed her; Rose's husband, was what we did to him really justice? No! Each moment of murder was a moment of madness.' I clear my throat realising this is the moment people can be swayed. 'Even now, this very weekend, our old headmaster, murdered and why? To scare me, to scare us so we don't confess. Even my father's killer, murdered. What about the poor boy fighting for his life as I speak, what kind of justice has been exerted on him? What did he do to deserve that? And even here, in the old house, above our heads, Fatima lies dead. All her hopes and dreams expired.'

I stare at them all open-mouthed, disgusted with them, disgusted with myself. They carefully avoid my gaze. 'We are like the Mafia but without their morality,' I continue, focussed on Jules. 'Put the gun down. Please.'

'What's done is done,' she says, solemnly shaking her head. 'It can't be undone.'

Orla tries to move but Jules, taller and seemingly stronger, grabs hold of her hair, bunching it into her fist, tugging hard and pulling her back. 'Don't be stupid, Orla. You're better than that. You all are,' she says, casting her gaze on all of us and puffing out her cheeks. 'I've sacrificed so very much for my little life with Costas. You were all kids when you killed the old man – a stupid mistake. And Chloe… well she was suffering… she was already dying. Costas put her out of her misery. Please, let God judge.'

'Zac!' Sian's voice splashes over the cracked and fraught atmosphere, brightly bleached jagged hair like a smashed halo about her head - a fallen angel. 'I'm so tired, please, let it go, for all of our sakes, let's not confess. All of this – it's killing us. Even now, we can leave it all behind. We can clean up. We can live our lives.'

Sian takes up a position next to Jules and Orla. Jules pulls Orla closer, yanking her head back again. Orla cries out. I'm paralysed by indecision for fear of Jules pulling the trigger, my mind imagining the explosion, Orla's face wiped clear of life.

Before I can respond, Jorge leaves his place at the window and strides around the table, to stand beside them at the back of the room. 'You have to listen to them, Zac,' he says. 'You can't confess on their behalf. They have lives to live, let them live them.' Then he asks Jules to let Orla go, a kindness of tone yet to be shared with me.

Jules takes a deep breath and exhales slowly, before lowering the gun and releasing Orla, apologising to her as she does so. Tomasz joins them, taking hold of Jorge's hand. Jorge smiles, eyes soft and considerate. 'Who else is with us?' he asks. I watch as first, Jessie joins them, even Rose, walking stick in hand, head down. Even Costas joins them, whispering, 'sorry' to me as he passes. My mind chugs like a tractor engine. Perhaps they are right. Perhaps we clean up the mess and go on with our lives. Without speaking, Harrison helps Helen, his arms wrapped around her for support, so they hobble to join the others collected next to the sideboard. Behind them my mother's giant, dark and gloomy painting of the Great Orme hangs on the wall. It seems they are in the painting, the Great Orme swelling around their heads, one pulsating heartbeat, the Great Orme in them, the history and sickness of the land in their blood. I feel my head will explode with the pressure. A hand, warm, takes mine, fingers entwine, squeeze. I see Choreji, beside me, gorgeous wide brown eyes, watery. She shakes her head. I blink hard, and see Orla stood next to me, the look on her face stark and despairing.

Jorge raises his arm and points the gun at me. 'Perhaps it's time for me to join the ranks of the killers. The final kill to end all killings?'

'That's the problem, Jorge,' I respond flatly. 'There isn't a final killing. It goes on and on. The only way we can step back from all of this is to confess – it's the only way out.'

I angle my head to peer at Harrison. 'Perhaps your girlfriend knows who the Leveller is?'

Helen pushes herself up from leaning against the table, a quick and knowing glance at Harrison giving her away. She smiles, even sniggers. It's the first time I've seen her flustered since we met.

Harrison makes a strangulated croak, preparing to speak, but Helen is sharper, quickly finding her composure. 'We didn't want to confuse the situation,' she says, talking to us but eyes fixed firmly on Harrison. 'I'm from Llandudno. My family live here. I did my police training in London. Harrison and I met in Windsor while I was on duty, nearly two years ago. Harrison worked the door at the Elephant and Castle. I managed to get a transfer to Llandudno – my mother still lives here, she's getting on and she's not well, I wanted to be there for her. Harrison told me he was coming up here. He told me about you. He also told me about the message you sent. I wanted to help… that's all, I just wanted to help.'

I'm incredulous. 'You wanted to help a bunch of killers?'

The Great Orme

She grapples with her hair, pulling it into a ponytail. There's an analytical calmness about her that unsettles me, and it seems a little more than her police training, more like that of a psychopath.

'To be absolutely honest, Zac – I admire you. You've only ever tried to exact justice. You've done your job. You've made the world a safer place.'

'It's too late to tell my old headmaster that, or the little boy lying in hospital with his head smashed in, or even Fatima, stone cold dead above our heads.'

Outside, I hear the occasional car pass by - the other world awake and going about its business, oblivious to the old house and the evil contained within. The old house creaks, its joints upstairs giving way to the cold. I can hear Smokey barking from the kitchen, my boy is locked up.

'Listen to yourselves!' Orla shouts, vertical lines of black tears spoiling her pale face. 'Are you all so cold and unfeeling? So selfish? Zac is right, God damn it! You have to listen to him!'

'Right,' Jorge says. 'And when was the last time you saw your husband before this weekend?'

Orla stares at him, her face scrunched up, perplexed.

'Six years ago, perhaps?' Jorge suggests. 'The same as the rest of his *close* friends?'

Orla's bottom lip is quivering.

Jorge continues. 'You think you know him? Can you appreciate just how embittered a man might get, living here on the Great Orme, alone in this *old* house?'

My head, it hurts. My brain too. His words derisory but now with logic of a sort. The only thing I have going for me is I know I'm not the Leveller. It's him. It has to be. Why though, doesn't he admit it and move on? Is he scared the others might turn against him if he does?

Jorge releases himself from Tomasz's grip and leaves the others, trailing his fingers along the curved edge of the table as he makes his way toward me. He stops before me and I can smell him. He's wearing my deodorant. 'Perhaps, just perhaps this one time, you're wrong.' I don't see the blow coming, the blunt metal handle of the gun striking my temple dazes me, a myriad of exploding colours inside my head, and I stagger, crouched over, but not for long. Another blow to my head, and I collapse to the floor.

My head is resting against the cold wall.

They are slipping away from me, all of them, and there's nothing I can do. My head throbs. I can taste blood leaking into mouth.

The force of a kick to my ribs knocks me over onto my side. I hear Orla scream.

I must open my eyes. Orla is nearby, I can smell her zesty scent. It invigorates me. I blink open my eyes, just in time to recognise the flash of Tomasz's white rubber trainer sole, and just before it strikes me in the face.

My head rebounds off the wall, and the light dims, faded to black, Orla's anguished howl the last thing I hear.

I wake with a sore head. Something is trickling from my nose. Blood, I think. I'm lying somewhere soft, a bed, damp, I try to move but my hands and ankles are bound together. Someone is lying next to me. I open my eyes, blinking rapidly to focus but the person's hair is stuck to my bloodied face. I rock my head back so the sticky strands pull from my skin. My head swirls with imagery, purple flowered wallpaper, two tall oak cupboards, an oval mirror set on my mother's dressing table – two bodies reflected in it, one of which is my own and the other lying next to me, not Fatima but Tomasz.

There's a hideous smell, a putrid combination of sweat and petrol fumes that make me gag. It's me. My clothes are wet. My waking calmness evaporates and I open my mouth to shout, but the sharp intake of air is trapped inside my head as Tomasz's hand slaps over my mouth.

I drive my knees upwards with as much force as I can muster, catching Tomasz in the midriff. It takes him by surprise. He gasps, hand dragged roughly over my face before he falls from the bed, the dull sound of his body hitting the floor and a chair toppling over.

I roll off the bed, landing, pushing out with elbows and thumping into Tomasz. He pushes me off, cool flecked eyes wild and staring.

'I'm sorry,' he says, the pair of us lying side by side on the carpet. 'I can't let you get inside my head. This place, this old house, it's trying to get inside my head, and I can't let it, either. Do you realise how scared we are, how scared I am?'

'Fucking hell, Tomasz,' I spit. 'You're scared!? I'm the one smashed in the face and trussed up like a Christmas turkey.' I try to pull my wrists from my ankles but it's no good, the tape doesn't tear, and it doesn't stretch.

'There he is,' Tomasz says, gazing as if hypnotised up at the ceiling.

'Wha... what?' I stammer.

'Bart,' Tomasz says flatly.

Lying on my side, I crane my neck to look up, and there he is, Tomasz's abuser, Bart, hanging from the light-fitting in the middle of the ceiling, a noose of tights wrapped around his neck, body and legs twitching beneath, the stench of his shit-stained shorts permeating that of the petrol fumes.

'I can't... I can't go to prison. I'd rather be dead.'

'And this isn't prison?' I ask, my lips and throat dry and raw with the stench and taste of petrol and shit. 'It'll be a relief for us, Tomasz. We can finally hand over control.'

Tomasz pushes up on an elbow and surveys the room with glazed eyes, staring from wall to wall, I don't think he's heard a word I've said to him. 'You've lived with the dead too long,' he mutters. 'There's another. Look.'

He points at the far wall. I see her. I don't want to, but I can. Choreji's face stares out from the purple-patterned wall, brown eyes flared wide at us. She lifts an arm and points at Tomasz while glaring at me.

I swivel my head and see he's shifted on to both his elbows, he's holding a box of matches clenched in his fist. A nervous grin creeps into his fearful expression. It's a different Tomasz, a dark menace entrenched in the fine lines of his face. I swear he's on drugs. Somehow, I punch forward with my head, my forehead connecting with his nose, a resounding cracking sound on impact and he screams in pain. I roll onto my back. He's let go of the matchbox to grasp his face but blood is rushing through his fingers, leaking on to the carpet. I think I've broken his nose.

'You stupid, stupid bastard,' he says, spitting into my ear. With one of his bloodied hands, he grasps me around my throat, with the other he's grabbed a handful of my hair. He pulls my head back, jerking my chin up. 'I thought as much, Zac – you are capable of the same violence as the rest of us.'

'Are you the Leveller?' I splutter.

He laughs, ugly, crazed. 'No, I'm not that smart.'

'Think, Tomasz,' I growl. 'Think what you are doing.' My taped legs and wrists are making my muscles burn along each side of my torso.

'I am thinking. This time thinking for myself instead of letting you do it for me,' he snarls. He grabs my head, jerks it up and slams it downward.

The back of my head, already sore, connects with the carpeted floor, stinging with old and new pain. There's blood in my mouth, I think I've bitten my tongue.

Tomasz's face is contorted, crazed and bloodied, the introspective footballer a man I don't recognise anymore, and in his hand, the box of matches. He shakes them, teasing. 'You are going to burn. On Earth, and in hell.'

Burning fingers of fear claws at my innards, the realisation of what this quiet man is capable of. I may not get out of my mother's room alive.

I press my face into the carpet, as if I've given up, and I nearly have, but with all the strength I have left, I spin my body, kicking the overturned chair as hard as I can, lifting it up off the floor. It strikes Tomasz with a satisfying clunk on the head, and he grunts.

The Great Orme

I look around to see him coiled in the foetal position as I am, his hands pressed to his face, this time covering an eye. I roll myself toward the dressing table, tumbling awkwardly at speed. I don't know how hurt he is. I don't even have time to look back, he could be on me any moment. I collide into the dresser's legs and immediately squeeze underneath it and push up, lifting and upending the whole thing so it crashes to the floor, spilling its contents over the carpet. I see the metallic glint of what I want straight away. Gasping for breath, I point and heave my body toward the tiny nail scissors. I can hear him moving, cursing under his breath.

I grab hold of the scissors between sweaty palms, adjusting their position so they point face down and, cocking my wrists, I stab at the tape, alternating between the bind on my wrists and ankles.

I hear the trudge of his feet across the carpet and his shadow looms over me, his laboured breath forced through a broken and bloody nose. He grabs my hair, pulling it tight.

I burst upright; the force tearing apart the semi-butchered tape, releasing my hands and ankles. My head connects with his chin, sending him spiralling backwards, toppling over the upended dresser and slamming his head against the wall. Groaning, he stumbles on to his feet before collapsing in a heap on the floor, where he stays, holding his head.

My first thought is for Orla. Where is she?

I step out onto the landing. All is quiet. I check each of the rooms along it, even the bathroom, all of them are empty, no bags or suitcases, no evidence of the others. From the top of the stairs, I see their luggage carefully arranged against the wall near the front door. I think I can hear voices coming from the lounge. I have to escape. I have to head for the door. The Leveller is in control. I am not. I lost control the day I sent the messages, and most likely a long time before.

I move stealthily, placing a hand on the banister to steady myself, but the stair underneath my foot creaks slightly. I wince, waiting for someone to come and investigate but no one does.

Hardly daring to breathe, I continue on, increasingly aware I have failed, all I wanted – a chance to persuade them, a chance to finally do the one right thing. If I reach the bottom step, I'll be first to the front door… I can escape. I can leave the old house. I can leave them. I can confess. It's over.

I descend the stairs and let go of the banister, my eyes are fixated on the front-door, and the inverse image of the bird of prey in the glass panel above it screams '*Go now! Go now!*'

I know I must, it's over, I must bring the terror to a close.

A shrill squeal comes from the lounge. I know immediately it's Orla, and she's in trouble, worse, she's in pain.

I turn to head for the lounge, but too late, I realise he's behind me, the heel of his shoe connects with the middle of my back and I lurch forward. Propelled by Tomasz's kick, I slam against the wall and smash into the assembled suitcases and holdalls, scattering them noisily.

An entrance to an exit

Chapter Twenty-Nine

Smokey is first to me, licking my face, his tail wagging furiously. Through the staircase's wooden spindles, I see Tomasz stepping carefully down the stairs. He's clenching his blond hair either side of his blood-smeared face, his eyes rimmed red and fixed with the countenance of a mad man. Perhaps we are all in the grip of a madness, a contagion of some kind.

I push some of the luggage away from me as the door to the lounge opens, instinctively pulling Smokey in to close to me, fearing for him as much as myself. These people, some I thought I knew, and others I have never known appear one by one, all of them wearing coats or jackets. Crowded in the hallway, they observe me lying amongst their luggage, stone-like expressions on their faces and in no hurry to assist. Orla's not with them.

Finally, Harrison and Costas attend to me, lifting me to my feet without a word. My entire body, my face, and my head, throb and sting like I've done a round with a cage fighter, but at least I'm not in flames. I imagine Tomasz tossing a lit match at me and I shudder. The two men carry me, hobbling, into the lounge. I still stink of petrol which doesn't help my churning stomach at all. I thank God on seeing Orla sat on the sofa, safely. Our eyes remain locked while Harrison and Costas escort me with great care, as if I'm an elderly man, and sit me next to her. Her hands are clasped together in her lap, and her wrists bound with tape. She is wearing a coat, my coat, the green one, still stained from her fall. I wonder for a moment if she had considered leaving with the others. Whatever the case, she hasn't and isn't, because like me she's considered a threat to their precious freedom.

The Great Orme

Tomasz staggers through the doorway, looks up at everyone else gathered, and promptly collapses to the floor. Other than from Jorge, he gets only half-hearted attention, a cloth thrown at him, which he takes to dab at his bleeding eye and nose. Even now, I find it difficult to comprehend how my friends have turned on us; the depraved lengths they are prepared to reach. Sian's guttural laugher breaks like a wave against the walls of the old house. I scrutinise her. How can she laugh? Her wife is dead.

She hands a roll of grey tape to Jessie.

Jessie has done something to her hair. It's sprung out, wilder, a shield of natural curls and kinks about her head, as it was when we were young. Her face is serious, deadly serious. I look about the room, all others remain still and grim-faced.

I must make them see things as they are. 'Tomasz intended to kill me,' I say, my throat sore from the petrol fumes, and sounding like a whining telltale kid. I pull at my petrol-wet jumper. 'He was going to set fire to me.'

'Are you really such an idiot, Zac?' Jessie's voice is plaintive. 'You as good as wanted to kill us. That's what sending us to prison for the rest of our lives would be like! Did you ever stop to think about the damage you'd cause our families? Their anguish in knowing what we've done. Their lives ruined!'

I shake my head in disbelief. 'You're making everything worse,' I tell her.

'All of these terrible things,' she says with force. 'They've happened because of you!'

It's true, the difference being I want them to stop, but I'm too mesmerised by Jessie unravelling the tape. Her eyes are like impenetrable hard shells. Where is the Jessie I remember? The one that cared so much for her boyfriend, so much so that she almost let his drug abuse kill her as well as him. She bites through the tape, snapping a long length so it dangles freely from her fingers. 'It breaks my heart, really it does, to see you so set against us,' she says, handing the tape-roll back to Sian.

She sneers at Orla. 'You too, Orla. After all, he's done to you.'

I regard Orla sat beside me, fresh scratches and bruises on her face. She's put up a fight. My heart crumples with pain as I wonder what she did to deserve me. Holding my gaze, she bites her lip, beetle eyes alert and laser sharp – she and I know we are fighting for our lives.

Costas moves toward us and reaches out to touch my shoulder, but I jerk it away. He nods as if understanding and I half-expect him to apologise for what they are about to do.

'Costas, you of all people,' I say, gazing up at him, the whites of his eyes scored with red lines. 'You know this is wrong. You can't handle this. You–'

'None of us want this,' Harrison says, his significant bulk occupying the space between me and the door. His eyes too, are blood-shot and his bald head shiny with sweat. 'But honestly, we just want to live our lives. What did you think we'd do? Trundle down to the police station with you?'

'It's either a goal or not a goal,' says Tomasz, sat on the carpet, one hand covering his eye, the edge of his blond fringe sticky with blood. 'There's no in-between.' He gazes up at me through one eye. 'Why are you so stubborn? All we want is to be able to live our lives.' He removes his hand, and I screw my face up at the sight of his blood-rimmed eyeball, the white of it washed pink.

'You need help – all of you!' I want to scream at them. I want to rip their heads open and shake their brains so they can see themselves for what they are. I get to my feet. 'It's a pattern. Can't you see? This is how you deal with things. You kill. It's crazy. You – we, we need help. Stop! Please!'

'It's been a long weekend. Let's bring it to an end.' Jorge's voice is solid and cuts through the room with ease. He weaves his way through the room like a motorcyclist through traffic, stopping at his lover on the floor. 'I won't have you condemn Tomasz to a lifetime in prison. You might as well kill him. You might as well kill me.'

The Great Orme

'You won't get away with this,' I tell him. 'They'll discover Fatima missing. They'll trace her to the old house. They'll find her murdered. They'll find you. All of you!'

'You're upset, Zac,' Jorge responds coolly. 'Understandable, given the circumstance. Honestly though, you don't have all the answers, and we don't have a choice.'

'So, you are the Leveller. After all this, why not admit it?'

'Because I'm not,' he replies, looking around the room.

I need to know who's in charge. It's going to be my only way through this. 'Who is it? For God's sake, stop hiding.'

'Answer him,' Jorge demands.

We wait, the old house waits, its bumps and groans a clamour in the silence. I understand Jorge needs to know who the Leveller is if he and Tomasz are going to have a chance at survival after whatever happens next. They need to know who is going to be watching in case any of them falter in their convictions.

Sian bumps the tape-roll on her thigh, drumming it at speed, a metronomic countdown to the revelation.

Click.

It's the door to the lounge.

Everyone is already in the lounge.

The silver handle twitches and lowers.

Click.

Click.

Click.

Next to me, Orla stiffens, leaning into me but I'm mesmerised by the handle, as are we all. It sticks as it reaches its lowest point.

'Who is it?' Costas blurts, unable to contain himself. 'We are all here!'

The lounge door gradually opens inward.

There's a collective sharp intake of breath.

Harrison staggers backwards, legs bumping against the sofa. Costas grabs him, the two men frightened by the appearance of a ghost.

Fatima stands in the doorway, one hand on her hip, the other on the door handle.

She's changed her outfit, no longer wearing the emerald blood-stained dress but wearing a black high-collared coat, black jeans and white trainers. Her hair is tied back in a ponytail and she's pouting her lips as if assessing the situation.

'But you're... you're dead!' Costas tells her, grappling for his antique crucifix inside his jacket.

The ghost laughs, letting go of the door and entering the room with the practised stride of the performer.

'But the gun... didn't I sh... shoot you?' Costas stumbles.

Fatima reaches out for Sian, and the two women embrace, sharing a kiss before the fireplace. Standing side by side and holding hands, the two women face the room.

'You forget, I'm an actress,' Fatima announces. 'A very good one it would seem, and one with a promising career ahead, a bright future, with the woman I love.' She turns to Sian and they kiss again. They are presenting a view of normality, of a love that will endure despite the situation. The others watch on with something like awe, and most-likely inspired. I feel the fear gripping my gut squeeze even tighter.

Fatima turns her gaze to Costas. 'During our *struggle*, I pressed your finger on the trigger,' she says. 'Making sure the gun was aimed away from me, of course.' She laughs theatrically, before adding, 'An Oscar-worthy performance, don't you think?'

Costas lifts his eyes to the ceiling, shaking his head in disbelief.

'I brought some fake blood bags with me, perk of the job I suppose, although my dress is absolutely ruined, cost an absolute fortune.' She waves her hand breezily. 'But it's been worth it.'

Still shocked by her sudden appearance, no one else speaks, and she's happy to hold court and comfortable with it. 'Now, listen to me,' she says, her face becoming serious, earnest. She casts her gaze around the room, assessing everyone present. 'We leave this... "old house", and we never come back. No one ever speaks of this weekend ever again. We go back to our lives and live them. We are blessed to have this chance.'

Fatima's voice isn't loud, but it projects, filling the room, each word and each consonant clipped, commanding, but she doesn't look at me or Orla at all. It's clear we aren't part of her plan.

'Anyone who would rather give up on life, please join Zac and Orla on the sofa.'

Costas looks from Jules to me and then to Jules, his moment of doubting quickly over. No one else moves.

Like a circus lion beaten and subdued, I feel cornered and desperate, but I know I have to change something before it's too late. One last roar. 'So, it was you all along? You are the Leveller?'

'Someone had to be, Zac,' Fatima says, buttoning up her coat. 'For all our sakes… someone had to be. Someone had to stop you.'

Smokey barks at her, and while I appreciate his sentiment, it's not going to be enough.

'Do something,' whispers an ice-cold breath in my ear. A small hand squeezes my bound wrists. 'You owe us,' Choreji says. Startled, Orla stares past me and down at my wrists. She's seen the little girl, too. Even dead, Choreji has an undeniable strength, one that will not give up.

Tomasz drags himself over the carpet toward the door. I can tell by the drop of his jaw he's seen the girl, but the others remain unfazed, not having seen her at all. I must keep the dialogue moving. It's the only chance I've got of affecting a change.

'Someone had to stop me?' I ask incredulously. 'Stop me, when it was you, all the threats, and worse, all you?'

Fatima angles her head. 'I shouldn't take all the credit.'

'You too, Sian?' I ask.

Sian nods and sighs, running her fingers through her spiked peroxide hair. 'Thank God for Fatima or we'd all be rotting in cells until we died. She's saved us from you. Now it's time to make you accountable. Finally, we get to relinquish your control over us.'

I'm dumbfounded. In that split second, I try to consider the how's and why's but can only conclude I was never in control, that it was perhaps they, only seeking affirmation from me to do what they were going to do, anyway. These people are scared and deadly. And I'm just scared.

'You gave us no choice,' Fatima says, shaking her head. 'You, of all people, should understand that.'

Then she's moving, first to Helen, who she exchanges a hug and a kiss with. Then Jules, who she embraces, sharing a brief whisper in her ear. Fatima hauls Tomasz to his feet. Still nursing his bloodied face, he dabs at the still wet blood around his eye and around his nostrils.

'You were in on it?' I ask him.

He shakes his head. 'I may be a performer of sorts, but I'm no actor. You were brilliant, ladies. Absolutely brilliant.'

'You do understand?' Fatima asks me, while weaving around the room, touching each person on the arm like she is doling out some sort of blessing.

'Understand?' I respond.

'Understand you had to be stopped. If you truly loved Orla, you would have understood. Look what you've done to her. Her friends don't recognise her anymore. You've destroyed her. You don't understand and you don't love Orla enough. You let her jump to her death rather than save her. A few well-intentioned words were all that were needed. You could have saved everyone, all the deaths this weekend. They are all your fault. Your lack of love for anyone other than yourself. You don't love anyone enough to put them first. You should have jumped instead of Orla, but you couldn't even do that. Well, it's over, Zac. We won't let you destroy us.'

She's speaking as if for all. Orla rocks her head back, staring up at the ceiling. She's exhausted.

I shiver, my skin is cold and clammy, my mouth dry. The faces in the room, those I thought I knew, those I thought I loved and who I thought loved me, stare back at me. I feel like the weight of the Great Orme is pressing down on me. I can't see a way out.

What if all the pieces of comprehension and memory that comprise who I am, Orla, my old *friends*, the ghosts that haunt me, are nothing but a tragic self-serving lie, a narrative my brain has compiled to protect me?

What if I'm losing my mind?

No. Stop.

I am not losing my mind. I am regaining it.

Beside me, the woman I love tilts her ghost-like face to mine, usual defiance entirely drained away. She closes her eyes, two black spaces. She smiles. Weak, but a smile. She leans in and kisses me.

I will not allow these people to get to me.

I will solve this problem.

I must know who are dead set against me, at least one of them can be persuaded. 'Who knew Fatima was the Leveller?' I ask them.

But it's Fatima who has them mesmerised, and it's she who continues to orchestrate the conversation. 'Let me explain. The thing is, Zac, we are modern women. We won't be played and we won't be treated unfairly. You certainly can't *tell* us to confess. Sian has suffered enough. What you made her do, it was awful. The same for Jessie. The same for the others, all of your so-called friends, you made them murder. You've already given them life sentences. We won't let you give them another on top.'

A dramatic shake of her head and a sympathetic smile pressed on her lips, Fatima returns to Sian's side. 'After reading your message, Sian told me everything. So, let's be clear once again, these people aren't responsible, Zac. You are.'

I let out an exasperated sigh. 'That's why I sent the message. I realised what I was guilty of.' I'm mindful that now is not the time to express my view no one needs to commit a murder because someone suggests they should. 'But we are all implicated. And that's why we need to confess. Let the law decide our punishment.' My voice cracks with the last few words, and I'm sure I sound desperate, and if I do, I have every right. Something terrible is about to happen.

'Look,' Fatima says, waving a hand in the air and rolling her eyes at me. I think she's enjoying her place in the limelight, maxing out on her performance. 'We knew how this would play out, me, Sian, and Jessie. Already on the same wavelength – not prepared to be sacrificial lambs. The law is already sort of involved… Helen.'

'Helen?' Harrison's face creases with confusion. Helen responds with an apologetic, tight-lipped smile.

'I called Helen before we arrived. We talked for a long time. Helen is smart, of course. She recognised the injustice. She loves you, Harrison. She'll do anything to keep you. And I mean, anything. You are one lucky man.'

Helen crosses her arms and nods her head. 'No one here is going to prison.'

An acid-steeped smile forms on Fatima's face. 'Harrison, you already told Helen about your past, our past. That really helped. Thank you.'

I suddenly feel giddy and the room falls to darkness, everyone a silhouette. A shape walks toward me. A stream of light from the gap under the lounge door stretches across the carpet to the figure. Panic glides into my brain like a sharp knife. The light spreads across the floor, spilling onto the leather sofa, and climbs up my body. The light pulses, glowing and spinning. 'Choreji,' I mutter. The girl walks toward me, blood dripping from her head, staining the carpet, but suddenly it's not Choreji. It's another girl, one I don't recognise, one half her age, similar jet-black hair, but paler skin, her face as if glass-sealed and lost. Every muscle in my body tenses like I've just looked up, and a wild animal is about to pounce. The house hums, straining. Something has to give…

'Zac…'

The Great Orme

Orla's voice inserts like a needle to the brain. The girl passes through me and is gone. I blink and see everyone staring at me. The morning light strains into the room from the big bay window.

Orla has a quizzical expression on her face. She hasn't seen the girl. I don't know what to say.

Fatima shakes her head, ponytail swinging violently behind her. 'You can see, Orla excepted, it's the women, trying to keep our families together. We're so grateful to you, Jorge, Tomasz, Harrison, for backing us, now, and always. As for Orla, well, Sian told me, you would stay blindly loyal to Zac. Apparently, you always have. Such is your downfall.'

'You fucking bitch!' Orla raises her manacled wrists, fists clenched, but Sian and Jessie are quick to press her down on the sofa.

'Helen?' Harrison's voice is mournful. The veins in his neck protrude thicker than ever. Stood next to the sofa, he rests a hand on my shoulder as if it might help him balance. I can smell and taste his odour – metallic perspiration.

Helen is leaning against the bookcase in the corner of the room, now with one hand pressed to her leg, clearly still in discomfort from the wound. She's put her bobble-hat on while we've been talking, yellow-blond hair framing her jaw and neck. She and the rest of them are ready to leave.

'I did it for you,' she says. 'For us. For our future.'

'Why? Why didn't you tell me?' Harrison's grip on my shoulder tightens.

'I didn't want to stress you unnecessarily.' I notice her eyes remain unchanged, thinking, searching the room, green slates of pure, cold menace.

I lean in to Harrison. 'Don't trust her,' I whisper. 'She'll kill you.'

She hears me. Of course she does. She adjusts her position, straightening, bumping against the grandfather clock, jolting the swinging pendulum within so it cracks the glass in the door. 'Zac,' she says, addressing me as if I'm a child. 'You know better than I do, the incapability of the police to bring to justice those who are deserving. In ninety percent of cases, you and I know who the abusers, rapists and murderers are, and they know we know too... but,' she sighs, 'establishing and collating enough evidence to prove their guilt *beyond a reasonable doubt*, is confounded at every point in the process to make it near impossible. Even if the resource is there to progress an investigation, any criminal with half a brain can obfuscate the evidence. Policing has abandoned the art of interrogation and intuition to the physical sciences. The modern police force are little more than cleaners, mopping up the aftermath, merely the recorders of death. You've been right all along, and I admire you for it. All you've done, and all we've done... it's for the greater good.'

'Not true.' I reply instantly. 'I may have agreed once, but a hankering for the dark ages is no way to the future. For all those years where we... where we killed, we did so because we had given up on what was right, given up because it was hard and we... I lacked patience. It's not too late, even now. Do the right thing.'

'Listen, Zac,' she says, her face stoic, 'because I don't think you are. Everyone murders, usually by proxy - governments, soldiers... police. We are their sponsors. Everyone is a hypocrite. We've become so desensitised to societal instigated murder, perhaps because it's justified as defence, done in volume and is decided by those within a wall of tradition, those who are privileged, those who are safest. It doesn't make our murders less morally substantive if the outcome is ultimately that of good.'

A thousand thoughts swarm around my head like wasps, each one impossible to hold on to and each with a sting.

Orla, staring straight ahead, deep in thought, speaks. 'That's the thing,' she says. 'Once people start attempting to justify murder, we've lost, we've all lost. Now, Zac has grown up, very fucking late admittedly, it's time we all grew up. We all bear a responsibility to one another and to our victims. Please, be honest with yourselves. See sense.' She casts her gaze imploringly from one person to the next.

The Great Orme

Harrison's removes his hand from my shoulder, letting it flop to his side. 'Maybe Zac and Orla... maybe they *are* right?'

'If only it were so simple, Harrison,' Fatima replies, her voice full of assumed authority. 'What's done is done. To be grown up, we have to deal with the consequences of our actions. We have to take control. We have to fight for what we want. We aren't cowards. I'm afraid our friends have become our enemies. Zac and Orla want to take the easy option. They want to give up. We can't let them. They would take our lives from us and we aren't ready for the end. It's them or us. It's that simple.'

She folds her arms and smiles, apparently amused at my seething countenance. I'm in a fight for my life, for Orla's. Perhaps if Costas, Harrison, Jorge and Tomasz can see her for what she is, they might side with me. I can still stop them. I can change their minds.

'So, you killed Josh? Josh Pinkney, our old Headmaster, the guy in Clonmel Street, a harmless old man?'

'I did,' she says. 'But what you didn't know, perhaps, is he had some indiscretions logged against him. Isn't that right, Helen?'

'Indeed, he did,' Helen nods. 'Just this year, two warnings for approaching school boys with improper suggestions.'

I shake my head, wondering if it's true and not wanting to believe it.

'It's true,' Helen says, as if reading my mind. 'I searched the police database. It's logged there.'

Fatima unfolds and claps her hands together. 'You see, Zac. We've saved innocents from abuse. I've done nothing but help you, Zac,' Fatima says. 'I killed your father's killer, because you didn't have the courage to do it yourself.'

'You pushed Yestyn off the pier?'

Sian has moved next to Fatima once more. Fatima nods a confirmation and gazes down at the small space between her and Sian. Choreji has reappeared, this time her mouth twisted, angry and upset, her face staring up at Fatima. Orla gasps, and when I look to her and back to Choreji, the girl has disappeared. Fatima's face has hardened, her eyes stiff, and she moves away staring at the space where Choreji stood.

Stood beside the sofa, agitated and pulling at her ponytail, Fatima eventually fixes her eyes on me.

'The boy...you attacked the boy. You smashed his head with a brick?' I can't disguise my disgust. I just can't.

'That was me.'

All faces turn to Helen.

'You?' Harrison puffs out his cheeks, struggling with the onslaught of revelations.

'We needed to scare Zac. To stop him. The boy is called Owain. He was a drug runner, the hard stuff, county lines and all that. He's been instrumental in the Llandudno drug scene... trafficking all kinds of shit into this town, a pedlar in misery. Of course, there's no hard evidence, but every kid and druggie on every street knows it. They are too scared to speak out. Owain was a nasty shit, destined to do worse, to ruin even more lives.'

'The old Zac would have approved,' Sian adds.

I wonder at Sian. Her once bright, lop-sided grin, brimming with fun, now seems corroded and bleak. I don't know what to say to her. I loved her. I loved all of my old friends. I wonder if I must hate them now.

I turn my attention back to Fatima, back to the actress, the woman who has orchestrated such evil and I wonder if I'm looking at a female me, me as I was, controlling... and so very wrong.

I pursue my line, the one to reveal her wickedness to the others. 'You've been a ghost in the old house? You put the mannequin doll in my sink, hacked it, wrote my mother's name on it. You filled the sink with cranberry juice to represent her blood. You wanted to remind me how I found her, how she died, how she killed herself.' I blink my eyes to stem the accumulation of water. 'Why would you do that? And then the goat's head in the sink? Why? All of it! Why?'

The Great Orme

Fatima stares back at me, the room's artificial lights reflected in her hazel eyes. 'Because, we are desperate. Because, we are fighting for our lives. Because, by reminding you of death, we hoped you might let us continue to live.'

I snap, lashing out at the coffee table with my foot, but it's heavy oak and it barely moves. 'For Christ's sake, Fatima!' I shout. 'You think I need to be reminded of death? I live with death! This old house is teeming with death! Y Gogarth, The Great Orme is carrying death on its back! I swear to God, unless we confess, the ghosts of those we've killed will haunt us for the rest of our lives!'

I'm trembling and it seems everyone is staring at me pityingly. I feel pathetic.

Quiet up to this point, Jorge breaks the tension, applying his own sort. 'Stop saying "old house" as if it's listening to us, as if it knows things. As for Y Gogarth, which I suppose means Great Orme in Welsh, it's a God damned rock, just like this is a God damned house, plain and simple. Anyone who thinks otherwise has lost their mind!'

The air in the room stiffens, the temperature seems to have dropped, it's as if the old house has taken one cold long drawn breath from below. I feel the sea serpent's ancient force crackle up from the ground through the floorboards and through the entirety of the old house and into my veins. Spectral glows emanate from the corners of the room, casting sepulchral shadows where none should be, the ghosts of those we killed desperate and yearning to share their untold stories with the living.

'Be careful, Jorge,' I say. 'The Great Orme, and this house, are connected. As are we, and those we've killed. Everything's connected. You think you can run away, but you can't. Tomasz knows that already,' I say, regarding the highly regarded athlete lying in a crumpled heap on the floor. 'I know you are scared.' Jorge bristles at my accusation. 'But hard as it is, in the long run, it's better to confess now, otherwise the ghosts will eat you alive.'

I offer up half a smile so he can't tell if I'm joking or if I mean it. I mean it.

'The problem,' he says, rubbing the back of his neck, 'is that while I might *feel* the *old house* is whispering, trying to tell me things, I know it can't be, I know it's impossible. Someone who's having an onset of psychosis believes it *is* true. You've become irrational. It's because you've lost control. Zac, you've lost your mind.'

His cold logic is tempting, always an appealing default when faced with overwhelm or experience beyond the normal realm. I know he hears the ghosts; he's in denial as are all of them.

'None of us are in control,' I tell him. 'Not before. Not now. Not ever.'

Jorge's eyes flick to the corners of the room, precisely where the ghosts hunker, restless souls cloaked in sorrow and reaching out to the living, their fingertips grazing the edges of reality, trapped between worlds while yearning for our confession, for their release. Choreji, Chloe, her mother, Ollie, Bart, Kenzo, Rose's husband, the small boy with face caved in. There are additions too, I see our old headmaster, and I see Yestyn, my father's killer. There are others too, presumably the faces of those burned to death alongside Kenzo by Sian. The room quivers with the weight of their longing, for the freedom they so desperately seek.

Jorge is scared, like I am. He sees, knows and feels more than he's letting on. He's scared of the Great Orme, he's scared of the old house, and he's scared of the ghosts. My concern is he'll run from them, not knowing it's impossible, you can't run from ghosts. You have to give them what they want, what they need.

I let him stew, turning my attention to Fatima. 'You tried to kill Smokey?' My old friend whines at the mention of his name. 'You strung him to my bedroom light.'

'None of this has been easy, Zac,' she replies, huffing. She's losing patience with me. 'None of this is what any of us would want. But you backed us into a corner. You left us no option but to come at you fighting.'

I open my mouth to defend myself but Fatima is forceful,

adamant, and she's not finished. 'I've been your neighbour and I've lived with you these past few days. I've followed you. I've left you messages… warnings – phone messages, written words in condensation on windows, the note in the pub, the doll and car outside the menswear store. Yes, it was me. I cracked the store's window. I was within touching distance of you, stood behind the owner in Maisie's chocolate shop when you spoke to her. The note thrown at you in the church – me. I took and printed off the photo of Orla crawling over the rocks. I did it. I did it all to scare you. Anything to change your mind. Anything to stop you confessing. I gave you every chance. Unfortunately,' she says, taking a deep breath. 'Jorge is right. You are insane.'

'I took the note up with me when we went up the Great Orme,' Jessie adds. 'Fatima gave it to me.'

'Congratulations,' I reply sarcastically. 'How did you get Orla off the rocks?'

'Luckily,' Fatima replies. 'We found someone who knows the Great Orme like the back of his hand. Someone who was able to skirt the edge and bring her back to the road, where I drove her home, isn't that right Costas?'

Costas merely turns his back on us to face the walls.

I won't give up. I won't be deterred. I turn my attention to the football star now sat cross-legged on the floor. 'As well as trying to kill me while we were upstairs, did you try to poison me too?'

'No, Zac. That never occurred to me. I only intended to set you on fire.'

'That's okay then,' I reply, hardly believing I'm having this dialogue with my best friends.

Someone clears their throat. Rose edges forward, walking stick thrust out before her.

'My dear boy,' she says, peering sternly over the rim of her glasses at me. 'It was me. I tried to poison you.'

I stop breathing. 'Rose?'

She uses her stick to clear a space between me and Costas;

the Vicar stepping aside for her. 'But I can't take all the credit, no.' She waves her stick around, finally pointing it at Jessie. 'She deserves some credit too.'

Jessie says nothing, lowering her gaze.

'Although young lady, you didn't tell me about Fatima did you now?'

'I'm sorry. I didn't want to embroil you more than was necessary.'

'Really?' Rose chastises her. 'Jessie is a chemist, don't you know? And I used to be a chemist. Now, the fact of the matter is we got talking this weekend, and it occurred to us it might be a good idea if we poisoned you.'

Orla reaches out and with bound wrists clasps my hands, her fingers, freezing cold.

Rose continues. 'It seems to me we are all so far down the road, that the way back is too far, therefore we must continue to the end. You are a lovely boy, Zac. And it pains me greatly, all of this, it's a dilemma. But when I think it through, I arrive at the conclusion there is a greater good to be had you are preventing. We're going to hell in a handcart, anyway! We might as well prolong the little life we've got left!'

'You tried to poison me?' I say, incredulous.

'Thallium, my boy. Oh, I have all sorts of bits and pieces next door, but thallium is definitely mine and Agatha Christie's preferred poison. You would struggle to get hold of it these days. You wouldn't believe how toxic that stuff is! Fever, delirium, convulsions, coma – and worse!'

'Stupid bitch,' Harrison curses, banging the wall with his fist.

The old lady smiles and ignoring him continues. 'You must have a highly sensitive system to notice it as soon as you did, Zac. We needed you to drink the whole cup for it to have impact… just as Harrison did.'

'Wait..! What?' Harrison slaps a hand on top of his head. 'What did you say?'

Rose presses down on her stick and shuffles around it to face the big man. 'How are you feeling, big boy?'

'You didn't?' he says, dragging his fingers down his face to his chin.

'Well, how about you tell me? Notice any *bits* in your coffee? The thing about thallium is it doesn't dissolve so well in water. I wondered if you might notice. Did you?'

'She's mad,' he says, shaking his head.

Clean white teeth in her craggy face, the old lady smiles. 'You killed Marmalade, my beautiful cat. Stabbed her like a sausage. I've never forgiven you.'

Harrison's face darkens, and he promptly marches over to her and snatches the stick from her. Costas and I are alert and we launch ourselves at him. Smokey yelps, scampering away as the three of us hit the floor and roll crashing into the coffee table upending cups and plates all over the place.

An almighty explosion destroys all other sound, gunshot.

I roll onto my back and look up to see Rose, still smiling. I don't think she knows or can know what's happened. Helen is stood next to her, arms raised, barely an inch between the gun and the side of the old woman's head. My neighbour's dark-green spectacles barely cling to her face, splashed red and skewed at an angle. Her smart grey perm is doused a fresh wet red. She raises a hand to adjust her glasses so they sit correctly on her nose, but she can't manage it, one of the arms won't hook onto her ear - because it's gone, a mangled bloody hole where it was moments before. With the other hand, she tidies her paisley silk scarf ignoring the fact it too is splattered with her own blood.

Her eyes have misted over and she begins to sway, but her expression is one of contentment, a slight smile forms on her lips as ruby red blood leaks into the corner of her mouth. 'Heddwyn,' she says, barely a whisper, 'I'm coming.'

She drops like a rag doll and we all cry out as her head cracks against the corner of the coffee table, a sickening thud. Unfazed, Helen spins and points the gun at Jessie.

Nothing left but faith

Chapter Thirty

Jessie throws her hands up defensively. 'I swear to you, Helen. Rose didn't tell me she poisoned Harrison. I would never have let her.'

Lying on my back, I somehow manage to roll against the sofa and push myself to my feet. I offer my bound hands to Costas and pull him up. Harrison declines my assistance, hauling his considerable bulk up himself.

Helen has turned her attention to Harrison, her eyes narrowed, knuckles white, such is her grip on the gun. 'How do you feel? Do you feel unwell?'

He stares at his hands and splays his fingers. 'To be honest honey, I've felt a lot better.'

'Jessie,' she says. 'How does this thalli… thing work?'

'Thallium,' she says, sighing, the strain showing on her face and in her sunken eyes. 'Manifestation of toxicity depends on the dose. Zac only sipped at it. He vomited it back up. Extremely lucky.' She hesitates, staring at me while rubbing her forehead. 'I only want a normal life. I only want to be with my family. Do you see what you've done, Zac? Do you see how you've ruined lives?'

'Never mind him,' Helen snaps. 'What about Harrison? Is he okay?'

Tears roll down Jessie's cheeks. She takes a deep breath. 'Harrison, you've not vomited, or collapsed yet, so there is some hope. That said, let's start with some simple symptoms. Do you feel any nausea, head or abdominal pains?'

Helen joins Harrison, wrapping an arm around his waist. 'Honey, you look a bit peaky.'

The Great Orme

He shrugs. 'I don't know. I don't feel great… but it's been that sort of weekend.'

'Well, if you *have* been poisoned, you will certainly have these symptoms,' Jessie says. 'Your nervous system will become the target of the poison. After that, coma, and, well…' her voice trails off.

'What's the treatment?' Helen asks.

'Prussian blue, it's an activated charcoal with forced diuresis to enhance fluid and faecal elimination of the metal.'

'Harrison,' I say. 'There are loads of old packets of pills in the cabinet next to the fridge. Maybe some laxatives.'

As he's about to leave the room, Helen calls after him. 'Get some for me.'

He stops in the doorway. 'What? Why?'

'You left half of your coffee. I finished it off.'

He punches the doorframe. 'It wasn't even me that killed Rose's bloody cat. Was it, Costas?'

Costas removes his glasses, and jams thumb and finger into his eyes. He leans forward and just as I think he's about to collapse; he pulls his hand away and straightens. He slides his glasses back on. He smiles.

'Are you okay?' Harrison asks.

Costas exhales, long, slow and steady. 'Yes, better than for a long time.' The smile stays.

'Our Vicar killed her precious Marmalade,' Harrison says. 'I thought I was doing him a favour by taking the rap for it. Some fucking rap.' He turns, his hulking frame bumping against the doorframe as he leaves for the kitchen. Helen holds out the gun for Fatima to take but it's Jules' hand that darts in and takes it from her.

'I think you'll find this belongs to me.'

Helen rolls her eyes and leaves the room, going after Harrison.

'No, Jules,' Costas says, alert yet calm. 'We've gone too far. In truth, it did the day we killed Rose's husband, the day you killed your mother. It's time we stopped. It's time we confessed, for the sake of our souls, for the sake of their souls.' He scans the room, but not at the people collected in it, not the living anyway. All those we've killed are amassed in the lounge with us, I can see them all watching us, stood still and silent in the corners, their wounds still raw and visible.

Neat white clerical collar stained dark at the top edge with sweat from his neck, Costas makes his way around the back of the sofa to join Jules, careful to avoid Kenzo, recognisable by his gold front tooth, most of him a blackened, charred skeleton. The ghosts who have made the old house their home lace the air with their dead breath. Outside, the winter sun is rising, its soft white glare casting the living inside, as sickly, pallid creatures.

Jules laughs at her husband, mocking, eyes half-closed, waggling the gun in her hand, seeming to enjoy the weight of the weapon. 'You are hopeless, Costas. These women are fighters, and they are right. "*Is there anyone without sin among us?*" Jesus said. "*Neither do I condemn thee, go and sin no more*". We do what we must, and then we ask for forgiveness.'

Jules moves, and she's around the back of the sofa with long, quick strides, and before anyone realises what's happening, she jams the point of the gun against the back of Orla's head.

Orla screeches.

'No!' I yell, reaching out with bound wrists. 'Stop!'

'Keep still, Orla,' Jules commands. She's caught hold of Orla's hair and not for the first time, is pulling it tightly. 'And keep quiet.'

Orla glares at me, pleading for me to do something.

'We've been a little disjointed in our attempts to persuade you, Zac,' she says. 'Now, don't let these brave women down again, not after all they've been through. What will it take, Zac? Just what will it take to stop you?'

'Jules, put the gun down.' Costas voice is determined.

Jules looks at him aghast, unable to hide her astonishment. 'How dare you? After all, I've done for you. For us. This life I've built. I've been through too much for it to get destroyed now, and certainly not because of these two woke fools. Only God can alleviate guilt!' Her words are spat out with such venom and feeling I think she'll pull the trigger any second.

'So true, Jules,' Costas says with a calmness and a freedom I haven't seen in him since he arrived at the old house. 'Only God can alleviate guilt,' he repeats, then reaching out and gently placing a hand on top of the gun, he says, 'She's here, Jules. She's watching us. Chloe wants us to confess.'

Jules tucks her angular jaw in to her neck. 'She's dead. Gone. Let her go. Let her rest!'

'She's watching us. She can't rest. And she won't let me rest,' he replies. 'Not until I confess.'

Finally, I think. *Finally*, a glimmer of hope!

'Chloe is with me every waking day and every nightmare-filled night. Zac is right. He's been wrong, but now he's right.'

'Please Costas, I want for it to be perfect like before. And it can. We can't… we aren't going to give up.'

'It wasn't perfect, Jules. We were sleepwalking, we were haunted by what we did, and by who we did it to. The weight of their longing gets heavier not lighter. Jules,' he pleads, shaking his head, beautiful brown eyes glistening with tears, 'It's time. It's time to confess.'

Orla emits a low moan, her pale white neck elongated, chin tipped backwards, Jules's hand clenched within her hair, pulling hard. I'm scared Jules will fire the gun, even by accident.

Costas glances toward the doorway. Helen and Harrison have reappeared. Jules, unaware, has her back to them. Helen approaches Jules, limping stealthily nearer. I'm unsure, it's too dangerous. I want to say something to stop her.

'I love you, Jules,' Costas says, and I know it's true. Both of them are crying silent tears. 'Stop,' he says calmly, but I can't tell if he means for Jules or Helen to stop.

Helen suddenly lunges across Jules at Costas, swinging her arm around his neck, crashing into Jules in the process. Released,

Orla cries out, and jumps up and away from them. Costas and Helen scramble to take the gun from Jules, the three of them stumbling and spiralling together in a macabre dance until the dreaded explosion of another gunshot halts them.

Jules and Costas are so close as to be practically touching lips. 'I love you. Truly I do,' Jules says, her long red hair splashed over her husband's shoulder. But Costas doesn't reply. He stares back at her, eyes and face wrought with pain. Jules tries to hold him up but she can't. Helen disentangles herself from them, and as she pulls away, Costas drops to the floor, out of sight behind the sofa.

Jules's heaving chest is smeared with wet blood. She is staring down at her husband, wrist limp, and in her hand, the gun.

Harrison disappears behind the sofa, soon rising up and shaking his head while biting his bottom lip. Hope, such a fragile thing, is quashed so easily; dread, fear, and all the other dark things, agile replacements that slot seamlessly into its place. The old house has two new ghosts to induct, Rose and now Costas. I see everyone and no one, all colours faded to grey. I am convinced I will never see colours ever again, nothing in the world can brighten the contrast before my eyes.

Jules is escorted by Sian to an armchair, and pandered to, as if she is the victim. My old friend, Costas, had fought his demons and was finally prepared to give up everything to do the right thing. The one person among them, persuaded to my reckoning, dead.

Jules sits in stupefied silence, while still constrained by the tape binding our wrists and ankles, Orla and I crumple into the sofa, both of us shattered by the horrors. The darkness at the heart of the Great Orme has infected us all. The sea serpent is in us, its stony black mouth sucks at the salty sediment in the sea, sucking at the little bit of life left in us, our evil secret the fire in its belly, the ghost-soaked old house a putrid spore on its spiny back.

The clock chimes. Noon. Twelve sonorous beats, stopping time and marking it as an imprint on forever, the moment Costas

The Great Orme

died. I straighten up, craning my neck to observe everyone in the room, their heads strange uninhabitable planets, and me, a dying sun in their solar system.

As the reverberations of the final chime fade, Fatima nods her assent at someone. She's looking beyond me. Something digs into the centre of my back, something sharp. I call out in pain.

Jorge leans over me, his tousled brown hair obscuring my vision. 'Every moment spent here is wasted time.' His voice is edgy, wavering. 'This place... the *old* house, the Great Orme, it's killing us. Look what it's done to us, what it's doing to us. You should have left this place a long time ago, Zac. It's made you sick. Sick and twisted.'

I can still smell the lingering scent of my aftershave he's wearing, but now it's mixed with the cloying sweet scent of sweat. He stands straight, and I see Fatima, once again, helping Tomasz to his feet. She whispers something in his ear and before I know what's happening, he and Jorge are prising Orla from me. She screams, but Tomasz slaps his hand across her mouth, hauling her roughly to her feet. Her pupils roll back and her lids squeeze shut in pain. I'm helpless to help.

'Maybe give them one last chance?' Harrison says, stepping around the sofa and stopping before Orla.

'It's too late,' Fatima replies.

'Are you sure?'

'There's no going back. Not now,' she says with an unshakeable surety.

My body is both numb and in pain, all that makes us move working at the extremity of endurance.

'Zac,' Harrison says, gazing down at me, his hand pressed to the side of his smooth bald head. 'I only ever killed those you told me to kill. The old man, the boy on the bike. No others. Once we killed the old man, there was no going back. I'd give everything to go back, but Fatima is right, isn't she? We can't go back.'

All this time, the skinny creature of our youth, now encased in muscle-bound armour, traumatised by his experience. He takes a kitchen knife from Jorge, and Jorge curses him.

'Harrison, you can stop this,' I urge, a sudden flare of hope within like a distant firework. 'I know you can.'

The air in the room tugs tighter on everyone's face, their muscles clenched and skin taught.

'It's not too late! It's never too late!' I splutter.

'Harrison!'

Helen's voice is sharp, it cuts deep, and I feel the air deflate.

'Harrison!' she repeats, this time softer.

'It's impossible,' he murmurs, tucking the knife in his back pocket and turning away.

In the distance I hear a rumble of a train. Jorge drags me off the sofa and I fall, cracking my head on the edge of the coffee table and slamming into the floor. A hand presses my sore head into the carpet. I try to shout, but my voice is muffled and hardly registers. Something solid smacks my head and voices blur to the hiss of one indistinguishable voice and I wonder if it's the sea serpent finally come to take me. A pain streaks along my shoulders as my arms are pulled up, yet more tape applied to my wrists, binding them together tighter still. I blink hard, desperately trying to focus, but all I end up seeing is Rose's deep fissured head, side-on and blood-splattered, and through the cracked lenses of her glasses, her eyes remain open, staring back at me.

Tomasz hauls me to my feet. He smells of rusted metal. I try to resist, but I'm dazed and my limbs feel numb.

Invisible hands grasp my body, pulling it as they want. I'm bundled onto the sofa, feet up. Orla is facing me. My wrists and ankles are bound together with Orla's. Her frantic pulling and twisting are as if nothing, a futile resistance, there are too many of them. Orla's shrieking amplifies the pain in my head, my mind an explosion of voices. Louder and more insistent than them all, creeps the voice of the Great Orme, rasping like a dying man, stiff-boned and slow. *You're not going to survive.*

The Great Orme

This is the place you die. The place Orla dies. Stop them!

The slosh and stench of diesel turn my stomach and cuts through my foggy thinking. Tomasz has unscrewed the cap from a green cannister.

'Help! Help us! For God's sake, someone help!' Orla yells. Her face is inches from mine, her eyes are blazing black-holes. She's pulling wildly, unintentionally hurting me in the process.

'Quiet! Fatima snaps, steel-cold intent on her face. 'Shut up!'

With a grunt, she punches Orla full-on in the face. I wince at the slapping sound of the contact, and again at the sight of blood pouring from my wife's mouth, her bottom lip split open. Gasping for breath and crying, Orla spits, spraying blood over me. A dislodged tooth rolls in slow, sticky revolutions down her chin, and hangs on a strand of bloody drool between us.

The blow has had the desired effect. Orla becomes silent. She's in shock, trembling. I try to hold her forearms, to steady her, but as much to steady myself, my thinking.

'Go on,' Fatima says to Tomasz. 'Time's up.'

Tomasz gives the cannister a swirl, peering at us through one blood-encrusted eye. Jessie rattles a box of matches. I am stupefied by their ruthlessness, their terrible capability for cruelty.

Harrison's voice, a plea, asks again if we'll be given one last chance to change our minds.

'Do more!' I say, desperate for him to act, but my words are slow and muffled. My head hurts but I guess Orla's hurts more. She's staring at me, her eyes timeless blackened tunnels through which I've willingly fallen so many times before, never reaching the end, nor do I want to. I can't let this be the end, but I don't know how to stop it.

Fatima claps, drawing attention to herself. 'Pour it,' she commands Tomasz.

Orla and I contort and twist, but it's no good, the putrid liquid splashes over us, soaking our clothes and burning our skin. I cough, a dry, heaving wretch, choking on the acrid fumes, my second dose of the day.

'Zac.'

I twist my neck to see Sian stood before the sofa, my notebook in her hands.

'Wow, this is interesting,' she says, turning the pages. 'A little too interesting… too revealing. We need to get rid of it. I've already deleted the message you sent us from your phone. "TheGreatOrme" isn't the best password you could have thought of, is it?'

She turns the book over in her hands, examining the green cover. 'I guess you hoped writing down our story would help when you came to confess. It's basically a written confession of what we did, what you made us do. Personal and sensitive information. As such, it too, must be destroyed.'

'You do that,' I say. 'Keep your damned secret. Let it eat you up from the inside. Let it destroy you. You are already half dead. I can see it in your eyes.'

She narrows her eyes at me. 'We were okay before you sent us the message to come here. You destroyed our lives. And while it can never be the same from here on, it's much preferable to the alternative. We have to destroy you. It's our only chance.'

'Why can't you see?' I insist, my heart a tribal beat of panic in my ears. 'One carefully thought-out decision now and we can finally face our demons. We can be free, really free.'

Perhaps sensing a wavering from Sian, Fatima takes over. 'Zac, we've made our decision. We've chosen *not* to rot in prison.'

I shake my head, try to speak, and fail. My head and heart are set to burst.

'It's over,' she says.

'It's over,' Jules repeats.

We all turn our heads to the hapless figure slouched back in the armchair. Her chest is smeared with her husband's blood. She's staring at her gun in her hand.

Fatima starts toward her but Jules responds quickly as if woken from a dream and points the gun at her.

'Come on, Jules,' Fatima says, stretching out her arm. 'Hand it over.'

'Zac's right. Costas realised that in the end. And now I do too. I killed my mother. I've killed my husband. What am I supposed to do? Return home without him? Deny all knowledge of his whereabouts?'

She regards everyone in the room, daring them to confront her. 'Couples all of you. And Jessie, you've got a family to return to… something to live for. All I've got left is my faith.'

'Jules!' Fatima states calmly but forcefully. 'Hand me the gun.'

An amused smile breaks out on Jules's face. 'I'm a coward. All of you are cowards. And like you, I can't go to prison. I can't go back there. God knows, I can't.'

She turns the gun slowly in on herself, pointing and pressing it to her forehead.

Harrison moves away from Helen and draws level with Fatima who sticks out her arm, preventing him from reaching Jules.

'We aren't cowards,' Fatima says. 'It's you who is the coward, Jules. You won't pull the trigger.'

'Fatima!' Harrison says, and, pushing her arm out of the way, he takes a step toward Jules and reaches out to take the gun, then recoils, jumping back at the explosion.

Jules's head slumps to the side. Her gun and hand drop into her lap. A dark red hole at the centre of her forehead oozes fresh red blood which leaks in rivulets over the contours of her pale face and merges into strands of red hair stuck to her neck.

Then Jericho

Chapter Thirty-One

I turn and press my face into the back of the sofa. My entire body is aching, and I'm doing my utmost to contain the silent scream in my head.

I turn back and see Fatima's hazel eyes, sharp and alert, staring back at me. 'Read it, Sian. Read Orla's sweet little entry in Zac's book, read it so we can all hear.'

Next to me Orla groans and her head drops, chin to her chest. She can't look at me.

Sian lets the book flop open to the back cover, before turning it back a couple of pages. 'I presume you've not seen Orla's small but significant entry at the back of your book?'

'Costas and Jules are dead,' I say, my voice breaking. 'They are still warm and bleeding… and you want to read me an entry from my book? You are mad.'

'Nah,' Fatima says, pulling in her chin to her neck. 'I think what Sian is about to read, you'll find riveting.'

Sian clears her throat. 'So,' she says. 'Here it is,' and she proceeds to read:

'Dearest Zac,

My heart is broken.
It cannot be mended.
I have to give up. I have to go. You won't know it but I've been in and out of hospital for years… six years to be precise. Diagnosed with clinical depression, I've attempted suicide many times. I've had my stomach pumped twice, I've had psychotherapy and I'm on

antidepressants. Neither work. The truth won't let them. Choreji won't let them.

I needed you. I need you. I'll ask you maybe one more time, but no more. If we can't live together, I can't live at all. If only you could love me like I love you.'

I can't help myself, the tears stream down my face. 'I do love you,' I mumble, but Orla keeps her chin tucked into her chest avoiding eye contact. I continue regardless. 'I always have. I always will. I thought… I thought you didn't need me. I thought I would hold you back, that you would resent me. I thought you were coping… successful.' Orla is crying too, the tears drip from her chin onto her arms. I wonder how we got so far apart, how everything else overshadowed our love for one another. How I let it.

Sian has hesitated, she and the rest of them watching me and Orla as if we are animals in a zoo. Sian takes a deep breath, lifts her eyes to the ceiling and down at my book before reading on:

'There's something else I must tell you. It's the most important thing. Life changing.'

Orla lets out a gasp as she catches her breath.

'I only hope you are able to forgive me,' Sian continues, wiping away a solitary tear from her own cheek. *'It won't change your mind about confessing. Nothing will. I know that now.'*

Orla howls, a cry of pain dredged from the bowels of the Earth ripped through her centre and released to the corners of the room and most likely beyond. Even the ghosts recoil at the agonised cry.

Fatima raises her hand, palm flat as if she can command the sound, the feeling. Exhausted, Orla stops. 'Go on,' Fatima tells Sian.

Wiping away a tear, Sian clears her throat. 'I'm sorry,' she says and focuses on the book in her hands. She seems to read silently before re-reading it out aloud:

'Zac,' she hesitates, taking a deep breath before reading on.

'You are a father. We have a daughter.'

The blood that moves my body, stops. My skin prickles. My heart lurches in my chest. 'Is it true?' I ask, choking on my words, unable to comprehend. Orla's lifts her head but her beetle eyes are clamped closed, her chest heaving with the effort of silent crying. Sian sniffs and continues to read on:

'I couldn't do it on my own... be a parent, not after what I had done to Choreji. How could I? A cruel animal like me, a parent? I left our new born baby in a bag at a hospital rest-room in London – a note with her: "Name: Jericho. Please find someone who will love her.". Her name is beautiful. It's burned into my heart. I'll carry it with me for eternity. It's an anagram – an anagram of Choreji.'

I pull Orla's wrists up, and take her face in my hands. I make her look at me, but we are both sobbing so hard. 'Jericho,' I say but my voice is hoarse, barely audible through my tears. 'It's a beautiful name,' I croak.

Sian, relentless, doesn't stop:

'Jericho is six years old, a final product of the old house, of the Great Orme. I leave you this message, Zac, my undisputable love, in the hope you can find it in your heart to leave all the bad we've done behind, and look to the future for the good. Please do not think I do not love our Jericho. I do. Painfully so. My soul aches with love. Zac, our girl is out there somewhere in this dark world. I am scared.

I saw in the media she's been adopted. I wrote her a letter. I sent it to the authorities. She'll receive it when she turns eighteen. Finally, I hope, I did as you would have done. I told her the truth. I told her what I had done. What you had done. What we all had done. I told her why, she might understand, even if unable to forgive. It's our confession, Zac. Whatever happens, you get your way in the end. We will end up confessing. Please don't hate me. All I wanted was for you to love me. For us to share our love with Jericho... I can't write anymore. Someone is coming.'

Sian lowers the book. Smokey jumps up on me. He knows I'm upset, but he's wary of the diesel fumes.

The Great Orme

'Did you give our names?' asks Tomasz. 'In your letter?'

Orla can only nod.

'Stupid bitch!' Fatima says, and swings the butt of the gun hard into Orla's face.

Smokey jumps off the sofa and launches himself at Fatima's leg. She shrieks, stumbling backwards, kicking out at him, shouting at me to get him off her. She edges her way around the sofa before tripping over Costas body.

Orla drops forward, pushing her face into my shoulder, and I catch sight of her visible eye bloodshot and swollen from the blow. Jorge orders Smokey off Fatima, and I hear my friend scampering away. The slightest of sounds stops all commotion and silences everyone – the strike of a match.

Don't let it end

Chapter Thirty-Two

The lit match is held up for all to see by Sian. She drops my book into a nearby metal basket, her haunted eyes fixed on the flickering flame.

Fatima has got to her feet. I hear her voice behind us as she tells Tomasz to pour the diesel on the floor. Tomasz does as he's told, kicking the diesel cannister over, letting the liquid splash over the carpet.

Fatima joins the others now gathered at the lounge doorway. Smokey is barking at them, short tail erect.

'Just a second,' Harrison says, coming back and picking up the cannister. 'We'd better take this… evidence.'

He leans over us, his touch on my back, stiff and cold like metal. He kisses me then Orla on the top of our heads. 'I'm sorry,' he whispers. 'I never wanted it to end this way.'

'Don't let it happen,' I say, feeling his warmth nearby but unable to take my eyes off the flame Sian's holding, eating up the matchstick. The flame has burned down the matchstick and nearly reached Sian's fingertips.

Helen appears, and taking hold of Harrison, tugs at him. His hand still on my back, he pats me – one last gesture before he retreats with her.

'Drop it, Sian,' Fatima calls from the doorway. 'There can't be a trace left.' Pulling the lounge door open, she adds, 'We have to find Jericho.'

Orla bucks as if electrocuted.

'What has Jericho got to do with any of this?' she yells at Fatima, some newfound energy driven up from the deep well within.

The Great Orme

'Everything. Don't you see? You two are going to get the blame for the murders this weekend. I've scheduled a post to the police's website, it'll go up any time now. It's from your account, Zac. Your confession. So, you kind of get what you wanted after all.' She smiles, eyebrows raised, amused by her cleverness.

'Of course, the police will track us down, but their focus will be on this weekend's murders... today's murders, not from years ago. We'll say you invited us back to the *old house*, a reunion, but you acted so strange, insular and scary. Too many years living alone. We'll say you rowed with Orla, you became abusive, we felt uncomfortable here, we had to leave. We'll say what a tragedy it is – to kill so cruelly. How shocked and saddened we were to hear you murdered dear Costas and his doting wife. Not to mention your lovely neighbour. And then you set fire to yourselves, put everything to flames. Leaving no trace... Just that damned letter to Jericho which complicates things a little. We'll have to ensure the letter never reaches her... one way or another.'

The flame reaches Sian's finger and thumb. She shrieks, flinging the match at us. Instinctively, I launch myself forward, yanking Orla with me. With our hands and ankles tied, we can't break our fall. I yell out at the pain shooting along my ribs on contact with the floor, Orla landing on top of me.

Smokey's barking reverberates off the walls, and beyond, I hear the front door slam shut. Footsteps peter away, car doors slam, and the sound of tyres on tarmac disappear into the distance.

I never expected a happy ending for me. Not for any of us. I only ever wanted to be honest. To write a new chapter. One that would right our wrongs. And now a new word, a new name, a new person, a new world is imprinted on my mind, that of "Jericho" – my daughter! And here I am, about to die, never to see her face, hear her voice, or to hold her hand. My daughter is out there somewhere, in need of protection – my heart is swollen with new feelings.

I think I'll faint, but will myself to stay alert, driven by the fierce heat. The fire has caught, and the sofa is alight with popping and cracking sounds as the fire takes hold. We can't move. Orla and I are fire-bait. Flames, wild and fast, snatch at the fuel-soaked fabric. I clutch hold of Orla and roll her with me as one, crashing into the coffee table. I regard the sofa, a raging fireball, spitting black smoke upwards. Even as we watch, it spreads, greedily licking at the carpet and feeling its way toward us. The room will burn, the old house will burn. Orla, Smokey, and I will burn. Even the book will burn, and no one will know what really happened here. The others will find Jericho and they'll kill her in the hope they might save themselves. There's nothing I can do. I'm helpless.

Next to us, Rose's feet catch fire first, her smart green shoes reduced to blackened stumps by the blaze. The flames creep up her legs, melting her tights. I wriggle so we can roll in another direction, any direction, as long as it's away from the flames. Orla is screaming, but we don't have any neighbours. By the time anyone notices the fire, it will be too late for us. I try to roll us toward the doorway. It's our only chance. The pain is immense, my body screeching for relief, but it doesn't matter. I rock us over and over, Smokey's barking cheering us on, the open doorway closer and closer. As I think we have made it, a searing wall of heat and flame scorches a path along the carpet from the sofa to the doorway, flaring up and grasping at the thick wooden door. Tomasz must have purposely poured the petrol from sofa to door to prevent our escape. All I can think of is Jericho. I must do something. We must live.

I deviate, tumbling us away from the doorway. The pair of us gasp for breath, but the smoke is chemical, black and thick. We cough, dry, gagging retches. I don't know what to do! I don't know what to do!

'The sofa!' Orla gasps, her face hot with sweat. I look back at the sofa. It's almost burnt itself out, already a glowing charred frame, the fire having moved on to consume the oak coffee table, creeping its way across the carpet toward us. There's no escape.

'Smokey!' Orla cries. 'Fetch!'

She's pulling my wrists with hers, pointing with her fingers at the sofa. 'Knife!' she commands, her voice desperate but authoritative.

At the edge of the sofa frame lies a knife reflected orange in the embers of the fire. I recall Harrison kissing the tops of our heads as we sat there, his touch on my back, cold, metallic. A knife! He left us a knife!

'Smokey!' I urge, pointing along with Orla's hands. 'Get the knife! Fetch! Knife, Smokey! Fetch!'

Alert, Smokey, stands rigid before us, triangular ears pointed, listening intently to our urgent demands. He sets to move away as if he understands, then he falters, looking back to us again for clarity.

Our commands become coughed and spluttered, we don't have long. The smoke and the flames are spreading faster and faster, crawling like Death's insidious fingers, searching us out in the unescapable gloom.

I'm barely able to speak, the back of my throat is clogged and burning, and as our last vestige of hope is about to burn to ashes, something clicks in Smokey's head, and he pushes off with a spurt toward the sofa, jumping through snapping flames and spiralling smoke. I hear him yelp, but the room is dark, the smoke so thick now I can't see him.

Bound and laid together, we wait for whichever comes first – the slow smother of a choking death or the scorch of our own flesh in the fire. Blackness burrows from the back of my head into my eyes as if my brain has been ruptured. I gulp and gulp, but the air burns, and the blackness I inhale merges with the blackness within me.

Smokey's furry head bumps against my hand. Barely able to see, I stretch out my fingers, wrapping them around the hot metal clamped in his teeth.

I turn the knife inward and sever the tape on our wrists. I'm imprecise and stab at our skin. Orla flinches, jerking her body. But I don't care. There isn't time left.

The tape snaps and our wrists release. Gasping and spluttering, I sit up, feel for the tape that binds our ankles and cut through it, somehow easier this time. I haul us to our feet and doubled over, drag myself and Orla away from the heat, toward the bay window. I wrench a handle upward and push the window outward. The air before us immediately thins from black to grey. I help Orla up and push her through the open window. I call Smokey, feeling below with both hands at my ankles for him. He's not there.

I call him again. The smoke, a scorching sandpaper cloud, is persistent, as keen as I to escape the room into the outside. It stuffs my mouth and nostrils, and scrapes my eyes. I'm choking, my lungs on fire. 'Smokey!' I scream for the last time.

I flinch – a moist touch on my hand. It's Smokey's tongue, something is in his mouth. I grab him, picking him up roughly, and launch us both through the window.

Bloodied but unbowed, Orla is already on her feet. She grabs hold of me, and we stare into one another's eyes, gulping on air that never tasted so precious and pure. I glance at the distant houses over the road, all quiet, not a soul to be seen on this early Sunday afternoon. Checking my pocket, I thank the Lord, my car keys are there.

'Quick,' I say, reaching down and picking up Smokey. In his mouth, my book. Tears fill my eyes. I blink them away and bundle him onto the back seat of my Jeep.

Orla is seated next to me in the passenger seat, staring straight ahead, drinking the remains of a can of cola she's found in the drink holder.

I'm trembling. I grip the steering wheel firmly and survey the old house. The big bay window to the lounge appears as if a portal to a universe of its own, dense black smoke within swirling and flashing with orange flames. Within, I see hands pressed against the glass, and what's left of my heart breaks again. For a moment I think I see Costas, Jules and Rose, their distraught faces like zombies clamouring to be set free. I blink to clear my mind and so I can see more clearly. This time I see the faces of our victims staring after me, and I pray the newly dead have been set free, that they won't linger as ghosts too. I fumble to start the car, but I know it's too late. The ghosts file one after the other, squeezing and clambering through the open window. The ghosts weren't confined to the old house; they are with me in the darkness of every dream and in every waking minute. There is no escape. Not until we've confessed.

'Where are we going?' Orla asks over the top of Smokey's barking.

'To the top,' I reply, pulling away.

To touch the sky
one more time

Chapter Thirty-Three

The view from the top of the Great Orme is beautiful yet desolate. There's something missing. Someone missing. Someone new.

In the far distance the ragged horizon oscillates as if the Earth itself is shaking, gasping with outrage at what came to pass. The closer to the edge we get, the better it is. There's nowhere closer to the edge than the Great Orme. Once you've gazed over it, things can never be the same.

Beneath the Great Orme's bruised skin, there's a power that feeds on fear, a beast that delights in pain, but only now I realise that's because fear and pain were all I had to feed it. I realise now I have love and hope for a new life, for my daughter, Jericho. This is what the Great Orme will devour from now on. I've been a slave to the alchemy of its deep driven drumbeat, the percussive sound permeating my body, pulsing through brain, blood and bones, like a sonic umbilical cord. I now know it was a part of me and always has been. The rush and roar of pure energy, a force greater than any other… almost spiritual.

Standing at the wild intersection, I glance up at the sky, and through the canopy of grey winter gloom. I think of the billions of stars hidden beyond. All at once, I feel heavy and floating, both alive and dead. I consider the deep vastness of space, diamond-clustered stars shining their lonely lights, doing little but magnifying the loneliness within me.

A sudden soft-curved wind catches me, swinging me around so I face the fear and horror of the land. And at my feet, beneath the stagnant soil, bones beneath my bones, a strange yet familiar sound drifts up from the dark depths, from the

The Great Orme

Earth's core, rippling through its brittle crust. Reason, blood, and soul screaming to be noticed. The Sea Serpent screams. It tells me what I need.

A golden ray of light breaks through a fissure in the winter clouds, and Orla squeezes my hand. I wonder what it means – an expression of love, a final acknowledgment before we jump, or an indication of regret. Her forefinger and thumb grip the ring encasing my finger.

'You're wearing our wedding ring,' she says, reaching up to stroke my hair.

The eternal circuit that connects us floods me with an unbeatable force, one I draw strength from. The wind driven up the Orme's solid vertical veneer, lashes her long black hair wildly about her head. I regard her face, fractured black lines of smoke stains and smeared mascara.

'I should be dead,' she says, turning away and peering into the distance as if examining something I can't see. 'Perhaps you too.'

A raven cries somewhere, and the ground beneath our feet shudders, the sea serpent, the sky, and the impossible screaming at me. Finally, I know what we must do.

'We have to find our daughter. We have to protect Jericho from the others,' I say.

'The ghosts will have to wait a little longer?' Orla replies.

'The ghosts have forever… We don't.'

Orla's face breaks, and like her head is on fire, she holds up her arms before collapsing into me.

'We have to find Jericho,' I state again, the agony slowly fading and my veins running free. I take the square patch of red wool from my pocket.

Orla gasps, eyes wild and alive, both sad and happy it seems to me; tears cascading down her cheeks. 'It belongs to Jericho,' she says, her voice breaking. 'So precious. I cut it from her knitted hat, the one the nurse put on her tiny head immediately after she was born.'

I squeeze the square patch of wool and I think I hear the

Great Orme roar from deep beneath my feet. In my other hand I hold my book rescued by Smokey, singed at its edges, and prepare to throw the words into the sea.

Orla clutches my wrist firmly. 'No,' she says. 'This story isn't over.'

My eyes smart from the nagging wind, eyes brimming with tears.

'We are doomed,' she says. 'But we won't give up. We will confess. Your words will be read… once we know Jericho is safe.'

Smokey barks, wagging his tail. I lean over and stroke his head, my gaze locked on the Great Orme's pock-marked terrain, its indelible map woven through my blood and bones. I feel its force anew, its energy coursing through bone, blood and brain – It knows what I want. I feel in control once more, although this time I know I can't be, and I'm thankful for my understanding. I think I hear soft sparks of sounds, Jericho's voice calling me.

THE END

Acknowledgements

I don't think I'll ever be able to thank her enough for everything, but this is a start: love and thanks to my wife, Claire, without whom, this strange book wouldn't exist, and for our adventures, but especially those in Llandudno, *The Great Orme*, where the seed was sown for this tragic tale.

The real Great Orme is a peremptory on the edge of the world, a towering expanse of limestone headland that dominates the space between sea and sky. It derives its name from the old Scandinavian Norse "sea serpent". I'm certain the Vikings knew something of the Great Orme and the ancient power it wields.

Love always to my two daughters, Millie and Eliza for being shining lights no matter what, proof that anything is possible.

Love and gratitude to my family, for their support, love, and putting up with my blathering about my stories.

My heartfelt gratitude to Northodox Press - Amy, James, and Ted, for accepting me into their wonderful empire of words. Thanks to Sophie Gregory for her kind feedback and proofreading notes.

And thank you to my readers - I know you are out there, and knowing so makes it worthwhile.

NORTHODOX PRESS
———————

FIND US ON SOCIAL MEDIA

www.ingramcontent.com/pod-product-compliance
Lightning Source LLC
LaVergne TN
LVHW031536060526
838200LV00056B/4525